I'm Not Making This Up, You Know

I'm Not Making This Up, You Know

◆ ◆ ◆

*The Autobiography of the Queen
of Musical Parody*

◆

ANNA RUSSELL

Edited by Janet Vickers

CONTINUUM • NEW YORK

To my bright and brilliant Deirdre

1985
The Continuum Publishing Company
370 Lexington Avenue, New York, N.Y. 10017

Library of Congress Cataloging in Publication Data

Russell, Anna.
I'm not making this up, you know.

1. Russell, Anna. 2. Singers—Biography.
I. Vickers, Janet. II. Title.
ML420.R925A3 1985   782'092'4 [B]   85-17150
ISBN 0-8264-0364-6

ACKNOWLEDGMENT

To my friend Janet Vickers, who has taken this amorphous mess of scribblings (I can't type and my writing is awful) and reduced it to such order as to make it acceptable to my publisher. Without her nothing would have been accomplished.

Contents

Prologue

"She's not very good-looking, but her overwhelming and sometimes exhausting vitality may one day take care of this. She's very companionable but shies away from demonstrations of affection. She has a nice figure and could look smart if she wasn't so damnably untidy. I don't know what she is cut out to do in life."

This quote is from a letter written by my godmother, Aunt Alice, whom I adored, to my mother, whom I hated. I was about fifteen years old at the time. The letter continues: "She turns out pages of ridiculous verse all the time, sets them to tunes, and sings them with a ukelele. I find some of them hilarious, but you can't make a career out of singing comic songs."

Well, now, dearest Aunt Al, I'm not so sure.

Anybody here remember Alberich? . . . And Wotan? . . . Mrs. Wotan? . . . Siegfried and Brünnhilde and my friend Erda? I've made a career doing my version of Wagner's *Ring*. Of course, I *tell* the story of the *Ring* and sing only bits of it, such as the Jo-ho-to-ho bit. While Wagner didn't exactly intend his opera cycle to be a comedy, I have made a career out of doing just that—finding the comical in serious music.

I have a go at lieder, French art songs, Gilbert and Sullivan, Verdi, folk songs, hey nonny-no and titty fa-las, as well as the pure-but-dull British nymph-and-shepherd items. Probably there are few forms of vocal expression I haven't tapped for their comic possibilities.

When I was a music student I was content to make up my comic songs and leave the rest of vocal music in pristine glory. In my youth, when I was still Anna Claudia Russell-Brown, I was terribly serious about music and singing, despite my strumming the ukelele to accompany my ridiculous verse.

I, Claudia, was born into a ridiculous situation. I enjoyed every musical and social advantage, but God gave me a tin voice. I'll always have a tin

1

voice. There's nothing I can do about it. A singing teacher can train a voice to be louder, or help a singer not to get laryngitis, but that's all a teacher can do.

I studied voice and piano at the Royal College of Music, in London, but when I sang, the students laughed. When I tried harder, my voice got louder and more hilarious. Sir Hugh Allan, who was the director of the college, said there was no room for students who weren't serious. Not serious? I was absolutely crushed.

Sir Hugh thought I got sillier every year, and had no hesitation saying so. I told him I really wanted to be a diva and was making every effort in that direction. All he said was, "Why don't you get an audition at the Palladium?"

People don't have to be good musicians or actors or glamorous personalities to be opera singers, and they really don't have to be intelligent, as long as they have a glorious voice. Without a glorious voice, nothing else matters, and I lacked the basic ingredient for a career in the profession I wanted more than anything else. The musical education I acquired and the social advantages I had could not compensate for what nature had denied me. But that didn't stop me from the adventure I made out of singing comic songs.

These first chapters are an introduction to my story, the beginning of my recital, as it were. I shall have to give you my family in some detail before we get on with me; then you will have an idea of why I was so ill-prepared for any other career.

CHAPTER 1

The only child of an unfecund crew

It has always amazed me how such a mixed bag of people as my family could be related, even by marriage. The Russells were rich and fancy Australians, the second lot of Browns were Spartan and "veddy" English, and the Tandys were modest Canadians.

When I was born, the eldest members of the disparate clans were Father's four Russell aunts; Tikka Gran, representing the Browns; and Granny Tandy. The Russell aunts had produced four children among them, and these cousins were already elderly when I appeared on the scene. All were unmarried, as were my mother's three handsome brothers. It seems to me that all the Russells, the Browns, and the Tandys had in common was that they were exceedingly unfecund. Out of all that crew came only me.

Most people's relations have children of their own to fuss over, but my relations had nobody but me. A family is usually a nice, comfortable pyramid, with brothers and sisters and cousins at the base. My family was like a pyramid standing on its head. I was the inverted apex, and the crushing weight was sometimes too much to bear.

Since I was the only child in the family, everyone had a say in my upbringing. Most children are answerable only to Mum and Dad, but my parents were always sending me to stay with some member of the family or another to relieve the burden of having me live at home, so that I became a conspicuous, even notorious, object of interest to my scattered relations.

All had very definite and diametrically opposed ideas as to how I should be raised. It was like being brought up by a jury that could never agree on a verdict. I tried, after my fashion, to please them all, but I never knew if I was guilty or not guilty, nor even what I was guilty or not guilty of. It was difficult not to get the wires crossed. I got far too much varied attention, and grew into a nasty, precocious, thoroughly confused brat. I did not have much "identity" until Aunt Al yanked me out of wartime England and I began to discover I had a comedic talent.

To get the ramifications and eccentric goings-on of my family down on paper would tax the ingenuity of a John Galsworthy, but I have neither ambition nor capacity to write the decline and fall of the British Empire as seen through the eyes of Anna Russell. I will merely dig around my roots a bit, which is what everyone is doing these days.

Andrew Russell, my paternal great-grandfather, was a successful Glasgow ironmonger who fitted out a ship and, together with some other Scottish colonists, sailed for Australia. The ship was well provisioned, and had cows and chickens on board. But no amount of planning could have prevented the disasters that befell the colonists. Some were swept overboard during terrible storms, and others died in childbirth. They all got scurvy when the ship was becalmed for weeks. It took four months for them to reach Van Diemen's Land (now Tasmania). The livestock died, the food ran out, and finally wine was all the survivors had left to sustain themselves. Imagine them arriving in freezing cold to colonize a new country, all smashed out of their minds. What a gorgeous picture it conjures up!

Andrew Russell kept a diary of the voyage in *A Tour of the Australian Colonies*, written in 1838–39 and published the following year. A few passages will give you a taste of what he and the voyage were like.

> *Nov. 24 [1838].* Haven't slept for two nights between the quacking of ducks, fowls screaming, pigs squeaking, and seasick retching under my cabin windows, there is no lack of discord.
>
> *Nov. 25.* Cook washed out of the galley and his fire too. No hot dish today. We got a bottle of wine and mulled it.
>
> *Nove. 27.* Poultry and pigs drowned in their coops. Ship's doctor seasick.
>
> *Dec. 10.* Fair weather, so got up a concert on deck. Sung some excellent duets and trios, accompanied with two accordions and a violin.
>
> *Dec. 13.* A calm. Provisions are much changed for the worse. [No wonder. They've all died or gone overboard.]
>
> *Dec. 24.* Took sea water today for an emetic, and a very good one it is. It is Christmas eve, some good sport on deck with

masks. What will not people do to dispel ennui. [Such as taking sea water for an emetic.]

Dec. 27. A calm—a new game—throwing buckets of saltwater at each other—although some decline this warfare.

*Feb. 17 [1839].*A passenger's cow goes berserk. It has rabies. It is nothing but skin and bone and burst out of its crib bellowing and foaming furiously, giving such tongue as to suppose we had got some tenant from the infernal regions on board.

Feb. 20. A heavy gale again. People and dogs and anything that isn't battened down gets swept overboard.

They finally arrive at Glenelg in New Holland, now South Australia. Another ship has arrived from Van Diemen's Land at the same time. My great-grandfather writes, "These people were employed in carrying their sheep to shore, but the sheep would drink the sea water, which often proves fatal. The beach was strewn with many carcasses."

They have been at sea 130 days, and they have to wade ashore into a lot of dead sheep—and *we* complain of jet lag!

Andrew finally settled in Melbourne. In 1847 he became the fourth mayor of the seaport capital of Victoria, and was one of the founders of the prestigious Melbourne Club. He is described in *The Chronicles of Early Melbourne,* by Gary Owen, as "a commonplace, persevering piece of ordinary respectability, slightly affecting the upper crust of society, but in a manner that could not be termed snobbish. He had an honesty of purpose and well-meaningness that rendered him a very desirable member of the community." Neat but not gaudy, I would think.

Andrew Russell married a Miss Jessie Fiskin from Ballarat, a city in South Victoria. They had two sons, who managed to kill themselves steeplechasing, and six daughters, who had to be married off. The daughters were the possessors of those enormous, British-type noses, which later prompted their precocious nephews, Claude (my father) and Frank, to nickname them the Beaky-Bullys. Such noses used to be portrayed by the cartoonist H. M. Bateman, but have died out nowadays. Early on, their mother announced that she felt it would be impossible to marry girls with noses like that to anyone of consequence in Australia. So after her husband died, she took them all except the eldest (who was already married) to live in the south of France, where she accomplished her purpose of marrying off the Beaky-Bullys to various minor European nabobs, no doubt with the aid of the Australian loot.

The dowager Mrs. Andrew Russell and her daughters were, I suppose, the nouveaux riches of that era. They spent money like water and had a wonderful time. Granny Russell, as she was called, made her home in Nice, where her French malapropisms became quite legendary. She prided herself on a mastery of the French language that she did not possess, but since she was a little forbidding, no one laughed or corrected her French, which consequently never improved.

Apparently Granny Russell's French maid understood that her mistress was sleeping underneath two coverlets and not between two sailors when she announced, *"Je me couche entre deux matelots."* The baker at the patisserie somehow understood that Madame Russell wanted the same kind of cake she had bought the last time when she asked for *"un gateau le meme que ma derrière."* Her most famous flight of fractured French occurred when she was being driven in a fly and, thinking the spring had broken, she ordered the coachman, *"Cochon! Cochon! Descendez de votre boite. Le printemps de votre mouche est cassé."* (Pig! Pig! Come down from your box. The springtime of your insect is broken.)

While Granny Russell had some obvious difficulty becoming Frenchified, her daughers had no trouble at all becoming very foreign. My paternal grandmother was the exception; Jessie Russell went to the other extreme and married a "fraffly" British type, Francis David Millet Brown.

The young officer in the Royal Munster Fusilliers first appeared in the Russell ménage as my great-aunt Mag's suitor. But before he could marry the woman of his choice, Jessie, the next youngest of the Beaky-Bullys, came back from some visit or other and fell madly in love with him, whereupon Great-aunt Mag, sacrificing her happiness in an excess of Victorian sentiment, informed Francis David Millet Brown, "I cannot allow my little sister's heart to be broken. I shall give you up, and you must marry her." And he did. The noble fellow took Jessie back with him to "Inja," where she gave birth to my uncle Frank and then Claude, my father, after which she promptly died of cholera.

The epitaph Grandfather Brown put on his wife's tombstone is strangely ambiguous: "Safe in the arms of Jesus May 13th is deeply mourned." Did that mean she was safe in the arms of Jesus only once a year? Or did Grandfather deeply mourn her only once a year? Or perhaps once only, and never again? Oh, well! I can't punctuate, either.

His obligation ended by Grandmother's death, Grandfather returned to the south of France, taking his two small sons with him. He proposed a second time to Great-aunt Mag, who informed him that, according to the tables of affinity in the prayer book, a man cannot marry his deceased wife's sister. So Grandfather parked my father and Uncle Frank with Great-aunt Bena (Rowena), another of the Beaky-Bullys, in Monte Carlo, and went back to "Inja" in dudgeon.

Great-aunt Mag remained a spinster. Perhaps she didn't really like Francis Brown. I don't think I would have liked him much, either. He sounds rather too virtuous for comfort, in fact, a prig.

He won the Victoria Cross for having distinguished himself "under the walls of Delhi" in the Indian Mutiny. He was handsome, brave, clean, courteous, reverent, honest, etc.—no end of a hero. All too Rudyard Kipling for words.

Aunt Bena was the most spectacular of the Beaky-Bullys, a tall and very baroque lady. Not the least of her distinguishing characteristics was the large family nose. She always wore enormous wigs: a brown wig on weekdays and blond for Sundays and special occasions. They were masterpieces of the coiffeur's art, having every elaborately and perfectly arranged sausage and spit curl in place. You saw her always strongly corseted and richly befurred and bejeweled, unless at breakfast, when she was all ruffled up in a glorious pink negligee.

The family naturally assumed Aunt Bena was bald, until she went into the hospital at the age of eighty-two. She was discovered to have a thick plait of her own hair hanging down her back, which no doubt accounted for the hydrocephalic appearance of her head. The only explanation she ever gave of her preference for wigs was that hairdressers chatter too much.

Aunt Bena never had children, so when Grandfather Brown parked Uncle Frank and Father with her, nothing was too good for the boys. In her kindness, she went as far as to try launching my father on a career as a concert pianist.

Aunt Bena adored my father, who was very musical as a child. Her husband, Albert Zeegers-Veekenz, was a Dutch pianist, quite famous at the time and very rich. They were quick to notice that my father was musical, really an infant prodigy. At the age of five, Dad was playing in public, all dressed up in golden curls and "Little Lord Fauntleroys," much to Aunt's delight.

The prodigy's concertizing might have continued, and Father might have turned into a genuine musician, had Grandfather Brown not come to fetch the boys home from Monte Carlo. As if Dad's playing in public wasn't bad enough, neither of the brothers spoke a word of English. The shame of sons of a colonel of the Royal Munster Fusilliers speaking only French and Dutch! There was the father and mother of a row about it. The little fellows, aged seven and nine, were packed off to military school in England, and Grandfather returned to "Inja" to produce more little Browns.

Grandfather had taken himself another wife. "A good and virtuous woman to take care of my poor motherless boys," he put it to Aunt Bena. His second wife, Doris, turned out to be a beauteous, godly, and quite dotty woman he had found working for the Zenana Mission in India. She was, of course, my stepgrandmother, known to me as "Tikka" Gran, or "half" a grandmother. Tikka is half of Pukka, which means "great" or "large" in Hindustani. Grandfather and Tikka Gran produced five children: my uncles Eric, Christopher, Wyn, Reginald Llewellyn (Llewyn), and my aunt Jessie. All rather eccentric, but darlings in a rarefied sort of way.

Grandfather Brown would write his "Dear Sons" in military school weekly letters full of stern, laconic questions and Polonius-like admonitions, each numbered as in a test:

1. Have you had a cough or been unwell since you last wrote? If so, what has been the matter?
2. What lessons do you like best, second, and third best? Give reasons.
3. Who are your best friends? Describe them.
4. Be sure to evacuate your bowels every morning after breakfast.

And so on. Imagine the poor little fellows chewing on that after having tasted Aunt Bena's colorful, extravagant life-style. But the letters must have had the desired effect of putting some iron into those young souls, because both went into the army. Uncle Frank was killed in the Boer War, but Father survived, an exemplary Royal Engineer. He was a great athlete, a Dead-Eye Dick at all sports. You name it, he could do it. He was a crack pistol shot; he played squash, cricket, and golf; and he competed in tennis for Canada in the Olympic Games of 1908.

Father's artistic tendencies, however, so briefly nurtured by Aunt Bena, were stifled by the rigid pattern of his conventional life. He continued to play the piano beautifully, but he confined himself to Gilbert and Sullivan, that being the only thing he considered suitable for an officer of His Majesty's Army. Many were the nights when I was lulled to sleep as a child by

Father rendering the whole of *The Mikado* or *Ruddigore* or *The Yeoman of the Guard* in assorted voices to visitors downstairs in the drawing room. Decades later, I was to render a reasonable facsimile of my father's virtuoso performance in my show. I called it "How to Write Your Own Gilbert and Sullivan Opera."

I heard my father play seriously only once. Everybody was out except Nannie and me, and I heard someone playing Beethoven's *Waldstein* Sonata in the drawing room. I crept in to listen. When Father saw me he was furious. He told me not to mention a word about it. You'd have thought I'd caught him *in flagrante delicto* with the maid.

After Grandfather Brown's death, Tikka Gran lived in England and, as you might suppose, her house in Yately was full of memorabilia from "Inja." One room was filled with shakos and busbys and all sorts of funny military hats, but the mice got into them, and they went the way of all things material. If I didn't watch out, I could get a jolly good jab from a blowfish with spikes, hanging from the banisters.

The house was fun to visit, but cold as blazes, and it had no plumbing, for Tikka Gran considered such things unhealthful. Plumbing was put in by her sons, however, who craftily inveigled her into going to a missionary meeting in Cheltenham before it was installed. There was a fine row about it, but Tikka Gran had to accept a fait accompli. She never used anything but the earth-closet, which remained.

In spite of (or because of?) her godliness, Tikka Gran disapproved of nearly everybody, and she was very critical of her only daughter, my aunt Jessie, who was extremely beautiful, which, I believe, aroused her mother's jealousy.

Tikka Gran had piles of white hair on which she would perch a hat. She would never be seen without it, even at breakfast. One day, after lighting the dining room fire, she started complaining bitterly that the smoke was smelling up the house. Poor Chapman, the maid, rushed in to see what it was all about, and there was Tikka Gran in a rage, her hat blazing merrily away, having been lit with the fire. Tikka claimed insurance on the hat; when the adjustor asked the price of it, he was told, in the year 1932, that it had cost four shillings and sixpence before the First World War. She looked very frail when I visited her just before she died, but she was sitting up in bed still wearing her hat.

Born Claude Brown, Father had later to tack the Russell on in order to inherit his mother's estate. From the age of seventeen, Father fought in all wars available to him, and still managed to find time to help Tikka Gran bring up the second brew of Browns. At the age of thirty-eight, he was sent overseas to the Royal Military College, Kingston, Ontario, as an instructor in map making. In Kingston he met Mother and fell in love with her. I don't think he'd had much experience with women, as he'd never had time to meet any. What with the wars and having to cope with the family, he wasn't as smart about women as about other things.

My father's family, the Russells and the Browns, eclipsed my mother's in affluence and eccentricity, but the Tandys' more homely virtues shall have their due in these pages. I loved fat, jolly Granny Tandy very much, as did the rest of her family. She was easygoing and certainly nothing like Mother, thank God. One of her most endearing traits was her faulty memory for names. She couldn't remember anybody's name, not even a child's. Granny Tandy would call me by one or another of her sons' names: Carl, Harry, or Bryer. She was apt to call Mother Tom, which was Grandfather Tandy's name. Father would get Percy, Algernon, Archie, and, once, Augustus, instead of his rightful name, Claude. When asked why she ever called him Augustus, she answered, "I know he has a pompous name, and it sounds something like a Roman emperor's." She would scream with laughter about her failing, and so would everyone else. Apart from this quirk, she was a very bright old woman.

Granny Tandy, the widow of a railway man, had great ambitions for her daughter, who was evidently one of the belles of Kingston. After Grandfather Tandy died, Granny lost most of their money, and the little that was left was spent on Mother. She was sent to finishing schools, given singing lessons, and generally spoiled rotten while the boys went to work. She had a rather beautiful voice, but never learned to read music.

When Father appeared in Kingston, he seemed like a good bet for marriage. He was socially acceptable, which was certainly an important consideration in 1910, and quite well off, too. And he was in love with Mother. He was wonderful with her. I never heard him raise his voice to her or lose his temper. But he was not one to be pushed around. When he put his foot down she would do what he said, and that was the end of it.

Mother loved him as much as she was capable of loving anybody. I don't know what their private conversations were like, but I do know that if anyone disagreed with her on even the most trivial matter, she would do one of two infantile things: burst into tears or throw a tantrum. Father seemed quite contented with her, however, which I suppose was the main point.

Mother and Father were married in Montreal, and then went on to New York, where they were given a magnificent wedding reception by Ernest de

Coppet, partner in the Wall Street firm de Coppet and Doremus, who, with his brother Casimo, was a patron of the Flonzaley String Quartet. Ernest was a brother-in-law of Aunt Bena's pianist husband, Albert Zeegers-Veekenz, but he was much younger than they, in fact, only slightly older than Father. They had been great friends since their youth in Monte Carlo, and now that Father had finally gotten around to getting married, Ernest insisted on putting on the bash. He took over most of the Plaza Hotel for the reception, which must have overcome Mother.

Almost nine months to the day, Anna Claudia Russell-Brown was born.

CHAPTER 2

Life among the "Mummies" while Father's over there

The scenes in my life are so many and varied that the places and houses where I have lived and the cities I have visited on my tours are sometimes a bit difficult to sort out. One place or person or thing suggests another, and soon I'm swept along on a stream of consciousness. I'm no James Joyce, however; if I tried to write his way, I'm afraid I should only produce another kind of parody.

One thing that has helped me immeasurably in putting together this grand tour of my life is the fact that almost all my ancestors were indefatigable diarists, pamphleteers, and scribblers. They collected family correspondence and photographs and cuttings from newspapers. Whatever happened to them, however inconsequential, was sure to be recorded in writing somewhere. None of them left me a red cent, but since I was the last leaf on the family tree, I fell heir to their outpourings.

Father started writing his diaries during the Boer War. There are graphic accounts of the Siege of Ladysmith, and how he got shot in the knee. But he is mostly preoccupied with wondering about the nature of God. His ideas were surprisingly ecumenical, considering he was born in 1870. In one entry, he says, "It is no use discussing the subject with my father, as he is firmly convinced that God is British." After Father died, we discovered that, in addition to the diaries, he had kept all family correspondence and had two trunks filled with cuttings from the *London Times*, all neatly tucked into little envelopes, carefully annotated and cross-filed.

The most illuminating experience was comparing Father's diaries with Mother's. Reading what he thought about her and she thought about him, I concluded that they could have been writing about two other people.

I think my mother's main interest, in fact, was writing her diary, though why this should have been I don't know. When she died, she left me seventy years' worth of daily records. They tell of no really vital interests, being just a timetable of events, useful but scarcely exciting. She never learned housekeeping, cooking, or sewing. She had no particular liking for clothes or frivolity, such as gadding about. She hated spending money on herself, although she would go to a lot of trouble to help people less well off. She was public-spirited and could always be counted on for a handout. Apparently uninterested in sex, she never flirted or looked sideways at another man, and was indeed not the least bit affectionate to anyone. However, she did like her women's clubs, especially if she could be president, make speeches, and open bazaars. And she did a very good job of growing plants in pots.

Mother was a prima-donna type, very personable when she wanted to be and much more attractive than the average, although not quite the beauty Father made her out to be. She was the eldest of the four Tandy children and dominated her three very handsome brothers. I suspect she was a small-town girl who found herself out of her element. With the best intentions in the world, Granny Tandy had created an image for Mother that she simply hadn't the capacity to live up to.

Mother was emotionally insecure, very competitive, and unable to bear anyone who represented a challenge to her. She was the sort of person who, if given an inch, takes a mile and, to mix the metaphors, swallows a person whole. Unless one was willing to be completely dominated by her, one had to take a stand, and then there was trouble. She was happiest surrounded by idiots who thought she was marvelous and flattered her up to the skies, and whom she was able to patronize. She probably had a monumental inferiority complex and was often very lonely, particularly after Father died.

Had Mother married someone of her own social class and been kept busy with a brood of children, she might have turned out to be a reasonable person. It was evident from her diaries that she had had a few encounters with men more dominating than she, but they had managed to elude her. That is why, I suppose, she was still single at thirty-four.

I think Mother took an instant dislike to me on my arrival. I loved her with all the trust a small child has in a mother who couldn't be anything but loving and kind because she's beautiful. But I no longer loved or trusted her after she had shown her rage and disgust over my not being pretty. Then I gave her a wide berth.

I gave Father a wide berth, too. I adored him, but reasoned that if I was as ugly, and consequently bad, as Mother said I was, he probably did not love me, either. He wasn't very demonstrative, so I couldn't tell what he felt. There's the family portrait: Father keeping a stiff upper lip, Mother having tantrums, and me pouting in the background.

It is true that I was a plain, unlovable child, and a smart-ass. My only talent was having total recall. And that irritated my family. When I was very small, I used to think I was quite nice, but that illusion was soon shattered. In one of her frequent tantrums, Mother said, "If you couldn't be a boy, why on earth couldn't you be pretty like me?" I don't believe I've ever quite recovered from those words.

One of the better entries in her diary was, "I should have been the mother of six proud sons, and all I have is the Toad." I don't know why she didn't try again, although I can't ever remember her even sleeping in the same room as Father. Did she expect immaculate conceptions? (When the time came, it was Father who told me the facts of life, adding, "Your mother doesn't believe in that sort of thing.")

When Mother got older, I think she was very sorry that she and I were not closer. Unable to see the funny side of anything, she was annoyed by my sense of humor, particularly after I had started exposing it in public. She came to only one of my concerts and hated it, and she refused point-blank to listen to my records. Poor Mum! She was probably a good enough person according to her lights. But her lights were a bit dim.

My first vivid memory is of Father, all done up in his dress uniform and riding a beautiful black horse. He was going off to the First World War, although I don't think I could have understood that, because I was about two and a half at the time. We were living in a large old house in Farnborough, a suburb of London. Mother and the maids and I went to the gate to wave him good-bye. I could not understand why they were crying and carrying on: it was all very exciting. Father had given me a teddy bear, which thrilled me, and I stood clutching it in the arm I wasn't waving. He rode off down Alexandra Road to join a big procession of mounted soldiers, gun carriages, bands, and all sorts of flags as it proceeded along Farnborough Road. It was Kitchener's army.

And so one parent rode out of my life, long before I realized how much I needed his love and attention. I was not particularly aware of my father again until many years later.

Besides Mother and me, the wartime household in Farnborough consisted of Nanny Stribbling; Nanny's sister Ada, our parlor maid; and Phoebe, a third sister, who was the cook. They were beautiful young women, only in their early twenties. Of course, they seemed old to me, even though they often behaved like playmates. They had dozens of nieces and nephews, thanks to their six siblings, and knew how to treat children. They were darlings, never too busy or tired to play, tell stories, and let me scrape out the cake-mix bowl. They even spanked me when necessary, but I knew where I stood with them, and adored them. This used to annoy Mother.

Not long after Father's departure, the household was increased by two of Mother's Canadian girlfriends, Mrs. Folger and Mrs. Wilgar, whose husbands were also in the war, and two nice little boys, about the same age as I was. Aunt Nancy Folger's son, Grahame, was gloriously beautiful, with big brown eyes and golden curls. Aung Gertie Wilgar was both aunt and stepmother to Billy, who was a delicate child, but very impish and a terrible giggler. He was full of ideas for fun and games, and all sorts of naughtiness. Grahame wasn't half so entertaining; in fact, he was a bit dull, but very good-natured.

I was just a skinny little girl. When Nanny took Grahame, Billy, and me for a walk, people were always stopping her and raving about how handsome Grahame was. One woman ended her paean of praise by saying, "What a pity the girl isn't the pretty one!" Don't grown-ups understand that even small children have ears and minds and feelings?

I suppose I took the stupid commiseration in stride—if a child of such tender years can be said to take anything in stride—because the remark was simply an echo of my mother's complaints. I was used to being made to feel inadequate at home, although I had as yet no vocabulary to express my feelings, even to myself, and so, apparently, took it for granted that the world regarded me similarly, with the exception of Nanny and Ada and Phoebe. I had the vague feeling that somehow they did not belong to the world "out there," and yet I knew they did not "belong" to me, or I to them, as I did to Father and Mother. However, what mattered to me, as well as to Nanny and Billy, was that the tactless woman had been struck by Grahame's handsomeness, and said so. We were all secretly very proud of Grahame's looks.

Aunt Nancy was mild and pretty, like her son, Grahame, but Aunt Gertie, Billy's stepmother, was my favorite. She was short and squarish, and usually wore a tweed suit and brogues. Her gray hair was cropped, which was very rare in those days. She had a loud baritone voice, the kind that so often belongs to women who breed dogs; in fact, she treated us, the children, rather like puppies. She was always very jolly, and inclined to "razz" Mother when Mother got terribly dramatic.

Despite Aunt Gertie's forcefulness, Mother was the dominant one among the "mummies," as Nanny called them; her unpredictability, I suspect, was the reason. She could throw almost anyone off balance, because one never knew what sort of mood she would be in. Adults usually gave in to her whims rather than have to weather an emotional storm. One day we would be sweet, darling babies, and nothing would be too good for us. The next day, she would be cross and cranky, and we would all catch it. I was beginning to be wary of her. I reached out, instinctively, to Aunt Gertie for the Rock-of-Gibraltar affection I needed, which, indeed, every child needs, but I got the back of Mother's hairbrush for announcing that in future Aunt Gertie was to be my mother, and the boys could fight over the other two.

The mummies never suspected they weren't nearly so important to their children's way of thinking as Nanny, Ada, and Phoebe. Apart from teatime, we hardly ever saw the mummies, who were doing their patriotic duty by working at the Red Cross.

It took us ages to figure out why the other children we knew had only one mummy per family, and we had three. We knew it was no good asking Nanny. She gave us a lot of guidance, and unceasingly admonished us to be better than we were, but ask a leading question, and we got an infuriating answer: "Curiosity killed the cat," "Don't be a nosy parker," or "You'll find out when you're older." I suppose the times were still too Victorian for Nanny to explain the mummy situation; it would have been too close to the facts of life.

Children's natural curiosity was never satisfied under the be-seen-and-not-heard tyranny. Any intriguing subject remained, for better or worse, a matter for speculation. The nursery curtain came down, and there you were, in the dark. If small matters were not dealt with early on, neither were larger ones, later. Communication, as we would call it today, was tenuous at best, and did not grow stronger with the years. Even in adolescence, I was behind the nursery curtain, a prisoner.

The daily routine was, I suppose, much the same for Grahame and Billy and me as it was for most children whose parents could afford servants in early twentieth-century England. Every morning, Nanny and Ada dressed us in red knitted jumpsuits and pompom-topped caps, and sent us out to play in the backyard of our Farnborough house. We were never allowed in the front garden, but had to stay where they could keep an eye on us from the kitchen. The neighbors knew us as the little red devils. All we had was a swing, a sandbox, and a hundred old petrol tins, but the backyard was a wonderful place to play in; it was amazing what could be achieved with that equipment. We built houses with the tins, or lined them up like soldiers. We drew horrible faces on them with chalk, or filled them with sand and water to mix the most delicious mud for making pies or dropping on pointy mounds of dirt to make fir trees. We were always filthy, but this was permitted in the backyard.

There was heaps to do while we waited for Mr. Okey, the milkman. He had a fierce gray beard and shouted "Milko!" as he drove down the drive in a Ben Hur-like chariot. He ladled the milk out of a great open can into a bowl Phoebe would leave outside the kitchen door. A number of flies were having a milk bath by the time she took it in; extremely unsanitary, but in those days people did not bother much about hygiene and those who survived seemed to be none the worse for it.

When we were tired of messing about in the backyard, we could hang over the wall and watch the grown-ups at their activities. Dr. Hunter-Dunn might go by in his Model T Ford, but more up-to-date were the Wright brothers, who would fly their airplane opposite our house, at the Farnborough Aerodrome. We would see an airplane, looking as if it were made of brown paper and string, go up fifty, or sometimes a hundred, feet into the air, and stay there for quite a few minutes. We were always hoping for a Zeppelin to fly over, but one never came. We did catch sight of Buffalo Bill Cody, American folk hero of the Wild West and a great aviator in his own right, who was one of the celebrities occasionally to be seen at the Farnborough Aerodrome, one of the earliest airfields.

One day, Billy and Grahame and I found a robin's nest in a bush in the backyard, and so began our ornithological period. Aunt Gertie promptly bought Billy a book entitled *Birds, Shown to the Children.* We spent weeks peering into the bush and watching developments while Billy laboriously spelled out extracts on the habits of the robin.

The brains of the outfit, Billy could read long before Grahame and I could. A delicate child, Billy was not allowed to spend as much time in the backyard as Grahame and I. Later he became a Rhodes scholar and died, tragically, of tuberculosis at the age of thirty-two.

Grahame hadn't much imagination, but he was a good listener, and I would tell him stories. He liked the scary ones, so I would get more and more gruesome in the telling, until finally I wound up scaring myself out of my wits.

There was an old wooden shack just the other side of our wall, but we could not see it from the yard except for a piece of black tarpaper that stuck up from the roof. I told Grahame that this was the hat of a wicked ogre who was crouching there, getting ready to jump over the wall and pounce on us, unless we could outwit him first. After skulking around a bit, acting very sinister, I would jump up on a petrol tin, lean over the wall, and, with a blood-curdling screech, bash down the piece of tarpaper with a stick. This was very popular with us, until one day I leaped up and screeched, and there on the other side of the wall was the ogre himself, who yelled right back at me. I howled with fright and Grahame burst into tears, while everyone rushed out from the kitchen to see what the fuss was about. I told the maids the ogre was there, but, of course, when they looked, there was no one. It was probably some poor pedestrian passing by on the sidewalk, whom I had startled just as much as he had scared me. Anyway, quite hysterical, I was put to bed, cossetted, soothed, and told not to let my imagination run away with me. I understood much later in life, when I began to do parody in earnest, that imagination is being able to see what other people cannot see until you point it out to them.

Gradually I began to believe that there had never been an ogre on the other side of the backyard wall, but for a long time the least thing would send me into a panic. For instance, there was an enormous coat hook on the back of the night-nursery door, which was always left ajar, and I could see the points of the hook silhouetted against the passageway light. One night it struck me that it looked like a woman's hat, which led me to imagine an old witch standing there. I called her the "Wo" lady. It wasn't long before I felt that she, too, was going to pounce on me, and I got hysterical all over again. I wouldn't tell anybody what was troubling me; it must have driven Mother and the maids crazy. Finally they presumed I was afraid of the dark and allowed me to have a night light. It was the Wo lady who frightened me, not the dark, but at least the night light turned her back into a coat hook.

When Granny Tandy stayed with us, she read the Bible to us children every night. This was very popular in the nursery, and Granny thought enough of our informal studies to note them in her diary:

> Grahame doesn't say much in my little Bible class for the children, but listens intently, looking like a little angel. He is a dear little boy, but I fear not as intelligent as Billy, who is the cleverest of the three, I think, and very studious. He can write much better than the other two, but is not as interested in the Bible as they are. He prefers to be read poetry or shown pictures in Mrs. Beeton's Cookery Book. Tonight, he said, "When I grow up I don't want to look like Jesus. I shall be big and fat and sort of watch-chainy." Other things he has said are: "I think I'd like Je-

sus better if he wore a bowler hat instead of a dressing gown."
"I've seen a picture of a sheep brain in Mrs. Beeton's, but I'd like
to see one with the think going on in it." "It's nice of you to
read to us, Granny Tandy, but I think the Bible was just written
for girls."

He is quite clever at writing stories, and wrote this little verse
the other day:

> *Mummy is short, Daddy is tall,*
> *Granny is big, Claudie is small,*
> *Grahame is curley, Ada is straight;*
> *I will be terribly strong when I'm eight.*

I am sorry Claudie is not prettier than she is. She is a solemn
little girl, but some of the things she says in all seriousness are so
funny I can hardly contain myself. She is the one most interested
in the Bible, and loves to discuss it with me. I have been trying to
get Bea to read it to her instead, but Claudie just won't listen to
her; she just dives under the bedclothes. When I asked her why,
she said: "I like Mummy to read the Bible, but I just can't bear
her explanations."

I'm sure Bea [Mother] could manage Claudie better if she
wouldn't get emotional with her. The child can't understand it.

Last night when I went in to Claudie, she was standing up in
bed with the cover over her head and under her chin, and she
said, "Do you know who I am, Granny? I am pretending to be
Jesus' wife. Have you got any 'woom' for me in your inn? I've
got my bed for a stable and seven covers."

She has Grahame completely awestruck, although they are
devoted to each other; but I think she's a little bit jealous of Billy.
She said the other day, "I can't write as nice stories as Billy or
write as nice 'pomes' as him, but I'm much fatter than he is."
She is working away at Poetry, but I'm afraid it isn't very good.

When it rained, we children wore gum boots and yellow sou'westers in
the backyard, and squatted under a big umbrella and listened to the down-
pour. We had to go in before lunch to get our baths and wash all the mud
off. Nanny and Ada would make us stand up in the tub to be soaped, but
Phoebe allowed us to wallow in the hot water and keep warm. She would

wash us catch-as-catch-can, getting hold of whatever bits of us she could. We didn't end up so clean with Phoebe, but we had a more comfortable time of it than with Nanny or Ada.

After the chimney sweep had been to our house, we would be scrubbed nearly raw to get the soot off. But it was a great treat to watch him at work, and worth the strenuous bath afterward. The chimney sweep was always pitch black with soot; all one could see of his face was a pair of very bright eyes. The household furniture would be covered with dust sheets. After attaching a long pole to his brush, he would let us push it up the chimney. Then we would rush out into the yard to see the brush come out of the chimney in an explosion of soot.

Every day after lunch the boys and I were dressed up in identical sailor suits, except mine had a skirt. They were complete with bosun's whistle, lanyard, and sundry other nautical equipment, and hats with HMS *Valiant* on the bands. After being taken for our daily walk in those outfits, we would have our hands and faces scrubbed and have to go to tea with the mummies.

Sometimes, when the weather was fine, which wasn't often in England, tea would be served in the front garden. There were flowers growing there, which we could smell but not pick, and we were not allowed to play because we had our clean teatime outfits on. Nanny and Ada would be in attendance, wearing their frilly uniforms and caps with streamers. Nanny and Ada would hardly talk to us in the front garden, and if they did, they would say Miss Claudia, Master Grahame, and Master Billy.

We could not make out why they behaved so strangely in the garden, as we were not yet old enough to grasp the Upstairs-Downstairs syndrome. In those days, life was still very like the television series of that name. Class consciousness was fully accepted and much more obvious a fact of British life than it is now, and everyone was snobbish; Downstairs was just as bad as Upstairs. It was called "knowing your place." As children we had only a foretaste of how our future lives would be governed by social protocol. You were Downstairs until you were about seventeen. Then you had to go Upstairs, and like it. Downstairs never spoke to you again except as Miss Claudia, and only if Downstairs was in uniform. I didn't like it. I was much fonder of Nanny and Ada and Phoebe and their friends and relations than I was of my parents and some of their friends.

On those al fresco teatime occasions, there would usually be a number of army officers, and among the regular guests, Red Cross matron Mrs. Gyes-Moores (everyone was hyphenated in Farnborough), a formidable woman, and nearly always the vicar, a frightening man with a booming voice, who played and joked with us a lot. One day he gave me a large felt dog to keep teddy company. The vicar was, I am sure, very kind, but he roared and shouted so much I was terrified.

Another frequent visitor was Auntie Wavell, a friend of Tikka Gran. Her husband had been in the same regiment as Grandfather Brown; she was the mother of Lord Wavell of Second World War fame, and my uncle Llewyn's godmother. She often invited us children to tea at her house, which was almost pitch dark, because it was completely covered with wisteria she absolutely refused to have pruned. The house was as full of things from "Inja" as Tikka Gran's; they were all the more fascinating for being difficult to examine in the gloom.

Actually, Auntie Wavell was rather like Tikka Gran: very contentious, especially with the vicar. They would have some terrible rows about the altar flowers, last Sunday's sermon, the popishness of incense, and so forth. We thought she was very brave to confront him.

When he was shaking hands with the congregation after the service, she nearly always got into an altercation with him, which would make him so mad he would go in and slam the door. Once he slammed it so hard it fell off its hinges. That was really worth going to church to see. It was one of my churchgoing periods I thoroughly enjoyed.

During the first years of the war, one or another of our fathers would turn up at our house on leave, but Grahame and Billy and I would hardly see them. My father and Uncle Bill Wilgar and Uncle Folger were usually so exhausted they spent most of their time in bed. They always brought with them their military sidekicks and batmen (their personal servants), however, who were accommodated under the same roof. When the batmen came out to the back porch to polish the uniform buttons and shine up the equipment, they made friends with the children playing in the yard and gave us stacks of cigarette cards with pictures of wild flowers, flags, military badges, and other things of an educational nature. These came in sets of fifty each, and some cards were very scarce and hard to get. Our new friends would take the numbers of the missing ones and case the canteens for them. It was thrilling when they brought us a new batch and one could complete a set.

The batmen would, of course, be entertained Downstairs. Nanny, Ada, and Phoebe were very popular with the soldiery. Men and maids sat around the big kitchen table drinking tea or beer, laughing, talking and singing, and having a jolly time.

One day Mother's youngest brother, Bryer, turned up. He was a great big blond, handsome, noisy fellow who had joined up in Canada as a private, been wounded, and was given a long leave. We saw a lot of him Downstairs because Upstairs were all the officers, so he had to keep saluting, which got very tiresome. He had a wonderful voice and, between mugs of beer, would roar forth "On the Road to Mandalay," "Excelsior!" "I Hear You Calling Me," and other sing-along favorites. He made a tremendous noise, which would rather rile some of the Upstairs officers and gentlemen, but they couldn't say much because he was Mother's brother. The maids Downstairs couldn't say anything, either—not that they wanted to—for the same reason: one didn't criticize Madam's brother. It was more or less bedlam all the while Bryer stayed with us, but it was one of the high points of the war.

Nanny, Ada, Phoebe, and the soldiery delighted in teaching us children the latest popular songs. I took to the new game like an early Shirley Temple. They would get me marching up and down on top of the table singing "Over There," "I'm Only a Broken Doll," and "There's a Long, Long Trail" for great rewards of soldier buttons, cigarette cards, and badges. Once I even got a German helmet. My most successful effort, done with energetic pantomime, put the kitchen light in jeopardy. It went:

> *Ginger, you're balmy, get your hair out,*
> *They all begin to cry,*
> *With nothing on your napper,*
> *Oh, you are a pie.*
> *Pies must have a little bit of crust,*
> *Why don't you join the army?*
> *If you want to look a don,*
> *Put a bit of something on;*
> *Ginger, you're balmy.*

Grahame couldn't hold a tune, and Billy wasn't allowed to sing on account of his chest, so the song-and-dance situation was the only one in which I was the undisputed star of the three of us. How would I know that it was the only situation in which I would ever win approval? I wanted approval desperately as a child; I wasn't to earn it until I was a grown woman. I was too sheltered, and certainly too young at the time, to know about music halls and the stage and that some people make their living singing songs—comic or sad. All I knew was that I felt happy performing in front of an audience.

I still do.

CHAPTER 3

A fairy-tale idyll in Folkestone

One day Mother discovered that I sucked my thumb. Since thumb sucking was supposed to be shameful, there was a terrific hullabaloo about it. Mother ordered Nanny to put bitter aloes on my thumbs, but I wiped it off on the sheet. Then Nanny tied my hands up in bags, which I bit through. Next, my hands were tied to the bedposts, but I wiggled out with the aid of teeth and contortions. I became a junior Houdini. Of course, it was actually more fun getting out of the restraints than it was sucking my thumb.

Mother made a dreadful fuss: Ada got scolded, Billy and Grahame were put on their honor not to let me wangle them into slipping in from their nursery to unloose me, and poor Nanny really got it in the neck.

One night, Nanny finally had it. She got very cross and said she didn't care any longer if I had buck teeth, and I could suck my thumb right off if I liked. She was going to give notice. I was appalled. There was no point in sucking my thumb if I wasn't going to get any attention. The fun had gone, so I stopped.

After all this, however, Mother was fed up with me, so she decreed that Grahame and I should pay a visit to the maids' parents, Mr. and Mrs. Stribbling. (We three children were less one member; Billy had gone back to Canada with his mother, my dear aunt Gertie, and his father, who had gotten out of the army before the other two fathers.) If our brief visit with the Stribblings proved a success, we would spend the summer holidays with their family at Folkestone.

Mother was quite willing to confide Grahame and me to their care, and yet she could write in her diary, "I think the Toad will grow up to be very common, as she prefers the company of the servants to her own mother."

In due course, Grahame and I went off to Ash with Nanny, Ada, and Phoebe. Everything seemed enchanted that day, for I was going on an adventure, leaving Mother behind, and I would meet Mr. Stribbling for the first time.

I suppose the Stribblings' house was just an old-fashioned laborer's cottage surrounded by a small garden, but I was stunned when I saw it. It was a fairy-tale cottage, the gingerbread house in *Hansel and Gretel*. Great fruit trees in blossom were hanging over the thatched roof, the garden was a riot of flowers, and there was a wishing well. (The well was the only water supply and the house had no plumbing, but such inconveniences have no place in fairy tales.)

Mr. Stribbling came to the door to meet us. He was a large man, with a luxuriant black beard covering most of his face and curling halfway down his chest. He worked as an engine driver on the Southern Railway and tended a market garden on the side. It was after tea when we arrived, and he must have already changed out of his work clothes, because he wore a maroon velvet smoking jacket and a pillbox smoking cap with a long gold tassel hanging from it. He looked so magnificent and impressive that I can remember him as if it were yesterday.

He said, "Hello, my girls," and kissed Nanny, Ada, and Phoebe. Then he said to Grahame and me, "And here are my two new little ones," and ushered us into the parlor.

The parlor was a dream. On the mantelpiece stood an enormous clock surrounded by the biggest seashells I have ever seen. There was a four-leaf screen, with Christmas cards stuck all over it, and a glass case full of stuffed tropical birds. Crest china mugs and jugs of all sizes occupied every available space. The walls were covered with pictures of King George and Queen Mary, Queen Victoria, *The Stag at Dusk*, and several sunset-and-wild-waves pictures. In the middle of all this was a sort of pope's chair. The room was a riot of color and I adored it.

I had barely begun to take in the splendor of the parlor when Mrs. Stribbling appeared, wearing a black dress buttoned up to the neck, with a lace collar and a large cameo brooch, her hair wound up on top of her head in a snail hairdo.

After the introductions, Mr. Stribbling sat in the pope's chair, took one of us on each knee, and announced, "I am Granddad, and that is Gran, and now I have two new little grandchildren. And soon we are all going to the seaside together, to have a lovely holiday."

Then we all went out to look around the cottage. We wound up the bucket in the well and had a drink of the coldest water I had ever tasted in those prerefrigeration days. We looked at all the flowers and were actually allowed to pick some. I had picked wild flowers, but had never been allowed to pick any in a garden. The roses were colossal; in fact, everything in the garden seemed to be bigger and brighter than anything I'd seen before. Then we peeked into the apple storerooms and saw shelves with rows and rows of red apples that looked about a foot across and smelled delicious.

Owing to the excitement, Grahame and I soon had to "go," so Nanny took us to a little shack almost covered with honeysuckle and old man's beard. It was nothing less than a three-holer—a big hole, a medium hole, and a little hole—and instead of the usual toilet roll, a great big Selfridge's catalog hung on the wall by a string. Nanny remarked that she had never known us to take so long, but how could one resist dallying in such fascinating surroundings?

After Nanny, Ada, and Phoebe let us have the fun of helping them pull up a huge supply of lettuce and radishes and cut lots of mustard and cress, they finally got us back into the house, where we had an enormous supper. Afterward, we examined every last Christmas card on the screen, listened to the sea in the giant shells, looked at everything in Gran's work basket and jewel case, helped Granddad wind the clock, and were finally put to bed. That was probably the best day in my life up to then.

The next day all the Stribbling family came to lunch. There seemed to be dozens of them, and quite a lot of children our own age. I particularly took to three little granddaughters: Elsie, Sissie, and Midge. I was used to playing with boys, but I'd never before come into close contact with girls. There was another huge meal before we got on the train and went home, exhausted but triumphant.

The visit had been a huge success. In a few weeks Grahame and I were to rejoin these transcendent people, and we could hardly wait.

The summer at Folkestone was a wild success. There were dozens of Stribblings of all ages, and we filled an entire boardinghouse. Every day would start with morning prayers, then Granddad would have a few words with each of the children: Had we been good? What had we done that was fun the day before? Had we been to the lavatory? Then off we went to the beach, where we had donkey rides, and bought ice cream sandwiches from the Italian in the little yellow cart; where we paddled, collected shells, built sand castles, and generally rushed about. All was supervised by Gran and Granddad, sitting in deck chairs under a striped awning. That summer had a glamor about it that I was never to recapture.

After our summer with the Stribblings home seemed very dreary, especially since Billy was gone, but now the mummies stood at three again, for Billy's mother had been replaced by my godmother, Aunt Alice Schuyler. When Grahame and I first found out about this, our hearts sank, but not for long.

Aunt Al was ten years older than Mother and infinitely more intelligent. She was one of five daughters of Judge Britton of Kingston, Ontario, an old rascal who had made a vast fortune in second mortgages. Her sisters were tall, Junoesque ladies, all suitably married to pillars of society. I suspect Aunt Al was the plain one, about five feet tall, round, not exactly good-looking even in her earlier years, but very chic. She was extremely clever and amusing, very peppery and inclined to be sarcastic, with a tongue like an adder when it suited her, and she had guts. She would have a go at anything, no matter what. She smoked like a chimney; she drank, sometimes a drop too much. She was a total person.

Aunt Al may not have had the family looks, but she had inherited the old boy's toughness. Judge Britton had prevailed upon her to marry one Valentine Schuyler, because he thought a classy American name like Schuyler would add a certain pizzazz to his Canadian family. Aunt Al couldn't stand her husband, so she made a deal that she would put up with him six months of the year provided she was given unlimited funds to do whatever she liked the other six months. Poor old Valentine was on the grog and finally killed himself drinking wood alcohol, after which Aunt Al's gallivanting knew no bounds.

She was an extraordinarily bracing influence on me, her five-year-old godchild. She paid me so much intelligent attention that I thought she must be a relation of Granddad. But I didn't say so, as remarks about him never seemed to get through to the family. When Aunt Al first turned up, I was at an age when my mind hadn't collected all the barnacles it has now, and I could see right to the heart of things. In those days, everybody gave me the ducky-wucky, cutie-boots treatment. "Little Claudia, come give Auntie [or Mother or Granny] a big hug! . . . Oh, what a pretty dress! . . . Let's see a nice smile, coochie—coochie-coo!" I used to think what fools they were. Aunt Al never went on like that. She would really talk to me and actually listen to what I said. Apart from Granny Tandy, who was a great expert on Jesus (in Whom I was passionately interested at the time), she was the only sensible person I knew.

She was different in other ways, too. For instance, she was the first person to give us children real toys. Mother was cross about this, and said that Father didn't approve of toys. Aunt Al answered that "Claude is an old poop." I liked that, and asked if I could call Father Poop. I was told no, that it was rude, but I could call him Pip. But why Poop should be rude and Pip not, I couldn't see. And I didn't understand the rather rude jokes Aunt Al would tell at teatime. But I do remember Mother would be shocked and say, "Not in front of the children, Al."

I didn't know it then, but this extraordinary woman was to play an important role in my life in the years to come.

The last thing I remember about the Farnborough period was being all dressed up and taken on a train by Mother to be a flower girl at someone's wedding. When we got off at our destination, I could not believe my eyes: there on the platform, in his dungarees, stood Granddad. I broke away from Mother, ran to him, and flung myself into his arms. I hugged and kissed him, so proud that he was driving our train. Mother was simply furious and dragged me away, although I protested loudly.

I can't remember the wedding at all, except that Mother, who could be quite a raconteur, spent a lot of time telling a funny story about me and an engine driver. This brought forth roars of mirth from the assembled company. I really think I hated Mother at that moment.

And I never saw Granddad again.

CHAPTER 4

"You've Never Done Your Bit
Till You're Dead, Dead, Dead"

About the third year of the Great War, Father was posted back to England, to be commandant of a soldiers' rest camp in Norfolk. So off we went to the east of England to occupy a house named Thetford Abbey.

Built on the grounds of a ruined abbey, it was a Victorian monstrosity, with the usual front lawns and backyard. All over the grounds were rows of huge Gothic arches and remains of what looked like Norman keeps, with spiral stone staircases inside going up to nothing. There were stone tombs, hunks of masonry and bits of carving lying about, all overgrown with weeds. It was a perfect place to play in, although it's a wonder we didn't break our necks.

Nanny Stribbling had left us to get married and had been replaced by Alison, who took care of Grahame's new little brother, John, as well as Grahame and me. But the family setup was still the same. My father and Uncle Carl Folger, Grahame's father, were both at Thetford Abbey, but we saw hardly any more of them than we did when they were at the front. Father spent most of his time at the camp, and Uncle Carl, who was a bit of a gallivanter, was always rushing up to London on some pretext or other.

The whole thing started again in Thetford about how lovely Grahame was and what a shame it wasn't me. Although I had always taken great pride in his appearance, and we both thought our mothers were silly to up-stage each other, I was beginning to realize the implications of being a rather plain little girl and the fact that he, being a beautiful boy, had definitely got the edge on me.

It had been said many times that Grahame looked like Gainsborough's Blue Boy, so Aunt Nancy had a blue suit made for him, which was an exact copy of the painting, then she had a photograph taken of him in the Blue Boy pose, which was blown up to the size of the original and colored and framed as nearly the same as possible. The reproduction was hung in the drawing room, so that when we went up for tea, Grahame and his picture were, naturally, the focus of attention.

The Blue Boy coup plus John, the beautiful new baby, made Aunt Nancy the top mama and my mother progressively more dissatisfied with me. To make a bad situation worse, Alison was definitely on Grahame's side, while Ada and Phoebe remained fiercely loyal to me, so there was a rift in the lute in the servants' hall, too.

Grahame and I were really fed up with it all. Most grown-ups were perfectly hopeless. We would keep on loving the ones we loved and take no notice of the others. Let them rant on.

At this point I fell in love with one of Father's officers, Captain Phillip Woolf Davis. He was tall, portly, handsome in a rather florid way. And could he play the piano! He had played at the Leeds Festival before the war, so I suppose he was a professional. I don't know what he did at the camp, but he seemed to be always at the house. Every time I saw him, even if it was just after breakfast, I would ask him to play, and he always did. Probably, like the rest of us, he liked to have an audience. I was the fan of fans, and would sit listening to him by the hour. He would explain what he was playing, tell me about the composer, and repeat my favorite bits over and over.

He was a bachelor and doubtless not used to children, but he had the same faculty as Aunt Al of talking to me as if I were a contemporary. I must have been a damned nuisance, though. Everyone was always telling Captain Davis to throw me out if he was bored; whether it was his innate courtesy or the natural-born teacher's aptitude, he would have none of it.

He sang in a rich, oily voice, making very funny faces as he did so, but his singing was most mellifluous. He could also paint very well. He took me off sketching, and gave me paper, pencil, and a watercolor box to mess about with. He explained perspective and how to apply color. When he wasn't there, I did my homework. Outdoors I tried to draw; indoors I would pick things out that he had taught me on the piano.

Poor old Grahame got very fed up with me, for he was tone deaf and didn't like drawing, and so he had no one to play with. Mother encouraged my new activities, as no doubt she was beginning to think I might become musical or artistic, and she would then have a Roland for Aunt Nancy's Oliver.

Then came a surprise. One day Ada rushed downstairs from the dining room at lunchtime in a great state of excitement to say that Captain Davis had said that I was a very clever child and might even be a genius. As you may imagine, I was thrilled with my beloved captain's pronouncement, and pretty well pleased with myself.

It wasn't until recently, however, when plowing through Mum's diaries, that I found out all Captain Davis had said: "Phillip said today at lunch that he thought the Toad was one of the most perceptive and intelligent children he had ever met, and he thought it possible that she could be a genius. We all agreed that it is a pity she is not a boy. He thinks genius is wasted on women. They either grow out of it, or become misfits for life. Oh, dear! What have I done to deserve such a child? If only she had been pretty!"

Mother never tired of that theme, and needed only such corroboration of her fears to harp on it. But dear Ada! Such a builder-upper! Trust her to leave out the rotten part. I am quite sure she took advantage of my rather questionable triumph to win the servants' hall skirmish, too, because after that Alison would say to me, "Eat your porridge, Miss Smartypants," or "Hurry up and clean your teeth, Miss Cleverdick, if it isn't overworking that bright brain of yours."

Neither his beauty nor my brain, nor indeed anything else, ever caused a rift between Grahame and me; we were always happy in each other's company. We used to sit together in class at Thetford Grammar School, where he developed a great talent for flicking spitballs. He would chew a bit of blotting paper to pulp, dip it in the ink, and flick it with amazing accuracy at some kid in front of him. He never got caught, because he always looked so cherubic, and the teacher couldn't believe he would do such a thing. I did it, too, but without Grahame's marksmanship, I usually wound up hitting the teacher. I was always the one to get caught.

The school's headmistress called on Mother to say that I was a very bad influence on that dear, good little boy. Once again, Mother's view of incorrigible me had been confirmed. Mother smacked my bottom with a hairbrush and sent me to bed without supper. I didn't mind because on supperless occasions Ada and Phoebe would sneak some ultradelicious snacks up to me when no one was looking.

I'm not certain how long we stayed in Thetford, but it was probably not more than six months before Father was sent to be commandant of a soldiers' rest camp in Crowborough, and we had to move again.

Our new house was next to one belonging to Sir Arthur Conan Doyle. Grahame and I didn't know who he was, but Ada and Phoebe knew, and were absolutely thrilled. Ardent fans of fictional detective Sherlock Holmes, they stopped reading us *Little Black Sambo* and *Strewelpeter,* which were getting a bit boring anyhow, and introduced us to the mysteries of *The Speckled Band, The Hound of the Baskervilles,* and *The Engineer's Thumb.*

Grahame and I immediately became sleuths. We had pictures of Sherlock Holmes and Dr. Watson pasted all over the nursery. Naturally, I was Holmes. Ada got Father to lend me an ancient deerstalker; it covered my whole head, down to my chin, but that didn't matter. Ada, who could sew or knit anything, made me an exact replica of Holmes's tweed cape. I had a meerschaum pipe, made of liquorice with sherbet in the bowl, that I clenched between my teeth. Not to be outdone, Alison found an old Homburg for Grahame to wear as Dr. Watson, and made him a fierce black wool mustache, which was held by an elastic band that went around his head. We each had a magnifying glass and an envelope to hold clues. We were in business.

Off we went spying through the hedge and looking for clues—but we didn't have a clue as to what or whom we were trying to track down. It wasn't long before our envelopes were full of fluff, twigs, snail shells, and other no doubt disgusting messes. We stalked numerous hounds of the Baskervilles, but we could see nothing going on behind the hedge that separated the Sherlock Holmes house from ours. The house next door appeared to be empty; it was undoubtedly Sir Arthur's summer home. But the absence of the great man in no way dampened our ardor for sleuthing.

When we learned Sir Arthur would soon be arriving at his house, we could hardly contain our excitement. Grahame and I were at our posts bright and early the day of his arrival. I don't know what we expected to see, probably Sherlock Holmes in person, but when Sir Arthur finally appeared in his garden, we were dumbfounded: he wore no deerstalker cap or tweed cape, and clenched no pipe between his teeth. This was not Sherlock Holmes, so who could it be? Of course! It was the archfiend himself—Professor Moriarty—the only one who could outfox Holmes.

The professor must not see me as the great detective. I knew Moriarty was a threat to me. Grahame and I, dressed in all our gear, spent the afternoon hiding up in the oak tree that dominated our garden. Sir Arthur walked over to our house, in a surprisingly neighborly way for one we thought was Moriarty. In our confused and fevered minds, we figured that if Holmes had not been able to "get" Moriarty, Moriarty was not going to "get" Holmes, certainly not if Holmes (me) was in our drawing room, with Father looking on. Later we learned that Father had been disappointed that we could not be found and had therefore missed the opportunity of meeting a great man. All we knew was that we had missed our supper.

At that time, in fact, Father had something more pressing on his mind than introducing us to a celebrated neighbor. There seemed to be a lot of lead swinging going on at Father's camp, a rehabilitation center for wounded soldiers just out of the hospital and getting ready to go back to the front lines. The men were saying they had done their bit and were too ill to go back to active duty. Their protests finally got Father down to the point where he gathered them all together for a reprimand and said, "You've never done your bit till you're dead."

One of the more lurid London newspapers pounced on the statement, and Father found himself in the headlines, all of which read much the same: "Harsh Colonel Brutal to Our Poor Boys." Suddenly, Sir Arthur Conan Doyle was not the only celebrity in Crowborough. Father's disciplinary reminder to the languishing men inspired a music hall comic to make a song of it, which was called, not surprisingly, "You've Never Done Your Bit Till You're Dead, Dead, Dead." Of course, we wanted to be taken to hear it sung at the London Hippodrome, but since it was apparently very vulgar and a slur on Father, that was out of the question.

Grahame and I were taken to London all the same, but for quite a different reason. The war had ended, and we went up to see the victory celebrations. Neither of us had ever been to a city, so you can imagine our excitement.

The mummies decided that we had to get dressed in our best, but the new outfit Aunt Nancy bought Grahame for the occasion was dazzling enough to divert attention from the Changing of the Guard. It was a red velvet Lord Fauntleroy, and he really did look adorable in it. I wore some sort of white smock with blue embroidery, and on top of my head a great blue bow, which I hated. I couldn't help thinking, "They're all going to start again saying how beautiful Grahame is, and no one will take any notice of me with this rotten bow," and I started to cry. Ada saved the day by reminding me that I was a genius, and "Geniuses don't cry," so the storm blew over.

All was forgotten by the time we reached London. Grahame had a passion for trains and I liked looking at the crowds of people, so when we got off the train at Victoria Station, we could have stayed there happily all afternoon. We were finally dragged away, protesting, to a taxi, which took us to the Savoy Hotel. We were to be entertained by Aunt Bena (my great-aunt Rowena), who stayed at the Savoy when she was in London.

I had never seen anything so grand: the doorman and liveried porters, the sparkling mirrors and great crystal chandeliers, and the lift, which fascinated me. I was too interested in going up in the lift to pay much attention to the smart ladies sitting in the lobby, but I heard them say, as we passed, "Look at the dear little boy . . . isn't he adorable?" and more.

Father rang the bell at Aunt Bena's suite, and the door was answered by an absolute scarecrow, wearing a very obvious ginger wig. Laughing and chattering like a monkey (in Italian, I suppose), Nina Leone, Aunt Bena's Italian lady's maid, showed us into a sumptuous anteroom.

Father had only slightly prepared us for Aunt Bena, a tall, elderly lady who swept in with towering majesty, her Duke of Wellington (or C. Aubrey Smith) nose preceding her. Her enormous head was covered with blond curls (she was wearing her best blond wig for this occasion), and her voluminous figure was draped with lace and sparkling with diamonds. She positively charged Father with cries of "My baby! My little Claudie! My own precious darling!" Father was a slim, elegant, six-foot-one forty-five-year-old. She enfolded him in an embrace and started up her cries again, this time in French.

When the paroxysm over Father somewhat subsided, I expected she would catch sight of beautiful Grahame in his gorgeous red Lord Fauntleroy and have another over him. But that's not what happened at all. Aunt Bena said, "Where's the darling baby?"

Grahame and I were standing close together, rather holding on to each other, like the two little babes in the wood. We were speechless with amazement. We had never seen anyone like Aunt Bena. Where's the darling baby? Who's that? Father pointed me out. To my utter astonishment, Aunt Bena sank to her knees, like a ship going down, and clasped me to her ample bosom. "Oh, what a darling!" she cried. "How adorable! What a pretty little thing!" A pretty little thing?—*I'm* a pretty little thing? And then there were many more cries, in French, which I couldn't understand. She ignored Grahame completely.

I felt shy and a little embarrassed and wasn't sure what to say. After all, I was quite unaccustomed to this sort of reception. Probably out of sheer nervousness, I asked her, "Are you one of the Beaky-Bullys?" I could hear Mother gasp. Gales of laughter from Aunt Bena.

"You've heard how your naughty father used to tease his poor old aunt about her great big nose!" She introduced me to Uncle Andy, her second husband, large and florid, with flowing white mustachios. He flung me up into the air and gave me a smacking cigar-scented kiss on each cheek. Then I had to stand in front of them and be minutely examined.

It appeared I looked like Father. I wasn't exactly pretty in the traditional sense, no. But what golden coloring! What a milk-and-roses complexion! Such bone structure! Intelligent! Witty! Not pretty in the chocolate-box sense, no. But, ah, attractive! Very attractive! So much better than mere prettiness, yes. Chic! Ah, *très chic!* Followed by a lot more in French. I could not believe my ears.

The next thing I knew, Father introduced Grahame to Aunt Bena, and I braced myself for even greater transports of joy. All Aunt Bena said was, "It's so nice of you to come, Grahame. We are delighted to have you." Her quiet, kindly tone fell on the room almost like a silence. Grahame grinned at me; he knew Cinderella had stolen the show from Prince Charming and, bless him, he didn't mind at all.

We then had a look around. The rooms were all crimson and gold, the way I imagined Buckingham Palace to be. I took a surreptitious peek at myself in one of the mirrors to see if some miraculous change had occurred in me, but no such luck. However, if Aunt Bena and Uncle Andy thought I was so attractive, maybe now some other people would think so, too.

Gluttony quickly superseded vanity when tea was served. What a spread! Sandwiches, crumpets, chocolate eclairs, iced cake, and cream buns. Grahame and I stuffed ourselves until we could hardly breathe.

When we came to the cakes, I expected Mother to say to me, as usual, "You may have only one," but she didn't. As soon as I had finished a cake, Aunt Bena would coax me to have another. Mother was probably intimidated. And overawed. And thoroughly outpomped. She had hardly said a word since we got there, which was most unlike her, as she usually dominated every conversation. Sitting there stuffing myself under Aunt Bena's protection, and not hearing a word out of Mother, was my idea of paradise.

In the evening, Uncle Andy ordered a carriage of the type used by royalty, and off we clattered to see the sights of London. Piccadilly Circus was the most exciting. The electric signs flashing away were not neon lights then; some of them are still there: Sademan's Port, with the Spaniard, and Bovril. Grahame and I thought the riot of light bulbs the most beautiful thing we'd ever seen. I asked Aunt Bena whether we could go around Piccadilly again, and she said, "Of course, darling, as many times as you like." She told the coachman to keep going around until I, and only I, decided when we should proceed further. I think we must have gone around twenty times. Still no word out of Mother. Young as I was, I realized that she could be silenced; I had won a victory.

The next morning we went back to Crowborough, and the return to normal was painful. The visit to Aunt Bena had been so fantastic that it almost seemed never to have happened. Grahame and I spent most of the day giving a detailed description to Ada and Phoebe, who were duly impressed. Nursery tea seemed very drab after the one we had had the day before. I clung to the knowledge, however, that there was something better than the gloomy house we lived in, and to the hope that someday I should live in a dear little cottage like Granddad Stribbling's or a grand suite at the Savoy like Aunt Bena's.

CHAPTER 5

From Sparta to Sybaris
and back again

Something wonderful, like our visit to London, was often followed by something unpleasant. Only a few days later, the blow fell. The war was over, and that was splendid for everybody except Grahame and me. He was going back to Canada with his parents and brother, and I was staying in England.

We howled because we wouldn't have anyone to play with, and put on a great old performance. When Ada and Phoebe had calmed us down, Grahame suddenly realized he wouldn't see *them* anymore, which started him crying again, and that set Ada and Phoebe off. The only one who didn't cry was Alison, who was disgusted and went to sit with baby John, leaving the rest of us to our misery.

It wasn't so bad for Grahame on the day of parting because someone had sensibly arranged for the young train buff to look inside an engine at Victoria Station, where our families were gathered to say good-bye. I had my own treat to tell him about: Aunt Bena was going to take me to the pantomime. We were so excited about our individual prospects that, as had been foreseen, we avoided sentimental melodrama on the platform and said good-bye in a civilized manner, with a minimum of tears.

I was not to see my dear, beautiful Grahame again for thirty years, not until he came to Eaton Auditorium, in Toronto, where I was doing a concert. He was six feet, four inches tall, still very handsome, but bald as a coot. Neither of us mentioned his beautiful golden curls.

The end of the war brought changes for everybody. Father was transferred to London, so we moved once again. Our new house at 39A Philbeach Gardens, Earl's Court, was in a row of typical London houses, about one room wide, with a basement and four floors above. There was a great gloomy kitchen in the basement, behind it an even gloomier servants' hall, and beyond that a small yard where a few sickly laurel bushes grew, surrounded by a ten-foot stone wall. The dark, depressing dining room was on the ground floor. The house seemed a bit grim until one reached the drawing room on the first floor. It was huge, with a fireplace, lots of mirrors, a crystal chandelier, and an elegant black concert grand piano (the house was rented furnished). In fact, it was almost worthy of Aunt Bena. The second floor had Mum's bedroom and boudoir; the third floor, Dad's bedroom and study; the top floor was for Ada, Phoebe, and myself. Not bad. Not bad at all.

Across the road was a high wall with a wrought-iron gate that opened with a big key and, lo and behold, beyond the gate was a large park where nannies pushed prams and children ran about and bowled hoops. Ada told me the park was only for people who lived in Philbeach Gardens—they were the only ones in the whole of London who had keys to unlock the gate. That gave me a sense of importance and a feeling that we might be moving up in the world, perhaps to Aunt Bena's style of living, which indeed proved to be the case. I understood that children in London could not be turned out to play by themselves, and the more fortunate had private parks where they were safe behind walls and locked gates. However, what little freedom I had enjoyed earlier I lost in a life of constant supervision.

A stream of relatives appeared now that we were living in London. Not one of them knew a thing about rearing a child, but each took me under his or her wing for a time—for as long, I suppose, as it amused them. Since I was the only child in a family that had stopped reproducing, some kind of atavistic urge must have compelled my uncles, aunts, and cousins to protect and nurture me as the last of the line. More often, though, it seemed that they regarded me as a very special toy, a conversation piece, a pet to be indulged and pampered and spoiled.

Glamorous and *exotic* are words that have become threadbare with use, but in their pristine meanings they applied to at least half a dozen members of my family. Uncle Reginald Llewellyn (Llewyn) returned from Germany, where he had been imprisoned all through the war. He was handsome and dashing and told me about all the things the British prisoners had done to while away the time. Many years later, television's "Hogan's Heroes" reminded me of the exploits Uncle Llewyn had so graphically described.

His eldest brother, Uncle Eric, was on leave from "Inja" at this time. He was a colonel of the Gurkhas, very pukka and romantic, rather like David Niven. His stories were, of course, about thrilling adventures. He wore a puggaree, or small turban, and a gray-blue uniform with a kukri, a sort of curved dagger, stuck in his belt. Instead of having some old Cockney batman, like Daddy's or Uncle Carl's, he had a dazzling Sikh body servant, Gumba Ding Poon, who had a great black beard and a turban. Even Uncle Eric's language was different from Daddy's and Uncle Carl's: regimental sergeant majors, corporals, and privates were Surbaders, Gemildars, and Rissaldars, not necessarily in that order. Uncle Eric drew for me wonderful pictures of these exotic army men.

Several of Father's aunts, the Beaky-Bullys, lived in London, and I was always welcome in their houses. Great-aunt Leila had a house in Lowndes Square, Knightsbridge, which was somewhat like ours in Philbeach Gardens, but three times larger and grander. It was there that Madame Nellie Melba, then Mrs. Armstrong, had sung in London the first time. Aunt Leila, who had been a famous hostess, was now an invalid.

Ada would take me to Lowndes Square and hand me over to Gardiner, the butler. He was very dignified and Arthur Treacher-like, as he bowed from the waist, with arms akimbo. Gardiner and I would solemnly proceed up the stairs to Aunt Leila's boudoir, where, looking like Lady Bracknell, the invalid would be sitting in a wheelchair throne. The poor old dear had had a stroke and couldn't talk. We would sit together for about half an hour, the silent old lady and the loquacious little girl, while I babbled on at her and she smiled and nodded and patted my hand. Apparently I pleased her very much, and she was a great success with me, as she was such a marvelous audience. Presently Gardiner would appear and conduct me downstairs to lunch.

Aunt Leila's children, all three unmarried and well past middle age, would greet me in the dining room. Gwynnie, a mother's helper-type old maid, must have been about sixty, with the mentality of a polite sixteen-year-old. Cousin Bob was fat and jolly, and Cousin Ernest handsome and charming. Not having to work for a living, the cousins spent their time visiting other social butterflies, or going to their clubs, the theater, or the races. Bob and Ernest were prone to entertain beautiful ladies of the chorus, a secret to which I was not privy at the time.

Aunt Leila's dining room was just as dark as ours, with the difference that ours was lighted by newly installed electricity, and hers by candles burning in two huge silver candelabras. Everything gleamed. On the table, polished until it reflected like a mirror, stood a colossal epergne filled with roses. It must have been spring or summer because the floral displays changed according to the season. Each place was set with a bewildering array of silver knives and forks on a Brussels lace mat; an individual condiment set, for salt, pepper, and mustard; and four kinds of sparkling cut-crystal glasses. There were silver dishes for nuts and ginger and all sorts of other good things. The dinner service was a beautiful green and gold.

Lunch was an amazing ritual. Gardiner and the two frilly parlor maids handed around each course. While we were eating they would go behind a carved openwork Indian screen and stand at attention in a line, pretending they weren't there. There might be a whole salmon, all tizzied up and decorated to beat the band with cucumbers, radishes, and lemons cut in fancy shapes; a roast of beef such as you might see being wheeled around the Grill Room at the Savoy; or, on special occasions, pheasant under glass. Caviar was commonplace. I hated it, and I still do. But the dessert! Charlotte russe topped with complicated patterns of cherries and angelica; mounds of profiteroles, filled with cream and covered in chocolate sauce; cakes decorated with sugar birds. Standing over the chafing dish, Gardiner prepared crêpes Suzette flambé or cherries jubilee like an orchestral conductor. We would have sherry with the soup, hock with the fish, Chateau Neuf du Pape with the meat, and champagne with dessert. I was given a quarter of a glass of each of the first three, but a full glass of champagne, because Cousin Ernest said it was good for me.

I can understand putting on a feast like that for a wedding, but every day! I often wondered what happened to all that food after we had ruined the appearance of it.

After lunch, Cousin Ernest would usually take me for a walk, which I think we must have needed. Perhaps we would go to the park and admire the flowers, and then take a cab to Bond Street to look in the shop windows. If I admired anything less than a diamond necklace, Cousin Ernest would rush in and buy it for me. We invariably ended the afternoon by going to the Park Lane Hotel to have tea and to listen to Albert Sandler, the violinist, whom Cousin Ernest couldn't hear often enough. Although I would have eaten more than enough food for one day, Aunt Leila and I would have supper together, which was served on a tray at six o'clock. After a proper interval for digestion, I was bathed, scented, powdered, primped, and put to bed by her lady's maid.

The luxurious holiday would end when Ada came to collect me at a prearranged time. We would arrive home clutching parcels and packages, boxes of chocolate, flowers for Mother, and for Daddy always a jar of the ginger he adored. Mother didn't approve at all; she took a very dim view of my excursions to Aunt Leila's or indeed to any of Beaky-Bullys' sybaritic households. But the formidable sisters had the power to overrule lesser authority and crush all opposition. On these occasions, Mother sent me to bed without supper, and probably with good reason, since I usually had a bilious attack when I got home, or felt like having one. Too much grandeur for someone only seven!

Another Beaky-Bully, Great-aunt Nell, lived in Bournemouth. When Ada took me to visit her, I enjoyed the same kind of luxurious holiday Aunt Leila provided, except for a little genteel paddling in the sea and listening to the brass band playing on the promenade. Cousin Maude, Aunt Nell's daughter, would take me to the band concert, a recreation her delicate health permitted. I never found out what was wrong with her, but I imagine it was a case of the Victorian spinster suffering psychosomatically. She was six feet tall, looked rather like Brünnhilde, and could put away just as much food and grog as the rest of the gourmets in the family.

I never saw my great-aunt Mag, who still lived in Nice, but, not to be outdone by her sisters, she used to send me ten-pound notes, a fortune in those days, with instructions to spend it all on whatever I liked, that Daddy must not be naughty and make me put it in the bank. No one at home approved of such wild extravagance, not even Ada and Phoebe, but they couldn't do a thing about it, for the instructions were there in writing.

Adding to this frightful orgy of indulgence was yet another relative, Cousin Fiskin, Granny Russell's niece. She would come to our house especially to take me to the British Museum or Kew Gardens, at least that's what she told Mother. We would go instead to the matinee at the Palladium, where I saw my first variety shows, or perhaps to see Maskelene and Devant, the conjurers. An avid theater buff, she introduced me to the comic stage. The impressions I received were to stand me in good stead many years later when I did my parodies and bridged the gap between the music hall and the concert hall. I nearly bit my tongue off trying not to tell Ada and Phoebe about all the exciting acts I had seen. Cousin Fiskin not only swore me to secrecy, but also boned me up on the edifying things we were supposed to have seen.

Whenever I had received too much attention from the Russell branch of the family, and exceeded the limits of insufferableness, I was sent smartly down to Yateley, where Tikka Gran very soon cut me down to size. There was certainly no love lost between Tikka and the Beaky-Bullys. Although I didn't consider a visit to Tikka exactly punishment, I perceived that some kind of penalty always had to be paid for having a good time.

My early life alternated between luxury and austerity, as my parents tossed me from sybarites to Spartans and back again. Life was either an icy morning bath or champagne for breakfast. It seemed that I had either a good time or a dreary time, and there was always too much of either, when there should have been a judicious mixture of delight and discipline. It was natural for an impressionable, lonely child to be attracted to glamorous relatives and delighted with their exciting, if sporadic, attentions and the luxury of their lives, but enjoying the high life scarcely prepared me for my later internment in the detention camps of English public school education. I was too young to feel anything but irritation, discomfort, and sometimes sickening insecurity.

My first was a convent school, which should probably have helped counteract my "worldliness," but the incense and holy water and statues appealed to my senses, not to my spiritual nature. In that respect the convent wasn't so very different from the Beaky-Bullys' houses. I am sure I was not supposed to "get religion," certainly not the Catholic religion, and probably had been sent there because a convent education is highly regarded in Protestant countries. I found it very pleasant to kiss the Mother Superior before going to Mass, join in prayers conducted by a nun, and be given lots of new holy pictures to paste in Granny Tandy's scrapbook.

After experiencing the joys of Catholicism all week, I was bored with our droning Church of England service on Sunday, with its long, dreary sermon, so I persuaded Ada to take me instead to St. Cuthbert's, Philbeach Gardens. She was quite agreeable, as it was just across the road from our house. It was very High Church of England, not to say altitudinous. There were three priests arrayed in gloriously colored embroidered vestments who waved censers, rang little bells, and ran around doing things up at the altar. There were lots of statues and decorations to look at if I got bored with the sermon. On special Sundays, the priests would put on different colored birettas and parade out of the church and up and down Philbeach Gardens, followed by the choir, adults carrying crosses and statues, and children carrying little nosegays. This was more like it, to my way of thinking; it was rather like taking part in a pageant.

Convent and church didn't consume all my time, though. I had forgotten perfidious Captain Davis and regained my interest in the piano. I attended a music school that taught the Fletcher method, which was great fun, a cross between jigsaw puzzles and building blocks. Two huge sets of five lines each were drawn on the schoolroom floor, and the students composed tunes by putting large wooden treble and bass clefs, notes, sharps, flats, and rests on the staves. The method must have worked well, for I soon graduated to playing pieces like "The Jolly Farmer" and "The Merry Peasant."

Aunt Bena, who saw in me a piano prodigy to replace my father, was thrilled and delighted with my progress. It wouldn't have mattered to her, a piano virtuoso or a diva, but a star I had to be. So she began taking me to concerts at the Albert Hall. What a huge place it was! And so glamorous! The artists were the most celebrated of their day. I heard Caruso, Dame Clara Butt, Paderewski (who had been a great pal of Uncle Albert, Aunt Bena's first husband), Chaliapin, Rachmaninoff, and a host of others.

Aunt Bena would usually take me backstage after the concert to shake hands with the artist. Caruso's hands were the softest I have ever felt. Chaliapin seemed to do a lot of carrying on and laughing. Sometimes he had laryngitis. Whatever else he sang, he always sang "The Song of the Flea." I clearly remember Rachmaninoff, perhaps because I was disappointed he didn't play the Prelude in C-sharp Minor. I learned afterward that he hated it, and if anyone asked him to play it, he would fly into a rage. This happened even at his farewell performance at the Albert Hall. He was encored again and again, but still he would not play the famous opus. Then people started shouting for it, but no, he still would not play it. Finally there was a riot and the police were called. In spite of everything, he remained adamant.

Occasionally, when Aunt Bena brought some of her artist friends to dine with us, I was allowed to stay up to hear them, as this was considered instructive. Mother or Father would plant me on a great pouf in a corner of the drawing room, out of the way, and there I would sit half asleep until the artists of the evening chose to perform. It was nice enough when I could stay awake to hear them, but one night I couldn't keep my eyes open.

Aunt Bena's guests were a couple from Berlin, who were to sing *Tristan und Isolde* at Covent Garden. They had been grogging away some special German beer that they had insisted upon having. Late in the evening they suddenly let fly with a loud Wagner excerpt that scared me nearly to death. I screeched and howled. Disgraced, I was ignominiously hauled away to bed by Ada. Aunt Bena was hurt and rather angry, and Mother was furious. They did not realize the shock I had received, being awakened from a peaceful doze at eleven o'clock at night by two *echt* colossal Wagnerians, full of beer, bellowing from a distance of only six feet.

Aunt Bena and Mother, agreeing for once, came to the reluctant conclusion that I was not musical after all. I was astonished that their judgment should be based on such slender evidence, if the Wagnerian colossi could be called slender. I felt I had been put upon, and went into a sulk for quite a long time. When Aunt Bena noticed this she got all remorseful over having spoken hearshly to her darling Claudie, and concluded that the incident had occurred because I was a little run-down from the cold weather and perhaps needed a tonic. And what do you think the tonic turned out to be? A split of champagne with my breakfast every morning for a week.

The champagne breakfasts were the last straw. Mother let go in her diary: "Since we have been in London and R-B's [R-B is what Mother called Father] aunts have been around, the Toad is impossible. They pander to her every whim and give her anything she wants. Aunt Bena was here last week and insisted on giving the child champagne for breakfast. It's insane. I never saw anything like the way those old things idolize R-B and Claudia. There's no sense at all about them. I spoke to Jessie C. [Jessie Crookston, a distant cousin of Mother's]. She's having the same sort of trouble with Andy [her son]. I suppose it's because they are 'only' children. We think we'll get them together. Was telling J. about Grahame and how he used to follow Claudia around like a little puppy dog. Andy's a year older, so he might be able to knock some sense into her."

It was duly arranged for me to meet Andy, who lived just around the corner from us in Philbeach Gardens. I thought he was marvelous. An only child, he, too, had done a lot of sitting around with grown-ups. We got on famously and were quite a success with our families until we started getting the giggles.

Andy was the most frightful giggler, and always getting ticked off for laughing at the wrong time. It would usually happen at afternoon tea, which we had to do from time to time. We'd be sitting there like good children, listening to the grown-ups gossiping away, and perhaps someone would say something like, "Poor Uncle Joe! He had only just got over his hernia when he got his thumb caught in the meat grinder." Andy would explode. His mother or aunt or one of the other ladies would draw herself up and say, "Andy! That's nothing to laugh at. Poor Uncle Joe! With a hernia and no thumb." By this time, Andy would be helpless with mirth and his relatives furious. When Andy let go, so did I, and we would both be sent out of the room in disgrace.

Mother was not amused. She confided to her diary that "C. and Andy were so tiresome this afternoon. This giggling is driving us all crazy. If you ask them what the joke is, they look at you blankly and then snigger right in your face. Little monsters!"

When we grew up, Andy and I remained the best of friends, although we met only once in a blue moon. He lived in Egypt, where his father had established an artificial manure business in Sofaja, and I remember his visiting London when I was first engaged to be married. He was an extremely handsome, sophisticated young man with beautiful teeth, and all my girlfriends thought him the last word in male attraction. When I took him to meet my fiancé, everything he said broke up Andy and consequently me. We still had that disastrous Bromo-Seltzer effect on each other. Afterward, my fiancé said, "What an extraordinary fellow! And I've never seen you behave as ridiculously as that before. What was the joke?"

I am afraid most of the people who were closest to me—or should have been—did not understand my reaction, and were puzzled that I found so much to laugh about. They never saw "the joke."

Bringing Andy and me together was Mother's major effort to rescue me from a life of indulgence by the Beaky-Bullys. This excerpt from her diary records a minor one: "Had Betty's youngest in for tea with C. yesterday—so pretty and dainty. C. would have nothing to do with her. Told me afterwards that Penny was 'wet'—whatever that means. She makes me sick. I just don't know what makes her tick."

Actually, I was jealous of Betty's little Penny because her mother had thought enough of her to make her look dainty and pretty. Mother didn't, and couldn't care less what I looked like in my rotten smock. Poor Mother! She didn't know it wasn't difficult to make a little girl look dainty and pretty. Not even me.

CHAPTER 6

Mother gives up and Father takes over—a great improvement

We had been living in London only a brief time when we had to move again, this time to York, where Father was to be commandant of Catterick Camp. Up until now, Mother had been the operative parent, and Father, although always very affable, had never taken much notice of me. But at York he took over completely. I didn't understand the sudden change and was too shy to ask him.

I believe Mother challenged him to do it, as this entry in her diary seems to indicate: "Had a long and very serious discussion with R-B last night about C. I told him he just doesn't realize how impossible his daughter has become. [I was always his daughter when naughty and hers when infrequently good.] But he just laughs it off. He is just as unrealistic about her as his ridiculous aunts are about him. If he thinks he can bring her up, I shall be interested to see how he manages."

When Mother and Father had a "discussion," she would usually fly into a rage, going on at Father, who would sit quietly until she had run out of steam. Then he would get up in the most amiable manner, pat her on the cheek, say something like, "Take it easy, old girl," and retire to his study until the storm had blown over. This "long and very serious discussion" must have been an absolute Donnybrook. Whatever had happened, he now took over my upbringing.

When we arrived in York, we went to live in yet another furnished house. Glenholme had a huge drawing room, going from the front to the back garden. Outside the rear drawing room windows was an immense rockery, at least twelve feet high; beyond that, a formal garden, which went on to another huge rockery, holding a pond in the middle; beyond that, a lawn with a willow tree so enormous you could climb up into it and completely disappear; after which came a long pergola, covered with roses and clematis, and leading to a kitchen garden; and, lastly, behind that, a paddock from which you could get on to the Knavesmire Race Track. It was a landscape gardener's dream (or possibly nightmare, when I come to think back), and a splendid place to play in. I grew to love the garden, and thought Glenholme a paradise of a house, probably because it was there Father really took notice of me.

A girl is usually partial to her father, and heaven knows I was partial to mine. After spending the first seven years of my life under Mother's erratic supervision and jaundiced eye, I was overjoyed that Father suddenly took a proprietary interest in me. Perhaps his interest was not so sudden as it seemed. Perhaps he had always wanted, in contemporary jargon, to communicate with me, but had been thus far prevented by several things: the demands of the military, which took him away from his family for long stretches; Mother's determination to dominate every situation, which he quietly concurred with until forced to assert his good sense; and his natural reserve, which probably took some doing to overcome. But once he had broken the reticence inbred in the English officer and gentleman, he was much more fun than Mother, with all her assumed airs and graces.

Father was very intelligent and clever enough to appeal to my own intelligence. That was something Mother had never done, perhaps because she couldn't. Although she pretended to be intelligent, she was in fact dictatorial and vain. Father, on the other hand, began to teach me and guide me, allowing me to think for myself and put questions to him. Because he was keenly interested, he made everything interesting to me. His enthusiasm for the disciplines he taught me aroused my own enthusiasm.

I became aware of the new arrangements the night we arrived at Glenholme. Ada and Phoebe were assigned sleeping quarters on the ground floor, Mother had her bedroom and boudoir on the first and, to my amazement, Father and I were to sleep in isolated grandeur on the second floor. Before I went to sleep that night, Father instructed me to go into his bedroom and wake him punctually at 7:30 every morning, without fail. I was too astonished by this new matutinal routine to make any comment.

Feeling the importance of my responsibility and determined to be punctual, I crept into Father's room at 7:27 to be ready to awaken him on the dot. I discovered that he was a very heavy sleeper, and it seemed an eternity until I managed to wake him. When I found out that a gentle shake didn't do it, I lost my timidity and leapt upon him with tomboyish abandon. That led to a lovely punch-up with the pillows. He threw me up into the air, and we shrieked and yelled and romped about for nearly ten minutes. This became known as our "rosh." I was ecstatic as only a child can be in the midst

of such exciting play, and amazed that Father would be so active, until I
remembered, with pride, his reputation as an athlete.

I had never seen him so jolly and, for want of a better word, informal. At
first I was afraid Mother would hear us. If she did, she never let on. Apparently she was doing her best to ignore the new regime and stay as much
apart from me as she could. In fact, she became as remote from my existence as hitherto Father had been. I met her around the place from time to
time, but had very little contact with her.

Now that Mother had withdrawn, as it were, leaving me free of neurotic
persecution, and Father had shown himself to be a loving, caring parent,
life was much less confusing than it had been. A kind of peace settled on me
that I had never known. I experienced emotional security for the first time.
I felt comfortable with Father's strict, but gentle, regime, and was proud
that I was beginning to make some progress with my studies. I was too
busy and exhilarated to miss the fatted-calf visits to the Beaky-Bullys.
Mother had been right about the dangers of excessive indulgence. No
longer exposed to the violent contrast between Sybaris and Sparta, I became more poised and less insufferable. But I was still no angel, and occasionally needed chastisement. Now, instead of Mother applying the
hairbrush to my backside, Father used a little riding crop to switch me on
the legs if he thought it necessary. It didn't hurt like Mother's hairbrush.

Father had a timetable for my training before breakfast, and we had to
get down to business as soon as our morning "rosh" was over. He was a
first-rate teacher and very methodical, but he didn't begin my educational
program with an explanatory preamble. We simply started, with tennis
practice on Monday, and that was sufficient unto the day. For the first
week, I didn't know what the morrow's discipline would be, and that made
it rather exciting. The second week I discovered that each discipline had its
own day, which remained unchanged for the two years Father was my tu-
telary genius.

Monday's tennis practice meant going into the garden and hitting a ball
up against a wall for half an hour, which was the time allowed before breakfast for my activities. A tennis player of such brilliance that he had represented Canada in the Olympics, Father was rather disappointed that I
wasn't better at the sport. But instead of humiliating me with unkind criti-
cism, as Mother would have done, he never ceased trying to improve my
game. Thanks to his great patience and teaching skill, I finally developed an
impeccable style, but it was still no good; I had a rotten eye. Even when
making perfectly coordinated swipes, my racquet seldom connected with

the ball. If you don't have an accurate eye in tennis, you don't have anything, just as in opera, if you don't have a glorious voice, the rest counts for nothing. I lacked but one thing to become, perhaps, a tennis champion, but there was no use crying over it. I learned a hard but valuable lesson.

On Tuesdays Father would produce a list of ten words. I had to look them up in the dictionary and write their meanings in a notebook. I hadn't been aware that he was surrounded by dictionaries and reference books, with the *Encyclopaedia Britannica* and *Webster's Unabridged* holding pride of place. What's more, he used them and expected me to learn to do the same. I took to it like a duckling to water, and I like to think my bibliolatry rather made up for my lack of tennis skill.

Father was frightfully good at teaching me methods and terribly keen on accuracy. "Write it down," he would say, "you'll never know it till you can write it down." He taught me how to do research, follow cross-references, and summarize the information I had looked up. I loved doing it, and still do. One reference leads to another, and you're off on a merry chase. Father would pursue a subject from source to source and book to book; he was an encyclopedic person. Because of his training, I'm terribly good at finding things out. My systematic use of the *Encyclopaedia Britannica* so early in my life has been a great boon. I never stop mining it for information I use in my work.

Father especially liked mythology and Roman history, and enjoyed making up genealogical tables of gods and Roman kings. It should be no surprise that as a Royal Engineer he admired the early Roman rulers' engineering feats. He liked to refer to Tarquinius, who had built the *cloaca maxima* that is still the main sewer of Rome, as the first plumber. The Roman roads in York fascinated him, and he had Ada or Phoebe take me to the library to learn as much as I could about the antique city's rich history.

Wednesday morning was given to mathematics, another subject in which Father excelled. He liked figures, drawing maps, measuring distances, calculating stresses and strains —all the things a good engineer has at his fingertips. He explained the relationship between mathematics and music, and so it seemed quite natural for piano practice to follow on Thursday and Friday.

Every Friday afternoon, Miss Coverdale would appear for my piano lesson. She was rather a martinet, and would rap my knuckles if I didn't pay attention. She started me on classics, instead of those insipid Maiden's Prayer-ish kinds of pieces, which suited me fine. My first attempt was Bach's Two-Part Inventions. For a long time I progressed at a snail's pace, but I very much preferred them to the Victorian horrors my friends were learning.

Saturday morning's half hour was music sight reading, which must have sounded hideous to the rest of the household. On Sunday Father would read me excerpts from a tremendously popular book called the *Art of Thinking,* by Abbé Ernest Dimnet. It promised that by faithfully exercising your mental capacities, you could be a genuine thinker and entitled to feel superior to nonthinkers. It was probably the first of what became an avalanche of how-to books. Father was a great how-to-doer, but I couldn't understand a word of the book, and hated it. I came across a copy a few years ago and still couldn't understand a word.

Every night after I had been put to bed, Father would come into my room for a chat, when he would want to know every last thing that had happened since our morning session. It was a very nice, relaxed checkup, and a profitable review of what I had learned that day. The curious thing is that Father left it entirely up to me whether or not I followed the morning schedule he had devised. If I did, he rewarded me with sixpence each time. Although "roshing" was more enjoyable than disciplining myself, cupidity overcame joie de vivre and mental laziness, and at the end of each week I would wind up with three shillings and sixpence. This munificent sum gave me status as the richest girl in the day school I attended in York. Most of the girls in the Mount School got only sixpence every Sunday.

Mount was a Quaker school, conveniently located just across the road from our house, and as different from the convent school in London as one could imagine. In fact, the diverse religious education I received in my early years helped prepare me for the wide variety of persons, places, and beliefs I was to encounter in my professional life. You might say that I learned tolerance and lost my prejudices, but I knew nothing about tolerance—an attitude that implies condescension—and I had no prejudices to lose. What I did learn was to adjust quickly to new environments and find something in common with people whose backgrounds were different from mine. The desire for change is still in my blood, and I welcome fresh panoramas. I love touring, traveling, and meeting new people.

Although the afternoon tea sessions with Mother and her friends had been discontinued, probably as part of Father's all-out effort to free me from her domination, he insisted that I go to church with her, in spite of the fact that he never went himself. For Sunday service, she bought me a particularly revolting hat. It was gray felt, shaped like a soup plate, with orange crochet around the brim and a huge orange tassel hanging from the top down to my shoulder. I was self-conscious wearing it while walking to church with Mother, but even more so during the hymns. People would turn around and look at us because Mother sang everything at the top of her voice, and I'd think, "Now they're going to notice this ghastly hat." The parson was a hell-firer who would bellow and roar and lean out of the pulpit and point, and I always thought he was pointing at my hat. I got such a thing about it that I persuaded Father to let me go to a Quaker meeting on Sunday, since I went to a Quaker school. He consented, and I didn't have to wear that hat, as Quakers tend to dress very plainly.

Ada took me to meeting, and once was enough. I had hoped it was going to be like St. Cuthbert's Philbeach Gardens, but I found it very disappointing. Everybody sat in perfect silence, until a man suddenly got up and said, "Jesus wept," and sat down again, and that's all there was to it. Fortunately when I returned to the other church I was without my hat—the dog next door had chewed it up. I always suspected Phoebe of engineering that "accident."

Father was at home a great deal during these happy days in York and he hosted many musical evenings in our drawing room. Guests always requested Gilbert and Sullivan, and, of course, Father obligingly rendered the only music he considered "suitable" for an officer of His Majesty's Army to play. For these musicales, however, he had also gathered a vocal quartet, consisting of a rather beady soprano; Mother, who was a contralto; a bass from the York Minster choir; and himself, a light baritone or tenor. A Miss Clark thundered out their accompaniments on the piano. It was all fairly earsplitting, but fun for me to listen to in my bed far away upstairs.

One can get a strange impression of words when heard lyrically wafted up two flights of stairs. I became very fond of "In a Persian Garden" by Liza Lehmann, the quartet's masterpiece, which begins, "Oh, the Sultan's turrets," but stirred by phonetic distortions, I imagined men and women that Omar Khayyam never dreamed of.

The singers started off with a whoop that sounded like "Oh, the Sultan's turds." To my ears, Mother's favorite solo began, "The Whirly Hopesman said there are Zapontonaches and Ikprosters," and Father's started off with, "Oh, Moonamida Light who knows Sir Wane." The bass sang, "Miss Selma Young did eagerly frequent doctors and saints with her great argument," and the soprano piped, "Alas, that Sprinkle Van is like the rose."

I didn't find out until years later that the Persian poet wrote, in the first instance, "The Worldly hope men set their hearts upon turns ashes or it prospers"; in the second, "O moon of my delight that knows no wane"; in the third, "Myself when young did eagerly frequent doctors and saints and heard great argument"; and, lastly, "Alas, that spring should vanish with the rose." I imagined Zapontonaches and Ikprosters to be something like unicorns, and wondered what Miss Selma Young was arguing about. I took Sir Wane to be Moonamida Light's boyfriend, but didn't understand turds at all, which was just as well. The Whirly Hopesman and Sprinkle Van sounded enchanting. I find Omar Khayyam admirable in Edward FitzGerald's translation, but I still have nostalgia for the Whirly Hopesman and his friends.

Mother soon gathered a group of teatime ladies around her and, as was the custom in those days, they would sing and play after drinking tea. Unlike the evening visitors, they never did anything as ambitious as the "Sultan's turds" or the "Whirly Hopesman." They were a bit on the pianissimo side, which presented a problem, since there was no one but the ebullient Miss Clark to play the piano. She was all right in the evening, when the quartet was going full blast, but she was overpowering in the afternoon.

Miss Clark was an immense lady, with masses of white hair and a bright red face, to which she applied white powder, thus making it purple. She usually wore bright green or magenta, and had a very loud, hearty voice and a heart of gold. Everyone was devoted to her. She reminded me of a verse by W. S. Gilbert:

> *King Boraleebungaleebo*
> *Was a man-eating African swell,*
> *His sigh was a hullabaloo,*
> *And his whisper a horrible yell.*

One day Mother hit upon the idea that I should accompany the ladies, and it surprised me that I thought her idea a good one. Having been spared her nagging supervision for a while, I was inclined to be more agreeable to her wishes. I had been promoted to playing the morning hymn at school prayers, which was a great honor, but I was still shaky at it, and this would be good practice. I played only about one note in three correctly, but since that was about what the performers averaged, it worked out splendidly. Our repertoire included "The Rosary," "The Lost Chord," "Mighty Like a Rose," "Roses of Picardy," and Tosti's "Goodbye." The ladies thought my accompanying them was just adorable, and Mother was pleased, especially as I was being clean and tidy as well as cooperative. In fact, I became

"My daughter" for quite some time. But my improved status was not destined to last, not after the episode of the two poems.

The first of my efforts was inspired by misguided literary ambition, the second prompted by sheer self-defense.

At school we were having our first go at Shakespeare and iambic pentameter, and were all straining away to write something in this meter for a prize. I marshaled all the words I'd learned Tuesdays mornings, paced the garden in a fit of creation, and came up with this:

> *This thing unseen, unheard, unfelt, untouched,*
> *That hovers in some grim and gruesome grot,*
> *And which the sun for very shame has left*
> *To breed, in darkness, things unspeakable,*
> *That creep and slip and crawl and slide and flit,*
> *Maybe 'tis found in unfrequented halls*
> *Of grey cathedrals, e'er the dawn has laid*
> *Its first pale ribbon on the robe of night.*
> *The windows high and small and slit, shed down*
> *Pale shafts of stardust, and the pillars tall*
> *Rear up their proud cold heads to where they meet*
> *Some flowered cornice bathed in chill moonlight,*
> *That's shining through a crevice in the roof.*
> *'Tis often found in wild and wooded dell,*
> *Peopled by leprechauns who dance and feast*
> *When bats, who spin in spirals, fill the night*
> *With the soft whirr of wings. The screech*
>   *owls cry*
> *And the chip-chip of grasshoppers is heard.*

Of course, I hadn't the slightest idea what I was talking about, but I thought the poem was spiffy, with all those Tuesday morning words in it. I proudly showed it to Father, who said he was glad I was learning to apply what he was trying to teach me.

At the next afternoon tea, however, Mother announced she was going to recite a poem by "my daughter." I nearly fell off the piano bench. Recite my poem she did—with all the stops out. Hearing it read, I realized it made no sense. Why had Father shown it to her? And why had she wanted to read it? Poor Mum, she never knew when to leave well enough alone. It was one thing for me to plonk away while the ladies were singing, but quite

another to sit there like a fool while Mama orated my nauseating poem.
The ladies thought it was just darling and made a great hubbub, but I was
overcome with embarrassment. I hadn't felt such a fool since the time of
that awful hat in church. I was appalled by the prospect of being Mother's
resident poetess.

To forestall any more effusions from Mother and consequent humiliation for me, I wrote a special poem for the following afternoon tea. When
she brought up the subject of poetry, as I had feared, I stepped in at once
and read my new poem. You might call it a protest song:

> *The ladies in their frilly hats*
> *All come and drink their cups of tea,*
> *And after they have had their chats*
> *My mother then produces me.*
> *I stand there while she reads my poem,*
> *Which makes me feel a silly fool,*
> *I wish that I was not at home,*
> *I wish that I was back at school.*
> *I'm fond of writing on my own*
> *And sometimes showing Father, that's*
> *Because he reads them all alone,*
> *And not to ladies in those hats.*

Some of the ladies pretended the poem was cute, others were frightfully
peeved, and Mother was furious. It wasn't meant to be rude, but I suppose
it was. Total warfare with Mother resumed. She gave me the back of the
hairbrush for the first time in ages. When Father came home I got a real
whaling, which hurt my feelings more than anything else, because he was always telling me to say what I thought. He explained that it was right to be
honest, except that one must never hurt people's feelings or be gratuitously
insulting. When I asked what "gratuitously" meant, he said, "Look it up in
the dictionary and copy it out fifty times."

Apart from these few eruptions, life in York was extremely pleasant. I
enjoyed it more than any other place I had ever known. There were lots of
children my own age in the Quaker school. We all had bicycles and sometimes rode around the Knavesmire Race Track. I could go shopping with
Phoebe and visit Mr. Peacock, the greengrocer, and play in the storeroom
with his daughter, Iris. I could walk all around York on the city wall, or

climb over the back fence and watch the races when they were on. Once I bet my whole three and sixpence on a horse and it won at five-to-one.

Until we moved to York, I had had only little boys to play with, and I had looked with great suspicion on the silly little girls who came all dressed up to our parties, with their doting mothers in tow. Now, for the first time, I acquired girlfriends—Marmie Rowntree and Mary Richardson. Marmie was a chocolate Rowntree. We would go to her family's factory and watch rivers of chocolate sludging about and fancy bonbons being stamped out by great presses. I shall never forget the smell of it all—delicious.

Marmie and Mary used to come to my house by themselves. In fact, I can't remember ever seeing their mothers. Was that a lovely change! If some of the boys came home from school with us, we'd play in the garden, but if we were just girls, Ada and Phoebe would show us how to knit and sew, or we might dress up and do each other's hair. It was thus gradually we became interested in how we looked. Suddenly I made a momentous discovery: if my hair was brushed, my nails were clean, and my legs were not covered with scratches, I didn't look too bad. I was no Grahame, of course, but it was a definite improvement. Even Mother remarked about it.

Father's before-breakfast training was beginning to pay off, too. Learning words from the dictionary had given me a great urge for reading, and I was plowing my way through Dickens. The piano playing and sight reading were improving quite a bit, but tennis remained, alas, a dead loss. I was writing poems like mad at school, but never read more than that one to an audience at home.

I gave a report on my scholastic progress to Aunt Al, who had just come back from China or Indonesia or somewhere. This peripatetic lady exhorted me to keep up the good work and always use my head, and finally considered that on the whole I was improving. Then she went off to see the pyramids.

As always, however, just as things were going smoothly and life was all organized, there came the seemingly inevitable upheaval. After only two years in York, Father was to be posted to Hong Kong. He and Mother were going there to live for five years, and I was to be shipped off to a detention camp—boarding school.

CHAPTER 7

Abandoned, detained, and at long last delivered

They began to arrive—the very real and ugly portents of my being thrust out from a reasonably happy life at home into a strange and hostile world. There were long-sleeved combinations, brown woolen stockings, a shapeless gym tunic, navy blue bloomers. Awful! To top it off came the school hat, a gray beaver soup plate with a big embroidered greengage plum around the initials S.F. (for St. Felix) on the front. It was almost as hideous as my church hat.

Everybody kept telling me how lovely boarding school was going to be, from which could be deduced it was going to be awful. My world had dissolved, suddenly and completely. Just as I was beginning to understand my father and love him dearly, he was going off to a faraway place where I was forbidden to go. I didn't believe what I was told—that the Orient was detrimental to the health of the Occidental young. I desperately clung to the hope that somehow I could change his mind before he and Mother sailed for Hong Kong.

St. Felix means happy, a misnomer if there ever was one. It was the bottom: the worst eight years I ever spent.

The day I had to leave York finally dawned, cold, gray, and raining. Ada took me to London, where I boarded a train in Liverpool Street, the gloomiest railway station on earth. She was planning to go back to her father and mother, dear Granddad and Gran Stribbling, in Ash, where I had spent my childhood's happiest holiday, and Phoebe was going to Canada to be in Granny Tandy's service. These separations wouldn't happen for a while yet, but I was already desolate. I said a wrenching good-bye to her at the station, and was handed over to a grim, bony individual in nurse's uniform, who was the matron of Centre Cliff, the junior school of St. Felix. I was herded into a compartment full of girls, who looked me up and down, asked my name and how old I was (nine), and then completely ignored me.

After about an hour I ventured a remark, only to be told that new girls mustn't speak unless they were spoken to; I wasn't spoken to for the rest of the journey. St. Felix is a very smart, up-to-date school (though Centre Cliff is no more, erosion having sucked it into the sea, thank heaven), but then it was more like a women's detention camp. There was hideous green linoleum on the floors and brown paint everywhere. The school wasn't heated, so everyone had chilblains and permanently purple hands.

The first day the new girls (there were three of us) were taken to meet Miss Anderson, the headmistress, who was very sweet, and the rest of the staff, a grim, rough-looking lot of old maids. Then we were given the once-over by the house prefects.

Children are conformists, who consider being in any way different a crime. It turned out to be fatal for me that my gloves were attached to each other by a string that went through my coat sleeves. I was at once pronounced a weirdo, and promptly named Claudia Russell-Glovestrings. Because she didn't like black, Mother had bought me brown stockings instead of the school's regulation black, and I had to pay for her mistake with further humiliation. I was also guilty of the crime of being two years younger than anyone else. With all this against me, I rapidly became the most unpopular girl in school. I couldn't even make friends with the other two new girls who, because they were good at games, were accepted almost at once. I might have ingratiated myself by being good at lacrosse or hockey, as proficiency in gym or games gave one status, but I was hopeless.

On account of Father's morning education sessions, I got promoted at once to the second form, where most of the children were eleven or twelve years old. The promotion gave me no status at all. On the contrary, I was looked upon as being a swot. In addition, I played the piano and was taking elocution lessons. This combination of activities put me absolutely beyond the pale. I was alone in the crocodile when we went for walks, and everyone shied away from sitting next to me at table or in class. I was seldom spoken to unless it was to be ticked off for something. No one wanted to be associated with a freak.

There was nothing in St. Felix's daily routine to ease the troubled heart, either. The day began with the getting-up bell at seven o'clock. You had to spring out of bed, wrap yourself in a towel and, without slippers or dressing gown, stand in line in a freezing passage, ready to take your turn in the shower, which was ice cold. There was nothing you could do to dodge the icy needles; Matron had hold of the chain that regulated them. (This practice was discontinued a few years after my time at St. Felix when one of the girls died of pneumonia.)

After we had dressed and made our beds, we had to go out for half an hour and play games, which I did not like. I much preferred deportment lessons, which we had three times a week. You had to put two books on your head and walk all through the schoolhouse without dropping them. If they dropped, it counted against your house, in which case you would be sent to Coventry or taken for a "rhubarb." Several of your classmates would take you behind the high rhubarb patch in the vegetable garden, where they would pinch you, pull your hair, and generally torment you. I doubt whether any of the teachers knew of this practice, but the house prefects did.

There was what was laughingly called the honor system. No matter what was done to you, you were not allowed to tell the teachers, because the house prefects were supposed to maintain discipline. What they did, in fact, was bully the unpopular girls unmercifully, while they let the popular ones get away with murder.

After breakfast, which was the best meal of the day, we had lessons until lunchtime. Lunch was horrible: boiled mutton, tough chicken, or stew. The desserts were revolting: soggy suet currant pudding covered with hot custard; bread and butter pudding; or deadman's leg, as we called it, which was a roll of rock-hard pastry with a dab of jam in it. You had to sit there until you had eaten every last bit, even if afterward it made you sick.

There were more games, which lasted all afternoon, even when it rained and we got soaked to the skin. For tea we had very coarse oatcakes, just thrown on the tables, without plates. The day ended with supper in the late afternoon, prep, and bed at eight o'clock. I would lie awake till all hours, listening to the waves and the foghorns, which gave me the loneliest feeling in the world. Many nights I cried myself to sleep.

Only one girl at Centre Cliff was more unpopular than I. Carol was a spiteful, ferret-faced girl, about twelve years old, whom I simply hated. One day she announced that I had to be her best friend, and unless I agreed, she would give me a rhubarb. I agreed, reluctantly. I suppose it was cowardly of me, but being black and blue from previous rhubarbs, and being much smaller than she, I had reached the point where I was terrified of everyone. I became her absolute slave, making her bed, sharpening her pencils, and carrying out her every command. The situation became so impossible that I used to read in the lavatory whenever I could in order to get away from her for a bit of peace and quiet. Probably it served me right for not having more guts, but by this time my spirit was broken.

The school made it our duty to write home on Sunday. One particularly dreary Sunday I wrote thirty-five pages to Daddy, begging him to take me away. The next week he came to see me, and I think he would have arranged to take me away, but the day after he left I came down with chicken pox. Persuaded by Mother, he came to the conclusion that I was suffering from nothing more serious than pre-chicken pox depression, and changed his mind about taking me out of St. Felix. I felt that my father had let me down. Now there was nothing to do but stick it out.

The first term finally came to an end. It was to be my last holiday in York, and it felt like the twilight of the gods. Father was being fitted for new uniforms, which included Duke of Wellington-type hats, with cock's feathers, and all kinds of finery. Mother was shopping for a veritable trousseau.

I went around with Ada and Phoebe saying good-bye to all our friends, and I had my last games with Marmie Rowntree and Mary Richardson. Finally we went down to London to see Father and Mother off on the boat to Hong Kong. Phoebe went off to Canada, and once again Ada took me to Liverpool Street. Back I went to school, where I was to remain for the next eight years.

Every term there were new girls, and some of the old ones left. My delight knew no bounds when my "best friend" Carol departed from St. Felix. I was almost as delighted when I saw Mary Nix the first time. As usual, we all went down to give the new girls the once-over, and there was Mary, the dearest little thing, with auburn hair hanging down her back. She was already being picked on because she, too, was wearing brown stockings, and she was absolutely terrified. I promptly yanked her off with me, eliciting such charming remarks as, "It takes a drip to know a drip," and "Now there's two rotten old brown stockings." I told Mary that insults didn't matter any more because after a bit one gets hardened.

Mary was rather quiet and a bit mousy, but absolutely brilliant. We were in the same form, and although I thought I was quite smart at schoolwork, I wasn't a patch on her. She was top of the class in nearly all subjects. There was nothing she couldn't do. When we both took up the cello, she was way ahead of me in no time, which rather put my nose out of joint, because I thought I was so musical. Still, Mary became my very best friend. I had someone to talk to at last, and Centre Cliff became fairly tolerable.

When we reached our last term at Centre Cliff, we all competed to win the scholarship for St. Felix's upper school. Mary won it and I came second. Scorn was heaped upon us for being such swots, but we didn't care. We were feeling glad that the next term we'd be away from Matron, who was a regular sadist, and from the dreary sound of the sea and the foghorns. The upper school was situated a little distance inland.

At Somerville we became new girls again, but it wasn't so bad this time because we had black stockings at last and had learned not to say or do anything out of line. I was appointed fag to the senior prefect, which meant making tea for her every afternoon and running messages. She was extremely nice, and the position carried a certain réclame. Mary and I were not popular, but no one was brutal to us, which was a change, and there were no more rhubarbs.

At this time Marie Olivier, some sort of cousin of Lord Olivier, was in the sixth form. A St. Felix student for years, she was a brilliant actress. Every year she played a leading role in the school's summer production, which was always of a classic. One year it might be John Milton's *Comus;* another year, Sophocles's *Antigone;* another, Shakespeare's *A Midsummer Night's Dream.* Because of her, the school had developed a reputation for theater.

When she left, which was in my second term, there was great consternation as to who would take her place. One day, quite unexpectedly, I was told that if I recited Book Five of Virgil to the drama teacher, I would get three stars and Saturday morning off. Being good at memorizing, I managed to recite Virgil's Latin verse without mishap or pause. I got my Saturday afternoon off, but it was the last one ever. I was to be the new star, not because I could act—nobody knew whether I could or not—but because I learned lines speedily and accurately.

I knew that most of the students and some of the faculty considered the drama department "drippy" and that my participation in the plays wouldn't leave much time for piano and cello practice. I was interested in music, not at all in acting. I didn't know the first thing about acting, and didn't want to learn. I had been beguiled into my new "career" by a very small carrot at the end of a stick, but I had committed myself. It was maddening.

I had assumed I was going to play women, but more often found myself cast in men's roles, perhaps because I was tall. I did play Iphigenia and Portia, but that hardly counts against an array of male characters, including Sir Anthony Absolute, Oberon, Caliban, and Charley's aunt. As the aunt, at least I had the opportunity of cavorting in skirts, although, of course, I was supposed to be a man in drag. At my senior boarding school, Harrogate College, I played Hamlet. Can you believe it? I know of only two other women who have played Hamlet, and I hesitate to mention my name in the same breath with Sarah Bernhardt and Judith Anderson.

I don't remember having any feelings of divine afflatus playing these parts. In fact, I don't remember my performances at all. I put them out of my mind, probably because I resented having to perform. It was a chore, an extra load of schoolwork unfairly put on me. I acted with a very bad grace and was probably awful. I feel certain, however, that something must have rubbed off on me—if nothing else, the feeling of being at ease on stage, which is akin to stage presence, or command of oneself and one's audience. It's ironic that I thrust aside whatever benefits I received from my early brush with drama. I was still oblivious of where destiny was leading me, and how I was being prepared for my eventual spot in the limelight.

Another event was to affect my future in an entirely unforeseen way. I had had a very good singing voice, and had indeed become the leader of the school choir, until one day in a hockey game someone hit me over the face with a hockey stick and broke my nose. It swelled and bled like mad, but nobody did anything about it, with the result that my acoustics were ruined. My voice now had the oddest sounds: F and E in the treble clef either didn't sound at all or came out in a sort of yodel. Then there was a very loud bit in the middle voice down to middle C, and under that was breath only. It was heartbreaking at the time, because it left me without a voice suitable for opera, but many years later my idiosyncratic voice, which could parody any kind of vocalism, proved to be a godsend for comedy.

I learned to write jingles at school, another thing that came in very handy when I started building my act. After hours of writing them I developed great facility. Our history subject for matriculation was the morganatic marriages of Charles V of Austria, which was so dull and complicated no one could learn it. I hit on the idea of writing my history notes in jingles, setting them to music, and singing them. It turned out to be such a good idea that I started applying it to all subjects. Suddenly everyone wanted my jingles, and I generously passed them around. We would roar them out all over the school. It was pandemonium, but it did the trick. That must have been the noisiest matric class in history, but our year had the all-time high average.

Hardly any of the subjects I learned in school, such as Latin, Greek, higher mathematics, history, or geography, with the exception of French, have ever been the least bit of use to me. Although a lot of erudition had been bashed into my brain, I couldn't type or sew, and I had no dress sense whatsoever. None of us had any conversation skills or manners. We were like the Belles of St. Trinian's.

I have often wondered whether this hearty, regimented, eighteenth-century-gentleman type of education is good for girls. It appears the training is entirely designed to make them as unfeminine as possible. Those who had the greatest success at school were the large, meaty, athletic girls; anyone gentle or pretty or both was considered a drip. I went only once, many years later, to an old girls' meeting, and I found it a bit horrifying. Most of the games captains and such had turned into most unattractive, lumpy women in tweeds, and the shy little girls, the drips and swots, had blossomed into sexy beauties. I'm sure many of the games gang got a terrible shock when they hit the outside world to find that the drips and the swots were far more successful socially than they were. Perhaps it was just as well not to have been popular at school.

One way or another, I suppose, all of us got some good out of St. Felix, but I feel I would have been a far better-adjusted person had I never been there. Most of my years at St. Felix were utterly miserable. I had a permanent cold and chilblains, and I looked like the devil, with nails all broken from playing cricket, hands always purple and grubby, hair wispy and untidy, and a red nose. My legs were covered with scratches and scars, and I'd reached the pimply stage.

Although the eight years I spent at boarding school were excessively unpleasant, the holidays, on the other hand, were rather fun. The first two years I spent all my holidays at Harefield, a small village between Uxbridge and Rickmarsworth, with a cousin of Father's, Uncle Race (Horace) Farquharson. Uncle Race, who was an architect, was a tall, thin, ginger-colored man with a marvelous disposition. He and Aunt Noel lived in a big Victorian house, less gloomy and formal than most, with wide passages, spacious, airy rooms, and full-length windows opening out onto a beautiful garden. There was a barnyard, a stable, and a pond to paddle in, and a very settled feeling about the place.

Aunt Noel had come over from Australia in a cast of *The Student Prince*. She was very nice but had a number of quirks. Rather a snob, she claimed to be related to half the British peerage. This seemed a little strange as she was an Australian, but if anyone with a title came to the house, she would put on a specially refined voice. She also claimed to be delicate and was always retiring to bed with some ailment, although she actually was as strong as a horse and lived to be over ninety.

The servant problem was a great bugbear to her. Nobody seemed to be satisfactory, and she was so autocratic that they gave notice about once a week, so there was a permanent crisis in this department. Most of the time the house was run single-handed by Lizzie Tinkum, or Zeum, who had at one time been both Father's and Uncle Race's nurse. She was a dear, placid old thing, and certainly had need to be.

Cousin David was at that time seventeen and going to Eton. He had acquired one of those accents, as they say, "If it was any more British he couldn't talk at all." It was almost impossible to understand him, and there was always a lot about "m'tutor" in it, which is Etonian for house master. He was a terrible tease, but I admired him enormously from a safe distance.

The other two children were Felicity and Denise. Felicity was the youngest, a very pretty little girl, much tormented and put upon by the rest of us. Denise was my age and just as plain as I, which was a great relief after being surrounded by so many beauties. She was very clever and particularly good at writing.

It was quite a new and wonderful experience for me to be with a normal family, instead of trying to follow conflicting directions from a bevy of aunts and uncles. We children were allowed plenty of freedom, but we knew just how far we could go. For all her quirks, Aunt Noel was a real mother, who adored her own children but never for a minute made me feel left out.

Once Denise and I got on a dressmaking kick. This was in the flapper era, when the bosom was nonexistent. Denise was given mauve crêpe de chine and I had emerald green. We had no bosoms, of course, as they hadn't started yet, and we felt very elegant in our new finery. Unfortunately, just then I started to swell out, right under my chin, it seemed. I tried everything, including slouching and strapping it up, to no avail. The fit of my beautiful dress was ruined; I had to give it to Denise, and Aunt Noel suggested a bra. I became thoroughly top heavy and have remained so ever since, while Denise became the elegant one until bosoms came in again.

Even when I spent my holidays with the Farquharsons, my godmother, Aunt Al, was actually in charge of me. She was usually abroad, but would come from time to time and take me on a trip. One day we went to visit some very wealthy friends who took a tremendous shine to me. Many visits followed, from which I would return horribly spoiled and laden with expensive clothes and extravagant presents. This caused a rift between Aunt Al and Aunt Noel, so Aunt Al took me away to spend my holidays with her. I hated leaving Denise, but apart from that it was wonderful.

I had no idea this was going to happen until one day Aunt Al descended upon St. Felix—that is the only way to describe her sudden appearance in the midst of that dreary waste. After several years of boarding school I was beginning to think all was lost, and was getting more sullen and pimply by the minute. She had just come from Angkor Wat, traveling, she told us, in the company of "Mr. Crane, the king of the bathroom fixtures." She promptly took me over, and very nearly the school with me.

She was driven by her elegant chauffeur, Egan, in her enormous Daimler limousine, of the kind used by the dowager Queen Mary. She lost no time informing St. Felix's headmistress, who was rendered absolutely speechless, that in future all school bills and communications regarding me were to be sent to her and not to my parents, and that she and only she was *in loco parentis*, as my parents were a pair of idiots and didn't know a thing about bringing up children.

It happened to be Guy Fawkes Day, so after giving the headmistress her instructions, Aunt Al told me to collect as many girls as would fit into the Daimler, and she took us out to a feast at the Black Swan, after which we went to the beach and let off fireworks she had bought for the occasion. I was suddenly the most popular girl in school.

At the end of the term, Egan and the Daimler came to fetch me. I was the envy of all the other girls, who were about to shuffle off on the slow, miserable, scruffy train ride to filthy Liverpool Station. I was conducted instead to my new abode: Queen Anne's Mansions, which were elegant service flats. Oh, the glory! Oh, the glamor!

The flats were housed in the then tallest building in London—seven and a half stories. Seven stories was the limit, but the builders had got half the eighth story done before the London County Council descended on them and told them to desist, so the half of the eighth story was allowed to remain. And where was Aunt Al's flat? In the half of the eighth story—where else?—where we could sit and look down on London. It was luxurious and exotic, and had a delicious smell about it—a combination of Turkish cigarettes, French perfume, and whisky.

Ensconced in the flat, I was briefed as to what was expected of me. "I do not like children," said Aunt Al, "so you are to grow up at once. Many women are married, with children. at thirteen. You are no longer going to bed at eight o'clock. I have many dinner parties, and I shall teach you to mix cocktails, which you are not to touch. You can have ginger ale, and you can hand around the canapés and speak when you are spoken to, but don't start off on your own. You will be meeting many fascinating people, and if you keep your ears open, you might enjoy it very much.''

And what parties she had! There were people from all over the world, speaking all sorts of languages and often in their native garb. Everyone Aunt Al had met on her gallivanting would pile in: artists and writers, actors and fakirs, swamis and psychics, real celebrities, phony celebrities, and little old ladies. My favorite little old lady was Miss Sylvia Delano Hitch, a cousin of Franklin Delano Roosevelt. She looked exactly like a chimpanzee, in a shiny black straw hat with a bunch of red cherries hanging over her nose.

The conversation at these parties was undoubtedly very intelligent, but I could hardly make head or tail of it. Aunt Al simply expected me to take in as much as I could, however, and not chatter, so I would learn to be a good listener, which she considered very important.

My relatives were horrified at these developments and certain I was going straight to hell. They all wrote my parents, but to no avail. My parents didn't give a damn—they were having too much fun in Hong Kong. Since Aunt Al was picking up the check, she told all the relatives to go and get stuffed, and we went our merry way.

Aunt Al was the first person with whom I could have an adult conversation. She would ask all sorts of serious questions and actually listen to my answers. She would talk to me about politics or painting or art. Often she would pick up some object in her beautifully furnished apartment, go into a long description of it, and tell me interesting things about the country it came from. Or she might explain in simple language what the dinner conversation had been about the night before.

Aunt Al was an enthusiast—she put everything into whatever she did, whether it was entertaining friends, learning languages (she spoke several), traveling the world, building houses, or being a substitute parent. She studied every aspect of parenthood, long before child psychology became prevalent. She was definitely an "I'll do it my way" type. It was a pity she had no children of her own. She would have made a wonderful matriarch. She told me that a godmother is someone who promises that if anything happens to your parents, she will look after you until you are grown up. She certainly lived up to her definition in the years to come.

Sometimes after our long conversations she would suddenly say, "Get out of here; I'm sick of the sight of you." She would then ring for Egan, the chauffeur, give him some money, and tell him to take me out and amuse me. He was very dashing in a smart blue uniform and highly polished boots. Egan was nice but always formal, being the old-style chauffeur who, as they say, "knew his place." He would never let me sit up in front with him; nevertheless, within the bounds of propriety, we would have a very good time. Often we went to Wembley Exhibition Amusement Park, and our conversation would go something like this:

"Egan, shall we go on the Tunnel of Love next or the switchback [roller coaster]?"

"I feel, Miss, if I may say so, the air in the Tunnel of Love may not be too salubrious owing to the crowds that have gone through; so if you would care to attend at the switchback, I would be happy to accompany you."

It must have been a funny sight. I would be shrieking and yelling at every dip, and Egan would sit there, completely impervious, just as if he were driving the car. I often tried to get more personal and pally with him, but if I overstepped the bounds he would say, "That is not within my province to discuss with you, Miss," or, "I should be taking a liberty to answer such a question." I finally gave it up and we stayed on these ceremonious terms.

Usually we had to converse with each other at the tops of our voices, as he was either in the front seat of the car and I was in the back, or he was a respectful three paces behind me. At the amusement park I was apt to become perfectly filthy and scruffy, but not Egan. He never had a hair out of place, and he sometimes must have felt ashamed of being seen with me, but never for a minute did he show it. He was a jolly nice fellow for all his pomp and circumstance, and always thought up jaunts that were tremendous fun. When I was due to return he would ring the bell and announce, "Miss Claudia, Madam," whereupon Aunt Al would take one look at my scruffy condition, and invariably say, "Oh, my Gaaad!"

One day Aunt Al gave me a ukelele, which I quickly learned to strum to accompany my ridiculous verse. I'd practice like mad all day until I became quite proficient. Aunt Al would say, "Write a song about Mrs. So-and-so," one or another of her bêtes noires. She'd roar with laughter at the result, then suddenly remembering her parental responsibilities, draw herself up and say, "It's rude to talk about your elders like that." She'd look very stern for about two minutes, until she could no longer keep a straight face. Then, like as not, she would add a few fancy touches of her own to the "rude" lyric.

One summer I was sent to France to spend my holidays with a very well-connected and matriarchal family, and this was rather a success. Charming as they were, this family was always bragging about their aristocratic relations, which was a bit putting off when I hadn't got any. So one day I took the bull by the horns and told them that my grandmother had poisoned my grandfather, which was only natural, as she was descended from the Borgias. They were hanging on my words and believed the whole thing, so it was great fun to enhance and embroider the story, which became such a masterpiece that they wrote to Aunt Al to say how sad it was for a little girl to have such a shocking background.

This cut the holiday short. Aunt Al ordered me sent home and gave me a frightful dressing down for being a wicked liar. She then insisted on hearing the whole story from the beginning, and finally pronounced it to be hilarious.

I thought Aunt Al and I understood each other perfectly, although she complained a lot about me. I didn't discover until after she died that everything that happened to me and everything we did together she wrote down and sent to my parents. After her death, Mother gave me the letters and said, "Look what a bitch you were."

It appears Aunt Al found me cold and unaffectionate. She was convinced that I much preferred Ada, who would come up from Ash now and then to mend my clothes and take me shopping or to the pictures. This upset her. I wish I had known at the time how she felt, because I was mad about her. Having adjusted to Mother when I was small, who either overwhelmed me with sickly sentiment or ridiculed me for it, according to her mood, I suppose I had become wary of showing affection. And kids are so self-centered. I should have seen that Aunt Al was lonely. I wish I had put my arms around her, told her how much I loved her, and thanked her. But I couldn't; it would have been considered sloppy. I was conditioned to good form and stiff upper lip, along with duty and honor.

At last the tocsin sounded—the parents were coming home—so great preparations began. Aunt Al bought me a regular trousseau from her Bond Street couturiere, Jeanne Penne, and after sending me to the beauty parlor came to the conclusion that the result wasn't too bad on the whole, and that my parents would be pleased with her efforts.

Her last report to them is the letter I quoted at the beginning of this book. It concludes, "I love her dearly, but sometimes she is so maddening I could cheerfully murder her. I beg of you, Bea, when you come home, not to get excitable or overemotional with her, or she will close up like a clam."

The great day dawned and all was excitement. We met my parents at

Victoria Station. Father looked much the same except a little thinner. He was very pleased to see me, but Mother took one look and said, "My goodness, you've grown into an unattractive girl." I was crushed. I could feel Aunt Al crackling with rage. She blew her stack at Mother, who burst into tears. I thought Aunt Al was going to shove her onto the railway tracks, but she simply turned on her heel and shot off in high dudgeon to New York. Father told Mother, "Take it easy, old girl."

After all this time we were right back where we started.

CHAPTER 8

"Une jeune fille musicienne"

Although I was glad to be rid of St. Felix, I was now stuck with my parents in a rented flat in a very dismal place called Artillery Mansions. I hated it. You couldn't get away from anyone and it was desperately gloomy. Father spent most of his time at his club, and Mother was on one of her "My child doesn't love me" kicks. Her tantrums started again and I sulked. It was as if darling Aunt Al had never been.

It wasn't long before the parents got fed up and sent me to another women's detention camp–boarding school, this time Harrogate College. Instead of a blue gym suit there was a green one; otherwise Harrogate was indistinguishable from St. Felix. This time, however, I was the oldest new girl (I was seventeen), I had my matric, and I was in the sixth form. I was an unknown quantity, so the other girls were a bit scared of me.

I went there to learn domestic science, but I soon discovered that only the morons incapable of passing matric were in the domestic science school. On top of this, being in the sixth form automatically made me a prefect. I was worried what might happen to a sixth-form prefect taking the moron course. Having learned by experience how to get on as a new girl, however, I kept my trap shut and played it very mousy, and it went off quite uneventfully, except that I absorbed very little domestic science, as I had to do sixth-form work as well. Another year of confusion.

In the meantime the family had bought a house in Baron's Court, and my darling Phoebe had come back from Canada. The only trouble was she had always been of the opinion that the kitchen was her private property, and she had never allowed anybody else to mess about in it ever since I could remember. It was the one thing she was adamant about. So when I shot into the kitchen to demonstrate to Father what I had learned in cooking class, she told him that unless I got out and stayed out, she would be forced, albeit reluctantly, to give notice. Father said to me, "For heaven's

sake don't go near the kitchen again. I can't have you upsetting Phoebe."
What little I learned at school faded out completely, and I have never been
any good at cooking since.

Aunt Bena was now a widow again and getting very old and too frail to
go out, but she still liked entertaining, so she would invite her friends to
come and listen to the opera with her on the wireless. Everyone would turn
up in full evening dress, sit on rows of chairs à la Covent Garden, and drink
champagne at intermission.

I was now eighteen, but I might just as well have been thirteen for all the
sophistication I had. This upset Aunt Bena, who was always on at Father
about it. "How," she would say, "is she ever going to get a husband if you
won't allow her to grow up?" They would go at it hammer and tongs, but
nothing was ever done.

Then one day her brother-in-law, Ernest de Coppet, turned up from
New York. He was staying at Claridge's with a retinue of servants and secretaries he had brought with him. Aunt Bena got together with Ernest to
do something about me, although I didn't realize it until later. The result
was that one day her lady's maid, Mina, took me to the beauty parlor,
where I received the entire treatment: massage, manicure, pedicure—
everything. They curled my hair and applied makeup to my face for the
first time ever. When I returned to Aunt Bena's, there, lying across the bed,
was a glorious, pumpkin-colored gown with a jeweled bodice, glamorous
underwear, and gold slippers. The final touch was a diamond necklace with
earrings to match.

The bell rang and in came Prince Charming, dressed to the nines in tails,
white tie, evening cloak, and top hat. This was Abel Smith, Ernest's secretary, who was to take me out on the town.

After I was wrapped in Aunt Bena's sables, we stepped into Ernest's
chauffeur-driven Rolls-Royce and were conducted to the Savoy for dinner,
followed by the theater. I can't remember what we saw, I was so bowled
over. Afterward we went to the Café de Paris, then on to various night
spots that I never knew existed, and finally to the Cavendish Hotel.

The Cavendish was presided over by a Miss Rosa Lewis, who was repu-
ted to have been a mistress of King Edward VII. We were ushered into a
room gloriously appointed in crimson velvet in the Edwardian style. Then
Miss Lewis herself appeared with a brandy snifter that must have held a jer-
oboam of champagne with whole peaches floating in it, and after a few, I
thought loaded, remarks, shut the door on us.

Well, I thought, here comes the big seduction scene. I was terrified, being utterly virginal, but it had to happen sometime, and after an evening like this what's the difference. It stopped just short of that, but he was a very charming fellow. I arrived back at Baron's Court at five in the morning.

The next day Father said, "How was the evening?"

"I've never had such a good time in my life," I answered.

"Did you find out anything you didn't know before?"

"I'll say!"

"Well, it was your cousin Ernest's idea, not mine."

There the subject was dropped. Of course, Ernest had set up the whole thing and had doubtless indoctrinated Abel as to how far he could go. It was a wonderful idea, because I could now see there were possibilities in life I had not yet dreamed of.

School was over, and it was nice to think that now I could settle into one place and concentrate long enough to become proficient at something, without getting yanked off to another type of existence. Some hope! Ernest and Aunt Bena must have gotten the message over to Father, because the next thing I knew, I was to go to finishing school in Brussels, to acquire some polish. It had taken eight years of boarding school to produce a rough, tough, scruffy hoyden, and now the process must be reversed. Here we go again.

Actually, it wasn't bad at all. Le Pensionnat Les Tourelles was an enormous, beautifully furnished mansion kept by two very elegant ladies—Miss Tungate, an American, and Mlle. Delstanche, who was Belgian. When we new girls arrived we were greeted with excessive politeness. I nearly fainted. They were charmed to meet us and we were charmed. There was curtsying and hand kissing from the masters (masters, yet!). I'd never witnessed so much charm going on in all my life. It was obvious one had better pull up one's socks in the manners department to cope with all this.

The next day we were introduced to the curriculum. Breakfast was at a civilized nine o'clock, followed by a history lecture by M. Ranci, during which we would sew or knit while he chattered on and gave us historical tidbits, which we never had to remember as there was so such thing as prep. There was literature with Mr. Ertz, and a gentleman with adenoids would conduct us around the galleries for *l'art*. At all times we were addressed as "mesdemoiselles." There was *l'elocution* and *l'etiquette*, when Miss Tungate held forth on how to enter a room, hold a cup of tea correctly, or talk to a duke (not that I ever anticipated meeting one).

After St. Felix and Harrogate College I thought, "That's a curriculum?"

Our beds were made for us, and we were definitely encouraged to change our clothes and primp about. After lunch we would go for a walk, but only if so inclined, and be fed with extremely rich cakes at some smart patisserie.

Each girl was asked on arrival at the school whether she preferred to be *une jeune fille sportive,* in which case she played ladylike tennis in the afternoon or did mild gym after breakfast or *une jeune fille musicienne.* If the latter, she would have piano lessons in the drawing room, and go to the Theatre de la Monnaie four nights a week to hear the opera. There had been enough *sportive* at St. Felix and Harrogate College to last a lifetime, so *une jeune fille musicienne* seemed the better idea.

The hairdresser would come in the afternoon to coif us, then, dressed in our best evening attire, off we would go in a limousine to be ushered into our private loge, where we would sit through all the usual operas. We saw numerous *Ring* cycles and many works that are seldom performed, such as *La Juive,* and we all had a mad crush on Jean Charles, the handsome baritone. I just adored the opera, and during intermission we would meet many people who would invite us to tea, so life at Les Tourelles became a social whirl. After the opera we would stand outside until the commissionaire called, *"La limousine des demoiselles des Tourelles."* Very grand!

I made a lot of friends at Les Tourelles with whom I have kept in touch over the years. There was one darling little girl, much younger than the rest of us, who was sweet, demure, and quiet, with beautiful long hair like Alice in Wonderland. She turned into that marvelous, mad comedienne with no chin and a squeaky voice, Alice Pierce, whom I met again in New York. That was certainly a sea change!

By the time the first holidays came around, Aunt Al had returned to England and had bought a sixteenth-century farmhouse in Buckinghamshire, which was surrounded by old tythe barns. Naturally, she'd had it restored and the garden landscaped, and getting carried away with the project as usual, had turned one of the barns into a concert hall, for which she bought two concert grands.

The next thing was to have a concert series. She engaged Ethel Bartlett and Ray Robertson, the duo pianists, to perform during my holidays, as well as Marion Kerby and John Jacob Niles, the American folk singers, who were staying at the house.

Ethel was exquisitely beautiful. She and Ray were both tiny like a pair of dolls. Marion Kerby was a big, heavyset woman with a deep voice, and John Jacob Niles played the piano and sang in a high falsetto. The effect was a bit startling, but marvelous.

Being much more at ease socially since Les Tourelles, I was able to become quite friendly with Marion. It was then that I made up my mind to be a concert artist—doing what, I hadn't a clue—but I was determined to find something. It took me another eighteen years, but I finally made it.

CHAPTER 9

The curtain comes down and the banns go up

I never expected to be sorry to leave any school, but I was sorry to leave Les Tourelles. What I'd absorbed there could be put into a thimble, and most of what I'd learned at the other two schools had gone by the board. On the other hand, my figure had improved and, though I was certainly no beauty, knowing how to do my hair and fix my face had made quite a difference, and for once I was quite approved of at home.

The next thing was to consider what I was going to do with my life. Father, bless his heart, went into this in depth, as he always did with anything he thought important, so we had a conference about it. "We must decide what you are to do until you get married," he said. Getting married seemed to me a most unlikely prospect. Not quite as unlikely as when I left St. Felix, but still unlikely. "That's no trouble," Father said. "Lots of the fellows in the regiment have sons of a suitable age, so I can soon fix that up."

As always happened when it came to making a decision, he got paper and pencil and said, "Let us write down the pros and cons of the situation and see if we can find a solution." The pros were, according to him, that I had my honor matric and was proficient in higher mathematics, so I could be a teacher. The cons were, according to me, that on account of the year at Les Tourelles and all that opera and social carrying on, all I had learned for matric had been forgotten, so I had nothing to teach. Besides, who would want to turn into a ghastly old crow of the type we had at St. Felix, and where would I go to meet all those mythical young men he was talking about if I went to a place like that?

"I see what you mean," he said, striking that possibility off the list. He was a very reasonable man, the old darling. "Then what about all this acting you've done at school?" he asked.

"Definitely not acting," I told him. After eight years of enforced drama at St. Felix, I had been immediately taken on strength into the drama group at Harrogate, where I became a shining star. Prodded on by my teacher, Nancy Brown, who subsequently taught at the Royal Academy of Dramatic Art (RADA), I had won the Associated Board scholarship to the academy, which I promptly turned down, much to her disgust. I had had the drama.

"Then what about music?" Father asked. "You could go and take the course at the Royal College." I told him that I was really not very good at music technically. There was never enough time to practice at school, because all my leisure was taken up learning those damn roles for drama. "Well! What would you like to do, then?" he asked.

"How about working as a salesgirl in Harrod's or Selfridge's," I suggested. "All my friends are doing it." This, it appeared, was absolutely out.

"I will not have my daughter going into commerce of any sort," he said. At this time Father was sixty, about twenty years older than any of my friends' parents, and his ideas on what well-brought-up young women should do were positively antediluvian. I pleaded with him for Harrod's, but he was adamant.

"Supposing no one wants to marry me. Then what?" I asked.

"They will. I shall see that they do." Confidence is a fine thing, I thought. That, however, was one of his great qualities.

It was a pity about Harrod's, but I consented to go to the Royal College of Music and was duly enrolled. It was arranged that I take piano, singing, and composition lessons with Marmaduke Barton (a pupil of Liszt), Madame Editha Grepe (a pupil of Jean de Rezke), and Herbert Howells (I don't know who he was a pupil of).

It all started rather well. I already had some dozen pieces, including the Liszt Hungarian Rhapsody no. 2, the Chopin *Revolutionary* Etude, three or four Bach preludes and fugues, and Beethoven's *Pathétique* Sonata. These were learned, I am ashamed to say, chiefly to show off at boarding school. They weren't bad, but since I'd practiced them almost daily for the last ten years, they should have been well-nigh perfect. The college held piano exhibitions in the first term, so I went and dashed them off in front of Sir Hugh Allen, the director at that time, who thought my performance was promising, and I was awarded a prize of ten pounds.

I was aware that it would take another ten years to prepare a fresh lot. By the next term all I had achieved was the first movement of Bach's Italian Concerto. Sir Hugh took a very dim view of this, and his views became increasingly dim as time went on, until I became a decided bugbear to him, for this and other reasons.

Madame Grepe did her best with my voice, but E and F still yodeled, no matter what she tried, and as most songs in the general repertoire contain these notes, I turned out a very peculiar performance. It was obligatory to do a concert each term, so I'd get out there twittering with nerves, which made the yodel even more pronounced. The students would laugh, which made me even more nervous, and it invariably ended up a disaster.

This is what used to annoy Sir Hugh so much. He was at all concerts, sitting in the front row. I would go on each time praying that no one would laugh, but they always did, because the yodeling had become a running gag. He would put his head in his hands, which would make me paralytic with tension. I would then not only yodel but go off key. Finally one day he walked out in the middle of it, and I was summoned to his study. He was enraged.

"When I first heard you I had hopes for you," he said. "What is the matter with you ever since you have put on these idiotic performances? It may amuse the students, but it doesn't amuse me. If you think you are as funny as all that, you can do it at the Palladium, but it's the last time you're going to do it here."

I was absolutely crushed. But he didn't know, and certainly I didn't at the time, how prophetic he was.

Herbert Howells had nothing but contempt for my considerable output of compositions. He said they would be all right for variety shows and ladies' afternoon tea parties, but hardly deserving of serious consideration, so the next term I went to Dr. Vaughan Williams. He was a great big countrified-looking old gentleman who was kind and charming. He said my compositions weren't bad, but very derivative. "For instance," he said, "that one is quite a creditable piece of Debussy." This got to be rather a joke: "Who are we going to be today," he'd ask, "Mozart or Wagner?" One day he asked me to please restrain the urge to be Gilbert and Sullivan, as he found himself humming my pieces, which interfered with his own musical thinking. After that he always referred to me as "Gilbert and Sullivan Russell-Brown." This was another portent of what I was to become, although nothing was further from my mind at the time.

Because of my shortcomings I had more time to spare than those who had talent. They had to practice, but no one cared whether I did or not. So I played the bass drum and triangle in the opera orchestra, and sang, or rather growled, the tenor part in the Verdi Requiem in Dr. Harold Darke's vocal ensemble class, as he was short of tenors. One term I even learned enough saxophone to play in Bizet's *L'Arlésienne* Suite with the third orcheschestra. Most of the time, however, was spent in accompanying anybody playing anything, people boning up on parts for the opera class, or getting ready for their violin exams so it was possible to be useful and it was a great way to absorb the general musical repertoire.

I was particularly useful to Dr. Herman Grunebaum (who was in charge of the opera class) for his Wagner ensembles. He usually had a crew of Valkyries, Rhine Maidens, and Flower Maidens going, of which various members would be absent, and for whom I would fill in accurately if not gloriously, to keep the ensemble together. Although I never distinguished myself in any way at the Royal College of Music, in fact quite the reverse, it all proved very useful and gave me a fairly wide musical education.

Then there was the social side, which was tremendous. I became friendly with Elizabeth Aveling, daughter of the registrar. She was a Rubensian woman of great personal attraction, and a splendid musician and singer, and was married to a man named Drubbles Rowe. They lived in my old stamping ground, Philbeach Gardens. She was the social leader of what one would call nowadays the "jet set" of the Royal College of Music.

Everyone thought we were terribly "fast," but looking back on it now, we were actually as pure as the driven snow compared with what goes on today. Nevertheless, we made a lot of noise. On Friday nights we would get dressed up in our evening clothes and repair to Philbeach Gardens, where there would be a musical evening for starters, then dancing and lots to drink. There were all sorts of love affairs going on, which we would all thoroughly discuss. Some of us would stay the night, so the party usually continued until Sunday.

Like everyone else, I fell in love, with a fellow who played the violin. He was nice, easy to get along with, and down-to-earth. You'd never think he was a violinist because he was so normal. We got along beautifully and he was my jet-set date for a couple of years. I was ecstatically happy. This was living! I took him home only once, and what happened was just as I expected. Mother said, "He's a nice enough man but not our class. He'd be more suitable for a relation of Phoebe's." (That may have been the attraction.) Father said I was not to contemplate marriage until I'd finished college. This didn't bother me, as I had plenty of places to see him without taking him home. Besides, I didn't consider myself Mother's class anymore. I was a musician and by now quite emancipated.

Because my practicing soon drove everyone at home crazy, Father rented a studio in the next block for me. It was a triangular, rickety-looking place with a fireplace and sink. The ceiling in the lavatory was only about five feet high, so you had to crouch down and back in, but that didn't matter—the plumbing was in order. The studio had a high skylight overlooking the railway. Every passing train belched smoke, so the place was impossible to keep clean, but never mind; it was a real studio and cost only thirty shillings a month.

Father had found another nice clean room for forty shillings a month, which he preferred. We had a great debate on the subject and I won. After all, mine was cheaper. Father said if I wanted a filthy place like that, it was my own head, but neither he nor Mother would darken its door again.

This was just the ticket, so the piano was moved in, and I was a householder and practically free from restraint. I had a key to Baron's Court and could come and go as I liked, except that it was obligatory to come home and dress for dinner in the evening. I'd rush in, have a bath, put on any old evening dress, and the three of us would solemnly sit down to a formal dinner by candlelight, served by Phoebe in her frilly apron and cap with streamers. Afterward, Mother and I would retire to the drawing room for coffee and polite conversation, while Dad remained with the nuts and brandy in the dining room. When eventually he entered the drawing room, I was free to go, so I would change back into my scruffy gear and tear off to the studio or wherever to rejoin my own social set. All in all this arrangement was pretty good, except on the rare occasions when we had guests and the men stayed in the dining room for ages, while I chafed at the bit with the women in the drawing room.

From time to time I would attend military balls with sons of Father's colleagues, the invitations doubtless set up by mutual paternal agreement. Inevitably, I would be invited out later by the young men I had met.

These outings had a regular format. Let's say we were to go dancing and to supper afterward, which was the done thing at the time. Father would say, "Ask him to come early and I'll take him to Queen's Club for a game of squash before you go, if he'd like that." They mostly did like it, as young officers by and large were great sports aficionados; also, some of them who fancied me thought it would be a good idea to get on the right side of the old man. Father was sixty and bald and looked mild enough, so they'd prance over to the club, and Father, who had never lost his touch with the racket and ball, would trounce the life out of them. The poor things would come back absolutely exhausted and would be practically useless to me for the rest of the evening.

When they took me home, I would naturally invite them in for a nightcap, but since the drawing room was upstairs on the same floor as Mother's suite, the only place we could go was the dining room, which was full of grim furniture, including straight-back chairs, hardly conducive to stimulating the tender passion. Also, we had to be very quiet, for if we woke Mother she would yell down the stairs, "It's one o'clock!" or whatever time it was. "Whoever you've got down there send him home." She would repeat this every ten minutes or so until the poor soul would get so unnerved, he would run for his life. Naturally enough, these encounters seldom got off the ground, but it really didn't matter.

What did matter was that my real boyfriend, as I considered the violinist, got fed up with the whole situation, as well he might, and married someone else, and I felt completely bereft. I saw him a few years ago. He was still playing in the orchestra and is now a grandfather and just as nice as ever, which makes me feel that if there hadn't been so much interference, I would have done a lot better in this department. But then there would have been no career, so probably what I lost on the roundabout I gained on the swings.

In our third year at college everyone was getting jobs with the BBC. If you were a student you had to get written permission from the college to audition, but I couldn't see Sir Hugh Allen doing this for me. Then I discovered that students from Canada, Australia, or anywhere else in the British Empire except England, could audition without permission, to broadcast on Empire transmissions to the folks back home.

I applied as a Canadian, which was half right after all, and sure enough I got the audition. The next thing was what to audition, so I went to see the marvelous Mr. Winchester at Chappell's Publishing Company, who was a great pal to all of us. I think he must have been familiar with every piece of music ever published. I explained that I must have something no higher than D or I'd hit the yodel, but I could do a very high note at the end. He came up with a book of songs, *Siete Canciones Populares Españolas* by Ocon. They were little jotas, zapateados, malagueñas, etc. With a comfortable range and charming accompaniments, they were all very chirpy and different. I learned a few so that I could sit down at the piano and dash them off, and they were rather effective.

I didn't really expect any results from the audition, as I had applied for it more in the spirit of fun than anything else. The great day came, however, and off I went to Broadcasting House. I was put into a room full of artists of every description, all talking to beat the band about their last appearance at Covent Garden, the Queen's Hall, etc., or what this or that conductor had said about their last great performance. They all seemed to know each other, but I didn't know any of them. It was the first time I had been in a group of musicians other than students, and I became completely overawed and paralyzed with fright, and almost turned and fled. But I pulled myself together when my name was called, and off I went to the Concert Hall. It looked vast. There were two work lights shining down on the concert grand piano, beside which stood the celebrated Mr. Berkley Mason, waiting to play for the auditioners. Apart from that were only what looked like thousands of seats fading away into the gloom. I said I was playing for myself. He looked pityingly at me and went out. Then someone fixed the mike and he, too, went out.

The studios in those days had that absolutely dead atmosphere, which made you feel as if your head was solid, your ears were stuffed with cotton wool, and you'd never be able to make a sound. I sat there miserably until a voice like thunder, goodness knows from where, said, "Announce the song and composer and then sing it."

After this godlike sound my miserable, scratchy little voice and scrabblings on the piano sounded just pitiful, but by then I'd gotten to the point, you know how you can, of feeling that you've made such an ass of yourself, nothing can be done, so you might just as well relax. After I finished, amazingly enough they asked for another and then another, so on I went, suspecting that someone in the bowels of Broadcasting House was having a jolly good laugh at my expense. But there was the comforting thought that it would be a very funny story to tell the pals back at college. In fact, I dined out on it for quite a time.

A few weeks later there came in the mail a great buff-colored envelope with "Contract Urgent for Signature" emblazoned in red across the corner. I was to give a half-hour recital of Spanish folk songs on a certain date at four o'clock in the morning, destined for western Canada, and I was to contact Mr. Horace Dann at once if not sooner, and I would be paid the princely sum of five guineas. This in itself was extraordinary, as my ballad-singing friends were starting at three guineas.

Mother and Father almost swooned away in sheer incredulity, having been exposed to my practicing from time to time. Father's comment was, "Doubtless what goes into a microphone sounds a great deal better when it comes out the other end, if the controls are manned by experts," a remark with which I privately agreed, although it was scarcely flattering to the ego. But five guineas! Up until now the biggest fee I had ever earned was half a crown from Father for cutting the lawn.

Then came the snag. I didn't know half an hour's worth of Spanish folk songs. There was no time to consult Mr. Winchester, as that week we were having opera orchestra rehearsals daily and all day, and I was on percussion. I daren't go to my professors in case it got back to Sir Hugh, who would probably kill me. So what to do?

I went to Dr. (later Sir) Percy Buck. He was a very handsome old gentleman who taught us all ear training. He had been the organist at Harrow, the boys' school, and was a very learned man and a celebrated musicologist. He had a wonderful and wicked sense of humor, and had been known to say very irreverent things about other members of the faculty. He was the only one outside the students who thought my efforts to sing at the compulsory concerts were hilarious.

I told him the whole story and he nearly split his sides. Then we got together a program, plus all sorts of other folk songs of various nationalities, and all sorts of reading matter by Cecil Sharp and other folk experts, and he told me to bone up on the lot. I asked him why all the rest of it, for I was no expert on the subject. He told me, very sensibly as it turned out, that if the first broadcast went well, I would be put on the list in that department, and my name would automatically come up from time to time, so why not inform myself now in preparation for future events.

It all worked out exactly as he had predicted, so there it was—Anna Russell had finally materialized and had earned five guineas! I continued hey nonny-noing every few weeks right up until the time I left the country. This was before folk singing was "in," when it was still considered highbrow. A few aficionados might be interested, while the general public would switch to Henry Hall and his dance orchestra. I doubt if I would have done so well now, but then there was very little competition.

When Sir Hugh finally found out about the first broadcast, as of course he had to, he was still very grumpy with me and said it was all most unethical, but since it was a fait accompli, perhaps now I would knuckle down and do some work and stop acting the fool all the time. I promised I would and really meant it, which I suppose were more famous last words.

It was about this time I got to know a very nice fellow who played the French horn. He had been a lawyer and had given consternation to his family, who were all of the cloth (Church of England), by giving up law and going in for music. This one I was able to take home, as his background was right. Bishops and clergy weld very well with the army. Sure enough, Father thought he was a splendid chap and they got on extremely well. It was very nice to have a boyfriend with whom I did not have to be schizophrenic. The question of becoming engaged came up, and Father said that if it had to be a musician, this was undoubtedly the one, so we did.

He was about six feet, four inches and nice-looking in a solemn, youthful sort of way, but exceedingly scruffy, which was the fashion then with orchestral players. He wore grubby flannel trousers and a tweed jacket, and a particularly shapeless brown felt hat that was so old it had a personality all its own and made him look rather like Jacques Tati of *Mr. Hulot's Holiday* fame. He had retained a whimsical, though slightly pompous sense of humor one associates with old family solicitors, which contrasted rather strangely with his appearance and tough orchestral behavior. His main characteristic, however, was ambition. He felt very sure that he was going to be a success, or else!

I doubt if he was madly in love with me. I think the main attraction was that I had a suitable background that would please the clergy. I wasn't wildly in love, either, but he was very attentive and nice and easy to get on with, and there was family approval on both sides, which was certainly a novelty for me.

We didn't see each other much, as he was always rehearsing or playing concerts, and I had become rather bored with the studio and besides was quite broke. In order to get a little cash, I rented the studio, unbeknownst to Father, to a couple of students who had just got married, and moved in with two friends, Audrey Langford-Brown and Mary Fitzgerald, a few doors up the street in Talgarth Road. Audrey was a coloratura soprano who finally made Covent Garden and now conducts a choral society. Mary was the darkroom assistant to John Everard, a famous photographer of nudes (artistic, not pornographic).

At that period John Everard was having a lot of trouble with his models. The fashions then required utter slimness, and he would tell Mary that everyone looked like a filleted fish when stripped—didn't anyone have breasts anymore?—and he hadn't seen a good bottom for years.

It so happened, although the face was nothing to write home about, I did have the body beautiful in those days. It didn't do me much good, as I was far too bumpy for the current fashions, but Mary suggested I go and show myself to Mr. Everard. I told her I couldn't, Father would disown me. "Oh," Mary said, "he only photographs bits of you at a time, all oiled and flocked through a wrought iron gate and things like that. It's all so artistic you can't recognize anyone, and you can ask him to keep your face out of it. Besides," she said, "it's quite respectable. Mrs. Everard works with him all the time and I'm always there. And the money is terrific. Why don't you go and talk to him?"

So of course I did. I explained to Mr. Everard that I didn't want to be recognized on account of Father. He said, "That's all right. Your face wouldn't do anyway, but the rest of it is marvelous," and gave me the job, so the money problem was solved.

He won quite a few prizes with bits of me. I remember one where I was oiled all over and covered with fluffy stuff, then I sat all hunched over on a table with my hands under my seat. He took me from the back and called the picture *Peach*. It came out in the *Tatler*. When Father saw it he said, "It's amazing what people will stoop to for money." Luckily I was not familiar to him from that angle.

About thirty-five years later I met John Everard in Johannesburg, at the height of my career, in company with Sir Malcolm Sargent. I could see he recognized me. It was very funny. He was far too much of a gentleman to come out and say I'd modeled nude for him, so we pussyfooted around, doing an "*Après vous*, Gaston" act which went something like this:

"How do you do," he said. "I haven't seen your performance yet, but I have your records."

"Oh," I said, "and I have your art books. They are fantastic."

"You know," he went on, "I'm sure I've met you somewhere before; your face is so familiar."

"Oh, yes," I said, "I was a friend of your one-time darkroom assistant Mary Fitzgerald."

"Of course. Now where did she introduce us?"

"She brought me to the studio," then a long digression on the merits of Mary.

"By the way," he said, "did you ever have the album with my photograph called *Peach*?"

"Of course. It was one of your famous ones."

"I won a grand prize for that."

"I know, and it came out in the *Tatler*."

"Shall we go to the bar and get a drink?"

At the bar, the barrier came down and we had a hilarious afternoon. He said he wouldn't tell anyone, but would I like to see the old pictures? I saw them, and some of them were lovely. I'd certainly gone off since those days.

To get back to my youth, I was very properly engaged for two years, during which time Father insisted that I be presented at court. I kept this terribly dark, as being a debutante just wasn't done in my circle, but a bass trombone player, Morris Smith, who was with the Grenadier Guards Band and later became the manager of the Covent Garden Orchestra, found out about it. He was slated to play in the throne room that night, and had seen my name on some list or other. Everyone thought it a huge joke and I got razzed unmercifully.

Since I was a debutante, my engagement was announced in the *Tatler*. I then went to dancing school to learn to curtsy to the floor right and left. You'd be amazed how difficult that is if you're not a dancer. There was the buying of the gown and train and feathers for the event, all sorts of outfits for going to balls and Ascot and goodness knows what.

On the day, I was beauty-parlored like I hadn't been since Ernest de Coppet sent me out with his secretary, and put into my finery. The Daimler limousine with two chauffeurs hired from Harrod's was waiting outside, and the guests began to arrive for the cocktail party. It was quite a production!

At the same time, on the opposite side of the road arrived a brewer's dray with some devils from the orchestra, who proceeded to play and sing and make remarks about the arrivals. I knew Morris Smith was behind all this and wondered what else could be in store.

Finally I got into the limousine with my presenter, a friend of the family, and off we went, round and round the Mall, with the public, including my revolting friends, looking in through the windows and making personal remarks.

On arriving at the palace, we were ushered to a row of seats, shown our places, and there we sat and waited. By this time everyone wanted to pay a penny, I'm sure, but couldn't. When my name was called, I went up a passage with my presenter. The Goldstick-in-Waiting took my train off my arm and flicked it out with his baton, and I was on.

My train was covered with rhinestones and lined with silver lamé, and not only did it weigh a ton, but it kept getting caught on the carpet, so I had difficulty walking gracefully. This, plus the fact that I could feel Morris's beady eye on me from the musicians' gallery, made me start my curtsy on the wrong foot, so it came out very much less than perfect. After the presentation we had supper and went home.

The following week Morris put on his act, "Brown Being Presented," and I must say it was a scream.

Of course, invitations followed for all the balls. I would be conveyed there all by myself, and on arrival would be announced up a grand staircase by the butler and footmen at the top of their voices, after which I would shake hands with the Duchess or whoever the hostess was, be given a program, and be shoved in to be confronted by the stag line, who would then sign up my program. Most of these fellows were spotty and chinless, or had big Adam's apples, they being at the age when this is most prevalent in males.

I felt like a fish out of water, as they either hunted, played polo, yachted, or had other pursuits of which I knew nothing, so there wasn't much conversation until I met one fellow who was also a fish out of water and bored with the whole thing. We sneaked out to the pictures and didn't come back until supper was on. After that we'd check whether we were both invited to the next one. If yes, we'd go to the pictures; if not, we wouldn't go at all. I never saw him anywhere else, but this saved us from a lot of tiresome evenings. It seems strange to me that people are so anxious to get into society when it is so dull.

When the season ended I went to Canada to see Granny Tandy before getting married. I was in the care of my cousin, Paul Davond, who was a fascinating fellow in the RAF. He was bored stiff about chaperoning me, as he had a girlfriend and didn't want to be bothered with a cousin. I was waiting to embark with a portfolio of photos for Granny under my arm, when a most handsome young man came up and asked me if I was an artist, as he was one, too. At this moment Paul came along and saw me talking to the man, greeted him with charm, and said, "If you are alone, do sit at our table." He was no doubt thinking that this would take care of Cousin while he visited the girlfriend, which it did.

I found the artist to be charming, and we became quite inseparable. After we reached Toronto he would come and take me out. It was all utterly pure because, being engaged, I would never have thought of getting up to anything, nor would he, being most respectable. Sometimes he would take me to visit his mother, who was a poppet. Nevertheless, Granny wrote and asked Mother and Father if it was all right for me to be going out with a Jewish man.

Obviously it wasn't. I was yanked home, the banns went up, my father-in-law officiated at my marriage, and off we went on a honeymoon to St. Raphael in the south of France, just like that.

We had a good time on our honeymoon and went back to a very nice flat in Roland Gardens, South Kensington. My husband returned to the orchestra and I became a housewife, aided by a fat, jolly Cockney lady, who came in the mornings. I got on very well with my husband, when I saw him, which wasn't very often, as he rehearsed all day and played at Covent Garden all night. But within our limitations we were a normal young married couple. I'd meet my girlfriends for lunch, visit my parents, go and stay with his family sometimes, and do all the usual things. Some evenings I would sit in the gallery at Covent Garden for the opera or ballet on a free pass.

My husband never got home until goodness knows when, as the orchestra had to gather after the opera to wet their whistles, and I was usually asleep. All the same we had a very steady ménage. He seemed to be getting on and making a fair amount of money; I was still doing hey nonny-nos for the BBC in a desultory manner, and it jogged on until he got a job as first horn in the BBC Midland Orchestra in Birmingham. So we moved up there and lived in quite a pleasant boardinghouse. I used to go to London once a week to visit Father, and it would probably have gone on like that, except for an unforeseen happening.

One day when I went to see Father, I found him in a particularly good mood. I was glad, because several things had recently upset him. He'd had an operation on a couple of his fingers, to do with something called Dupitron's Contraction. He'd had a rather rotten time with it and had gone over by himself to the battlefields in Flanders to recuperate. To add to this, Phoebe, our long-time servant, had been going to the doctor for the past two years to be treated for indigestion, but had been getting worse and worse. She was suddenly taken to hospital and died in a week of terminal cancer. The doctor at the hospital wanted us to bring charges against the local GP for malpractice, but Father thought that since Phoebe was dead, there was no point in that. It was all rather nasty and sad.

This particular day, however, he seemed to be right back to his old form. We lunched at the Savoy, went to a matinee, and did all sorts of things that I liked to do and that he usually never did. I went home so relieved and delighted about how well he seemed. The next day he blew his brains out.

I went completely to pieces. Of all the people in the world, he was the last one I would have thought of doing a thing like that. He must have planned this for some time. All his affairs were in order, and he left a note saying that Mother should go to her brothers in Canada.

Why did he do it? It was all so desperately out of character. He was a charming, intelligent person and everyone liked him. He had no vices: he didn't drink or smoke or run around; he'd had a good career and enough money; he had taken care of his old aunts, his stepfamily, and us. In all ways he had been the most exemplary person, and this is how it wound up.

It didn't make sense to me then, and it still doesn't make sense to me now. Perhaps he had been trying to play God and suddenly found he wasn't; perhaps he'd given out so much to us all and we'd never given anything back, so that he had nothing left of himself; perhaps he couldn't stand being retired with a war coming on and not being in it. I don't suppose I shall ever know the truth. One thing I am convinced of, though, is that he was a first-rate, sincere man who cared a lot and did his best for a bunch of raving egotistical maniacs who finally got him down.

CHAPTER 10

"O Canada"

War was going to be declared at any moment, so my husband gave up his job in Birmingham and we went to stay with his parents at the rectory until he made up his mind what to do.

My father-in-law was just what one imagines a rector ought to be but so seldom is. He was a big, strong, calm man with wiry gray curly hair and a deep, though not churchy, voice. He was the British croquet champion, of all things, and he must have had a tremendous intellect, although he didn't parade it much, for he could do the Torquenada crossword puzzle in the *Observer* without batting an eyelid. You need a degree to understand the clues for this one, let alone fill them in.

My mother-in-law was a tall, slim, pre-Raphaelite sort of woman, very sweet in a sighing, wistful way. Their daughter, a big, husky girl, was engaged to the curate, a bright, birdlike little man.

The rectory was old and spacious, surrounded by lawns and tall trees. There was always a great deal of gentle activity going on between it and the church—ironing surplices, arranging flowers, and setting out cups and saucers for the ladies' meetings. It all had a dreamlike quality about it, considering that everybody knew that war could be declared at any time.

The day before it happened we all went for a picnic in the country. It was one of those hot, sunny days with a cloudless blue sky that is so very rare in England. We spread out rugs and unpacked hampers full of cold chicken, hard-boiled eggs, cheese, and all the typical British picnic fare. After clearing the ants away, we stuffed ourselves and then lay around sunbaking among the debris. It all seemed so permanent and traditional, but we were all wondering if it would ever happen again. The next day war was declared and almost immediately the air raid sirens sounded, all the more ominous in those peaceful surroundings. It was the end of an era.

My husband made up his mind to join the officer's training corps of some crack regiment and not wait to be called up. He was too ambitious for that. He tried to get into the Scots Guards, but that required a private income, which we didn't have, so he went into the Somersets, which are known for wearing their caps straight on the head instead of tilted over one eye like all the rest. Meanwhile I went down to Yateley to stay with Tikka Gran.

When I got there I discovered that, to occupy their time while nothing was happening, the retired colonels living around (of which there were quite a few), were setting up do-it-yourself booby traps on their properties in case of an invasion. Some of them were very ingenious, and any invader of Yateley would have been surprised, to say the least. One man had dug tremendous trenches at intervals across his lawns, then covered them with plywood and put the turf back on top. Tank trap! Another had electric wiring all over the property, which could be turned on by a switch in the house.

I joined the women's transport, but that didn't last long. After I got a six-wheel truck wedged in a driveway so that it wouldn't go forward or backward, I was sacked ignominiously, so I joined an amateur show in Camberley, from where we would drive all over the country in the black of night with only a slit of light to guide us to the various army camps. The show rather reminded me of the goings on in the kitchen at Farnborough in the First World War. We had Road to Mandalays, Tipperaries, and very much the same program. I even rendered "Ginger You're Balmy" on occasion.

I couldn't get a real job, however. In those days people were very persnickety about whom they took on; if you weren't sufficiently qualified they looked down their nose at you. I had no real home, as Mother by this time had gone to Canada to live with her brothers, and wives were not allowed to join their husbands where they were training, or so I was led to believe. Actually, my husband had requested that I not join him, as he was too busy with his career to bother about me. Once in a while he would turn up in Yateley for the weekend, with his cap on straight and a huge RAF mustache he had grown. Apart from planting a victory garden, I had nothing to do and there seemed no future.

All of a sudden, from Samarkand or somewhere Aunt Al Schuyler appeared like Nemesis and summoned me preemptively to London. I hadn't seen her for a few years nor had I heard from her, so I flew off to London thrilled and delighted. I found her in a towering rage.

"You make me sick," was her first remark.

"What have I done now?" I asked.

"I am going to tell you something," she said, "that I promised never to tell anyone, but in view of your father's death and your subsequent behavior, I feel absolved from that promise." It appeared that all the time Mother and Father were in Hong Kong, Aunt Al had paid for everything—my schooling, my clothes, my holidays, the lot. After they returned she continued to pay for my schooling.

"So," she said, "I think I have some say in this matter. I tried to bring you up to think for yourself when you were with me, and thought I was having some success until your family came home. Then you reverted to being a silly little girl again. Can't you do anything of your own volition? Are you always going to wait to be pressured by someone else? You've got no guts."

What did she expect me to do? "This is your last chance," she said. "I am going to Canada and I want to take you with me." I felt I couldn't do that with a war on even if I could get an exit permit. What would people think?

Aunt Al didn't care what they thought. She considered herself to be a citizen of the world. Nationalism was all bunk and war was a waste of time, and it would be all the same in another twenty years when this one was forgotten and another would start.

"Then what about my husband?" I asked.

"You're not in love with him and you'd never have married him if it hadn't been for your father. Anyway, you won't do any good with him; he's not your type."

We went at it hammer and tongs all night long and finally concluded that I owed it to her to go. I wasn't really attached to the way of life I'd had up till then. I would do it! But how? The only way I could get an exit permit was to be pregnant.

"Well! So get yourself pregnant," Aunt advised. I told her that I thought it unlikely with my family history. "Well! Get yourself declared pregnant," was her next remark.

"How am I going to do that?"

"That's your problem, and you have a month to think it out; then I'm going for good." And with this flat statement she closed the subject.

Sure I had the family talent for nonpropagation, I took to crime. Remembering the row over Phoebe's death, I went to the GP who had failed to diagnose cancer and told him quite bluntly that if he didn't declare me pregnant that instant, I would reopen the case and bring charges against him. The decision was his. He declared me pregnant.

I said good-bye to my husband, who didn't seem to mind. I bade farewell to the rest of the family, quite a few of whom set upon Aunt Al for daring to take me away at such a time. She couldn't have cared less, and told them to mind their own business. So with scorn heaped upon us, for leaving at such a time, we packed our things and took off for Liverpool.

That night there was an air raid warning, so we all went down to the cellar of the hotel in Liverpool. You never saw such a motley crew in their nightclothes, all being served with coffee and sandwiches by waiters in dinner jackets and tails. The next day we sailed off to a new life.

The voyage, though blacked out, was vastly entertaining. I met a charming man, and we had an affair, which absolutely amazed me. Up till then I had been pure and faithful unto death, and would never have considered such a thing. But having committed the ultimate crime of leaving England in wartime, one more peccadillo didn't seem to matter much. Instead, I felt liberated, and about time, too. I was already nearly thirty.

As soon as we boarded, Aunt Al had gone off to the smoking room, where she played bridge from dawn to midnight, except for meals. She told me, "Look, dear, if you want anything, charge it to me but don't, for heaven's sake, interrupt the bridge game." We would both get back to our cabin at about midnight, slightly tiddly, and have a talk and a giggle over our nightcaps. She was about seventy-five at this point, but you would have thought we were a couple of teenagers.

The extent of my worldly wealth was currently fifty pounds and a through ticket to Toronto. The small income left me by Aunt Bena when she died I had to leave behind. But she had also left me mountains of valuable jewelry, so having already become a blackmailer and traitor, I thought I would have a go at being a smuggler, too. When we disembarked in Montreal, my underwear was studded with diamond brooches; I had a multiple string of pearls in one side of my bra, and a diamond and ruby necklace in the other; a string of rings hung around my waist; and short of an emerald in my navel, I was bejeweled from top to toe under my clothes.

At Customs I felt a little apprehensive, but they were so busy giving Aunt Al a going over (for they knew her of old), that they took no notice of me. She had purposely put in a few pieces of contraband for them to find, reasoning that they would be so elated catching her out that it would take the heat off me, which is exactly what happened. They promptly confiscated the goods and imposed a mild fine on her. I'm sure she would have made a very successful crook.

After stopping off in Kingston for my great-uncle Kenny's funeral, I went on to Toronto and met Aunt Al, and the next day we went to Unionville, a little village about twenty miles out, where Mother, Uncle Harry, and Uncle Bryer were living at Cedar Trees Farm.

I could see that this part of the family didn't approve of my turning up in Canada any more than the other part approved of my leaving England. Mother said, "I don't know what your father would have said about this."

Aunt Al answered, "Since he is absent by his own choice I don't think the question arises." Then the subject of "your poor husband" came up, to which Aunt replied, "I think his time is fully occupied learning to be an officer and a gentleman." Aunt Al had a ready temper, so by this time she was in one of her incandescent rages. Her eyes flashed, her voice had a certain edge, and her command of sarcasm and innuendo was second to none. Having wiped the floor with Mother she said, "There's nothing you can do about it, so just don't get emotional," after which, in her usual style, she hopped in the car and went off to Honolulu.

When she was gone I had a look around. The farm was enchanting. There was an avenue of enormous fir trees up to the house, and the garden was a riot of flowers. Beyond the dwelling was a big red barn and meadows as far as you could see. The house was comfortable and scruffy. Among the beat-up and Victorian furniture, was Mother's oriental furniture with knickknacks to match. On the walls were Chinese scrolls and Japanese prints, alternating with reproductions of *The Stag at Dusk*, *Love Locked Out*, and pictures of waves and sinking ships. There were plants everywhere in various stages of growth and nongrowth, papers and magazines on every available surface, a few perfect cobwebs in the corners, and over all a fine film of dust. The effect was an air of down-at-heel coziness.

Then there were the uncles. Uncle Harry was very handsome, and dressed smartly every day when he went to his advertising agency in Toronto, but at home he wore shapeless trousers and old sweaters. He never said much, but what he did say was exceedingly amusing. Uncle Bryer, who was the one who sang "Road to Mandalay" in our kitchen during the First World War, was tall and heavyset with a bald head. He looked like a very large edition of Sydney Greenstreet.

Uncle Bryer looked after the place, and when I say looked after, I mean he did everything, including the cooking and housework, which probably accounted for the dust and cobwebs. Apart from these occupations, Uncle

Bryer had his nose in a book or listened to records. There was no subject on which he could not converse intelligently, and he knew far more about music than I did.

The uncles had nothing in common, but they got on very well together. They would sit for hours not saying a word, just puffing contentedly on their pipes. Mother did nothing except try to reorganize them more to her liking, but she got nowhere, because they would retreat in silence to the kitchen. I think they were a little afraid of her, particularly when she got emotional; then they would go to the barn or Uncle Harry's hideaway. This was a little hut he had built in the garden. It contained two decrepit chairs, thousands of pictures of nude ladies cut from old calendars, and one of Hitler framed in a lavatory seat, which was used for a dart board. By mutual consent no one could go in there unless expressly invited.

The first month I was there the uncles regarded me with grave suspicion. Mother was put out with me for being there and with the uncles for refusing to talk, and I was put out with Mother for taking this attitude and with the uncles for being, as I thought at the time, so stuffy. It was rather like *The Fall of the House of Usher.*

Then one day Mother announced that she was going away for the weekend. The uncles and I sat in stony silence in the living room as she departed. No sooner had the noise of the car faded out in the distance, however, than Uncle Harry reached behind the sofa, brought out a gallon bottle of rye whisky, and announced, "We are all going fishing."

I never saw such a change come over two people. It was as if someone had pulled the cork out. We had a few snorts, then Uncle Harry launched into some perfectly wild stories, and Bryer gave a rendition of "Road to Mandalay" with almost as much bravura as he had done twenty years previously. After picking up Freda, who I discovered had been Bryer's lady friend for the last twenty years or so, and whom he visited every Thursday and Saturday, we took off for Murray Bay, where there were more of the uncles' cronies. I never had so much fun in my life. When the uncles had ascertained that I was not madly keen on Mother's church ladies and enjoyed the odd drink, I was accepted as a member of the club. We arrived back on Sunday night, tired, filthy, and rather hung over. Uncle locked away the grog and said, "Don't you ever mention this to your mother." The next day when she returned things went back to normal. Armed neutrality.

Poor old Mother, I felt so sorry for her. If she only could have relaxed and not tried to be the Lady Bracknell of Unionville, we could all have had such a good time. I think she was very lonely without Father to dance attendance on her, and she would never in a million years get that from the uncles. I tried many times to make her to understand this, with no success whatsoever. She would just get mad at me, complain that I always liked common people and common behavior, and wonder why I couldn't act like a lady and be more like my father's people, so I finally gave up.

The uncles couldn't understand her attitude, either. Apparently she had been a grand girl when she was young. Bryer had looked forward to her coming, hoping she would keep house for them, and I think they were both bitterly disappointed at the outcome.

I was now taken to visit Freda on Thursdays and Saturdays. We'd have a few drinks and a big feed, then I would play the piano and everyone would sing, or we would go to the pub or the amusement park at Sunnyside. I felt that I was part of a family in the sense that most people are part of a family; if only we could have gotten Mother to join!

After I had lived on the farm for a few months my money had practically run out, so I made up my mind to leave for Toronto and find myself a room in a boardinghouse from which I could start making my fortune.

CHAPTER 11

My career gets off to a shaky start

I was packed and ready to go the next day, when who should turn up but a girlhood friend of Mother's, Alice Rolph, and her daughter Maire. Although this Aunt Al had never been to Ireland, she was as Irish as Paddy's pig and had the raciest line of chat I'd ever heard. When I told her what I was going to do she said, "You will do nothing of the sort. You will come and live with me and Uncle Ern," and that was it. You disagreed with Aunt Al's pronunciamentos at your peril. I had not yet met Uncle Ern and wondered whether he would be consulted on the matter, not that it seemed to make the slightest difference.

The next day I went up in a taxi with my baggage, and there on the front lawn was the gardener, who told me there was no one at home, but that I was expected, and took my bags in for me. He was a dear old fellow with a mop of white hair, a broad grin, and a very peculiar accent. I went outside and chatted with him. He certainly knew all about plants and how to keep the lawn in good order, and he gave me a very technical lecture on setting up a compost heap. I asked him how long he'd been with Mrs. Rolph. "Man and boy, fifty year," he said. "She be a right fine lady to work fer." We kept this chat up for about half an hour, until a car drew up with Aunt Al, who got out, promptly kissed the gardener, and said, "Hello, Ern."

Although Uncle Ern would have made a wonderful actor, he was actually one of Canada's leading architects and had built the Royal York Hotel. He was also a well-known collector, and had one of the finest collections of Chinese snuff bottles in North America. He and Aunt Al had a huge house absolutely stuffed with beautiful things. I don't think Uncle Ern ever missed an auction, or ever failed to buy something at one. Not a week passed without some stupendous objet d'art being delivered. This riled Aunt Al, who had no more respect for art than for anything else. She would complain that the place was nothing but a warehouse, but he'd just laugh and keep on collecting. As fast as he would bring things in through the front door, she'd give them away through the back.

Nevertheless, it was the most cheerful house I had ever lived in. There were two more daughters besides Maire: Pat, the youngest, and Billie, who was married, with two children, and lived close by. There was something happening all the time: dinner parties, dances, the theater, the symphony, outings. If we had a day off, Maire and I would start at 11:00 A.M. and go to three different movies.

Pat and Maire had their various boyfriends, and one day Aunt Alice said, "Clard [her rendering of Claudia], can't you find yourself a man? I like my parties to come out even." I told her no. After all, I was married. "That's got nothing to do with it," she said. "Go and pick one up for yourself."

So I thought, who do I know, and I suddenly remembered the artist I met on the boat when I came to see Granny seven years ago, when I was engaged. Charlie was probably married by now, but it was worth a try, so I called him up. There he was, still a bachelor, and he promptly invited me to dinner on Saturday with his ma. I got on very well with Ma, so Saturday night became an established custom. Charlie, who was by this time a well-known artist, was a great success at the Rolph ménage, particularly with Uncle Ern, who also collected paintings.

After a few months of living with the Rolphs I told Aunt Al that I simply must find myself a place and get some work, but she couldn't see any point in that. "Why don't you get into the show at the Active Service Canteen?" she asked.

"Because I have to earn some money," I answered.

"Why? Aren't you enjoying yourself here?" I think by that time she had convinced herself that I was one of the Rolph girls, but I insisted, and found the most enormous room in a former mansion on Bloor Street called Belvedere Manor. It was unfurnished, but it was the only place I could find. "Good!" said Aunt Al. "Take it and leave the rest to me."

I moved in with only a camp bed that the landlady lent me. The next day a huge pantechnicon arrived, out of which came beautiful carpets, a set of dishes, brocade curtains, and a grand piano. When it was all set up it looked like the salon of Madame de something or other, it was so elegant.

I thanked Aunt Al and said I would take great care of all the lavish things. "I don't care what you do with them," she said, "so long as you never send them back here. I now have a little room to breathe until your uncle Ern fills it up again with more junk."

So I settled into Belvedere Manor. It was owned by an enchanting and permissive woman named Ann Miller. There were dozens of boarders, who at times became very quarrelsome, but usually only in the dining room, as the landlady had the sense to put all the noisy ones in the front of the house and the quiet ones at the back. On one side was a trombone player, a few singers, a dull young RCAF man named Lonergan, myself, and a very pompous Englishman named Syd Dixon, who worked for the CBC.

Syd was pompous all week, but on weekends he would invite everyone in and get roaring drunk. This caught on, and it wasn't long before Saturdays became absolute bedlam. The uncles would come up with Freda; Charlie and I would have a quick bite with Ma and be there pronto. Everyone brought their friends and some grog, and it became a weekly institution. The quiet boarders complained like mad, but it made no difference because Ann preferred us, so one by one they slunk away to be replaced by more noisy ones.

Before long I was doing a few hey nonny-nos for the CBC and some bit parts in soap operas. The money wasn't lavish, but it was a start. Then I collected a few comic songs and went to audition for the Active Service Canteen, where I began performing on Sunday nights.

I was teamed up with Ruthie Johnson, a woman of only four feet eleven. She wasn't squatty, but was built completely in proportion to her height, and had a loud contralto voice. I wore a white embroidered lawn dress with long sleeves and a boned-up collar, and a pair of high-heeled shoes. My hair was piled on top of my head and topped by a hat with white osprey feathers sticking up. Ruthie wore the same sort of dress, flat heels, and droopy hat. This made her about half my size.

We sang some nauseating Victorian duets such as "All Things Are Beautiful," and "Trust Her Not, She Is Fooling Thee," all dripping with sentiment. We also rendered the duet out of the opera *Norma*, "Hear Me, Norma," which is actually composed for two women, but Ruthie and I sang it as a love duet; she wore a walrus mustache, tails, and trousers with a pillow stuck inside. Then there was a number in glorious Spanish costume, where she was also the gentleman. This last routine, especially, used to bring the house down.

Around this time I received an offer to sing old music hall songs on CFRB's radio show "Round the Marble Arch." I was a bit dubious at first. The comic turn was fine for club dates and the Canteen, but I didn't want to spoil the hey nonny-no image I had been painstakingly building for so many years on the BBC and now the CBC. I was making a lot of money with the comic songs, however, while my hey nonny-nos had never set the world on fire, so I took the job.

The show consisted of Roy Locksley and his orchestra; a pretty, plump soprano singing light operetta favorites with cadenzas up to the ceiling; Wishart Campbell, Canada's lover-boy baritone; myself with "Knock 'Em in the Old Kent Road" numbers; and Ruby Ramsay-Rouse at the console of the CFRB organ. The men wore red tails and the girls red dresses. There was always a studio audience to capacity and hanging from the rafters, as a great deal of horseplay went on that didn't register on the radio.

The program had been on for ages, so when I arrived they were just about scraping the bottom of the barrel for music hall songs, as all the best ones had been done. The songs finally got so abysmal that I came to the conclusion that even I could write better ones than these, so I came up with my first opus, "Don Bonzo Alfonzo the Matador." It was complete with castanets, flamenco, double talk, and olés.

Roy Locksley, who was responsible for finding the material, said he thought it was jolly good and I could just get on with it and write myself a comic song each week. This was rather a tall order, but it's amazing what one can do if there is a deadline coming up. After a while I got the hang of it, and I found the numbers very useful for my club dates as well.

Now that I'd collected some material, I thought I'd go back to England and join an ENSA show (ENSA was the British equivalent of the USO), but the red tape made this well-nigh impossible. At the same time Roy Locksley joined the navy and began recruiting across Canada for the Canadian Navy Show. "Round the Marble Arch" went off the air, but Roy said he would probably recruit me if he didn't find another comedienne. So I waited for the next few months, getting broker and broker, as there were few conventions at that time of year. Then one day J. Walter Thompson approached me to write comic songs for "Jolly Miller Time," a show sponsored by the Maple Leaf Milling Company. I held off until my last red cent had gone, hoping to hear from Roy, but I finally decided to sign the contract. Two days later Roy turned up with an offer, but Maple Leaf Milling wouldn't release me.

Anyway, I bashed out some more songs and went up to see Winston McQuillan at J. Walter Thompson, who was in charge of the program. He blandly informed me that they didn't want comic songs after all, as they had Al and Bob Harvey on the program, a celebrated music hall team. What they wanted was a six-minute comic monologue. I asked him where I could find one. "I don't know," he said, "you'll just have to go and write it, won't you? But I've dinged them seventy-five a week for you, which might be an incentive." That was a lot in those days.

Here we go again, I thought. I got *Joe Miller's Joke Book* and old copies of *Punch*. I tried to remember what I'd learned in drama class at school, and who I'd seen that was funny. I pored over Stephen Leacock and all the comic writers I could think of, burning the midnight oil for weeks.

I finally came up with a dotty housewife, Mrs. Virgil Denison, who was full of household ambition, which always wound up a shambles. At the beginning of each monologue I would rush on and yell "Virgil!" then unburden myself as to the particular tragedy that had occurred. In the first program, however, because of nerves I yelled "Virgil!" with such force that I blew the station off the air, electronics not being what they are today. For a long while after this, I was the station engineers' nightmare.

My friend Charlie had by now joined the RCAF and was the commanding officer of the Historical Section. Ann Miller had got married and sold Belvedere Manor, so I had to move. I had met a charming woman who was a home economics expert, and she suggested we share an apartment. All my friends who knew her said, "Watch out, she drinks!" That didn't bother me, as I had been exposed to the uncles on Thursdays and Saturdays and later to Syd Dixon in Belvedere Manor, so we got a lovely little place in St. Mary Street, and everything worked out very well. She went out to business during the day, so I could practice. When she came home she would cook the most delicious meals. She knew all the household tricks to make everything pleasant and comfortable (which I never could do), and she was great fun into the bargain.

Everyone was asking how we were getting on. I told them marvelously, and as for drinking, I'd never seen her touch a drop. Then Christmas came and she must have gotten into the rum while baking cakes, because she went off like Sputnik, drinking everything in the apartment plus bottles she had hidden in such weird places as the laundry basket and toilet tank. Then she disappeared, with no clothes, in below-zero weather. When she returned two days later, with the most awful jitters, I told her about Alcoholics Anonymous, which was just starting in Toronto, and which I had heard about from a policeman. She was a bit afraid to go at first, but she soon took over the meetings, in her usual efficient style, making cakes and sandwiches and fixing the clubroom up. Then she started organizing other AA branches and writing a newspaper column answering migrants' problems. Soon she got a job with one of the big department stores as an interior design consultant, and finally had so many projects going that she had to have a secretary and an office and move to a larger apartment. The last I saw of her was in New York at an AA convention. She never touched a drop of anything again for twenty-five years, until she died.

After she moved out I got a new roommate, Dorothy Parnum, who ran the North American Artists' Bureau all by herself. She had quite a good list, including the Hart House String Quartet and some artists who later did very well in the United States. I never saw anyone work as hard as she did. The whole place was piled with photographs, press books, and circulars, and we would spend every spare second putting these into envelopes and mailing them away. The artists would be forever coming in and complaining that they weren't getting enough work, or she'd be auditioning violinists and singers and such in the front room. I doubt if she made a nickel out of it, as she seemed to be always broke, but it was a joy for me to see another aspect of show business.

Came the day when the Canadian Federation of Music Teachers was to hold its convention in Toronto, and it all worked up to a frenzy of activity, as Dorothy was the secretary. In the midst of the hurly-burly she asked me to suggest a performer for the last-night dinner. They'd had the Hart House the previous year, so that was no good. We discussed a few more, which she said she'd think about. A week later she came in looking stricken. "The deadline for the printing is this afternoon," she said, "and I've forgotten to engage anyone to perform at the dinner, so you'll have to do it."

"I'll have to do it!" I said. "You can't sing 'Don Bonzo Alfonzo' to a bunch of music teachers."

"Well, if you don't, I'll get the sack," she said. So of course I had to.

Luckily the dinner was two weeks away, so I had time to cogitate. I suddenly remembered my Gilbert and Sullivan Russell-Brown period with Dr. Vaughan Williams, and wondered if it was still possible to write some derivative music. So I went to work and came up with an aria, "I Wish I Were a Dickybird," after Bellini; "Je ne veux pas faire l'amour, j'aimerais mieux manger," after Debussy; "Schlumph ist mein Gesitzenbaum," after Schubert; an eccentric rendition of "Liebestraum" on the piano; "The Tragedy of Lord Ernest," a dramatic poem with a musical background; and to start it off I polished up the radio script of "The Lady President." Aunt Al Rolph lent me some wild Victorian costumes for this, and as the elocutionist I was done up in cheesecloth drapery. Dorothy got a violinist to play while I was changing, and that was the program.

The cream of the Toronto musical world was present, including Sir Ernest MacMillan, the conductor of the Toronto Symphony Orchestra, who was quite a humorist himself. Sir Ernest laughed so much that he fell off the head-table platform. After the performance we talked about my uncle Llewyn, who had been in prison camp with him during the First World War, and he asked me to tea the following week. He was ultimately to play a large part in helping me establish my career.

Dorothy Parnum's artists' bureau was making a terrible mess of our apartment, so we cast about to find a cleaning woman, a commodity hard to come by in Toronto. A friend offered to send hers, as she was going away for some weeks, but we found there was a lot of protocol involved in the employing of Mrs. Carthew. In the first place she didn't do cleaning, she "obliged," and I had to write a polite note to say I was a friend of Mrs. Barrington, who had recommended her most highly, and would she be good enough, etc.

Sure enough, one morning the bell rang, and when I answered the door there stood Mrs. Carthew. She was the perfect charwoman as George Belcher used to depict in *Punch*. She had a weather-beaten but somehow rather dear old face with red veiny cheeks and no teeth. She wore a battered black hat with three tired roses wobbling about on the top, a moth-eaten fur around her neck, stout black boots, and under her coat I could see several skirts of different lengths.

"Mrs. Barrinton 'as arst me to oblige for yer, Mum," she said.

"Why, Mrs. Carthew, you're English," I exclaimed with delight.

" 'Ow didjer naow?" she asked. "My sister wots just come aover, she sez, 'Em,' she sez, 'yer've got that Canydian I can't unnerstan a word wot yer torking abaht.' Yer must 'ave ever such a good ear."

We then had a cup of tea and some more conversation. It was all very ceremonious. It appeared she belonged to the Unity Church presided over by the Reverend Mr. Hawkey, for whom she also obliged and whom she admired, for she quoted him incessantly.

"I mike it a rule only to oblige for 'igh clarse people," she said. Apparently I qualified, for as she rose to leave, she said, "I can fit you in Thursdays," and then sailed out with dignity.

Mrs. Carthew turned out to be a gem. She never took her hat off, but after pulling a pair of men's socks over her boots, she would work like a Trojan, at the same time giving me the benefit of her philosophy. "Mr. 'Awkey sez we can't be syved till we've 'ad a new vibrytion," she would tell me, or "It's a lucky thing I'm not Gawd. I'd mike an 'ell of a mess of it." One day the boiler blew up and we had no water. "Ah!" she said, "Mr. 'Awkey sez we've all got our crawses ter bear, and I recon' that's yours." I asked her what her cross was. "Carthew," she said, " 'asn't done no work fer ten year 'cos ev'ry week 'e thinks 'e's dyin. 'E won't, a course; a creakin' gyte 'angs on fer ever; but when 'e duz go I ain't gonna give 'im no plumes at 'is funeral." If she was a bit down she would sing hymns because, as she said, "A nice 'ymn does me good; it gets me on an 'igher vibrytion."

My mother had joined the St. George's Chapter of the Imperial Order of the Daughters of the Empire, whose war work it was to make waistcoats out of scraps of leather to send to the troops. I went quite often to do a bit of machining, and one day the lady president asked me if I would put on an entertainment to raise some money for them. Thinking it would be held in someone's drawing room and that the hat would be passed around afterward, I said I'd be glad to. I could probably get together an hour's worth of something or other, and it would be jolly. The next I heard, they had booked Eaton Auditorium. I nearly had a fit. That was where the Celebrity Series went on, and I certainly didn't feel up to that standard. They assured me, however, that it would be all right, that I would have plenty of time to think up something during the next four months, that it would be such a good way to raise money. It's on their own heads, I thought, and it *is* for a good cause.

By this time I was used to having unlikely projects thrust upon me, so I started off once again to see if it could be done. I went to a very keen and businesslike lady who taught speech and drama, Gladys Shibley-Mitchell. Her aim was to get immediate results, as she was used to coaching protagonists for eisteddfods, and people who had to learn to do one thing well, even if they couldn't do anything else. She gave, you might say, a crash course for a particular event, and you could study the flapdoodle later if you wished. It wasn't very profound, but it was effective.

The first thing she advised was to get the script written. In the opening number I played various people at an art show. I collected remarks I'd heard and things I'd seen while at the art gallery with Charlie, and we bashed those into shape. The next one was "The Street Car." Then there was a very dramatic monologue about the war, with organ music in the background, followed by some of the "Jolly Miller Time" monologues. In the second half I did a musical skit based on the Active Service Canteen, where I was first the auditioner and then all the different artists auditioning. To end up I did an impersonation of Mrs. Carthew, my cleaning lady, where I scrubbed my way in pantomime across the stage, philosophizing. I wore a variety of costumes for the show. I suppose I was trying to be the poor man's Ruth Draper.

Mrs. Carthew was fascinated with it all, so with some misgivings, I gave her a couple of tickets, hoping she wouldn't be offended by my takeoff of the charwoman, but I took the risk, as she was a very good sport and didn't mind a laugh at her own expense.

The great day came, and we had a full house. It was my first performance in a large auditorium, and the first time I ever felt that wonderful warmth that comes from an audience that is enjoying itself. All the subjects were, of course, thoroughly familiar to Torontonians, and the next day I got an excellent press of the "local girl makes good" type. They even liked the dramatic one with the organ, which is something I would never dare do now.

Mrs. Carthew, as usual, had a great deal to say. "It was very nice play-acting, I thought, and the sad one with the organ was loverly. I 'ad a nice cry in that. 'Ow I luv a nice cry; it relaxes me. But do you naow wot I liked best? That old charwoman you done at the end. Cor! She wasn't 'arf comical! I larfed! I dunno 'ow yer thinks up all them funny things ter say."

After my successful benefit performance, Dorothy Parnum signed me up with the North American Artists' Bureau, and we got busy on do-it-yourself promotion. We sent a brochure to all branches of the Ontario Federation of Music Teachers, as they were the only ones who had seen me, and the first thing we knew, we had a tour booked all over Ontario.

I had finally managed to get all the odds and ends of things I did into one show, and for the first time in my life was not going in six directions at once. It was all very gratifying. I suppose this was really the lowly start of what was to become a very enjoyable professional life.

CHAPTER 12

My husband turns up and divorces me

To assist me on my first tour, I chose Ruby Ramsay-Rouse, the organist from my "Round the Marble Arch" days. She had been a great celebrity in Toronto for years and years, and used to come billowing up on the Wurlitzer in a blaze of lights from the bowels of Loews State. But she was most widely known for her performances at the organ on radio.

Although everyone in Canada had heard Ruby, hardly anyone had seen her, except for her back view riding up and down on the Wurlitzer, so when the tour was announced with her as assisting artist, everybody and his brother turned up to see what she looked like. Although I had top billing, I could have stood on my head, for all anyone would have cared. She was really the star. Luckily they also took to me, however, and by the end of the tour we had had so much exposure that I was set for the concert circuit, and bookings were coming in splendidly.

Meanwhile, Sir Ernest MacMillan had asked me if I could think of anything new for the Toronto Symphony Christmas Box Concerts. After years of performing carols, orchestral novelties, and any funnies that Sir Ernest or the orchestra could think up, they were getting a bit low on comedy ideas. So we selected some of my arias, such as "Anaemia's Death Scene" and "I Wish I Were a Dickybird;" we arranged "Liebestraum," which I played as a piano concerto with all sorts of unlikely interpolations by the orchestra; and there was "Caro Nome" with bassoon obbligato, and various monologues to do with the musical scene. I didn't wear costumes this time, but came on as an utter prima donna, which added a new dimension to the performance—playing it absolutely straight. This I continued to do on tour, with great success. John van Vucht, the librarian, orchestrated the whole thing, and it was a smash hit. The press was tremendous. In fact, Hector Charlesworth, the music critic of the *Globe and Mail* and a great friend of Uncle Ern Rolph, wrote an absolute rave review. Unfortunately, he died of a heart attack the next day.

I took part in the Christmas Box Concerts for quite a number of years. It was at one of these that I started what was later to become the talk on the *Nibelungen Ring*. I narrated, and the orchestra played the excerpts. For the first performance I put in a little joke regarding the Siegfried horn call, which necessitated that the last long part of the call go all wrong at the end. I explained what I wanted to the first horn, who got simply furious and said I was trying to ruin his reputation. Since he wasn't the most accurate player on earth, I thought the chances were good that he'd mess it up anyway, so I let him do it. Unfortunately, for the first time in his life he played the Siegfried horn call absolutely flawlessly and completely ruined the gag, so I took it out. Horn players have absolutely no sense of humor.

The war was finally over and my husband was coming to Canada. Dorothy Parnum moved out of St. Mary Street, and Mrs. Carthew and I got the place all spiffed up. When I told Sir Ernest that my husband was a horn player, he said he could certainly use a good one in the Symphony (as I well knew), so the future looked quite promising. I hadn't seen my husband for several years, so during the weeks I spent alone in the apartment I thoroughly mulled over the period of our courtship and marriage, preparing myself, I suppose, for his arrival. Then, at 7:00 A.M. on Christmas Day, I went down to Union Station to meet him.

I don't know what I expected—I suppose to see him in flannels and tweeds and the funny hat, carrying his horn case. Instead, this immaculate vision emerged in an Anthony Eden hat (in fact, he looked rather like Anthony Eden), rolled umbrella, and well-cut overcoat (my father's, incidentally). It was all rather a shock. He had come to take me back to England, it appeared. He hated Toronto, and had no intention of playing the horn anymore, as he had made important connections in London and was about to join the British Arts Council.

I could see then that it wasn't going to work out. If he had been with the Arts Council when we were first married, I have no doubt I would have loved all the socializing and entertaining, but by now it was I who was involved in rehearsals, nighttime performances, and ambitious projects. Besides, I had no domestic arts at all, so I would have been useless in this future setup.

It was all very sad, but life doesn't go backward. He was a very nice man, but our timing was quite wrong for each other. He stayed only a week, about the worst week I ever spent. Mother didn't help much either. Her reaction was, "Who is going to look after me when I'm old?" I felt guilty and miserable, as if the world had come to an end.

In due course, though, things went back to normal. Dorothy Parnum moved into the apartment again, and Charlie reemerged and we resumed the Saturday night dinners with his ma. There were the concerts, the club dates, and the Christmas Box Concerts, so I was very busy for a number of years. I no longer toured with Ruby, as she had been snatched back to the console at the radio station, but I had a very fine young concert pianist to accompany me, John Coveart. He was handsome and golden blond, and was as much a success with the audience in his way as Ruby had been in hers. I had done away with costume changes, so I could now keep the audience under my beady eye at all times, which made it much easier to build the show to a climax.

I have always been a great believer in having an accompanist with audience appeal. It helps enormously. I know many concert artists prefer some dim and anonymous type playing away in the background. But I like them to have personality. The more they come across the better. In fact, what I need is not so much an accompanist as a straight man.

I had by this time concocted a folksong called "I Gave My Love a Cherry Without Any Pit," and I bought an Irish harp and took enough lessons so I could accompany myself for this one number. The song lasted only three minutes, but I still had to cart the harp around and spend at least an hour tuning it before each performance, which was a terrible nuisance.

One day as we were going across the border to Detroit, the Customs officer impounded the harp, saying that he couldn't release it until he found out from the chief Customs officer, who was away, whether the harp came under the heading of a pipe organ or a wind instrument. I told him I needed it for a concert that night. He was sorry but adamant.

When we got to the hall with no harp, I suggested the pianist play the accompaniment and I would pantomime the harp. I had done the number so often I more or less knew where to play the harp in thin air, so to speak. It brought the house down; they thought it was a splendid piece of mime, and it suddenly became one of the highlights of the show. I thought, why cart a harp around and spend hours tuning it, when an invisible one works much better, so I picked it up on the way back, and it immediately became "the harp that once . . ." I never touched it again, and I have been shedding props in my show ever since.

Since I had refused to go back to England with my husband, we now had to be divorced, so Charlie, who stood as corespondent, and I went to the lawyer for instructions. Apparently, to furnish proof, my bed had to be turned down, we had to be in our dressing gowns, and the detectives would call upon us at such and such a time.

When the time came, we didn't know quite how to behave, so we lit the fire, got in some drinks, and made some sandwiches. The bell rang and two little men came in, one with a very strong Yorkshire accent. After we sat them down and gave them a drink, I found out that the Yorkshire one had been to the Mount School in York where I had gone when I was seven. The upshot was that we all had a very pleasant evening discussing York. When they got up to go, they said, "Oh, yes, we've got to look, haven't we?" So they glanced into the bedroom to see the bed was turned down, noted we had dressing gowns on, and my Yorkshire friend said, "I wish all our cases were as pleasant as this one has been. We've had a wonderful evening. Thank you so much," and they left.

During the last few years Mother had completely washed her hands of me. She had decided I was no good, would never be any good, and was in fact a lost cause. Charlie's mother, however, had come into very strong focus in my life. Ma was a tiny, thin little lady, very down-to-earth and unflamboyant. She had a charming way with her, and a beautiful if somewhat sarcastic sense of humor. She was a very real sort of person, completely unprejudiced. It isn't often a Jewish mother will look with any favor on a prospective *shiksa* daughter-in-law, particularly one as devoid of domestic capabilities as I, but ever since I'd known her she had been the most welcoming, charming person.

The day after the detectives came about the divorce I went over to see her. She behaved as if it was the most ordinary, everyday occurrence, and wanted to know all about it. I told it exactly as it happened, and she was very entertained. That was the beauty of Ma; one never had the feeling of "I'd better not say that, it would upset her," or "Perhaps she wouldn't understand." Ma liked the bald facts, to which she would react in a realistic manner.

About this time there was a radio program in New York called the Fitzgeralds' Breakfast Club. The first of the ad-lib shows, it featured a husband and wife chattering over breakfast, and it was enormously popular. Whatever NBC did, the CBC was bound to follow, so in due course they teamed me up with a most amusing man, Syd Brown, to do half an hour Monday through Friday. It was a hotchpotch sort of program where we sang a bit and played a bit and did whatever came into our heads. Up to this time, radio had been scripted to the last comma, so this was a great innovation and got a lot of attention, which proved to be a mixed blessing.

Since we didn't know what we were going to do, it couldn't be passed by the CBC first, so we'd get onto all sorts of controversial subjects, for which the powers that be in Ottawa would sharply reprimand us. The listeners preferred the controversial programs, though, so it wasn't long before we were walking the tightrope between being too dull for the listeners or too vulgar for the CBC.

The CBC carried sponsors at that time, and since we didn't have one as yet, this being a new network, we invented one—"Wheat Smoochies, the breakfast food that explodes in your face." We did Shakespearean commercials, operatic ones, and all sorts of comic jingles. It was great fun. That, however, was in the days when all commercials were deadly serious and no one dared send up the product. So naturally we got into trouble about it. "Besides," they said, "people are starting to ask for Wheat Smoochies at their grocery stores." I don't know why someone didn't bring out a product and cash in on our free publicity; anyway, they didn't, and we could plainly see our days were numbered, so that was when I made up my mind to take a giant step and go to New York.

By coincidence, Mother was all set to go back to England for good. According to her, the uncles were peasants, I was no good and refused to go about with the "right people," most of the friends of her youth were dead, and she was going back to England, which was the only civilized country. So off she went in one direction while I got ready to go in the other.

After many farewell parties and with lots of encouragement from Charlie and Ma and my collection of friends, who were sure I was about to make it in a big way, off I went to New York. It was rather like stepping off a cliff. I knew only one person there and had absolutely no connections. I hadn't the slightest idea what I would be up against, which was just as well.

CHAPTER 13

My first U.S. tour. My second marriage

When I first got to New York, I stayed at the Taft Hotel until I could find a permanent place. Space was very scarce, so I could stay at the hotel only a week, and apartments were very hard to find. The only person I knew in the city was Kay Carleton, who was the director of the Rehearsal Club, a residence funded by the Rockefeller Foundation to keep actresses off the streets.

I had known Kay when I was a child. She was Grahame's cousin and used to turn up in Farnborough all done up in furs and jewels, fresh from triumphs on the London stage. She was beautiful and charming and immensely popular, and she ran the Rehearsal Club on a very light rein.

When I phoned her, she asked me to lunch, but she said she regretted I couldn't stay at the club. First, I was overage, and second, it was full, and the waiting list was a mile long. I went back to the hotel very disappointed, and started adjusting to the fact that I would probably have to go back to Toronto.

That night the telephone rang at 4 A.M. It was Kay, to say one of the girls had had a nervous breakdown and was hallucinating, and she was in the process of being taken to hospital. If I would pack my bags, check out, and arrive at the club forthwith, she would put me in this girl's room before either the board of directors or anyone on the waiting list found out. "Possession is nine points of the law," she told me, "so if you keep a low profile for a couple of weeks the chances are no one will notice." That is how I moved into the Rehearsal Club, which became a home away from home for the next few years. I am glad to say that my benefactor, the girl who had the nervous breakdown, recovered completely, went home to Montreal, got married, and had a splendid family.

Although the inmates of the club were technically actresses, very few of them were acting. Jobs in the theater at this level were well nigh impossible to get, so most of them were working as typists, waitresses, or shop assistants while waiting for their big break. There were, however, one or two ballerinas from the Radio City Music Hall ballet, and a couple of Rockettes. The stars of the club at the time were Bibi Osterwald and Frances Yeende.

Bibi was a comedienne who had been in a number of Broadway shows, a tremendous performer with great audience appeal. I never could understand why she didn't become one of the top stars, although it was probably because she was always helping other comediennes with introductions and so forth. They would then scheme and plot to get the jobs and keep Bibi out. I saw this happen a number of times. Alas! It isn't always practical to give a helping hand in such a dog-eat-dog business.

Frances Yeende was a glorious creature, with yards of golden hair and a magnificent voice, who had recently signed with Columbia Artists Management as one of the new crop of opera singers. She was most humorous, which was unusual in the operatic world.

There were also two excellent pianists: Dorothy Lee, who had started as an infant prodigy in Chicago and was then accompanying for various distinguished singing teachers in Carnegie Hall and playing in a cocktail bar on Fifth Avenue at night; and Christine Johnson, a music teacher from West Virginia, who was taking a very advanced course at the Mannes College of Music. She was a bit of a genius and could do anything whatsoever on the piano. It took her no time at all to absorb my repertoire, so it was only a matter of days till I was able to join the after-dinner performances that went on almost nightly in the Rehearsal Club drawing room. On the rare off-nights I would play Chinese checkers with Kay Carleton and Sara Enright in Kay's study.

Sara Enright was a theatrical agent who knew absolutely everybody in the theater. She was a rather acid little lady, but most amusing. "When are you going to start looking for work?" she asked me. I told her I'd start the next day. "Well, I can tell you right now you won't get anything," she said. "I've nothing for you, and you won't even get in to see the agents unless you have press notices." I said I had a lot of press from Canada. "Who ever heard of Canada?" she said. "Besides, your act isn't commercial; no one would understand it in a nightclub. That might not matter if you could play up the sex angle, but you haven't got it in that direction." I explained that what I had in mind was comedy connected with classical music. "I daresay you'd be all right for Carnegie Hall," she said, "but you'd never be let in; it's a closed shop."

She came and listened to me nonetheless and knew my repertoire inside out. She was cranky and great fun and gave me all sorts of introductions, but nothing ever happened. "You see," she said, "no one is going to take an interest in you. Why don't you go home and get married?"

Her gloomy predictions were fully justified. I'd traipse around the booking agents' offices day after day and sit for hours waiting to be told there was nothing. No one would audition me. They said if I got a job they might come and see me, but since no one would audition me, I never got a job. It was hopeless.

Apart from this daily pilgrimage, I was having a very good time in the evenings. Through my pianist friends Dorothy and Christine, I got invited to many a musicale or soiree to hear a lot of distinguished artists. Occasionally at the end of these functions, when either everyone was fed up with too much serious music or the wine was flowing, I would be invited to render an excerpt or two. This proved to be of interest enough for my friends to be asked to bring me along to these affairs (for which they were usually paid) to provide the light relief. Thus I met a lot of interesting people.

One time Dorothy was to accompany Salvatore Baccaloni at a benefit at the Lotos Club in aid of some charity. It was a lovely musical evening, and many of the top artists and concert managers were there. Signor Baccaloni, the celebrated basso buffo, emceed the show. I had met him years before at Glyndebourne when my husband was playing the horn in the orchestra there, so while he was waiting, we had a lovely gossip about old times. When I told him what I was doing now, he said that since Miss Lee could play for me, he would announce me as a surprise guest, and I could finish the concert up, as he said, *"Con piccola* laugh." The results were astonishing. I was introduced to Mr. Martinelli, a leading tenor; to Mr. Marks Levine, president of the National Concerts and Artists Corporation (NCAC); to the charming Miss Maggie Teyte, who was currently having an enormous success with her recitals of the French art song at Town Hall. She and I had a great deal to talk about, as I had known one of her first singing teachers, M. de Mest, when I was at finishing school in Brussels, and had seen her at the Hammersmith Theatre in London starring in *Tantivy Towers*, a musical by A. P. Herbert and Reynolds.

The absolute highlight of the evening came when I was invited to the table of Mr. Arthur Judson, the president of Columbia Artists Management. An enormously tall, elderly, white-haired man, he had a reputation for being tough and ruthless, but he seemed to me very dignified and charming. I later discovered that he was highly respected, even revered, by people who usually had no respect for anybody or anything.

I was in a great dither at meeting him, but he soon put me at ease. We had a long talk, and I told him how I had not been able to get through to any theatrical agents whatsoever. He said he could well understand why and suggested I hire a hall and put myself on, which was the only positive idea I'd been given since being in New York. It eventually turned out to be the right one.

Shortly after, at another musical evening, I first met Dolores Pallet. Dolores was an entrancingly beautiful Russian who was assistant musical director to Russell Markert at Radio City Music Hall. She was a marvelous pianist and arranger with a tremendous sense of humor, and one of the most outgoing people I have ever known. We hit it off immediately, and I later saw a lot of her and her family. One day she said, "Why don't you come in every morning to Radio City, and I will coach you and get your show streamlined and polished up, and then we will see what we can do with it." It sounded like a wonderful idea, but where would I get the money? Being coached in New York is a very expensive business, as I knew full well. "Oh, not for money," she said, "just for fun. I spend a lot of time just sitting around up there, and we might as well do something productive."

As often happens when you are learning from someone with whom you are very *en rapport*, I started churning out mountains of new material, which we'd shape up and switch around, usually shrieking with mirth because we thought we were being very funny. Russell Markert would come in from time to time to see how we were getting on. He thought it was fun, too, but not right for the Music Hall.

Dolores set up auditions for me all over the place. We tried the Roxy, all kinds of night spots, club shows, everything, but nothing worked. Most of the auditioners admitted I had something, but no one could think what to do with it.

Then we thought we'd try the concert field. This probably wouldn't have worked either, except that it was just after the Florence Foster Jenkins boom. She was a very wealthy woman and patron of the arts who would dress herself up in operatic costumes and, to the impeccable accompaniment of Mr. Cosme McMoon, give earsplitting and completely out-of-tune renditions of arias such as "The Queen of the Night" or "The Bell Song." No one has yet determined whether she did it to be funny, whether she was dotty, or whether because she had given so much money to support opera, she felt entitled to get up and carry on like that. At any rate, in the recent past, shortly before she died, she had filled Carnegie Hall to capacity, with people lining up around the block for standing room.

"So," said Dolores, "let us try the Foster Jenkins approach." Concert and theatrical booking don't overlap at all, and Dolores had no concert connections, but she did know a promoter. That's when I met Jack Petrill.

Jack was a big, fat, rather good-looking Italian, very rambunctious, who could talk the hind leg off a donkey, albeit very entertainingly. His conversation was sprinkled liberally with four-letter words, and he was the world's greatest optimist. He had written a large tome on factory management and had promoted everything from spaghetti sauce, cookbooks, and beauty contests, to crooners, opera singers, and stand-up comics. You name it, he'd had a go at it. At times he would get so enthusiastic that he would promote something up to the heights and back into the ground again, ending up flat broke. He was in one of these low periods when I met him.

"Yes," he said, "I shall promote you into Town Hall. Have you got any money?" I said I hadn't. "Nor have I," he said, "but never mind. We'll manage."

The next day I was sent over to book a date at Town Hall. The lady in the office seemed a bit doubtful about it all, but admitted that since Madame Foster Jenkins had performed there she supposed it would be all right, and after muttering something about "the lowering of standards," she gave me the contract to sign. I paid the down payment, which practically cleaned me out. Where the rest was to come from I hadn't a clue.

Jack got the printing done with promises to pay later. Kay Carleton agreed to let my rent wait till after the concert. It all made me feel very apprehensive and certain that I was headed for disaster. Not so Jack, although he was just as broke as I was; he went into his promotion act, and to hear him you'd think the whole of New York was waiting with bated breath for my debut. We nearly came to grief a week before the concert when neither of us could raise $250, but I managed to borrow it from Aunt Al Schuyler's nephew in Connecticut, and disaster was averted.

One thing about Jack, he always made such an uproar about whatever he was currently engaged in, it did sell tickets, so when the great night came, to my utter relief we had over twelve hundred paid admissions. We got a very good review in the *Times* and a superlative one in the *Herald Tribune*. At last I had something to show for my efforts.

Kay Carleton and the Rehearsal Club board members were very pleased with me. Sara Enright said, "Of course, notices from music critics won't mean a thing on Broadway." Dear Sara, I'm making her sound very hard-boiled. She wasn't, though. She was one of those people who would say the most terrible things to cover up the fact that she was really an old softie. She was dead right in this case, though. No one was any more interested than they had been before, and I was right back where I had started.

By this time Jack Petrill was on to his next mammoth promotion, and Dolores Pallet had done everything she could think of, to no avail. I suppose had I had any sense I would have packed up and gone back to Canada, but after all this effort I had got the bit between my teeth and was determined to press on.

One day a pianist friend of mine took me to the Brooklyn Academy to hear a talk by the opera singer Mary Garden, now a very old woman. She tripped on dressed in bright scarlet from top to toe and gave a most amusing and racy talk. My friend took me to meet her afterward. She was enchanting. He was telling her of all my vicissitudes when she said, "What you must do is go into the lecture business." I'd heard of the lecture business, of course, but it all sounded so dull and academic. "Nonsense," she said. "Everybody who doesn't fit in anywhere goes into the lecture business. Why, they have everything from comic waiters who spill soup over you, to deposed European royalty. They have conjurers, weight lifters, people playing antique instruments, chefs, interior decorators, politicians, beauticians, morticians, ballet dancers, professors, practically anything you could mention, including ex prima donnas with no voice left. I'm with a lecture bureau and am making a lot of money for just talking, which I'd probably be doing anyway."

She told me to get *Program* magazine, which is to the lecture world what *Musical America* is to the concert world. This was an eye-opener. I thanked her very much indeed and got *Program* on the way home. It was full of people doing the most extraordinary things.

A few days later I called on Mr. Bim Pond, the proprietor of *Program*, who was delighted to see me, which was rather a shock in itself. I showed him my Town Hall program and the two little reviews. "I know," he said, "these reviews might not do you much good on Broadway, but they're just the ticket for this business, just the ticket. There's no doubt you're on your way." Then he gave me a cup of tea and a long list of lecture managers to see, introduced me to the staff, and ushered me out, saying he expected to hear some good news from me shortly.

The next day I started on the list. Lecture managers were a great deal easier to see than agents and seemed much more interested. Mr. Colston

Leigh said it sounded very good, but at the moment he was concentrating on authors. Miss Selma Warlich of NCAC said she'd sign me like a shot, except this season she was concentrating on a comic dancer. Everyone was very interested, except that for a variety of reasons, they couldn't do anything. It didn't take me long to see it was the same old runaround, just done more politely.

Then one evening I had dinner with my cousin Denise and her husband, Freddy Bryan, a lawyer. By chance, Freddy was then representing Clark H. Getts, the manager who advertised on the back page of *Program*, in his divorce case against Osa Johnson, the aviatrix. Freddy said he was pretty sure he could arrange it so that Getts would sign me. I don't know how he did it, but it worked. I was summoned to meet Mr. Getts.

Such an elegant office! It was on Park Avenue, and it was the last word in decor, with vast photomurals on the walls, a carpet that came up to my ankles, and the biggest light mahogany desk I have ever seen. Everything about the place was outsize. I was expecting some giant to emerge, but in came a tiny, immaculate, white-haired man.

Clark Getts said he would be happy to sign a contract. He would get 40 percent off the top, and I would pay all costs for transportation, hotels, and publicity material. The fees would range between $250 and $350. I could not travel a pianist, but the agency would arrange for one at the place of the engagement. I wasn't altogether happy to sign the contract, but I did anyway. In a few months the tour was arranged. I received my itinerary, a list of people to contact, and bundles of tickets, and off I went. I had taken the precaution of thoroughly practicing my accompaniments because of the pianist situation, and it was just as well.

I don't know how Clark arrived at his bookings. Although the itinerary was quite well arranged, I never knew what sort of engagement I would run into next. One day it would be a women's club, the next some crummy night spot where, in addition to doing my own material, I would be expected to sing with the band and mix with the customers. There were Rotary lunches; club dates, where everyone was roaring drunk, agricultural fairs, where I had to perform across the race track to the audience beyond. I didn't play a burlesque house, but I bet I would have if Clark had the contact.

It was lucky I knew my accompaniments, as some of the pianists were frightful. The women's clubs usually provided some ancient person. On three separate occasions I was proudly informed that Mrs. Whoever-it-was had been a pupil of Leschetizky. I don't know about Leschetizky, but these three women were the worst of the lot. They couldn't read a note. Then there were the pop pianists who could play only from a figured bass. Some could play in only one key, and some I really don't think could play at all, so five times out of six I wound up playing for myself. Once in a while, like an oasis in the desert, a really splendid accompanist would turn up and make me feel that maybe it was all worthwhile, but the next date would be back with the Leschetizky bunch.

The tour did have its highlights, however. In Minneapolis I found myself in the Flame Room at the Radisson Hotel for two weeks. I had no band parts, and the pianist–band leader couldn't read a note, but a friend of Dorothy Lee was at the university there, and he kindly consented to play for me. At first the band gave us an introduction and windup to each number, but after a few days the band started to join in with us, and shortly we had a great act going and packed the place. I wish we could have gotten the ultimate arrangements down on paper, but nobody could write them.

Another high spot was the Harvard Club in Boston. Everybody was in *grande toilette*. There was a cocktail party and dinner first, where I met a lot of perfectly charming people, then I gave my performance. It was a splendid evening. From there I went into the Oval Room at the Copley Plaza to share the bill with the dancer Eric Victor. I was fêted and entertained by my newfound friends from the Harvard Club, who came to see us in the Oval Room and sent flowers and champagne. It was all terribly grand. Ever since, Boston has been one of my very favorite cities.

Of the low points on the tour, the lowest was the lumbermen's stag night at the Sherman Hotel in Chicago. They were all drunker than hoot owls. The show started with a group of baton-twirling girls, after which came a stand-up comic with the most filthy jokes, then a stripper, and then me. By this time I was panic-stricken. The audience had been roaring "Take it off!" to the stripper, and when I went on I was told to take it off, too.

Being neither the size, shape, nor age for this sort of thing, I almost turned and fled, but it's funny how often one gets a brainstorm. I was working in the center of the room, surrounded by tables, so when "Take it off!" had reached earsplitting proportions I held up a hand for silence and said, "I shall not take it off. I shall put it on!" and snatched one of the cloths off a table and wrapped it around myself. All the glasses and bottles fell on the floor, the dishes smashed, and cutlery went everywhere, making a terrible noise.

The evening was at the point of inebriation where noise was the big thing, so a large man stood up and said, "Okay, honey, put it on!" The cry was taken up while I went on snatching tablecloths and wrapping myself up, until I couldn't manage any more. As a finale I picked up the mat we were working on and put it over my head. The band struck up some exit music, and I waddled off, dragging my carpet train behind me, overturning tables as I went, and left the place a shambles.

It was a great success that evening, but it was just as well that I left the following morning, as it presumably wasn't such a success later when the Sherman Hotel presented my sponsors with the breakage bill. That was one date I didn't get paid for.

The tour lasted about four months. It was, I suppose, a valuable exercise in keeping my wits about me, but it didn't do a thing to advance my future, and over the entire time I made about $500. I got back to the Rehearsal Club exhausted, but nothing had changed. The tour was good for a laugh and that was about all; it kept Sara Enright and Kay Carleton in stitches for days. Sara said, "I told you you'd never make it, but it could be a funny book or record."

"No," I said, "I shall now, belatedly, take your good advice, shut up, go home to Canada, and get married." And I did just that.

CHAPTER 14

Bitten by the bug again, I return to New York

When I got back to Toronto, I first went to stay with Mother and the uncles at the farm. Mother had found England rather bleak and lonely without Father, so after six months she had come back to Canada. While in England she had seen my first husband, who had married again and had a small daughter. The child had been told to call her Granny Canada. This gave rise to a lot of pointed remarks at my expense, and since she was also furious that I was going to marry Charlie, I soon left the farm and went to stay with him and Ma while we waited for the great day.

We were married in Rabbi Feinberg's study at Holy Blossom Temple. Charlie had his sister Anna and her English husband as his Jewish witnesses, and I had Aunt Al Schuyler, who by this time was very, very old and deaf, and my newspaper friend Gwen Barrington for my Gentile ones. We had the full ceremony with the breaking of the wine glass. When this part came, Aunt Al, who hadn't heard a word, said, "No one offered *me* a cocktail." The Jewish witnesses were supposed to sign the register first, so the rabbi handed the pen to Aunt Al, as my lot looked a great deal more Jewish than Charlie's. Otherwise it went off very smoothly.

Dear Ma, like the perfect mother-in-law, had moved out to stay with Charlie's brother, and there I was back in the domestic scene. I'm afraid I was a pretty poor substitute for Ma in the house, and she wasn't very happy sitting around while her other daughter-in-law kept house, so we finally sold the house and bought another one in Cooksville, and Ma came with us.

The new house had an enormous white-tiled kitchen, in which I hardly ever cooked a meal. Ma always beat me to it. I loved that house; it had a very settled family mansion atmosphere—one felt one easily could have been born there—and it was a wonderful place for entertaining.

My career picked up quite nicely again once I had settled in. Although the work I had done in the United States didn't mean much in the States, it had quite an effect in Toronto. Dorothy Parnum started the tours again, I resumed the Christmas concerts, and I was very much in demand for club dates. This time I was paid a great deal more, as befitted someone who had worked in New York, and I started to write a lot of new material.

About this time I decided to do a talk on how to play the bagpipes. Of course, I had to learn them first, so I made an appointment with an ex pipe major of the Toronto Scottish regiment. When I got there, he took one look and said, "Ye'll no learn the pipes a' your age." I asked him why that mattered, as long as I payed my tuition. He said, "It's no' respectable for a middle-aged woman," which was a bit unsettling, as I was a sprightly thirty-three. "Besides," he said, "when ye've lairnt the chanter ye'll have tae practice the pipes down at the armories, and the Toronto Scottish Pipe Band will be up in the gallery laffin' at ye." I told him this was exactly the idea, but he was still doubtful about the whole thing. He was very dour and obviously took his bagpipes seriously. Finally he grudgingly consented and ordered me a chanter and a set of Toronto Scottish army issue pipes.

Learning the chanter is rather like learning the penny whistle with lots of twiddly bits in, or cuttings, as they are called. When I had duly learned "The Road to the Isles" on it, we went down to the armories to start on the pipes proper. To begin with, I nearly blew myself inside out and couldn't make a sound on them but gradually I got the knack, and after a period of banshee wailings and screechings (during which the pipe band was in fact laughing at me from the gallery), I managed to keep the drones going. Then we'd march—two steps you blow, two steps you squeeze—but you have to start squeezing before you stop blowing to keep the air pressure constant. It's rather like patting your head while rubbing your stomach.

Having got this far I had to write the talk, so I looked up *bagpipes* in the *Encyclopedia Britannica*, and there it all was. It only had to be reworded a little. In the nearly forty years I have done this routine, I have always announced my source, but no one seems to believe me, and I have yet to meet anyone who has checked on it. Every time I start a new routine I look the subject up in the encyclopedia first, and nine times out of ten it is there. I've given the *Encyclopedia Britannica* so much free advertising they ought really to have presented me with a complimentary set.

I gave the pipe major tickets to Eaton's Auditorium for the first performance of the number. Although it went over very well, he was still rather disapproving. He said, "It's no' vurra respaictful to the pipes." I suppose he was right.

At about this time I became involved with the people who were promoting the "Great Canadian Theater." Their efforts would start with great enthusiasm, struggle along for a few months, and then collapse, usually from a lack of funds, but also from an unwillingness to pay local talent, although fortunes were paid to artists from the States. One of these projects was the Civic Theatre, started by a local columnist, Roly Young. Another group was started by Lorne Green, who was then the chief Canadian newscaster, long before he became Pa Cartwright on "Bonanza." None of these groups got anywhere, except for one, which in spite of all the ups and downs managed to keep going. That was the New Play Society, run by Dora Mavor Moore, who would go to any lengths to keep the NPA afloat.

She had, I think, originally been with the Ben Greet Shakespeare Players. She stayed in Canada, battling on against fearful odds and in the teeth of all kinds of opposition. Most people in the theater in Canada have been through her school, I should think. She was a gallant and dedicated woman, and I loved her. She invited me to stay with her while I was learning the bagpipes, so she could make certain I did the requisite amount of practicing, and you must admit true friendship could go no further.

Dora belonged to the Toronto Zonta Club, whose members are businesswomen of top executive standing. Each year the club had a special project, so one year she persuaded them to bring Tyrone Guthrie over from England as an adviser on starting a Shakespeare company in Stratford, Ontario. There had been many previous attempts to start a Stratford Festival, with no success.

To raise the money for this project, Dora asked me to perform for free at the Museum Theatre because, as she said, "You don't need any stagehands or union help, so you are cheap to produce." Fair enough. On I went, and the money was raised. My reward was membership in the Zonta Club, where I felt rather inferior and out of place among top executive women. "Nonsense," Dora said. "You are quite eligible. You own your own business because you are the only one in it." Nonetheless, they had to send to the head office in Chicago to find out my category, which turned out to be "arts, liberal."

Guthrie was to stay with Dora while he was here, and she invited me as well. Although I knew him by reputation and we had a good many mutual friends in England, I had never actually met him. To say he had impact is an understatement.

He must have been at least six feet, seven inches, with dark hair and a neat military mustache. In fact, with his appearance and upright stance, he looked very much like an army officer, except for his clothes.

The first night Dora had a dinner party, and although everyone else was dressed to kill, he had on a white shirt, open at the neck with the sleeves rolled up to the elbow, rumpled gray flannel trousers, no socks, and sand shoes, but he still managed to look more impressive than anyone else in the room. A most amusing and fluent talker, he kept everyone in stitches, yet he didn't dominate the conversation, as some great people understandably do, but would listen as well as he talked. Having created a great feeling of joie de vivre and bonhomie at dinner, after dessert he said, "I shall now go in and wash the dishes, as I am the only one dressed for it." Then he said to me, "Come on, you're the youngest. You can help me." So we went into the kitchen and washed up mountains of plates and pots and pans, while he continued to be simply fascinating as well as extraordinarily efficient at the sink. Had I not known who he was, I doubt that I would have guessed; he could have been a writer or a general or a scientist. He was so down-to-earth and spontaneous, in spite of being such a brilliant talker, that he was somehow completely untheatrical. Usually it sticks out a mile, particularly to anyone in the business, but certainly not in his case.

This was forcibly brought home to me the next day when the great and grand of Stratford were giving a very posh cocktail party for him at the Royal York Hotel in Toronto. In the morning one of the columnists from the Toronto *Globe and Mail* called me and said, "You're coming with Guthrie, aren't you?" I told him yes. "Well, I want to write a column about him, so will you introduce me?" I said I would.

It was a grilling hot day, and Dora and I were sweating into our cocktail gear, but Tony as Tyrone was called, said he was going as he was, namely in the same outfit as the night before. When we got there, I introduced him to the columnist, and off they went to the window, where they stood talking away for about half an hour, meanwhile watching a regatta on Lake Ontario. We left soon after, as cocktail parties at the Royal York in the height of the summer are sheer, unadulterated hell.

Well, a week went by and no column came out. Then two weeks. So I called the columnist to ask why not. "Because," he said peevishly, "you never introduced him to me."

I said, "You've got to be kidding. He was the very first one I introduced you to."

"What? You mean that long beanpole with the mustache?"

"Yes."

"You mean the one with the open-neck shirt and the rumpled bags?"

"Yes."

"With no socks on and the sand shoes?"

"Yes."

"Good God!" he said.

"Well," I said, "you were over there talking to him by the window for half an hour. What on earth were you talking about, then?"

"The regatta," he said. "That fellow knows more about sailing than anyone I've ever heard. He was fascinating."

"Well, who on earth did you think he was?"

"I didn't actually catch the name when you introduced him, but I had the idea he was the Royal York house detective."

In due course Guthrie went up to Stratford to have a look. Although he had been brought to Canada only to advise, he fell in love with the project and said he would undertake to get it going. Everybody was thrilled. He also said he would do it for such money as could be afforded, which was precious little, on condition that he get no interference from politicians or the CBC. He would have the complete say as to how the theater would be built and who would build it, he would audition anyone in Canada who wanted to audition, and thereafter he would supervise the casting, and if at any time the aforementioned bodies were to interfere with him, no matter at what stage, he would immediately pack his bags and go home. And this was the beginning of what is now one of the great theater festivals.

At first there was just the stage and a sort of tent arrangement, but in due course the theater was finished, and it is quite wonderful—semicircular, with a stage built on various levels, and the acoustics are splendid. I did a Community Concert there years later and found that, although it seats fifteen hundred people, I got the feeling that no one was more than twenty feet away from me.

At this particular period, my life was very pleasant. I wasn't exactly setting the world on fire, but I had plenty to do. I was extremely fond of my in-laws and enjoyed the novel sensation of being part of a normal family group with lots of people my own age, instead of being the family problem child and juvenile delinquent. Charlie was taken up with teaching and art shows and what have you, and I was busy performing.

I must admit that culturally, Charlie and I didn't exactly communicate. Visually I am completely hopeless. At boarding school I was the only one ever to be excused from art classes, as Miss Lilly, the teacher, said on my report, "Claudia seems a very intelligent girl in many respects, but I have never encountered in a pupil before so little aptitude for art. Perhaps she needs glasses." Father had my eyes tested, but they were perfect, so art made way for tennis coaching, at which I was equally hopeless. Charlie, who was a very good teacher, used to make me do blind drawing, where I'd look at an object and, without taking my eyes off it, let my hand draw it on the paper. It is supposed to work wonders in almost all cases, but not here. I couldn't get even the faintest resemblance. It probably means no coordination between the eye and the hands, which might also explain being rotten at tennis. Finally, patient as Charlie was, even he gave it up.

On the other hand, he was tone deaf and couldn't carry a tune. He would listen valiantly to all sorts of music, but when he thought no one was listening would sneak back to the "Beer Barrel Polka" and such like. Finally we made a pact that when I went with him to some art show, as I had to at times, I would shut up, state no preference, and make no smart-aleck remarks, and he would do the same for me when in the music department.

I expect that life would have continued much the same to this day, had not the Met come to Toronto to play at Maple Leaf Gardens, which could be described as Toronto's Madison Square Garden—used for anything from wrestling to symphonies. At the time the New Play Society was doing *Spring Thaw*, a topical review that had been going on in Toronto for years. It was produced by Mavor Moore, Dora's son, who was then the drama critic of the *Globe and Mail* and a very clever and creative fellow.

Since the Met was going to be in town while we were playing, I concocted an operatic spoof called "Potted Met." It started with a prologue, pinched from and after the style of *Pagliacci*, to the effect that if you were rich folk in tails and white mink you could go to the Maple Leaf Gardens every night for a month and hear all the operas, but if you were poor folk like us we would give you the whole rundown in half an hour, at the same time proving that the tenor is actually the villian in grand opera, as the women who tangle with him never survive. Then we rang up the curtain, and the tenor, Rodolfo, came on and sang "Your tiny hands are frozen" to the three consumptive ladies—Mimi, Violetta, and Manon (actually Manon had VD, but it all amounts to the same thing). Then the three ladies die on their dying music. Then he sings "Your tiny hands are frozen" to Nedda, Carmen, and Gilda, and because they won't buy it, he murders them on their murder music. Then he sings "Questa o Quella" ("There's plenty more where they came from"), whereupon Brünnhilde turns up, and he sings "Your tiny hand is frozen to her." She sings "No, it isn't, but you look chilly," and she conjures up the Fire Music and burns *him* up. By now it's Walpurgis Night, and Mephisto is singing "The Cloth of Gold," interspersed with the three consumptive ladies and the three murdered ladies. Salome enters singing "My Lord, my Lord, give me the head of Rodolfo." The head is pushed onstage on a dinner wagon and sings "Your tiny hand is frozen." So Salome covers it up with a big silver lid, and the show winds up with a rousing operatic medley. It happened that there were some very good voices in *Spring Thaw* that year, so it came off rather well.

When I was in New York I had got to know quite a lot of people who were now playing in the Metropolitan Opera Company, and they all duly came to see *Spring Thaw*. They thought "Potted Met" was absolutely hilarious. The word must have gone round, because gradually the stars started to come on their off nights, and finally Edward Johnson, the manager of the Met, turned up. He thought it was tremendous, and asked me if I was going back to New York for another try. I told him I thought not. He gave me his card and said that if I should ever go back, he knew just the right people for me to meet and would be glad to give me introductions.

A few nights later Alec Guinness, who was that year the star at the Stratford Festival, and who is my absolutely favorite movie star, came backstage to see me. Well, that did it: I was bitten with the bug again.

I suppose show business is like alcoholism or drugs. You think you've got it out of your system completely, then you get a little taste and you are right back where you started. After being perfectly happy and contented pottering around Toronto for a few years, I got terribly restless and couldn't wait to get back to New York. So, of course, I hashed it all over with Ma.

We sat in the garden by the hour and went over the pros and cons. We came to the conclusion that it would be rather an intrepid move, as I was no spring chicken, being at the time thirty-six, but on the other hand I had some good connections. It might not be a sound idea to go when I had been married such a short time, but on the other hand, Charlie was frightfully busy and had been a bachelor for so long, being quite a few years older than I, that it wouldn't affect him as it would a young husband. We didn't have any children, and Charlie didn't depend on me to keep house for him, since Ma did the housekeeping.

So, having come to the conclusion that I was not indispensable (in fact, I think up till then I could have taken the prize for being highly dispensable to everybody), we decided I should go, and I told Charlie, then went to the farm to tell Mother and the uncles. Uncle Bryer produced a bottle of whisky for a farewell celebration, which Mother made us drink in the kitchen. Uncle Harry produced some stories he'd written in the *Saturday Evening Post* and copies of a column he used to have in the *Globe and Mail*, in case they might be useful (he had been a very good comedy writer in his day). They promised to look in on Ma and Charlie, and wished me all sorts of luck. Mother's only comment was, "Now I'll never be a grandmother," which, since we were all feeling very nicely, thank you, I'm afraid made us laugh. Poor old Mum! Everything I did made her furious.

I had written to Kay Carleton, who wrote back that I was very welcome to come back and that, oddly enough, my old room was vacant again, so off I went. The Rehearsal Club hadn't changed at all: a lot of the same people were there, still battling away to get the big break. The first night back I went in, naturally, to play Chinese checkers with Kay and Sara Enright. "Oh, my God, I can't bear it!" said Sara, as I appeared in the doorway. "It's the poor man's Brünnhilde. You're looking very well." Then realizing the last remark was not at all in character, she added, "But you won't for long if you stick around this place. There's absolutely no work, you know," and we sat contentedly down to our game of Chinese checkers just as though I'd never been away.

CHAPTER 15

The great Eastman Boomer takes charge

The second time around in New York started much more auspiciously than the first. An acquaintance from J. Walter Thompson in Toronto, who had been transferred to the Madison Avenue office, gave me some very valuable introductions for television. Thereafter I was on a lot of Goodson-Todman game shows, had spots on "The Gary Moore Show," served on the panel of various gab fests, and played Lady Bracknell in *The Importance of Being Earnest* on Kraft Television Theater. This was all very well, and I was better off financially, but I was doing too many diverse things to be building any sort of specialty.

The D'Oyly Carte company came to New York about this time. This was very nostalgic for me, as many of the cast had been students with me at the Royal College of Music, my first husband had played the horn in the orchestra under Isidore Godfrey, and Helen Roberts, the leading lady, and I had both studied singing under Spenser Clay in London in our youth.

One evening I went along with the company to the home of Dr. and Mrs. Hellman, where I was asked to perform after the Gilbert and Sullivan. This led to regular visits and I became very good friends with my hosts. Dr. Hellman even arranged for me to give a concert for the American Medical Association, of which he was president. Its success convinced me I should concentrate on this field of endeavor, rather than allow myself to be sidetracked by the odds and ends I was doing on television. So I decided to try the Columbia Lecture Bureau, feeling it might not be as eccentric as the Clark Getts bureau and since I had already met the manager, Arthur Judson.

So I pulled some strings and got an interview at Columbia with a Miss G., who was extremely agreeable but gave me the feeling that she was not very impressed with me. Then the door opened and in came Mr. Judson. I never saw such a metamorphosis. From being brisk and efficient, Miss G. became coy and giggly. Mr. Judson was charming and said no doubt Miss G. was going to set up an audition for me. She immediately arranged one for a few days later in Steinway Hall.

At the audition I was nobly supported by the Hellmans and their friends, and most of the Rehearsal Club were there rooting for me, so the hall was nearly full, which made it much easier, as I am not at my best at auditions. When I took my final bow and walked off, there in the wings was a tall, handsome, cheerful-looking man who announced that he was Eastman Boomer and that he was to be my manager. He said he had a terrible hangover because he had just signed Tallulah Bankhead for a lecture tour, but that didn't seem to impair one with his perfect charm and mad sense of humor. This was the beginning of a long and close partnership.

After Boomer started his promotion, I didn't have long to wait for developments; in fact, it was all I could do to keep up with him. In a month I was to have another Town Hall Concert, and in the time intervening there were endless rehearsals with the pianist Harry Dworkin. Boomer had me on every available radio and TV interview show, and life suddenly became a whirl of activity.

It is usual for everyone concerned to get nervous and uptight before an important concert, and certainly that was how I'd felt before the first Town Hall. But with Boomer somehow this didn't happen. He simply took everything in a spirit of fun and games. Although what he did was efficient, to the point of being brilliant, one felt one was assisting at some huge party. This used to annoy some of the more solemn managers, but they couldn't quarrel with his effectiveness.

The concert went off in great style, and I got a wonderful press. Even Sara Enright admitted that it was conceivably possible that I maybe could make it this time by a fluke. There was no anticlimax, either. The next day, bids from record companies started pouring in. We began working in a studio on a demo with RCA Victor, but since I simply cannot work without an audience, we decided to record instead at a repeat concert on January 13, 1951.

Meanwhile, when Mr. Judson heard about the negotiations with RCA, he said he preferred me to sign with Columbia. Although they were one of the few companies that hadn't made an offer, this was apparently immaterial. A contract came over by special messenger within the hour, and I was told the concert would be recorded live for the Columbia Masterworks label. I believe I was one of the first recording artists to do this.

That was a very exciting Christmas. Boomer and I were invited to all manner of parties, and I was even taken to dinner by Dmitri Metropolis, the conductor of the New York Philharmonic. Wherever we went, everybody seemed to know who I was, which is a most heady feeling when it happens for the first time in a place as big as New York.

The concert on January 13 was, if possible, even more exciting than the one in November. It was completely sold out, and more than five hundred people had to be turned away at the box office. In the audience were Jeanette McDonald, Ethel Smith, Nita Naldi, Hermione Gingold, Ethel Barrymore, Giovanni Martinelli, and all sorts of other people who had been only names to me up till this time. Columbia recorded the concert live, and RCA Victor was there too, as in the excitement Boomer forgot to tell them that I was already signed with Columbia.

As a result of all this, the William Morris office and all the Broadway agents whom I could never get to see before started calling with offers of this and that, but they came too late, as I was very happy with things the way they were.

At this point there was something of an exodus from the Rehearsal Club. Arthur Jacob, a rather sweet but somewhat eccentric photographer who was more or less the Rehearsal Club boyfriend and spent most of his waking hours there, suggested taking an enormous apartment in the Osborne on Fifty-seventh Street, so seven of us clubbed together and moved in. It was a beautiful place, with enormous high-ceilinged rooms, inlaid floors, marble bathrooms, and mirrors everywhere. It was a little shabby with an air of departed grandeur.

There were Arthur and myself, a baritone and his coloratura soprano wife, two actresses, and a nightclub singer. Arthur had a loudspeaker in his ceiling blaring out Wagner all night while he developed pictures, the baritone would start his setting-up exercises at 8:00 A.M. to the strains of "Jezebel," sung by Frankie Laine, after which there would be coloratura exercises, dramatic declamations, or nightclub act practice, depending on who got the floor first. It was absolute bedlam, but it never seemed to bother anyone, perhaps because on the corner of Fifty-seventh Street and Seventh Avenue there was so much noise going on outside, that a little more inside made no difference.

On the rare nights Arthur's Wagner kept me awake, I would go in and let him take ridiculous pictures of me. It's astonishing how ridiculous one can get at 4:00 A.M. The others used to think we were both crazy, but the photos came in very useful in the years following. He took the one where I am dressed as Brünnhilde reading the *New York Times* and the one on the record cover of *Guide to Concert Audiences*.

I had a very erratic time that spring. Since I'd joined the management in the middle of the season, it was too late to book a tour for me. Instead, I took over dates that had been canceled by other artists. A few times I re-placed Elsa Maxwell, who was suffering from chronic dysentery, probably because of all those parties. I also stood in for Adolph Menjou and Charles Laughton, and covered a prodigious amount of territory.

The first concert was for a conference at the Chateau Frontenac in Quebec. It was -4 degrees Fahrenheit outside. I caught the flu and the next day had a temperature of 102. The doctor said I had to stay in bed, but that was out of the question, since the next night I had a performance in San Angelo, Texas, which is right across the continent.

This is where I demonstrated mind over matter, or perhaps it was sheer hysteria. It was impossible to cancel on my very first tour or I would be thought undependable; therefore, it was impossible to have a cold. I got all rigged up in snow boots, wooly pants, and fur coat, and sallied forth, sniffing and coughing, to the airport. In New York it wasn't so cold, so I shed my wooly pants and my sniff. In Atlanta I shed my fur coat and my cough. In Dallas I shed everything I could. And I arrived in San Angelo, where it was 85 degrees, stripped down as far as decency would allow, with my cold quite gone. Then I noticed that the committee waiting for me at the airport looked at me rather strangely. I had forgotten to take off my knee-length fur snow boots.

I did that concert and three or four others quite successfully and arrived in Chicago for a week's break, which I spent in bed finishing the flu. It had rejoined me as soon as the curtain came down on the last concert.

Touring for Boomer was as different as could be from touring for Clark Getts. For one thing, I was getting more money, and for another, my pian-ist, John Coveart from Toronto, came with me, which helped relieve the monotony of traveling. What was rather dreary last time became a lot of fun this time.

One day Boomer asked me if I would like to become a Steinway Artist. I thought at first it was one of his jokes, for although I do play the piano, I am certainly no virtuoso. But no, this was for real. A few days later we went to Chambord, a very expensive restaurant of the old school, and met John and Uncle Billy Steinway and some of their directors. For nearly four hours we went through course after course with appropriate wines for each. It was absolutely delicious, but far too much. Uncle Billy gave me some very charming little presents as the meal progressed, and we tottered out, stuffed to the gills, at about three. That was it! I was now a Steinway Artist, which meant I was entitled to buy a Steinway piano at a great reduction and to use the Steinway wherever I was performing, if there was one available in the town. When I went to a concert the following week at Carnegie Hall I was fascinated to see an ad in the program saying "Anna Russell uses a Steinway piano."

The tapes for the record were now ready, so we went up to Columbia Records to hear them. It was a very traumatic experience. One can never hear one's own voice as it really is, so one is apt to imagine in the enthusiasm of the moment that one is pouring out glorious, pear-shaped tones. Alas, this wasn't the case. I knew my voice was loud, but had hoped it would come out rich, or at least lyrical, but I think the best description of it would be "penetrating." I listened miserably to forty minutes of this, punctuated by shrieks of mirth from the audience. I didn't think it was funny at all. It made me very nervous. Unaccountably, the Columbia Records people were delighted with it.

To this day, I don't really enjoy listening to my own records. In my heart of hearts I would love to have had a great voice, and to listen to mine is rather wounding to the ego. This may account for my initial bitchiness toward singing, even though I later learned to appreciate the undoubted advantage of being a comedienne in this field, where there isn't much competition.

After listening to the tapes and then trying unsuccessfully to come up with a title for the record, Boomer and I were about to leave the studio when Dave Oppenheim, head of Columbia Masterworks, said he wanted us to hear a very funny "under the counter" record. No one knew who had made it, but it was all over the country. I recognized it before we had heard two sentences. Syd Brown had made it for a CBC stag night, at the time we had our program in Toronto. It was entitled *The Crepitation Contest,* and to put it delicately, it was a wind-breaking competition set up in the form of a boxing match between the British contender, Lord Windershmere, and the Australian contender (whose name I had suggested, incidentally), Paul Boomer. It was exceedingly vulgar but very funny. Someone (certainly not Syd) pirated it and made a fortune. I even saw it later in Texas, done up in a very fancy album.

I was shortly to go back to Toronto to give a concert at Massey Hall, which I did occasionally. This time was going to be different, since Boomer was coming with me. It certainly was different.

The local musicians' union suddenly decreed that although I used only a piano, I was to pay an eight-piece orchestra to play "God Save the Queen." Had I been on my own, I would have bowed to the inevitable, but not Boomer. He went storming down to the office and told them they could play the Queen, after which he would cancel the concert and send everyone home. Then he called a press conference on the mezzanine of the King Edward Hotel. The Queen was therefore played as usual on the piano. All the resultant publicity, plus the fact that I was accorded the concert Steinway from the T. Eaton Company instead of the beat-up Heintzmann I usually used, had a very beneficial effect on the box office.

A few days later, I was asked to perform at some club date that the Robert Simpson Company, one of the two big department stores, was putting on, for which they offered me $50, a huge amount for Toronto at the time. The rest of the entertainment was to be a package deal bought from a big New York agency. Boomer promptly turned our offer down, got in touch with the New York agency, and had me included in the package, where my fee was $250. Thus I learned quite early that, given a reasonably competent performer, managerial tactics and merchandising have a lot more to do with success than many artists would care to admit.

I felt very secure within myself at this period, probably for the first time since Father had died. Boomer had very definite plans for me, and I did whatever he told me. Just as I had had complete faith in Father's judgment up till the time he died, I had the same sort of confidence in Boomer, and I realized it was something I had been missing for a great many years. Possibly if either of my husbands had given me some sense of direction instead of waffling about, one or another of my marriages might have worked out.

I had been staying at home while in Toronto, but I could feel even then that things were not the same. Ma could sense this, too. Charlie and I were starting to go in different directions.

When Boomer and I got back to New York we discovered that I had started a ruction. My French art song, "Je n'ai pas la plume de ma tante," had caused great offense to a very well-known singer of this type of song, because she thought I was making fun of her. Actually, when I wrote this number I had in mind Maggie Teyte, who had thought it very amusing. As to the other woman, although I knew who she was, I had neither heard her nor set eyes on her. Nonetheless, she started a petition to keep me out of Town Hall and Carnegie Hall on the grounds that I was ruining great music, and she had persuaded a lot of artists who probably hadn't the least idea who I was, to sign it. I was a bit alarmed at this, although I really couldn't fathom how I could be ruining great music, when all the music I used I had written myself. Boomer thought it was hilarious and pointed out that any controversy was good for business, and I suppose it was. At any rate, it all wound up as a big joke and the petition was dropped.

This same sort of suspicion kept me from performing for community and civic music associations for a long time. Although there was a lot of interest from these groups, inevitably someone would claim that I was lampooning what they were trying to sell seriously, so over quite a few years we had only four or five of this kind of date, until Ward French, president of Community Concerts, bought over two hundred tickets to one of my Town Hall concerts for the Community representatives who were in town for a convention. After that I was frequently put on a "bonus" concert in towns that had taken the maximum number of artists, or as a "come on" in towns where they were trying to build up the audience.

During the summer we did a great variety of things. I played the lead in *Travellers' Joy,* a rollicking farce for Billy Miles at the Berkshire Playhouse. I went to the Tanglewood Festival, where I met Eleanor Roosevelt. Boris Goldovsky was conducting, and after the performance we gave out the prizes together. I remember Sam Levinson won a very minute pair of bright red ladies' pants. Then there was the Aspen, Colorado music festival, where I first met Dr. Rosenstock, director of the City Center Opera Company, and renewed my acquaintance with William Primrose, the violist, whom I hadn't seen since Royal College of Music days. After Aspen I went to the Brevard Festival in North Carolina.

When I got back to my apartment in New York after the Brevard Festival, I discovered that work had been very scarce that summer, so, to meet the rent, everyone had taken on a roommate. Someone slept on the hall sofa, two people were in the pantry, and there was even somebody in the loft above the pantry, which had no window and could be reached only by a ladder that pulled down from the ceiling. The apartment, though it was huge, was bulging at the seams with perfect strangers. Voices singing, violins, pianos, and radios were all going at the same time. The din was appalling. The other tenants had complained about us, and the elevator men had christened us the Snake Pit. Feeling our days were numbered, I moved over to the Woodward Hotel to room with a friend, Chiquita Leberman.

Chiquita rented out her living room for people to practice in, so it was noisy, but not as bad as the Osborne, since they weren't all going at once. There was a little Chinese man who would sing "One Fine Day" in a piercing soprano; two Mexican singers, Nestor Chaves and a fellow called Cassanova; and a Spanish dance troupe.

After I moved in, Chiquita took me down to the Woodward bar. The owner, Martin, was a Maltese whose English was well-nigh impossible to understand, although he'd been in the States for ten years or more. He was about five feet tall and looked like a pint-size George Raft. I think he was some sort of small-time gangster, because he had heaps of money and seemed to know everybody. He took a tremendous fancy to me and began taking me to dinner. We looked quite ridiculous together, as I was about a foot taller than he. Nonetheless, he used to call me Baby! We had absolutely nothing in common, but he remained my faithful admirer for years.

I had a tremendous tour booked for the fall, so I went back to Canada for a breather. When I'd see Mother on weekends, she would act very strange about my work. On the one hand she liked the idea of having a daughter who was a celebrity, but on the other hand she hated me holding the floor. She'd introduce me to her friends, mostly the local church ladies, with great aplomb, then when they came twittering about and I was halfway through my best anecdote, she would tell me to keep quiet because I was talking rubbish, and she would send me out to join the uncles in the hut.

I was to do another Town Hall Concert at Christmas, so I went over the *Nibelungen Ring*, which I had not yet done in New York. I read every book I could find on Wagner, went through the analysis of the music and the translation of the libretto, and pared it all down to a twenty-minute routine. This was exceedingly hard to do and was just the bare bones of the story. I often think I could do another talk about all the things I had to leave out, like the Tarnhelm, the Treasure, the Spear, Nothung the sword. I don't mention Donner, Loge, or Froh, or that Wotan lost the same eye on three occasions. There was Mime, Alberich's brother who brought Siegried up, and all the cries, by the Valkyries, the Rhine Maidens, and Hagen, who is the only fellow with a downward cry and the only one among all these people wearing a helmet with horns turning down. To have given the complete story of the *Ring* would have taken at least two hours. Oh, well, one day I may have another bash at it!

CHAPTER 16

Fun and games on Fifty-second Street.
My first big national tour

When I went back to New York to start my first big tour, I moved from the Woodward to an apartment on Fifty-second Street, which I shared with Audrey Gillespie (nicknamed Auntie), who later married my cousin David Farquharson. The apartment was even grander and shabbier than the Osborne. It had two enormous rooms divided by carved mahogany sliding doors, a grand piano lost in an alcove flanked by two mahogany pillars at least a foot across, two great green marble fireplaces with huge mirrors over them, and a marble bathroom with an immense toilet that looked like a pope's chair. All this grandeur was spoiled by a terribly slummy kitchen built in a passageway about four feet wide. If we wanted to use the oven we had to do it sideways. The apartment was in the last brownstone next to the new Esso Building, against which it leaned rather drunkenly, so that all the floors slanted. When you came in the front door all the rest of the flat went uphill.

Strip joints occupied all the basements on our block, so as we came home from Sixth Avenue we had to run the gauntlet of barkers standing outside shouting, "No cover, no minimum, drinks at the bar!" This was the noisiest place I'd been in yet. The band in the basement thumped on, shaking the house, until four o'clock every morning, invariably ending with Ravel's *Bolero*. The drums would build up and up to a big climax for the last bump or grind, at which point our bathroom tap would fall off with a crash. We never found a plumber who could make it stick on through this onslaught, so we got used to putting it together ourselves every morning.

The apartment certainly had its faults, but it was a very good place for a party. Auntie was a Cordon Bleu chef and the only female chef ever to have been employed by the Ritz Carlton. After she had set out the family silver and put flowers in front of all the cracks and deficiencies of the place, and our beloved maid, Myrtis Clare, had tricked herself out in her daintiest cap and apron and put her teeth in, we could produce quite a grand effect if we could get the guests in without running into the very strange witchlike woman who had a Collier Brothers establishment upstairs, and could get a few drinks into them fast enough so they would think the slope of the floor was just their own impending inebriation.

When our domestic arrangements became too onerous—when we weren't able to get the bath tap back on at all; when there was no hot water or worse, when the water was boiling and there was no cold water; when the gas stove blew up in our passage kitchen; when the ancient fridge began belching clouds of evil-smelling gas; or when the cockroaches got the better of our rather primitive exterminating methods—we could always go over to the Rehearsal Club for a free bath or a meal, while we gathered our strength for the next crisis.

We both had our methods of dealing with the noise downstairs. Fortified with a bit of gin, I would practice or write material between 10:00 P.M. and 4:00 A.M., and Auntie would take sleeping pills.

One night Boomer and I were going to Philadelphia to put on a concert at the Academy of Music for the twenty-fifth anniversary of the Emma Feldman Management. It was a very grand affair. Important New York managers were at the reception at the Belleview Stratford afterward, as well as Eugene Ormandy and a bevy of artists, and the champagne was flowing. Before I left, Auntie warned me that if I disturbed her when I came home in the wee small hours she would be very annoyed, as she knew when Boomer and I got together we were apt to make rather a noise. I told him this as we left the reception. We were feeling quite good after the champagne, but not unduly so, and he said he'd remember.

In the restaurant car on the home-bound train, we ran into Franchot Tone, an old buddy of Boomer's whom he hadn't seen for some time. This called for more celebration, which tended to increase our decibels. In the taxi home I begged him to lower his voice when he escorted me to the flat, and to make doubly sure of being quiet, he left his shoes in the taxi, which he asked to wait. We crept up the stairs, shushing each other as we went. We opened the front door and negotiated the up-sloping floor without making a sound. I motioned him to a chair, which he slumped into with a sigh of relief.

As he did so, the chair slid downhill and knocked over an enormous standard lamp with three Victorian globes and a glass shade. The noise was deafening, there was glass all over the place, we both got the giggles, and the taxi driver must have heard us because he started blaring his horn outside. I was expecting Auntie to rush out in a dudgeon and tell me to go and live somewhere else, but there wasn't a sound from her. The next morning she sadly surveyed the debris.

"What happened to you?" I asked her.

"Oh," she said, "I was afraid something like this might happen so I took four sleeping pills last night."

John Coveart joined me for my big tour that fall. We went to New Brunswick, where it was freezing. Our trains kept getting snowed in, and we often had to change in the washroom, surprising the other travelers by emerging in full evening regalia, wearing ear muffs. The sponsors would yank us off the train, and we'd arrive at the hall with red noses and frozen fingers, just in time for the curtain.

We went to Montana and Wisconsin and Texas and Colorado and Washington, D.C. Half the time we didn't know where we were, we just followed the itinerary. Sometimes it was freezing and sometimes stifling. We could be playing to an audience of ten thousand in St. Paul, Minnesota, or in a school hall in Wausau, Wisconsin, where the hind leg of the grand piano fell off and the piano had to be jacked up with orange crates before we could continue. We met every sort of local manager—Daddy Hooks in Denver; Hazel Oberfelder, who sent me down to the supermarket to buy her some celery that was on sale; Ruth Seufert in Kansas City, who insisted I have four eggs and eight rashers of bacon for breakfast to keep my strength up.

This tour taught me a few useful facts. Physical strength and endurance are the most necessary attributes for a touring performer. Talent is fine, but I've met some good talent that went to pieces because the strain was too much. Giving the concert is only a small part of it. Actually, one is more like a commercial traveler, which is a very hard grind.

You get off the plane, rush to the hotel, and stand in line to get your room. You fill the bath with boiling water and hang your gown over it to get the creases out. A durable and uncomplicated wardrobe is best, because there's never time for valet service. When it's time for a press conference, or a TV or radio interview, or all of them, you rush down to the auditorium, set out the props, and try the piano, which has probably not yet been turned. Somewhere about 5:00 P.M. you try to fit in a meal, if there is anyplace open. You dress and do the concert, and go to the party. There is always a party. Although you go through this routine five and six days a week, the place you are in probably has only five concerts a season; therefore it is an occasion and, to be fair, most of these people are kind and sweet.

There are parties where you are expected to sit down and plow through a colossal meal, or ones where grog of all sorts is flowing like water, but there's nothing to eat but a peanut. There are the coffee and cake ones, where everyone sits around making polite conversation, ones where no one but the hostess has been to the concert, so everyone wants you to do it all over again. They can be highbrow, lowbrow, or downright binges. You will be the center of attraction, as it is all part of the deal. They have bought you for the evening, so you must be in top form. If for any reason you are not, or you do anything untoward, every concert manager in the country will know about it in the next few days. The party will go on till two or three in the morning and the next day you will most likely have to be up at dawn to catch the plane to the next place, where it will start all over again.

I found the parties a little difficult until I got the hang of it, because everyone asks you the same questions. Where, how, and why did you start your career? Do you know Bob Hope, Danny Kaye, the Duke of Windsor? I would like you to meet my daughter, who sings, who acts, who baton twirls; my aunt Bessie, who knew Rudolph Valentino; my grandmother, who was a Ziegfeld Follies girl; our organist Miss Jones, who was a pupil of Leschetizky. Have you played at the White House, Buckingham Palace, Carnegie Hall?

Then there are people with ideas, who will say, "Here's a wonderful idea, a new sketch you could do in your show. There were five people getting into a bus. And the first one says . . . and then somebody else says . . . and that person does this and somebody else. . . . I think you could do that marvelously!" These ideas seldom concern less than four people at once, and no one has yet elucidated how they can be done by a solo performer. Then there is, "Why don't you sing a few serious songs?" If they'd ever heard me try, they would know at once why not.

These questions are, of course, perfectly legitimate and the sort of things everyone wants to know about an artist, and ones I have frequently asked when the positions have been reversed, but what people don't realize is that when one is asked the same thing six times a week for four months, it gets increasingly hard to look animated and give fresh, crisp answers, and not get that "Oh, my God! Here it comes again!" look on one's face.

So I hit on the plan of writing special material for the parties. I knew the questions, so I kept at my fingertips a selection of sprightly, well-rehearsed answers that sounded on first hearing as if I had just thought them up, for as every comedian knows, the better rehearsed the act, the more ad lib it will sound. The only thing I had to watch was not to do this in earshot of my accompanist, or it would be he who would get the "Oh, my God! Here it comes again!" look.

Another good idea is getting your accompanist to do a party piece. With John Coveart it was the Chopin Polonaise in E-flat; my next one, Eugene Rankin, did *La Maja y el Ruisenõr* by Granados with all the stops out. But Frank Bartholomew was probably the most successful in this respect. He could take peoples' telephone numbers and improvise them into a Bach fugue, and by the time he had done all the women's numbers, he was the center of attention, and everyone had forgotten about me.

On this first big tour for Boomer, he turned up from time to time to see how things were going. This was tremendous, because having been around the territory for years, he knew everyone in the vicinity, and the women doted on him. He usually had some big joke going on and would say dreadful things to people, but they loved it. One time in Dallas he referred to the Trapp Family Singers, whom he had managed, as the Dirty Dirndls, and the critic John Rosenfield printed it in the *Dallas Morning News.*

Often the joke was on me. He would call me on the hotel phone and say something like, "Toscanini is staying in the hotel and would like to meet you." I always fell for it, but of course there was never any Toscanini, just Boomer laughing himself sick.

One time in Houston, Texas, he called and said, Leopold Stokowski would like to meet me. This time I was not going to be caught. I had met the maestro many years ago when he was conducting one of the selections at the command performance for King George V and Queen Mary at the Royal College of Music. He was more generally known at the time as Mr. Stokes, the organist of one of the churches up near Piccadilly Circus, so you can imagine how long ago that was! I said I would be glad to receive him in half an hour. I put my hair curlers in, creamed up my face, and generally looked as awful as possible, which can be pretty awful. A knock came on the door, I flung it open, and there stood Leopold Stokowski! I must say he thought it was funny, too, as he knew Boomer of old, and in spite of his reputation as the great Polish conductor, Stokowski was actually brought up English, with the good old British sense of poking fun, and was perfectly charming about it.

A lot of people I knew used to say Boomer was sadistic because of his practical jokes. I don't agree. He was a great manager, and I think his way of protecting his artists from the shocks they would inevitably receive was to get his cracks in at you first.

I was told that it was not sufficient to have a good New York press to be successful on tour. You also had to be approved of by certain critics in Boston, Chicago, Dallas, San Francisco, Washington, etc., because what they said about you in these key cities governed the likelihood of bookings in that part of the country. I was very lucky to meet one of these great people beforehand in New York, John Rosenfield of the *Dallas Morning News*. He was enormously stout and seemed rather terrifying and portentous at first. Tremendously well-informed about everyone in show business past and present, he was inclined to orate, creating the initial impression that he never listened to what others were saying. In fact, he never missed a syllable of anything that was said, and his word pictures of the behavior of various celebrities were priceless. He and his wife, Clare, were devoted to Boomer, and later, when I had a concert anywhere near Dallas, John would drive the lot of us there, write a beautiful review, then drive us back for a delirious late night at his place.

Another important critic was Paul Hume in Washington, D.C. He was the intrepid man who panned Margaret Truman's recital and got ticked off by Daddy for doing so, and it all wound up in *Time* magazine. Just before I got there he had criticized very strongly some German coloratura. He said she "eeked" on her high notes. (Personally I think that's a brilliant description!) I was a little apprehensive, as Constitution Hall was a very grand place to be playing, but I needn't have worried. He said in his review that he'd been ticked off by the President in one case and by the cognoscenti in the other, but he enjoyed me the most, because even though *all* the concerts had been funny, he was allowed to laugh at mine.

Relations with the critics had been going pretty well up to now, and I was probably lulled into a false sense of security (which is of course a great mistake), so I wasn't in the least apprehensive when I discovered I was to appear for three nights in Kimball Hall, Chicago, where I would encounter the artist's downfall and terror of them all, Claudia Cassidy of the *Chicago Tribune*. The stories I had heard about her were legion. Some of the world's very greatest would catch it from her. I don't know why I wasn't worried; I think it was that deep down I didn't really believe she'd come.

We had a full hall, and sitting in the front row right under my nose were those two absolutely delicious women, whom I had met for the first time that afternoon, Mmes. Rosa Raisa and Edith Mason, who had been great stars with the Chicago Opera Company. When one is aided and abetted by people like that, the show is apt to go off with a bang, and we thought it had.

Well! You never read anything like it the next morning. The review was terrible. And not only that, Miss Cassidy was a very good writer. It was more, you might say, literature than journalism, which made it all the more devastating. She started, "This big, bosomy, blowsy, Britisher . . ." and ended up, ". . . I thought I had seen the most repulsive performance last month, Liberace, but this woman is more revolting than Liberace."

I could see, of course, that Chicago in future would be out, but then it suddenly struck my accompanist and me during the morning that "This b, b, b, Britisher" sounded like the beginning of a recitative, say, "Ritorna Vincitor!" or some such. So just for fun we spent the afternoon concocting a Verdi-type recit and aria, "I'm more repulsive, I'm more revolting, I'm more disgusting than Liberace." After all, we were dead anyway, so what did it matter?

That evening we had a full house, because everyone had come to see how revolting I was. The aria was a smash hit and was encored several times. The next day it was mentioned in someone's (not the *Tribune*'s) gossip column, so the third night we were packed out. The Mmes. Mason and Raisa were in the front row again, and when we did the aria they looked as if they were going to have a stroke.

Also that evening, Harry Zelzer, a big concert manager, came to see what all the fuss was about. It seemed we had started something. Not on purpose. We were only having a bit of fun. Harry Zelzer said if I could think up another number in this vein he would book me into Orchestra Hall the following season, because, he said, a lot of artists wouldn't come to Chicago on account of Mme. C. and it wasn't very good for business. I could see his point.

When I was announced on Harry's series the following year, the Madam didn't wait until the concert, but started lambasting him beforehand for daring to bring such dreck to Chicago, letting the standards down, etc. Of course, the hall was full, since I'd had so much publicity. The number for this occasion was one of those arias that singers are prone to start recitals with, entitled "Madama Tribune." My local restaurateur Curley helped me cook up the lyrics, and the Italian was impeccable.

The next day everything was as revolting as ever, but no mention was made of this number. So Harry called up and translated it to Mme. C.

The next I heard, John Rosenfield in Dallas knew about the feud and what's more, he was also in the doghouse. He had recently had dinner with

Mme. C., whom he described as an embittered sentimentalist. Apparently a favorite conductor of hers, Rodzinsky, whom she thought was simply marvelous, had just died. At dinner, John was sitting on a big carved chair, feeling very fat and full of food, when Mme. C. said wistfully, "John, do you know who was the last person to sit on that chair?" It had been the conductor. So John heaved himself up, turned around, and solemnly kissed the seat of the chair. It apparently caused dreadful offense.

At the time he told me this story, I was in the middle of writing a travel article for *Musical America*, so John suggested I put something in it about her. All I said was, "Watch out for Chicago, as you will probably get the treatment from Acidy Cassidy." But because this was a national magazine it went the rounds and the name stuck. The next season Harry Zelzer had me booked into the Tenth Street Theater, and I was wondering what would happen this time, as so many people had gotten into the act. Nothing happened. Nobody came from the *Tribune*, and that was the last that was heard of the whole affair, so I reckon I won in the end.

CHAPTER 17

The girl of the Golden West.
A master class with Lotte Lehmann

After that first great safari around the country, it was very pleasant to get back to the apartment and Auntie's meals. A perpetual diet of steak and salad, which is all anyone seems to eat on the road, gets very monotonous.

The day I arrived she was concocting one of her special home brews for a friend who lived nearby. Ed was a poor, lonely soul, but a tremendous hypochondriac and a dreadful complainer. Although Auntie spent a lot of time cheering him up and cooking meals for him, nothing was ever quite good enough. She had arranged a beautiful party for him a few weeks before, but all he had done was complain bitterly that the punch had no kick. Nonetheless, he expected Auntie, as usual, to cope with another party he was having the following week for his church choir, in which he sang tenor.

On this occasion she had for once gotten absolutely fed up. When I came in the door, she was muttering imprecations over a big plastic bath in the middle of the floor, into which she was pouring whisky, brandy, vodka, liqueurs, and bottles of wine with abandon. "This," she said, "will teach him to say my punch has no kick." Alcoholic fumes fit to knock you over were rising from the bath.

"One glassful of that and they'll all be dead," I suggested.

"No they won't," she said. "When I've finished with it they won't be able to tell it from my kickless punch. This time I'm jolly well going to teach him a lesson."

I helped her move this evil mixture onto the balcony, where she covered it with plastic and left it to mature for a week. It seemed to me likely to go up in spontaneous combustion or eat a hole through the balcony. When we brought the mixture in the following week, it had mellowed somewhat, but was hardly the thing to give a church choir. I was sure that when the vicar got downwind of it he would forbid it, so what was the point? "Wait," she said. She then put in pounds and pounds of strawberries and piles of sliced cucumber, covered it again, and put it out on the balcony for a couple more days.

On the day of the party I got the job of filling the punch bowl, which stood in the middle of the elegantly set table. "Funny," I said, "the fumes have gone." It was a beautiful, delicate pink, with the strawberries bobbing around in it.

"Now taste it," Auntie ordered. It was the coolest, most delicious punch and didn't seem to have any kick in it at all.

"What happened to it?" I asked her.

"You may now eat one strawberry and one slice of cucumber, but don't touch either during the party." It was the most strawberry-tasting straw-berry I had ever tasted, but it nearly knocked my head off, and the cucum-ber was delicious, but fizzy. "That," said Auntie, "is where the alcohol has gone."

The party started to arrive, a collection of earnest and rather plain women, and some men who were either adenoidal or paunchy, shep-herded by the vicar. Everyone was offered a choice of drinks—a highball or punch. "I think," said the vicar, "you'll find that not many of us care for strong drink." Then he caught sight of the punch, and beaming around on us all, said, "The punch, I think, would be more our sort of tipple."

After everyone was served, they gathered around the piano for a few rousing hymns to start the party going, while Auntie, Myrtis, and I kept the punch flowing. It wasn't long before the hymns got very rousing in-deed. A few halfhearted attempts were made on the food, but the punch was the big seller. In due course half the party got riotous, and the rest got either contentious or sick. The vicar sat in the corner and went to sleep for the entire evening, which was probably just as well. Ed, who had once again complained of the weakness of the punch and had not been let into the secret, got very drunk, sang some exceedingly dirty songs in a loud voice, and passed out. Some unlikely flirtations started, the place was rap-idly becoming a shambles, and the noise was deafening. Auntie, Myrtis, and I spent a good part of the evening escorting casualties into taxis. The upstairs neighbors complained and finally called the cops. We were able to mollify the two who arrived by showing them the sleeping vicar and administering beer mugs of punch. I suppose as a party it was a success, but as a choir outing, I'm not so sure.

Boomer had recently got wind of the fact that a Broadway producer, Mike Meyerburg, was about to make a movie of the opera *Hänsel and Gretel*, using fully articulated and electronically controlled puppets, which had just been invented. He was using the original Humperdinck score, but the characters were to be gimmicked up in various ways, and some parts were to be spoken, others sung. Mildred Dunnock was the mother, Frank Roget the father, and the Vienna Choirboys the angels. In fact, the whole show was cast, except for the witch. Franz Allers, who was to conduct, was getting rather impatient, as he had other things pending, but the lack of a witch was holding up the production.

It is a dramatic, or mezzo soprano role usually, and everyone who had ever witched had auditioned, to no avail. Meyerburg, being a theater rather than an opera man, maintained that rich, fruity voices, though they might be great for Brünnhilde or Tosca, definitely didn't sell him a witch, and until he found someone who sounded like a witch he would hold up the production indefinitely.

Since my voice had been variously described as being "of acid timbre," "shattering glass," or "like a cracked temple bell," Boomer thought I might fit the bill, so he sent my record over and an appointment was set up with Mike and the directors. They had all listened to my record and had agreed unanimously that I had the voice of a witch, but definitely! They gave me the score, and we went on to discuss dates and rehearsals.

It was an exciting project, and I was bubbling away about it on the way home, when Boomer said, "I have news for you. You are not going to do it." I was dumbfounded. Why not? I'd been given the score to learn and everything. "Because Meyerburg is negotiating with RCA Victor to record the sound track, but you are a Columbia recording artist, so you won't be permitted to do it."

Shortly after, I started on my first California tour, which I was looking forward to tremendously, since I'd never been on the West Coast before. On the trip out, John Coveart was reading *Billboard* and discovered that my album *Anna Russell Sings?* had been a top-selling classical LP for forty-eight weeks. To begin with, fancy being considered classical! There it was in print, though. I had topped Sir Thomas Beecham and the Philharmonia, and all kinds of august personages. Furthermore, I had always thought of my performance as being more visual than auditory. Of course, I had hoped that people who saw the show would buy the record, but I never expected it to go the other way, which in fact it has.

When we arrived in Los Angeles, we were met by Dr. Mary Bran, the local manager who was presenting me at the Philharmonic Hall. Mary was Russian, a dear soul, and an excellent promoter, but full of Slavic intensity. She would run the gamut of emotion from deep despair to wild buoyancy in the matter of a few minutes, which on first meeting was most unnerving. While she was promoting me, I was the focal point of her existence, the most fabulous artist that ever lived, the only topic of conversation permitted in her vicinity. From crack of dawn until I fell exhausted into bed at night, there were interviews, press conferences, luncheons—any method of blazoning my name around. She had put a great banner across Sunset Boulevard announcing the concert. Every time we passed the banner we had to stop and admire it.

She was an enthusiast of whom I have seldom seen the like. Everything she did was perfect and brilliant, and everything I did was perfect and brilliant. I sometimes felt she might become incandescent and explode, and I would collapse into dust at her feet. Mind you, it was rather fun a few days, but I certainly couldn't have kept it up permanently, which she evidently did. The point was that it was effective. My concerts were always packed.

She would come to New York from time to time for the Concert Managers' Convention. I remember one occasion when I was going to meet her at the Russian Tea Room on Fifty-seventh Street. On the way there, I met Ilya Motylieff, at one time a director of the Moscow Art Theater, who was then a drama professor at Hunter College. Like Mary, he would run the gamut of emotions in five minutes flat. I told him I was going to meet the Los Angeles concert manager Mary Bran, and he promptly went off like a squib. He had known Mary Bran . . . they had worked together in Danzig thirty years ago . . . how wonderful she was, how marvelous! There he was, dancing up and down and shouting away on Sixth Avenue. It was getting late, so I suggested he come with me to renew their acquaintance.

You never saw anything like it! I thought Boomer and I could make as much noise as any two people, but we weren't in it with this pair. They fell upon each other in the middle of the bar with cries of ecstasy, and you

know how Russians talk to each other, particularly if they are excited—
they change each other's names all the time.

For instance, where we would say, "Well if it isn't Joe Blow!"

"Maisie Jones!"

"Joe Blow, you look great!"

"Maisie Jones, it's wonderful to see you!"

"Joe Blow, what a surprise!"

"Maisie Jones, it's been years!"

In Russian this confrontation would go something like this: "Ilya!
Ilyulya!"

"Marya! Maroushka!"

"Ilyulya Motylieff!"

"Maroushka Clavdovnaya!"

"Ilyulya Davidovnavoff Motylieffskovitch Bodeen!"

"Marushkaya Clavdovnaya Dushka Branskayova!"

It takes a bit to startle anyone in the Russian Tea Room, but this did.
Everyone at the bar turned their stools around to watch the show. We sat
down at one of the horseshoe-shaped tables with me between them. Ilya
and Mary wept their way through the Revolution and rejoiced about their
great productions in Danzig and other parts. Every now and then, when
nostalgia became too much, they would leap up and embrace. Once in a
while, when they remembered I was there, they would both fling their
arms around me and say what a marvelous, sublime artist I was, what a
dear friend! Then back to the Revolution, the suffering and the merry
triumphs. I can't say I understood much of it, but the noise was incredible. I don't think we had any tea, as the waitress was too fascinated to stop
the flow. I eventually had to go, as I had an appointment, but I don't
think they noticed. I rather envy Russians. They seem to be able to squeeze
so much feeling out of so little, and have such a good time doing
it.

At that first concert in Los Angeles I really grasped the fact that movie
stars are real people. In the intermission I told Mary that there was a man in
the front row who looked exactly like Charles Coburn. It was, in fact,
Charles Coburn, and he sat in the same seat every time I played there. A lot
of movie stars would come because, rather strangely, there isn't much entertainment in Los Angeles.

After this concert I performed an extra one with the Beverley Hills Philharmonic. They asked me to do my Brünnhilde routine; I was standing in

for Kirsten Flagstad, who had canceled at the last minute. I suppose they thought any old Brünnhilde was better than none.

After the concert, Marion Kerby turned up, whom I hadn't seen since she and John Jacob Niles had performed at one of Aunt Al Schuyler's do-it-herself concerts in Buckinghamshire when I was a teenager.

"Marion Kerby!" I screamed.

"Have we met?" she asked rather blankly. When I told her I was Claudia, she was thrilled and promptly took me under her wing, introducing me in time to all sorts of people. So she produced Ethel Bartlett and Rae Robertson, the duo pianists who had also been in Aunt Al's concert series years before, and we had a great reunion. She also introduced me to Bill Swan, who became one of my closest friends. He was an enthusiastic amateur baritone, with a lovely voice, who spent a lot of time singing at funerals. Since funeral parlors abound in Los Angeles, he was kept very busy. He invited me to stay with him and his family, and thereafter Bill's house became a home away from home.

Perhaps I have such a special feeling for California because it was the first place I ever went that was even slightly tropical. Cold and dreary countries, where I had mostly been up till now, seem to develop cold and inhibited people, full of virtue and energy, no doubt this being the best way to keep warm. But I like a warmer place, where life doesn't seem so grim and earnest, and California is like that. Up in Nicholls Canyon, where Bill lived in a beautiful house cantilevered off the mountain, the air always smelled of frangipani, and the sun shone, and I had that joyful feeling of suppressed excitement that everything was possible, that one's most extravagant pipe dream might well come true.

After playing a concert in Veterans Auditorium in San Francisco, plus several others in the vicinity, I headed back to Bill's place for a few weeks' rest. The day I returned, everyone was getting ready for the party they were giving for me the following night. The whole family were tremendous cooks. Bill's mother, who had her own kitchen on the level below, was baking up a storm of cakes and pastries; in the upstairs kitchen Bill, his sister Leah, and even his little niece Anne were concocting elaborate dishes. I began to feel very lazy and useless in this hive of activity, and kept asking if I could help. Finally, probably to keep me out of their hair, as I am a lamentable cook, they gave me a bowl, led me to a counter with shelves and shelves of every known herb and spice, and gave me instructions how to make the salad dressing. I thought I followed them to the letter, but I must admit the mixture looked very strange when I had finished; it was diarrhea brown. When I showed it to Bill he said, "Never mind, I'll do it later," and was about to throw it out, when he tasted it, and said, "This is certainly not what I told you, but it is simply delicious."

So we looked at all the bottles I had out, deduced what I had put in it, and made some more for the party. The salad was a tremendous success, and I was terribly proud. Bill later gave it to the chef of a restaurant he had an interest in, and they used it and named it after me. So now there is Peach Melba, Chicken Tetrazzini, and Salad Dressing Russell. Well, you have to start somewhere. Here is the recipe:

salt   a level teaspoon of curry powder
pepper out of the grinder   wine vinegar
a squeezed clove of garlic   olive oil
a dollop of Dijon mustard

Don't worry about the disgusting color, it doesn't show when it's mixed with the salad.

One morning Bill said he would have to be away the next day to go to Santa Barbara for Lotte Lehmann's master class at the Academy of the West. Lotte Lehmann! The most glorious lieder singer that ever was! I had never missed a recital of hers when I was at the Royal College, and had heard her in all her great operatic roles at Covent Garden. I said, "You miserable amateur funeral baritone, how dare you be able to go to her master class when I am such a *fan*." He knew her very well apart from class, so he rang her up and asked if he could bring a house guest to listen in. Lotte said, "If that is Miss Schlumph Russell, tell her I would be delighted if she came."

I sat spellbound through the master class. Although there were some outstanding voices there, as soon as Lotte opened her mouth to demonstrate, even though she was old and hadn't a great deal of voice left, everyone else's paled into insignificance. Years later when I went to her class in New York's Town Hall, and she was just speaking the words to the music, the same thing happened. She had magic.

The class looked as if it were coming to an end when Lotte said, "And now, Miss Russell, we shall interpret 'Schlumph ist mein Gesitzenbaum,' which means, for those who don't understand German, 'Dumb is my sittingtree.' " I got up there amid roars of laughter from the class, and there was the number, all beautifully written out. They had taken it off the record. Lotte said sternly, "Please, I want no laughing," and proceeded to take me through "Schlumph" just as thoroughly and just as seriously as she had taken someone through "Die Erlkönig" minutes before. I must say, my little nonsense was a hundred percent improved ever after.

CHAPTER 18

The movie, the opera, the Broadway show. The United Fruit Company

When I got back to New York, I really had to get down to work. The next Town Hall concert and recording was not far away, and I had to make sure it was at least up to the standards of the previous one. Mr. Judson had told Boomer that the career span of a performer like me would probably be about two years, and I myself had seen artists come out one year with a big splash and be a great success, only to fail miserably the next and vanish from the scene. So if I didn't want to be a one-shotter I really had to deliver.

I needn't have worried, though. Town Hall was sold out, and the audience was a delight. I felt more secure this time, as I had gained experience, and the audience was with me. They didn't miss a trick. When I am holding forth and everyone is reading me loud and clear, I feel that I am really communicating. I am giving them something, and they are giving something back, which, I suppose, is what it is all about.

Alas, things are different for me in real life. People make me nervous. It is probably a hangover from youth and trying to comply singlehandedly with that horde of relatives and Father. Audiences are different, somehow. They are easier to talk to than individuals, and the footlights are always in between, providing a kind of barrier. Don't they say that all comedians are neurotic?

In this concert I had included, for the first time in the States, my explanation of Wagner's *Ring*. Some people were shocked that I would send up this august piece of music, but I don't consider it a sendup. I merely tell the story as accurately as possible and play the bits of music exactly as written. I can't help it if the story is absurd. Sometime later, Ernest Newman, erstwhile critic of the *London Times* and one of the world's great experts on Wagner, said that, although he wouldn't have expressed it in exactly the manner I had, my facts were completely correct. It wasn't until then that the routine became respectable, and it is now in the curriculum of a number of universities where The *Ring* is studied.

After the concert who should appear but Mike Meyerburg, asking if I had yet learned the witch in *Hänsel and Gretel.* I told him no, as I thought I couldn't do it, being a Columbia recording artist. He said he had switched to Columbia in the meantime so that I could, so I had better hurry up and learn it.

I couldn't sing the role properly, as a lot of the notes in it were the ones I yodel on, so when they came I would substitute shrieks, peculiar noises, or wild remarks. Meyerburg thought this was great, and had me make a tape of solo shrieks, groans, and gibberings that could be superimposed on the main tape, and then decided he would give me top billing in the picture.

It was exciting to see my name blazoned across a wide screen all by itself, because the only other movie I'd ever appeared in was a Terry Thomas whodunit, where I played an old woman who got murdered early on.

About this time I had to find a replacement for my accompanist, John Coveart, because the McCarran Act had just been passed and he was not an American. Boomer and I were always arguing about accompanists; he seemed to think any old pianist would do. I, on the other hand, think a good accompanist is absolutely vital. This time he said he didn't want any more nonsense about it—he was sending me one from Mrs. Hannenfeldt's accompanists pool at Columbia Artists, and this was the one it had to be, so Eugene Rankin appeared on the scene.

Gene had a bright orange tweed suit and a North Carolina accent you could cut with a knife. If you have seen "Gomer Pyle" on TV, that was exactly what Gene was like at the time. Lovable, but a bit simple. He wasn't anything like the virtuoso John Coveart was, but he played very sympathetically and was a good sight-reader, so we made the deal.

Gene had quite a few talents besides playing the piano. He was a travel enthusiast; he would bone up on anyplace we went before we got there, so he would know where the hotel, the auditorium, the radio station were, where the sponsor lived, and what to do for fun on our days off. He took care of all the tickets, which he would constantly switch around if he found an easier way to go. He was a brilliant driver, and would go about ninety miles an hour, but I always felt quite safe, and we got places fast. He was an expert packer of suitcases, so he mostly did mine too, and besides, he had audience appeal. Everywhere we went, someone would say, "Love your pianist!" He kept names and addresses of everyone we met whom we liked and wanted to see again, and was generally a lot of fun and a very good traveling companion. He would have been marvelous for conducting those world-traveling, purple-haired ladies for a travel agency.

As time went on he lost the North Carolina accent and picked up mine, and the orange tweed suitings gave way to quiet elegance. I remember the time in London when he bought a Savile Row suit. The first time I saw it we were walking out of the Savoy Hotel. It was dark gray, he had with it the British white shirt and a restrained tie, and the good old rolled umbrella, and it struck me that all he needed was a bowler hat to become the complete and traditional Englishman. He stayed pretty British after that except when we went down to North Carolina, where he would immediately revert to Gomer Pyle.

Everyone liked him except Boomer, who for some reason was inclined to ignore him completely or call him "Thumper," which hurt Gene's feelings. So one year he quit.

Boomer came up with a complete monster to replace him, ugly and scruffy, who held his dress pants up with a brown belt that showed under his white waistcoat. He couldn't follow, he played too loud, he lost the tickets, was a shocking driver who couldn't find his way out of a paper bag so we were always late, and I hated him. I hated him so much that it began to show in the performances, which caused the bookings to fall off, so Gene had to come back. I was never so glad to see anyone. I got a note from Boomer while I was on this trip, saying I was not to go staying with my pals when the tour finished, as I was to sing the witch in *Hänsel and Gretel* at the City Center Opera on Easter Saturday. What? I thought he must be pulling my leg. Juxtaposed with proper singers I could sound crazy.

Dr. Rosenstock, who ran City Center and who was a friend from the Aspen Festival, thought it would be fun to have me because, he said, after two acts of little girls singing syrupy songs in thirds and sixths, he got fed up with pretty noises and wanted a change.

Hänsel and Gretel had already been performed that season, so everyone knew what to do except me. I had one week to get rehearsed. The first piano rehearsal was with Mr. Tarrasch, who disapproved of the whole idea, the second was with a mad fellow who said he didn't like *Hänsel and Gretel* anyway, so let's louse it up. The third go was an orchestral rehearsal in the studio with Tommy Schippers conducting; it had to go straight through with no stops, as that's all the time the Musicians' Union were going to allow. The performance was the following afternoon, but so far I had had no stage rehearsal; in fact, I'd never been on the City Center stage, and what the set was like I hadn't a clue, nor had I seen my costume. Tommy said doubtless someone would go through the motions with me on Saturday morning, but no one was worrying about it except me.

I got there early, and there wasn't a soul around, so I poked around in the wardrobe and found what looked like my costume. It was far too big, so I cobbled it up with an upholstery needle and some string I found. I wandered about all morning, but no one came, until people started arriving for the performance. I was sent down to Mr. Arshansky, the makeup artist, who stuck a large rubber nose and chin on me, and gave me the most horrendous makeup, and I went back to my dressing room. No one came near me, and the performance started. The first act went, and the second act, then a voice said, "Miss Russell on stage please." I went down, and there was Dr. Rosenstock, Tommy Schippers and the stage manager.

Dr. Rosenstock said, "I'm sorry you didn't get a stage rehearsal, but in the witch's ride, you go round there, and up there and out there."

"She can't," said the stage manager, "there isn't an exit there; she must go up there and round that and through here and out there."

Tommy Schippers said, "I doubt if there is enough music for all that."

"Well anyway," I asked, "where is the broomstick?" It wasn't there, so someone had to go up to props to get it.

"That is the oven," said Dr. Rosenstock, pointing to a very small door.

"Will I be able to get in?" I asked.

He said, "I should think so, Madame Votipka can, but hurry up and get through the back, because sixteen bars after they push you in, it explodes. You really should have had a stage rehearsal. Anyway," he said, "in the gingerbread house there is a hole in the roof through which you can see Mr. Schippers for your cue."

I gathered up my candies and rope, and went in. Goodness knew what was going to happen, but I was past being nervous; I was just numb.

The curtain went up and the third act started. It was coming up to my part, so I looked through the hole for Mr. Schippers, but all I could see was the back of a tree. I knew I entered on a trumpet note, but what sort of tempo I was to take, I hadn't a clue.

The trumpet note came, and I thought, Here goes nothing. I shot out of the gingerbread house like a bat out of hell. Hänsel and Gretel really looked scared, and probably were, wondering what this idiot was going to do. A good question, since I didn't know myself. I pranced around, sang what bits I could, whooped and shrieked the bits I couldn't, and generally carried on as witchily as I could think of. I got through it somehow, and only just managed to wedge myself through the oven door to be grabbed by a couple of stagehands just before it exploded. My nose came off, so I had to rush up to makeup and get it stuck on again to take my curtain.

Charlie had come down from Toronto to see it and thought it was dreadful. Boomer thought it was a riot. Gene Rankin had almost always heard it better sung, but had never seen it more witchy. And I was a wreck.

In the next day's reviews I got the headlines. I was the most original witch ever seen, it was splendid, it was different, it was just what the doctor ordered. The reviewers were evidently of the same mind as Dr. Rosenstock: thirds and sixths are all very well, but something has to give.

A few days later, Dr. Rosenstock called me in to say that after my efforts, all the proper witches had struck and refused to sing the role again, so I would have to become a member of the company, and the permanent witch. I served in this capacity for two years, and even went on tour with the company.

By this time Boomer and I were getting very pleased with ourselves. Everything so far had gone our way, and we were beginning to think we were infallible, always a great mistake! Boomer thought it was time I had a Broadway show, so he sent a man named Arthur Klein running around collecting the backing. When Boomer asked if I knew anyone who would put up some money, I suddenly thought of Martin at the Woodward. I didn't think he would, as he had been to all my concerts and had slept soundly through them, not having understood a word, but he had been trying to give me a mink coat for a long time, which I wasn't about to accept, for obvious reasons, so I thought he might be worth seeing anyway.

Martin told Arthur that what I was doing wasn't any good at all. He thought I should be in a girlie show! Arthur assumed it was no go and was about to leave, when Martin said he had offered me a mink coat, which I wouldn't have, so if Baby wanted a Broadway show, even if it was going to be a sure flop, Baby could have one, so he came across with the rest of the money.

I should have done my first Broadway show by myself. This is where we made our big mistake. I didn't think at the time I could do eight shows a week. I could have, of course. I've done it a million times since then, but I didn't have that much confidence yet, so in the show we had the Jean Louis Destinee Dancers and a magician.

I had been put on pills to lose weight. I'm sure they must have been Benzedrine, because I went down like a pricked balloon and got so jittery I couldn't sleep or sit still for a minute. It's a wonder I didn't get hooked. In no time I was a large, raw-boned skeleton. I wasn't svelte, because you can't get any thinner than your bones allow, and I looked terrible. In the show I was doing groups of my usual stuff; "How to Play the Bagpipes" in full kilts and a sporran; and a new number, "The Prince of Philadelphia," which was how to write your own light operetta, with a very unfunny baritone. I had a lot of flamboyant gowns, which were so un-me it was pitiful, and I looked awful in kilts.

We opened at the Vanderbilt Theater on September 13, 1953, the same night as *Carnival in Flanders,* and it was a bomb. The second-string critics roasted us to death. Some of them liked the rest of the show but hated me, a few tolerated me and hated the rest of the show. The one who came off best was the magician. All the press loved him for swallowing and then regurgitating a lot of razor blades on a string. He printed all his great notices (with my rotten ones included) for a throwaway to upgrade his club act. Some woman tripped over a dog in the theater and broke her leg or something, and sued Boomer as the producer. Charlie was down for the week from Toronto, and he didn't help much. He hated the show and everyone connected with it, and he also got it firmly fixed in his head that I was having an affair with a particularly repulsive Polish man named Wachtell, who was hanging around at the time. The man in question was the last person on earth I could ever imagine in this connection, but as Ma used to say, "When Charlie thinks he knows something, don't argue." Anyway, he was as cranky as could be all the time he was there.

That seemed like the end. I had flopped on Broadway and everyone all over the country knew it, so no one would have me again.

Since my career had taken a nose dive, Boomer suggested I try something new. *The Nellie Melba Story* had just been released, with Kathryn Grayson in the title role. She wanted to do a concert in Carnegie Hall, so I decided to handle the booking. There seemed to be no risk. If the public was interested, they would come; if not, the movie company would buy the house out. So I engaged Carnegie Hall and signed all the contracts for printing, etc., but no sooner had I done it than something happened that none of us had foreseen. Katherine Grayson canceled out. There I was with Carnegie Hall on my hands.

So I did the only thing left to do. I wrote another show (which became "Guide to Concert Audiences"), and presented by Boomer's friend Ed Oman, I went on myself. Carnegie Hall is a step up from Town Hall, and it sold out. Doubtless a lot of people came to see me fall flat on my face again, but I didn't. I was back in my own element, in a great big auditorium with a nice flood spot from the back of the hall, instead of a flea box with those ghastly bright lights that nearly blind me and prevent me from seeing a soul in the audience.

I know it's all against Stanislavski and the fourth wall, and that's why I am a terrible actress, but I hate not seeing the audience. Basically, I suppose, I am more the evangelist type. I love to harangue the mob, but to harangue them you have to be able to see them, and in an auditorium you can. I don't care if it seats ten thousand, it is far preferable to any theater, with those ghastly lights.

That fall the *New York Herald Tribune* sponsored the seventh annual Food Forum. This was a big advertising clambake, which ran for a week at the Plaza Hotel. Tuesday, it appeared, was to be given over to motivation research. In the morning there was to be a talk by Vance Packard, and in the afternoon talks by Drs. Dichter and Cheskin, all big experts and writers of books on the subject, but not exactly the most electrifying speakers in the world. Dudley Anderson and Yutsy, who were the PR for the Forum, felt that Tuesday was going to need a little pepping up, so they asked me if I would do a show that day. I felt that what I did was so out of the picture with advertising that it wouldn't be suitable, so I suggested writing something special for the occasion. Thereupon I was invited to a brainstorm session to find out the best thing for me to do.

Advertising people have fooling the public down to a real science, and their jargon is quite unbelievable. The room I was ushered into was yellow. There were yellow pads and yellow pencils in front of everyone at the table. Yellow, I was told, is the color of "ideation." In a brainstorm session everyone sits around and thinks up ideas, most of which are crazy, but now and again a good one comes, which you write down on your yellow pad. Then you have a debate on the written-down ideas, when *the* idea is supposed to emerge.

The Food Forum was sponsored that year by the United Fruit Company, which at that time was advertising bananas. The emblem was to be a big 88 (which is the amount of calories in a medium-size banana) with little bananas hanging from it. It appeared in posters on the walls of the Plaza, and on earrings for the women and tie clips for the men. So, after we had all brainstormed, it was decreed that I should write, after reading the books of Dr. Cheskin, Vance Packard, and Dr. Dichter, a practical banana promotion through every psychological level. I would be announced on the program as Dr. Russell, fresh from the London School of Economics, with a new slant on motivation research.

So duly on Tuesday I put on my lady-executive outfit and a very smart hat, and sallied forth to the Plaza. I heard the talks by the three men and was introduced around as Dr. Russell, the one with a new slant. Everyone thought I was for real and were looking forward to my talk, so I had to be very careful what I said, but I managed not to give myself away.

After being announced, I went up to the speakers' desk, put on glasses, and fiddled around with bits of paper, as the others had. The audience was sitting there with pencils poised, waiting to write down my pearls of wisdom. I launched into my talk, and you wouldn't believe how much nonsense I was able to get through before the penny dropped that it was a sendup! It wasn't until I mentioned the first advertising agency in the world, J. Walter Belshazzar, who invented the writing-on-the-wall technique—"You have been weighed in the balance and found wanting, and you are going to be made to want whatever they have made up their minds to sell you"—that it really got through.

The following week, as a little bonus, the United Fruit Company sent me a crate of bananas, five feet each way, and if you can give away, or otherwise get rid of that many bananas before they go bad and leak through the crate, you're a better man than I am, Gunga Din. I had a terrible time with them; they stank the place out and stained my carpet, and our super was furious when he had to get rid of the mess.

That fall the question came up of putting out a record of the *Hansel and Gretel* movie soundtrack. Columbia weren't about to do it, as they had just released *H and G* done by the Met. So RCA Victor came out with it on one of their pop labels. This time it was all right for me to be in it. Record companies are so mysterious.

Just before Christmas there was a concert at the Waldorf-Astoria, given by the contest winners of the Federated Women's Clubs of America. That year they hadn't enough winners to make a full evening, so I was engaged to do the *Nibelungen Ring* as a makeweight. I felt a bit strange when I saw right under my nose at the head table Mrs. August Belmont, founder of the Met Opera Guild. I wondered how she would take it. She loved it, and afterward she came backstage and said, "Dear, is that what really happens in the *Ring?*" When I told her it was, she said, "I've heard the cycle at least ten times, but after the first quarter of an hour of *Rheingold,* I give up trying to understand what it is about and let the music wash over me. But now I know, I wonder if I'll be able to sit through it again without laughing."

One day Boomer took me out to lunch with a lawyer, Mr. Myerson. In the middle of the meal he suddenly said, "I want you to arrange a divorce for Anna." I was speechless. Such a thing had never crossed my mind.

Charlie was being quite hopeless and uncooperative, but I thought it was only temporary. He had just done an eight-page art supplement in *The Lamp*, the magazine of Standard Oil of New Jersey, which had been most favorably received. Out of this had come a big commercial art job for J. Walter Thompson in New York, for a series of advertisements for Lever Brothers, and I really had hoped he'd come to New York and join me. He could have taken a sabbatical—he had one coming—but he wouldn't. Boomer was of course being realistic. He said if he won't come now when everything is going his way he will never come, so I would have to make up my mind either to go back and be a wife and forget my career, or get a divorce. I wasn't really needed at home, so Mr. Myerson and I went down to Dade County, Florida, and I got the divorce. When I told Charlie what I had done, he was furious and said it wasn't legal. Boomer said it was legal enough for me to apply for American citizenship as a divorced person, and when I had that it would wrap up the whole thing, which it did.

I wish Charlie had joined me. I'm sure he would have had a nicer life than he has. He lived in Toronto in a great big house all by himself for more than twenty years, which seems such a waste. We remained quite friendly and would visit each other from time to time. I think the trouble with all the men in my life has been that I appeal to the types that like to be big fishes in small puddles, whereas I prefer to be a small fish in a big one.

"Dad [holding Anna]
is just off to World War I."

Colonel Claude Russell-Brown

Anna's mother, Bea

Anna's parents on their wedding day

Uncle Bryer, Granny Tandy, Uncle Harry
at the farm in Unionville, Ontario

Anna at age 8

Anna's godmother,
"Aunt" Alice Schuyler

Anna about to be presented at the last court of King George V and Queen
Mary. Photo: Tunbridge, London

"My first N.Y. publicity photo. I was shapely, wasn't I? But I don't think much of the face." Photo: Bruno of Hollywood, New York City

Concert in Hobart, Tasmania, on Anna's first Australian tour

"Eastman Boomer, the great manager, turns up, and we are in business."

Cleveland Pops concert. Photo: Rebman Photo service, Cleveland

Albert Hall concert with accompanist Joseph Cooper. Photo: Dezo Hoffman, London

As the Witch in San Francisco Opera production of *Hänsel and Gretel*, conducted by Carmen Dragon. Photo: Lew Balon, San Francisco

Photos: Arthur Jacob

With Lotte Lehmann before concert for the Academy of the West

With Jack Cassidy in *Half in Ernest*. Photo: Burriss Associates, Bucks County, Pa.

On the *Dick Cavett Show,* March 1981

Deirdre's wedding, with (*left to right*) Deirdre's brother, George Hibbert; Deirdre; her husband, Fred Prussak; Anna's accompanist, Gene Rankin; and Anna

Anna's New York farewell concert at Carnegie Hall, April 15, 1984.
Photo: Robert Maass

With accompanist Frank Bartholomew and manager Arthur Shafman at
Carnegie Hall. Photo: Ed Kashi

On the street where she lives in Unionville, Ontario

CHAPTER 19

"I pledge allegiance . . ."

The new year brought another phase in my life. Boomer had arranged a season for me at the New Watergate Theatre in London, through Emmy Tillett of the Harold Holt Organization, and he was coming with me. It was my first trip back to England in fourteen years, and Boomer's first ever.

We sailed on the *Queen Elizabeth* in great style. Everyone came to see us off, there was a press conference on board, and we were photographed all over the ship, peeking through life preservers and going through all the usual capers that press photographers dream up. In the next cabin was an old friend of Boomer's, George Stinchfield, known as Stinkey, who ran a chain of barbershop boutiques in New England, and who seemed to know everyone on board. He turned out to be a great addition to the party. The trip was so festive that we were practically worn out by the time we got to England.

I was glad to arrive in Southampton. It felt so strange to get once again into the funny little railway carriage on the boat train, which seemed so much smaller than I had remembered, and to have the familiar cold meat and salad, heavily overloaded with beetroot, and tea, served on the heavy old British Railway china. I found it very nostalgic, but Boomer simply hated it and was almost ready to turn around and go back on the return trip immediately. It was raining, of course, and I had forgotten how dazzlingly green England can be. I had also forgotten how filthy London railway stations are. After the antiseptic and polished American ones, Liverpool Street looked incredibly down-at-heel, with its sooty old glass roof, the inevitable clock, and rows of old-fashioned ticket windows with their paint peeling.

We were staying at the Savoy and were warmly greeted by what looked like the same green-uniformed doorman who had been there in my youth.

When we got in we were surrounded by a bevy of frock-coated assistant managers who ushered and bowed us up to our suite. Then we went down to the Grill for dinner, where we were hovered over by numberless waiters and busboys, as is the custom. I thoroughly enjoyed it, because it brought back memories of Aunt Bena queening it around there when I was little, but it nearly drove Boomer mad.

"All this bowing and scraping wears me out," he said. "Every time I turn around there's someone fidgeting about behind me. I can't even pick up an ashtray for myself. Do they think I'm a cripple?" Up in the suite he said, "Look at that damn bath!" The tub was surrounded with old-fashioned but expensive purple marble and had an enormous tap out of which both hot and cold water deluged at once like Niagara Falls. The shower resembled an inverted tin soup plate.

"Well it works, that's all I care," I told him.

"Well it looks awful," he said, as he leaned against the towel rail, which was heated, of course—in fact, boiling, as they always are at the Savoy. He leaped about two feet in the air. "I can't stay here," he said. "They've even got the place booby-trapped!"

So we moved into an elegant private club, one of those heavily carpeted, highly polished, discreet Victorian places, where the service was so perfect it was invisible. It was full of moribund elderly gentlemen in armchairs, reading newspapers, who hardly moved a muscle between breakfast and bedtime. Boomer didn't like this much better and christened it the morgue. As I said, it was the first time he'd been abroad, and he was definitely not impressed with England.

The Watergate Theatre in London, where I was to play, was a theater club underneath the Strand, seating a hundred people, which seemed tiny after Carnegie Hall. Attached to the theater was a restaurant that served beautiful food, but permeated the whole place with a strong effluvium of garlic. It wasn't bad once you got used to the smell, but Boomer christened it "The Sewer with the Fringe on Top."

After rehearsing the show with my pianist, David Titbold, I went to my first British press conference. Astonishing! I'd had many press conferences in the States, and knew what to expect there. It was usually possible to spot U.S. newspapermen on sight; they all looked and sounded like Jimmy Cagney, and although they asked rude and rough questions, one could have a fair idea of what the questions were going to be. I never in a million years would have spotted the London reporters as press. There were elegantly tailored gentlemen with Anthony Eden homburgs, scruffy chaps with beards—rare in those days—little old ladies in shapeless sweaters, fashionable beauties, and nondescript men from the BBC. Every last one of them asked me how old I was, a thing they'd never ask in the States, probably because in that land of perpetual youth they know that they would never get the right answer. I told them, and told them correctly, as they gave me the feeling they would verify my statement anyway. The British press can ask some extremely curvy questions, in the most charming manner possible, which can easily catch you out if you don't keep your wits about you.

The opening night arrived. I was wearing a beautiful gown from I. Magnin's in San Francisco. It was a sheath of black lace over flesh-colored satin, with a big pouffe of tulle at the back of the skirt, making a little train. The first time I wore it in San Francisco, as I went on to take my final bow, Gene Rankin accidentally put his foot on the train. As I walked on, the whole thing pulled out, and there it was, stretching from my behind right offstage like a fence. It apparently looked very funny and got a big laugh, but it took ages to gather the tulle up again and sew it in place, so I told Gene in future to watch his big feet. It didn't happen again until that first night at the Watergate. I'd forgotten to tell David Titbold to mind his feet.

After the show a little American sailor came backstage. He had enjoyed the show, but what actually killed him, he said, was the last act.

"You mean the *Ring?*" I asked him.

"No, the last bit where your skirt stretches across the stage," he said.

"That wasn't an act," I told him. "That was an accident."

"The hell it was an accident," he said. "I saw you do it in San Francisco."

I found the London audiences quite different from the North American. They were very quick on the uptake, and had to tighten up my material considerably or they would get the point before I'd come to it. They would also pick up asides and little details that had never before been noticed, and there was no need whatever to belabor the punch line. It could have been that my British accent was more familiar there than in the States.

In addition, I had come to think of myself as a sophisticated performer and was inclined to gather an eccentric and rather "in" audience. People would say, "Yes I saw Anna Russell, but did you get a load of the audience? What a bunch of weirdos!" Here the audience was more Ma, Pa, and the kids. One old man of about eighty came backstage hobbling on two sticks. "Ee it wur looverley," he said. "A 'avn't seen noothing lak thut since Florrie Ford." She was a famous music hall artist during the reign of Edward VII. So there it was: I wasn't sophisticated at all. I was corny.

We got a wonderful press, and Boomer was trying to set up further bookings in England, without much success. Ian Hunter positively refused to have me at the Edinburgh Festival. There was a special for ITV and a few things for the BBC, but not much else, so we booked Festival Hall for a little while later, and went on a trip to Europe.

In Paris, where we had very foolishly neglected to book our accommodations in advance, we wound up in the middle of the motor show. There wasn't a room to be had, and it looked as if we were going to sleep in the station, when finally one of the big hotels relented and put us in a perfectly enormous attic with nothing in it except four huge brass beds and a bidet on wheels. Boomer amused himself by whizzing around the attic on the bidet at a terrific speed until requested by the management to desist.

From Paris we went to Rome, then Venice. From Venice we had tickets to fly back to London for the Festival Hall concert on a Wednesday. When we phoned about the limousine to the airport, we were told there was no plane that day—it went only on Mondays and Fridays. Since our flight had been confirmed, we were naturally very annoyed and, what's more, we had a deadline to make. The only possible way to get back was to drive to Milan, and there wasn't much time for that, either.

So we got a taxi and explained our predicament to the driver via an interpreter. I must say that what the Italians lack in efficiency they make up in goodwill. The taxi driver was a real sport. He was going to get us there in time no matter what happened, and it's a wonder nothing did. He didn't stop for anything—red lights, policemen blasting on whistles, cross traffic. It didn't matter which side of the road, round blind corners, with everyone honking and shouting at us. It was terrifying, but we just made it with nothing to spare.

When we got to London there was a newspaper strike, so the attendance at Festival Hall was very poor, and of course there were no reviews.

When we'd first arrived in London, someone had said that I had a great admirer in Arthur Benjamin, the composer. This I simply couldn't believe. He had taught me piano for one term at the Royal College, when my regular professor was sick. In those days he was a brilliant young man with a future and not much patience, who liked good students but hated the hopeless ones, like me, with a passion. I was struggling that entire term with Bach's Italian Concerto. I could play the first movement but not the last, and then after Herculean efforts on the last, I'd forgotten the first again, and so it went round and round and drove Arthur mad. An expression of agonized boredom would come over his face each time I appeared. He would stand by the window and look at his watch every two minutes, which made me paralytic with nerves, and would shoo me out on the dot after the allotted half hour. Even when I met him in the corridor, he would get a pained expression as if he couldn't bear even to look at me. So naturally his newfound admiration came as a very odd piece of news.

"Does he remember me?" I asked.

"Well," said his friend, "he thinks he once met you."

"You're darned tooting he's met me," I said.

"That is as may be," said his friend. "Anyway, he would be very pleased if you would dine with him at his house next week."

On the appointed day, off I went in a taxi, and there was Arthur on his front doorstep to welcome me. When he saw who it was, his expression changed to one of horror. "Claudia Russell-Brown! Oh, my God, not you again?" he said.

"I'm sorry, Arthur," I said humbly.

"Well in that case," he said, "there's got to be hope for everybody."

Talking over the old days, I reminded Arthur I had sung the beggar in his opera *The Devil Take Her* at the RCM. "And which movement of the Italian Concerto are you currently engaged upon?" he asked.

I saw a lot of him on that trip and thoroughly enjoyed him. He put me up for membership in the Musicians' Club at 14 North Audley Street, whereupon my first husband promptly resigned in protest!

That trip home was a bit sad. Everything was smaller and shabbier than I remembered.

On returning to New York, the first thing I had to do was to go to the Immigration Department to be quizzed on the contents of the citizenship book, which I'd been studying for the past few months. I'd memorized the presidents by fitting them into several verses of that old British folk song "Old Uncle Tom Cobley," which goes:

> *Tam Pierce, Tam Pierce, lend me thy grey mare*
> *All along, out along, down a long lea,*

for I want for to go to Widdicombe Fair
With Dan Brewer, Tom Stewer, Peter Gurney,
Peter Davey, Dan'l Widdon, Harry Hawk,
Old Uncle Tom Cobley and all.

It's very good for the presidents:

George Washington, George Washington,
lend me thy grey mare.
All along, out along . . .
I want for to go to Widdicombe Fair
With John Adams, Thomas Jefferson, James Madison,
James Monroe, John Quincy Adams, Andrew Jackson,
Old Martin Van Buren and all.

This was rather fun, and I put it into my program once or twice, along with the states and capitals, which went to another tune. The history, however, was very difficult. We had done the War of Independence at school, where we were the goodies and they were the baddies, but now it had to be learned in reverse.

I went to the Immigration Department rather quaking, certain I'd forgotten it all. The official came in, looked at me rather ominously, and said he hoped I'd studied the contents of the book. I told him indeed I had. "Very well then," he said, "here are the questions. Can you write?" So I wrote "Now is the time for every man to come to the aid of the party." "That's very good," he said. "Now, who was the first president of the United States?"

"George Washington," I said.

"Okay," he said, and stamped the paper.

"Is that all?" I was flabbergasted.

"Yes," he said, "but I had you rattled there, didn't I?"

Early the next year I was to be sworn in as an American; therefore, at nine o'clock one morning off I went to the Central Court of New York. It was very impressive. We all sat in pews, as in church, looking up at the flag and the judge's podium, while a little man chattered away to us about what to do and what to say, where to stand and where to sit, and the rest of it. After about half an hour of this, he suddenly said, "Is there a Miss Anna Russell here?" Oh, Lord, I thought, don't tell me I am on Red Channels. (This was round about Senator McCarthy's time.) I held up my hand

and the little man came round to where I was sitting in the back row and said, "I understand the presiding judge is a cousin of yours. He'd like to see you in his chambers after the ceremony." It was going to be Freddy! Frederick van Pelt Bryan was married to my cousin Denise Farquharson.

"Yes," I said, "he's my cousin."

All of a sudden the little woman sitting next to me piped up, "Vell, so the judge is the cousin?"

"Yes," I said.

"Vell, you ain't an American."

"Not yet," I said.

"So if the judge is the cousin 'e ain't an American neither."

"Yes he is," I said.

"It don't sound no good," she said.

She proceeded to make such an uproar about it, that it took the combined efforts of the little man and an attendant to shut her up, and even so, she muttered and mumbled all through the ceremony, thoroughly unconvinced. I'll bet she got sworn in again later just to be on the safe side.

Freddy was a handsome, leonine fellow with iron-gray hair and a mustache. He has a splendid, resonant voice with a somewhat British accent, probably picked up from Denise. He's a little pompous, but has a great sense of humor. If he talks to more than three people at once it tends to become a speech. On this occasion he made a great entrance in his black robes, but I am sure he would have preferred to be in scarlet with the full wig of a British judge. That would have knocked us all dead, but as it was, he was extremely effective. He harangued us on the solemnity of the occasion, how privileged we were to be forsaking all others, and generally whipped us into a state of euphoria. It was splendid, and I was now an American!

I went up to his chambers, walking on air, expecting him to say, "Here's a new American, congratulations and hurrah!" or something like that. But instead he said, "How did I do?"

I said, "You were a smash hit, you old ham!"

(By the way, he was the judge who permitted *Lady Chatterley's Lover* to appear in the States in the unexpurgated edition.)

Each summer during this period I did summer stock. This year I went to the Pennsylvania State Playhouse in New Hope and did my own show for Mike Ellis, who usually had a part for me in a play later in the season. It was generally an old aunt, or maid, or some other small character part, so I always agreed to do it sight unseen. This year he said he had a part in *The Children's Hour*. Being mostly a concert or operagoer, I am not very up on the theater, so I thought this part might be some sort of nanny or governess, and I agreed to do it.

When I told Boomer he seemed to think it was a big joke, but since he thought most things were a big joke, I didn't take much notice. But then I got funny reactions from a lot of other people when I mentioned *The Children's Hour*, so I thought I'd better hurry up and read it. I nearly had a fit! It was heavy drama, and I was to play Aunt Lilly, who starts all the nasty insinuations.

When anyone is seen purely as a comedian for any length of time, people are apt to laugh even before anything is said—it's a simple reflex action. If this happened in *The Children's Hour*, it would be a disaster. Besides, I had never played drama before. It was a terrifying prospect, but it had to be done, as the contract was signed.

The two leads in the play were Linda Darnell and Margaret Phillips. You never saw such an ill-assorted trio. The director was an avid fan of Linda's and concentrated entirely on her. She was a sweetie, but very Hollywood. Maggie Phillips was an extremely accomplished actress whom I found rather terrifying at first. But someone had to help me, so I decided to tell Maggie of my plight.

After I explained my difficulty, she said, "Well, actually, when I heard you were going to be in it I nearly cut my throat."

"If you'll tell me what to do," I told her, "I'll endeavor to do it and we might be able to avert disaster." Luckily, most of my scenes were with her. So we repaired to the cocktail bar and got properly stuck into the martinis while she explained what had to be done. She was a splendid teacher and I learned a lot, which stood me in very good stead later.

Since it was summer stock, and not really a matter of life and death, she suggested we play the scenes differently every night for practice. One time we'd hiss and spit, the next yell, or be coldly sarcastic, or whatever she had in mind. At the end of the week Mike Ellis said, "Funny, this play seems to come out differently every night." It went very well actually, and I got a good, if surprised, writeup in *Variety*.

I had to pay ever so great attention not to get laughs, though. It was a weird sensation, rather like wanting to throw up and knowing you can't. I could absolutely feel the laughs about to come and had to keep tight control to force them down. It was really quite exhausting.

When I got back to New York I moved into a new apartment with my friend Janet Hall, with whom I'd been living for the past two years in a much smaller apartment. For once I had the time and the money to decorate a place just as I wanted, and it turned out marvelous.

Auntie gave us a linen shower, and besides the linen she gave me a very smart black tulle cocktail hat with a pink velvet rose on the top. It wasn't very me; it was more the style of thing my friend Frances Yeende would wear, who was noted for her very modish, if way-out hats. I couldn't think why Auntie gave it to me at a linen shower, but it didn't look bad and I wore it quite a few times, including once to a cocktail party at her place. When she saw me she had hysterics. "That's not a hat," she told me, "it's a lavatory seat cover." I have to admit in all fairness, when it finally got where it belonged, it looked much better on the lavatory than it did on my head.

The orchestral scores of all the Christmas Box Concerts I had done with Sir Ernest MacMillan and the Toronto Symphony had been sent to New York at Mr. Judson's request, and I had quite a few orchestral concerts booked for that fall. I was a little apprehensive about the conductors, though. Sir Ernest was quite a comedian in his own right, but perhaps the more serious-minded ones would feel it rather *infra dig* to have to conduct for me. Nothing could have been further from the case; they were all delightful. In fact, it was the ones who had the most serious public image who were usually the most likely to get into the act.

For example, in the middle of a piano routine with the Indianapolis Symphony, Fabien Sevitsky, who had terrified me in the rehearsal by being so insistent on perfection, walked grandly onstage with a tiny Liberace candelabra, ablaze with birthday cake candles, placed it on the piano, and as grandly walked out again. It brought the house down.

In my rendition of Rossini's *La Danza,* where I shoot the conductor and conduct the last verse myself, various conductors have died some very showy deaths. At a children's concert with the New York Philharmonic, Wilfrid Pelletier took a nose dive into the cello section, disappeared, and didn't surface until half the orchestra got up to look for him. With the Philharmonia at the Albert Hall, Sir Malcolm Sargent keeled over with much grace, and when he got up for us to take a bow, he had a whacking great bloodstain on his bosom. Anything was likely to happen.

The boys in the orchestra would always enter into the spirit of it and we'd have a lovely time. There was one terrible occasion when I had a date with the St. Louis Symphony on Sunday afternoon and the Minneapolis

Symphony on Monday night. There was a cyclone in St. Louis just after the concert, and all the planes were grounded, so I had to go by train via Chicago. The earliest I could arrive in Minneapolis was five in the afternoon and, of course, I had all the orchestral scores. I was going to miss the morning rehearsal, so I couldn't work with the orchestra, and Gene Rankin had gone off somewhere where I couldn't reach him, so I had no pianist.

I duly arrived at five, and Antal Dorati, the conductor, whom luckily I had met before when he had conducted the Ballet Russe at Covent Garden, said he hadn't the least idea what was going to happen. They had rehearsed an overture for that evening, and that was it. The rest was up to me. The hall, which was enormous, was sold out. Well, someone produced a pianist, who luckily could read like a dream, as all my music is in manuscript, and we shot through one of my solo shows like a dose of salts, once through and that was it.

That evening the concert started with a spirited rendition of *La Gazza Ladra* overture by the orchestra, after which Maestro Dorati announced that since I had not turned up for the rehearsal that morning, that was the extent of his responsibility, whereupon he and the entire orchestra filed off the platform and sat in the orchestra pit right under my nose while I did a show I hadn't done for weeks all amongst a welter of instruments, chairs, and music stands. The strange pianist did a perfectly marvelous job, and what with that, and a lot of lighthearted heckling from the orchestra in the pit, it turned into a wonderful evening of banter and audience participation.

Gene and I had a very long tour ahead of us, right across the country and then on to Australia and New Zealand. There was the usual crop of adventures this time. At one point we had a flight booked over the Gulf of Mexico which we had to postpone at the last minute. It's lucky we did, because the plane disappeared without a trace. While we were in California we drove to Santa Barbara to see Lotte Lehmann. As a result of this visit, I established a scholarship at the Academy of the West for someone to study with Lotte, and she gave it to Grace Bumbry, the mezzo soprano.

Our next stop was Vancouver, where Hugh Pickett presented me every year. Hugh brought a tremendous number of artists to Vancouver, anyone from Rubinstein to Elvis Presley. He had a funny but wicked tongue, and a great gift of narrative. This time we were also playing Victoria, so we went over on the night ferry a couple of days early. During the trip he was telling me about one artist who insisted on being driven around in a Rolls-Royce. "Right," I told him. "Then you can also have a Rolls-Royce for me when we arrive."

"But the Empress Hotel is only about half a block from the quay," he said.

"I don't care," I told him. "If you do it for them you can do it for me. It's a question of status."

"All right," he said, "I'll wire ahead and have one meet you."

I was only joking, of course, and thought he was too, but not a bit of it. When we disembarked there it was, with a smart liveried chauffeur. I was tucked in with an elegant lap robe and waited for them to get in. "Not at all," said Hugh. "We're just the hoi polloi; we'll walk."

I arrived in state at the Empress Hotel, the doorman and the manager rushed out, and I was bowed into the lobby. It was the full Savoy Hotel bit, and I was beginning to think there was something in this status business after all.

In a few minutes Hugh, Len, his assistant, and Gene arrived, and Hugh started to carry on like Gatti-Casazza. I had become Madame Russell, the diva. Every time he spoke to me he'd give a slight bow. Gene was running around behaving like the traditional obseqious accompanist, which he definitely was not, and Len was directing the bellboys where to put everything. They'd obviously cooked this up on the walk to the hotel. Well, if they were going to do it, I was going to do it, so I started being gracious. We were being quite ridiculous, but it certainly was selling. The people in the lobby were gaping at us, obviously impressed, and every bellboy was running around doing our bidding.

Usually I have just a room when I'm on tour, but Hugh had booked a suite. It must have been the royal or presidential suite, because it was enormous and very elegant. We went in and shut the door and were having a good laugh when there was a knock. "Watch it," said Hugh, and we all went back into character. I was stretched languidly on the chaise longue, Len had opened his briefcase and was immersed in paper work, Gene was emerging from the bedroom with a mink stole to wrap around the diva, and Hugh opened the door like Jeeves. It was an enormous basket of fruit, compliments of the hotel. Moments later another knock: several bellboys with enormous vases of flowers. That is usually all, but not this time. Another knock: two waiters, one with an ice bucket and one with a magnum of champagne for Madame.

The concert wasn't till the next night, so the subject of eating came up, and I suggested we go down to the dining room. "Not on your Nelly," said Hugh. "It's going far too well for that." He called room service, and believe it or not the chef came up. "What would Madame fancy?"

"You are, of course, the genius in these matters," I told him graciously. "Why don't you consult with Mr. Pickett, my manager (flicking my hand at him disdainfully). He knows my preferences." So Hugh and the chef went into a long confabulation in the corner.

In due course a lot of waiters arrived with an enormous meal, all served up in great silver dishes. The Canadian Pacific and Canadian National hotels are great on silver. If you order a cup of tea and a bun, the table is covered with it, and in this case the table would have done justice to Henry VIII. The waiters wanted to stay and serve us, but Hugh said, "No, Madame prefers to be served by the management," so we all sat down and had a blowout.

The grandeur persisted for the rest of our stay, and the concert was sold out to overflowing. All that because of half a block's drive in a Rolls-Royce!

Our last date before leaving for Australia was three nights in War Memorial Opera House in San Francisco. This was when I met Sally Stanford, the famous madam. By this time she was married to an importer and antique dealer named Gump, who was very *comme il faut*, and she owned a restaurant, called Valhalla, in Sausalito.

During my performance, when I was doing the *Nibelungen Ring*, I mentioned that Valhalla had since moved to Sausalito, which brought the house down. On the third evening I got a message from Sally Stanford, thanking me for the ad and inviting our party to supper at Valhalla.

She was a charming woman, with an overwhelming personality, who greeted us with a large parrot perched on her shoulder. While we were having drinks, the parrot gave a floor show, hopping all over Miss Stanford and making the most extraordinary remarks. When she thought we'd had enough, she unbuttoned the front of her dress, stuffed the parrot in, and buttoned it up again. The bird apparently stayed there for the rest of the evening; at least I never saw her take it out.

It was a large party, and we had all been furnished with a dinner partner. We were still having champagne at 3:00 A.M., which surprised me, as closing time in San Francisco was midnight. I asked my dinner partner what would happen if we got caught.

You won't get caught," he said.

"How do you know?" I asked him. He put his thumb through the armhole of his waistcoat and inflated his chest, which had a star pinned on it.

"Because I'm the sheriff," he said.

CHAPTER 20

I discover Australia and the Russell relations

All my youth I had heard about Australia from the old great-aunts, and I used to spend hours in those days poring over their photograph albums. There were pictures of Great-grandfather's house in Collins Street, Melbourne, with all the aunts and Grandmother looking young and fetching in complicated Victorian dresses, playing croquet on the lawn and indulging in other suitably ladylike pastimes. There was one of Aunt Leila in a ballroom full of tremendous crystal chandeliers, shaking hands with the Prince of Wales, later Edward VII; pictures of race meetings with everyone dressed up to beat the band; even a photo of Aunt Leila with a Mrs. Armstrong, who later became the famous Nellie Melba. The Russells appeared to have lived a most luxurious life in Australia.

We flew into Sydney over the famous harbor and bridge; the extraordinary Opera House had not yet been started. Spread out below us for miles were little red-roofed houses, like the ones you see in England.

We were met at the plane by Mr. Lamb, the concert manager; Bill James, the Head of Music; and Charles Moses, the general manager, all three very charming and affable men of the Australian Broadcasting Commission. They took us immediately into a tin hut for a press conference. (This was before the days of elegant airports.)

The ABC looked after their visiting artists in a truly magnificent manner. During the fortnight until the tour was to start, our days were filled with publicity and sightseeing and our evenings with dinners, concerts, and plays. We visited the wineries and were photographed sampling the produce, which is of a very high quality. We marveled at all the sights: the gum trees, the fantastic cloud formations and sunsets, the completely different lot of stars at night, the beaches with their tremendous breakers, and of course the nearly continuous sunshine.

The opening concert was at the Sydney Town Hall. The audience was wonderful, and we had a truly riotous evening. After my performance, I was surprised to have a lot of flowers handed up to me while I was still on stage. This had rather gone out in the States; if I received any, they were sent to the dressing room. The old-fashioned way is much nicer.

There was a tremendous basket of flowers from the ABC, various normal-size bouquets, and one that was so huge I could scarcely get my arms around it. It was from my friend Bunny Musgrove in the Australian consulate in New York, and was like a shock of wheat in size—all roses from about three feet long down to miniature ones. She had gone into our favorite restaurants and bars, collected a quarter from my every friend and acquaintance, and made them sign a card. There were, in fact, ninety-six signatures. She had obviously forgotten that roses, which can cost up to two dollars a bloom in New York, were by no means that expensive in Australia, hence the extraordinary bouquet.

After the concert I was taken upstairs, sat at a table, and armed with a pen, while dozens of people filed past for autographs, after which the concert manager and various people detailed to look after my well-being (this was something quite new—it usually fell to Gene to do this) put me into the limousine with the basket of flowers and the light on, and instructed me to throw the flowers out to the people congregated on the sidewalk to wave me off. I'm sure the great-aunts would have been proud of me.

When we went on the road we found the accommodations in the small towns very primitive. Nowadays there are comfortable motels everywhere, but then one usually had to stay in a pub. They had to have rooms by law, or they couldn't get a license, but these were more or less token rooms, and people seldom actually stayed in them. If you were lucky there might be linoleum on the floor. There would be a brass bed with a lumpy or saggy mattress, a straight-backed chair, a naked light bulb in the middle of the ceiling, a hook on the back of the door, or maybe even a coat rack to hang your clothes on, and that would be it. The bathroom would be on another floor or out back, if indeed you could find it at all, and the uproar from the bar beneath had to be heard to be believed. I remember that in one of these rooms there was actually a built-in wardrobe. Naturally there were no hooks or a coat rack. On opening the wardrobe I found it hadn't a rod, a shelf, or a hook; so short of dumping my clothes on the floor of the wardrobe, there wasn't a place to put anything. I therefore went down to my host, borrowed a hammer and some tintacks, and tacked everything to the wall. One had to be very flexible on these occasions.

In one place the Town Hall was being altered and had not been finished in time for the concert. It was a freezing cold night, and there was no back to the stage—just a tarpaulin between us and the elements. The seating part was full of metal scaffolding, which I had to peek through to see the audience, who were sitting in their greatcoats with rugs over their knees. Before the first number was over I was purple with cold in my décolleté gown, so I said, "Now you've seen it," and put on a football jersey that Gene had acquired, which was far too big, and which had red and yellow horizontal stripes that contrasted oddly with my beautiful cyclamen lace gown sewn with brilliants. I then had a good swing on the scaffolding to restore my circulation sufficiently to continue. Despite these measures I got a horrible cold.

The next concert was a Saturday matinee in Sydney, which I was afraid might have to be canceled, as I could only whisper. The ear, nose, and throat specialist said it was a bad case of laryngitis, but that I should come back the next morning and it would be perfectly all right. In the morning I was still speechless, so he got a hypodermic of something, and blithely saying, "This will do the trick," plunged it in. I should think it did the trick! Vavoom! I nearly shot through the roof. My voice snapped back and had, in fact, more ping to it than usual. The concert went like a charm that afternoon, after which we went to a party where I went roaring around all night, and it took Gene's best efforts to get me to go to bed at four in the morning, and then I didn't sleep. All Sunday we were out and about, and I felt splendid. The doctor had said there might be a slight recurrence of the cold, and armed me with a phial, with instructions to call a doctor at the next port of call. By Monday the cold was slightly back again, so I popped into bed and phoned a doctor. When he came I gave him the phial. He took one look at it and collapsed with laughter. "Don't tell me you got all this?" he asked.

"Yes indeed I did," I told him.

"And what happened?"

"I nearly shot through the roof."

"I should think so!"

I asked what it was, and he told me a stimulant.

"What does it stimulate?" I wondered.

"Everything," he said. "I never thought of the vocal cords before, but I suppose it stimulates them, too."

It was Benzedrine in camphor, the sort of thing given to people bleeding to death from terrible accidents, or who are otherwise in the last stages. He didn't think I was sufficiently in the last stages for another go, so he pocketed the phial and prepared to administer penicillin. When he looked in his bag, he found he had forgotten his alcohol, so he asked if I had any perfume. I hadn't, but there was whisky, which was apparently all right, so he turned me over, put a good slosh of it on the appropriate spot, and gave me the injection.

After he left, Gene came in rather nervously, wondering if there was going to be a repetition of the weekend, had a good sniff, and said suspiciously, "You've been drinking." I hadn't done badly at that over the weekend, either!

"I have not," I said.

"Yes you have. I can smell it," he said, unconvinced.

"Yes, and I bet you can't guess where it is," I said. That, then, was the end of the laryngitis.

After we had finished in New South Wales we were handed over to Victoria, to start in Melbourne, staying in Menzies Hotel. Although I'd never been to Melbourne before, when I went into the main dining room that evening, there was something very familiar about it. It was all white and gold, with many exquisite crystal chandeliers hanging from the ceiling and sconces on the walls. I couldn't have seen the room before, yet it was familiar. I was mystified—not being the least psychic, or having ever experienced déjà vu—so I asked the maitre d'. He said it was a very old hotel, and the dining room had once been a ballroom. That was it! The picutre I had so often seen of Aunt Leila shaking hands with the Prince of Wales had been taken in this very room!

I mentioned this at the press conference the next morning, for want of something to say, and it created quite a lot of interest. Mr. Selleck, the Lord Mayor of Melbourne, had done some research on the Russell family and Great-grandfather when he was Mayor, and he made me photostats of his writing in the civic books. I was taken to see where his house in Collins Street had once stood, and to the Melbourne Club, which he had helped to found. In fact, it was beginning to seem like "Hometown Girl Makes Good." I had developed a root! I had an ancestor!

While I was in Melbourne, Pat Jarrett, the women's editor of the *Melbourne Sun* told me that I was to have a column in the paper twice a week. It would be ghostwritten, but would come out under my by-line. The *Sun* apparently had an arrangement with the ABC that all visiting artists did this, but I flatly refused. It was all right for artists like Isaac Stern or Artur Rubinstein, since they didn't talk in their performances, but I talked all the time, and I'd be hanged if I was going to have a lot of other nonsense, written by someone else, coming out with my name on it. This created somewhat of an impasse until Pat asked me if I was willing to do the writing myself. I agreed.

The upshot was that I had to join a guild and become a *Sun* writer, at a salary of thirty pounds a week. Anna Russell a newspaper woman!

I wired to Boomer, "Guess what? I am a newspaper writer for the *Melbourne Sun*?" He wired back, "Guess what? I have closed the deal with the publisher for your forthcoming book." What forthcoming book?

The column turned out very well. Among my other duties, I had to go to other people's press conferences, with my little notebook and my photographer. I got a great kick out of asking them all the questions I'd been asked for years.

The funniest press conference was the one for the Barbirollis. Evelyn had been in my year at the Royal College of Music, when she was still Evelyn Rothwell, first oboe of the London Symphony Orchestra, long before she met John, but I'd never seen her since. When she saw me with my pad and photographer, she said, "Claudia, what on earth are you doing here?" Charles Moses, who was with them, looked rather startled, not of course knowing who Claudia was. "Claudia," she went on, "I never knew you'd become a writer. What happened?" and we went gabbling on, with everyone looking at us as if we'd taken leave of our senses.

Charles said, "You see, she's the one before you."

"What?" said Evelyn, vaguely.

"Anna Russell is the artist before you on our series," he said.

"Anna Russell—oh, yes," said Evelyn. "I've got some of her records. Is she here? Do you know her, Claudia?" By this time everyone was certain we were crazy.

"Oh, yes, she's here," I said, just to add to the confusion.

Finally Charles said, "That is Anna Russell, her, the one you are talking to right now."

Evelyn was astounded. "I know you, but I didn't know it was you," she said, "and if it's you, why should you interview us?"

"I don't understand this cross-talk," said Charles. "I think we'd better get on with the press conference."

Every time I had a concert, the ABC would broadcast six minutes of it, so for the first one in Melbourne, we decided on a section of the *Ring*.

There are no wings in the Melbourne Town Hall—I entered center stage through a little passage—so no one could see me performing from backstage. In the middle of the *Ring,* which was going very well indeed, some poor woman sitting on the aisle was laughing so hard that she choked, went purple in the face, and started to pass out. I felt very sorry for the poor woman, but everyone was laughing so hard that this sent them into complete hysterics. I dried up, and we all sat and laughed for six minutes. I know, because we had just gone to air when this happened, and all that went over were shrieks of mirth, and not a sound from me.

The next concert was in a country town, and they were going to broadcast the *first* six minutes so there would be no repetition of the fiasco. I walked on, took the first deep breath to launch the opening remark, saw what was before me, did a frightful doubletake, and dried up again. The entire audience was priests. There were gleaming dog collars as far as the eye could see. Of course, you know what happened. Seeing my discomfiture, the audience broke up again, and the same thing happened as before. I think they might have warned me that we were playing in a Roman Catholic seminary.

Gene was having a wonderful time. He had gone on an art kick and bought himself a Dobell and a Russell Drysdale, two top Australian painters, and a lot of aboriginal carvings that weighed a ton. He'd done a few piano recitals for the ABC, met a lot of people on his own hook, and was visiting all over the place on his days off and loving it.

On most tours no one would invite me anywhere without Gene, and vice versa, so after a bit there was nothing for us to talk about. In the United States we used to spend a lot of time gazing into space. Mind you, Gene was a darling, and a very nice person to be vacant with, but in Australia, when we each went our separate ways, we had a much more lively time.

One of the Melbourne concerts was a command performance for the governor of Victoria, Sir Dallas Brookes. Everyone was to stand while he entered and the Queen was played, he would sit in a roped-off space in the Town Hall, and in the intermission come to the green room, where champagne was waiting and I would make my curtsy and polite conversation. I asked someone beforehand if Sir Dallas had ever been in the Royal Marines, but no one could tell me.

The great moment came, and after the formalities I asked him if the name Christopher Brown meant anything to him. "By Jove, it does," he said. "Old Kit Brown and I went through the Royal Marines together. The old warrior was one of my very best friends. How do you know him?"

"My uncle," I said. He looked at me hard, and the penny dropped.

"By Jove, if it isn't good old Corkie!" Corkie was my uncle's version of Claudia.

I had met Sir Dallas when he was Major Brooks and I was about twelve and spending the holidays in Yateley with Tikka Gran. He and Uncle Kit, who was a bachelor and living at home, used to breed setters and pointers. The place was swarming with dogs—eight grown ones and puppies everywhere. My job was to run the eight dogs twice a day down to the paddock and back. It was quite a coincidence that the governor of Victoria was attending the concert of his former dog runner on the other side of the world.

The intermission was all too short to catch up on everything, so Sir Dallas invited me to brunch at Government House the following Sunday. Everyone in the hotel was very impressed when the gubernatorial car called for me at nine-thirty in the morning; they wondered, no doubt, what could be going on there at that time of day. I was shown around in the approved style, then Sir Dallas told everyone to go, and he, Lady Brookes, and I went into the kitchen, cooked ourselves a lovely breakfast, and had a good chatter about the old times in Yateley.

While I was in Australia I also met Dame Sybil Thorndike, who is without a doubt one of the world's most fascinating people. She and her husband, Sir Lewis Casson, came to one of the concerts and invited us to spend the day at the house of their son, John Casson, in Toorak. John was then managing director of J. C. Williamson Theatres, the biggest theater chain in the world at that time. We had a riotous time and laughed so much I was a wreck. We discovered, among other things, that John's mother-in-law lived in—you guessed it—Yateley, and was a friend of my aunt Jessie.

I don't know what it is about Yateley—it's all-pervading like garlic. Years later I was staying on a property in Queensland, when the son of the house brought back a fellow he'd just met in a pub—from Yateley. I get the feeling that, were I to live on Mars, my next door neighbor would be from Yateley, yet it's a village of only a couple of thousand inhabitants. Very odd.

After stops in Tasmania, Perth, and South Australia, we returned to Melbourne, where I was to do a benefit for one of the hospitals with the Melbourne Symphony. Melbourne was about to host the Olympic games, so the bartender at Menzies Hotel had invented an Olympic cocktail and I was to christen it. The drink consisted of orange juice, lemon juice, the yolk of an egg, maraschino, Pernod, and iced Cointreau. I had caught a dreadful cold, but never mind. At ten o'clock that morning, I descended in the lift to the ground floor, where I was met by a piper and piped into the bar, where the press and various dignitaries were gathered. On the bar were rows of wine glasses containing what looked like something to make an omelette out of.

After various speeches, we all swigged one down. It tasted like a drink you'd give your Aunt Minnie when she comes to town to live it up. It was sweet, slightly perfumy, and I would have said quite innocuous. Suddenly my bagpipes were sent for, and I had to drink another toast clutching my pipes and linking arms with the other piper. We did this two or three times and consumed a couple more cocktails, but they had no effect at all.

After this I had a radio interview sponsored by Noon Pies, who had recently been in trouble with the authorities because of rats' tails in the meat. The interviewer, who was at the party, suggested I wrap up well, as it was very cold outside. As soon as we got out of the door, the cold and the Olympic cocktail hit us simultaneously—it was one of those delayed-action drinks. We reeled over to the studio and sat on either side of a table. There at my right hand was a box containing the commercials. "I thigk," I said, "with by cold, I cad do a better job od Dood Pies thad you cad."

"Be my guest," he said. I can't remember exactly the words, but there was lot about what "Dood Pies do for the Idder Bad." The program was a complete shambles, and the sponsor complained about me to the ABC.

Immediately after, I was to go to the hospital to donate a pint of blood. I was still up to the gills with the Olympic cocktail, and my cold was getting worse. I was laid out in a Porsche, which had just made its appearance in Australia. I say laid out, because sports cars always make me feel as if I were in a coffin. I was taken to the hospital and laid out again. On one side I had a needle stuck in my arm, draining away my life's blood, when suddenly from the other side an ABC interviewer sprang up with a microphone and said, "Miss Russell, do you think that whoever gets your pint of blood will become a comedienne?"

"Doe, I don't thigk so," I said. "They'll doe doubt get dubodia ad alcoholisub." It wouldn't have mattered, except that this was going out live over the network. It was a rather disastrous morning, but how was I to know the Olympic cocktail was loaded?

You see, I'm accident-prone. In the days before I hit on the idea of becoming a comedienne, exactly the same sort of humiliating things happened, and people would look embarrassed and try to cover up for me or pretend not to notice. But now they know all is for laughs, so when these disasters occur, there is no embarrassment. They just think I'm a bit dottier than usual.

CHAPTER 21

I visit New Zealand and find the perfect martini

As they are so frequently mentioned together, we expected New Zealand to be just like Australia, but it wasn't at all.

We arrived in Auckland late at night and went straight to the Grand Hotel, the most old-fashioned place you ever saw. At seven in the morning, my bedroom door was flung open, no knock or anything, and a large woman in cap and apron with starched cuffs, looking for all the world like a hospital matron, bounded in with a pot of tea and about a dozen slices of bread and butter. I presumed this was breakfast, so I ate it all, as it was delicious, turned over and went to sleep again. At a quarter past eight the desk called and asked if I was going down for breakfast. I said, "Haven't I had it?" No. Apparently all that bread and butter was morning tea, so I went down and joined Gene in the dining room.

Every meal was announced by great bashings on a brass gong suspended between two elephant tusks and situated in the dining room under a huge picture of a rather old-fashioned looking nude, called the Oracle of Delphi, which was a strange contrast to the utilitarian appearance of the hospital nurse waiting on table.

The menu was enormous and had everything on it, including soup, which I'd never heard of for breakfast before. People all around us were shoveling it in, but I couldn't manage much after the mammoth plate of bread and butter, much to the disapproval of our nurse.

After breakfast the New Zealand Broadcasting concert manager took us to a reception the Lord Mayor was giving for us. They were very keen on mayors' receptions in New Zealand; there was one every place we went. It was eleven o'clock and there was another great spread, only this time it was sandwiches, scones, cream buns, cakes, and Pavlovas, which are concoctions of meringue, cream, and fruit, and are terribly rich. I've never heard of them anywhere else but in Australia and New Zealand. I don't know whether they were invented or eaten by the famous ballerina, but I wouldn't fancy the chances of dancing *Swan Lake* on a diet of these. I didn't feel like eating a thing at the reception, but was urged to have a little for politeness sake, after which we went back to the hotel and sat in the lounge.

All of a sudden the elephant-tusk gong shattered the refined atmosphere, and everyone leaped up and rushed for the dining room, as if they hadn't eaten for a week. I couldn't manage a thing except Creme Soubise. This was soup, and we had it every day. No matter whether it was brown, orange, or beige, on the menu it was always Creme Soubise. Everyone but us was having soup, fish, meat, dessert, savory, cheese, fruit, and after-dinner mints, and our waitress was not pleased with us. Coffee was served in the lounge afterward. After lunch I went for a brisk walk to exercise off all the food, and got back just as the tea gong blared out for sandwiches, scones, cream buns, cake, etc. It was hopeless, so I fled to my room. At six the gong reverberated again, and immediately I could hear footsteps running past my door and down the stairs, but I was going to give it a miss. I wasn't allowed to, though. After they'd called me three times from the desk, more in sorrow than in anger, I hadn't the nerve not to go down. The dinner menu was colossal, and I don't think anyone missed a course except us. After dinner I went to bed stuffed to the gills, and was awakened at nine o'clock to be told it was time for supper. In spite of the disapproval, I declined. Gene told me later that supper had been cold beef, cold lamb, chicken, salad, cream buns, iced cakes, etc., etc.

New Zealanders are strong, sturdy people, and no wonder. I am a large woman, but I didn't feel so large in New Zealand.

We stayed in some very strange hotels, for the most part great big early Victorian structures, with spires, tower rooms, stained glass windows, all very cold and gloomy in the Charles Addams tradition. It would have been quite in keeping should Herman Munster have appeared to serve the drinks. I counted sixteen dried flower arrangements in the hotel lounge at Invercargel, which was so vast and high that the ceiling was lost in the gloom.

Gene and I always liked to have a dry martini before dinner on the nights we weren't working, so we'd order them hopefully, to find that either the bartender had never heard of them, or if he had, would turn out the strangest concoctions. Eventually we kept ordering them more for the fun of seeing what would appear than anything else. There was a bar attached to this great lounge in Invercargel, and we were laughing about what we would probably get. To our amazement, the bartender got two glasses of the correct shape, suitably frosted, out of the refrigerator, and proceeded to make about the best and strongest martini I have ever tasted. We expressed our amazement and delight and asked how he had become so expert. Apparently when the Queen Mum came out, word was put around that she liked her martini, and liked it right. This fellow, who was a medical student, was the only one to be found with the necessary qualifications, so he was hired as special bartender during her stay. He liked the extra money, as medical students are always broke, so he had stayed on ever since. The Queen Mum, by the way, likes her martini twelve to one.

When we finally returned to Auckland after our tour we decided to throw a farewell cocktail party at the Grand Hotel for all the people who had been so good to us. The food looked very nice, and Gene took the bartender aside with the Fleischmann's gin and showed him how to make martinis. All went well until halfway through the party, when someone asked Gene whether he thought the martinis were starting to look rather strange; they were dark brown. We discovered that the bartender, having run out of Fleischmann's gin, had started to make them out of Fleischmann's whisky. After all, he said when asked about it, the name on the bottle was the same, and it was all the same to him if a lot of crazy foreigners wanted him to make a lot of crazy drinks. The party went on unabated into the wee small hours, brown martinis or not.

On the way back home we stayed a few days in Fiji, then went on to Honolulu for two concerts. It was at the first concert in Hawaii that a curious thing happened. I started with two tried and true jokes that so far had never missed, but this time they did. The timing was off, and then I suddenly realized that we were back in the States. In England it had been necessary to tighten up my material, which was also true for Australia and New Zealand. Now that I was back at home, it was necessary to put back the *Luftpause* before the punch line, after which it was all right again.

Timing is a strange thing. It's a sort of instinct or feel for riding along on the audience reaction, like verbal waterskiing. If you can't find the right pace, it won't work.

CHAPTER 22

"The Power of Being a Positive Stinker"

W hen we got back to New York I learned that the wire Boomer had sent me in Australia was true: I had a deal with Citadel Press to write a book. I hadn't a clue what to write about, and it seemed quite a tall order. It's one thing to write a column, but a book? Browsing around book stores in search of ideas, I noticed that picture books were very popular and looked as if they would be quite simple to produce. Uplift books were very much the thing, too. *The Power of Positive Thinking* had just come out, and there were all sorts of books like *How to Be Gorgeous After Forty, How to Win Friends, How to Be Marvelous or Sexy or Brilliant or Whatever with the Least Possible Trouble.* Just for a gag, we postulated that perhaps some people were fed up with being so positive and would prefer to be negative; thus *The Power of Being a Positive Stinker* took shape, the idea being that if you were to follow my directions, you'd wind up in jail. I was to write it, and Arthur Jacob, my friend from the Osborne days, was to take the pictures.

Getting the book together turned out to be far more of an epic than the book itself. To begin with, it was almost impossible ever to find Arthur. He always had dozens of projects going at the same time and was the world's worst procrastinator. I had spies all over New York keeping tabs on him, and spent a lot of time dragging him out of all kinds of strange places back to the studio, where he'd take a few pictures, run out of film, go tearing off to get some more, and disappear again, when I'd start my sleuthing all over again. It was like trying to hang onto quicksilver, and very exhausting, particularly as we had a deadline to make.

We came to the final day, and the book was all finished, except for the last two photos, a full face and a side face with a number under like the ones they take when you go to jail. That morning word came through my grape-vine that Arthur was being dispossessed, and the marshals were at his apartment. It would be a disaster if his photographic equipment were impounded, so Bob Grimaldi, a big, powerful friend of mine, offered to go up the back stairs, collect the equipment, and take it down to the basement where a girlfriend of Arthur's lived. She was a little prone to the bottle, but luckily it was early enough in the morning for what we said to penetrate. While Bob and the girlfriend were salvaging the stuff down the back stairs, I went round to the front to try to head off the marshals.

Arthur was not to be found, as usual, and they were standing on the front steps, so far unable to gain admittance. I chatted with them a while and suggested a few places in the vicinity where they might look for Arthur, where I was sure he wouldn't be, which gave Bob and me a little more time. We got everything out except the lights when Arthur appeared, sauntering down the street. He would! The one and only time he should have stayed away!

The marshals impounded the lights and locked up the studio. We now had Arthur, the cameras, no lights and no studio, so I went over to the Rehearsal Club and was able to borrow someone's boyfriend who was a prizefighter and had a car. By now it was pouring with rain. The prizefighter packed Arthur, the girlfriend, her grog, and the equipment in his car and drove them up to my place, promising not on any account to let them out of his sight. Grimaldi managed to borrow some lights from the photographic store around the corner, as the girl who worked there had a great crush on him, and we ran with them through the deluge and joined the others at my apartment. We moved the beds, so as to have a plain background, and set up the cameras, considerably hampered by the girlfriend and Arthur, who had by now joined her on the grog. All of a sudden there was a ring at the front door. It was my cousin David Farquharson, who had arrived that very minute from England. I said inhospitably, "For heaven's sake go away for a few hours, you can't come in." I knew the sight of a fresh face would ruin what was left of Arthur's concentration, not great at any time. David looked rather startled.

"What's going on in there anyway?" he asked. "Are you having an orgy?"

"No," I said, "I run a lunatic asylum," and slammed the door in his face.

The last two photos were finally taken. My hair was soaking wet, but for a prison photo it didn't really matter. The prizefighter had turned out to have all sorts of abilities, and had taken complete control of the whole ridiculous situation. It was he who removed the last two plates from the camera, as he considered Arthur was a bit past it by that time, and leaving Arthur, the girlfriend, the grog, Grimaldi to keep an eye on things, and Cousin David pacing around in the passage outside wondering what was going on, he drove me through the ghastly storm at breakneck speed to the publishers and got the last two photos in three minutes before the deadline.

Arthur immediately vanished for about a month, and if I hadn't finally done another sleuthing job on him to get him to remove his cameras and other equipment from my place, they would probably be in my possession to this day. The last time I saw him he was living in a warehouse loft over a Horn and Hardart, in what looked like the height of discomfort, but happy as a clam.

The book duly came out and was quite a success. It was one of those you could read over the drugstore counter in twenty minutes, but it had a record in the back, so if you wanted to hear the record you had to buy the book. A very good gimmick and probably Boomer's idea.

It is curious how some people are photogenic and some are not. I definitely am not. In fact Mr. Goldberg, the *New York Times* critic, remarked in one of his reviews that I had a face like a collapsible camp chair, which I guess about describes it. In the early days I tried all the photographers, but I came out looking either like a vapid hunk of lard, or manic and ready for the psycho ward, according to the amount of retouching. Once I even went to Ottawa to be taken by Karsh, at enormous expense. The results were just as frightful as anyone else's. It was very wounding to the ego.

When I found that even Karsh couldn't do me, every time a photographer came near me I'd purposely put on some zany expression, and this has worked very well over the years. Friends often ask why I allow myself to be photographed like that, but I tell them I don't allow it—it just comes out that way, and I'm used to it by now. In fact, sometimes it works to my advantage when I'm going to a new place. After being heralded by a lot of crazy pictures, I have often been greeted by my sponsor with remarks like, "You look much better than we thought you would. Why don't you have photos like you really look?" Which is very good for the ego.

The first Johannesburg Music Festival was coming up, and Boomer was going with me to South Africa via London. Boomer had been trying to negotiate a tour of the British Isles through Wilfred van Wyck but was getting nowhere fast. There didn't seem to be much communication between them—a case of speaking the same language but not meaning the same thing.

For example, Boomer would say, "I don't know what the hell he's talking about. He writes two pages about the weather, the London scene, and enquiries after my health, and he mentions business in the last paragraph as if it were an afterthought."

Subsequently I had a letter from Wilfred, who was an old friend. He said, "What's the matter with Boomer? He writes when he wants the tour, how much, yours faithfully. Hasn't he got any manners?" I told Wilfred to write back in the same style. He said he'd try, but he felt it was very rude. A bit later Boomer mentioned he'd at last had a letter from Wilfred that he understood, and we might be going to do business.

"So when you answer," I suggested, "tell him what the weather's like, ask him how he is, and throw in a little schmaltz." Boomer thought it was ridiculous but did so, and when I next saw Wilfred, he said he hadn't liked the sound of Boomer at first, but now he found him a very likable chap.

We made full use of our short time in London, arranging bookings for later concerts. I was at last going to go to the Edinburgh Festival, the first comedian ever to be actually in the festival, as against "On the Fringe," as it was called. I gathered that a lot of people in the music scene felt that because of this the whole festival would shortly go to pot, but no matter.

We felt I must also appear in London at that period, so Boomer went off to book Festival Hall again. He came back enraged. Apparently it was too far in advance, they had to save so many dates for the BBC and various other bodies, and he was gently reminded that I had done very poor business at my first Festival Hall. He reminded them right back that there had been a long newspaper strike, but they were definitely not enthusiastic to have me there again and suggested I try the Wigmore Hall, which is a lot smaller and would be easier to fill.

Boomer fulminated at some length about all this and came to the conclusion that it was better not to show at all than to show in a much smaller place. With him it was onward or nothing. Then I suddenly had an idea.

"Why," I said, "don't we take the Albert Hall?" The Albert Hall! What an idea! Of course it was ridiculous, it holds nine thousand, but still . . . and we began to hypnotize ourselves. That was where I'd seen the world's greatest artists in my youth . . . that was *the* place in the old days . . . it had status . . . we could pull all the curtains on the boxes and just play to the stalls. We had a bottle of champagne and made up our minds. We would book the Albert Hall! Excelsior!

Mr. Hopper, the manager, was a sweetie, very jovial, with a lovely north country accent. Boomer asked if we could book the hall a year from September 15. Mr. Hopper looked in his book, found the date was free, and asked what we wanted it for. Boomer didn't want to tell him right then, as he was still rather smarting from yesterday's encounter, and we weren't feeling quite so exalted about it as we had been the night before. This didn't seem to worry Mr. Hopper at all.

"All I need to know," he said, "is that it is not against the Constitution, antireligious, or pornographic." We assured him it was none of these, so He got out the contract and we signed it. It was the same price as Festival Hall. While Boomer was signing his bit, Mr. Hopper looked at him speculatively and whispered to me, "Is it going to be a prizefight?" I nearly collapsed. So that was how Boomer appeared to an Englishman—a fight manager! Well, in a sense he wasn't too far off.

Since Wilfred van Wyck was taking care of the Edinburgh Festival, he would be the logical one to manage the Albert Hall concert, so off we went to see him. When he heard what we'd done he nearly had a fit. He said the only type of thing that went in there now were the Prom Concerts, *Messiahs*, and big spectacles. Very few solo artists played there anymore. He wouldn't consider managing it on a percentage basis, as he didn't think we had a hope of getting a house. He huffed and puffed, which he often did when disturbed, and finally agreed to take care of it for 240 pounds flat, but took a very dim view of the whole proceeding. This was a bit discouraging, but never mind; it was a long way in the future.

Shortly after that we packed up and went to South Africa. Gene wasn't with me, so I was to have a Johannesburg pianist, José Rodriguez-Lopez. My goodness, I love Spaniards. Not that I'd ever been to Spain or met any, other than the meat chef in our cafeteria on Sixth Avenue when I was at the Rehearsal Club. He was tall, slim, aquiline, serious-looking, and utterly gorgeous. We would gaze into each other's eyes over the counter while he made me a corned beef on rye. The kids used to think I was nuts, but I'd get about half a pound of corned beef in my sandwich for ten cents, which is a help when you're broke, as I was in those days. And, after all, you can dream, can't you? So naturally I couldn't wait to meet José Rodriguez-Lopez. A matador type maybe. Bound to be tall, dark, and handsome. Perhaps he'd look like the meat chef! Olé!

José Rodriguez-Lopez turned out to be a small, plump Dutchman (apparently the Spaniards overcame the Dutch at some point in history, and left a lot of their names in Holland), a very serious little man and a fine musician, and he played wonderfully for me, but he was no matador. So much for my overactive imagination.

We stayed at the Carlton Hotel, together with Sir Malcolm Sargent, Victoria de los Angeles, La Scala opera company, and other artists appearing at the festival. On first arriving it seemed very like Australia, but not for long. It was around the time of the Mau Mau uprisings, and we were told on no account to roam very far from the hotel after nine at night, as it was dangerous. You could feel the antagonism and suppressed violence in the air.

One night I invited the La Scala company to my suite for a party after the show. When one of them remarked he wished I had a piano, like a fool I said I had a guitar. That started it. There was a good player in the company, and off they went. You can imagine the impact of an opera company in a hotel suite! In the Carlton Hotel they were of the "don't make a sound after ten o'clock" school, so in no time flat they called up from the desk and asked us to stop. Have you ever tried to stop an opera company with a certain amount of grog on board when it feels like going? There was silence for about a minute, then little hummings would start, a few "Ahoi! Ahois!" from a baritone, a coloratura trickle or two, and off they'd go again. There were several more calls from the desk, some delicate tappings on the door with polite requests to desist, then louder tappings with less polite requests, bangings on the ceiling, and finally the manager in his dressing gown and a towering rage. I couldn't do a thing. It was like trying to put out a forest fire. You think it's out, then there is a little smoulder, a little spark, and vroom! It's blazing again.

Finally two enormous Afrikaans policemen turned up and we were all going to be arrested. We offered them a drink, which they refused, then some of the lovely ladies of the opera went to work on them, but blandishments were no good either—they were very stern fellows. They must have had a little twinkle somewhere, though, because after some negotiation and offers of tickets for La Scala, which they refused, as neither of them liked opera, they vouchsafed that what they liked best was a popular radio comedian from Capetown, who was indeed very funny (and with whom I played on my last South African tour). But they were still going to arrest us for disturbing the peace.

Then someone had an idea. "La Signora Russell, you go to her, you will laugh, you will have a good time." Can you imagine a diva from La Scala trying to use me as a bribe to prevent a couple of Afrikaans policemen from arresting us all for disturbing the peace? I mean one can invent gags, but nothing is funnier than what really happens. Finally the deal was made: four tickets for the policemen and their ladies, and not another sound from us. So everyone slunk away and that was that.

CHAPTER 23

High jinks at the opera.
Full house at the Albert Hall.
Enter Deirdre

Before I went to South Africa, I had been approached by a promoter named Dario Schindel to sing the witch in *Hänsel and Gretel* for the Cosmopolitan Opera Company in San Francisco.

The opera company was backed by a wealthy industrialist whose wife was mad about opera. A typical American setup—the Madame had gone all cultural, so Daddyo had to put up the money, whether he liked it or not. It turned out he didn't like it; opera bored him stiff, so he kept out of the way while Dario and Madame were being impresarios. Daddyo had heard, however, that I was a very funny witch, so he said that if he was expected to sit through the rest of the season, he was going to get at least one laugh, so *Hänsel and Gretel* had to be included in spite of Madame's protests.

They were having the same old jazz for their season: *Tosca, Rigoletto, Bohème, Carmen, Butterfly,* etc. At this time my old pal Frances Yeende was singing *Turandot* with the City Center Opera. She had also done it in San Antonio and had gotten glowing reviews from John Rosenfield. But when I suggested to Dario that he include *Turandot* in his season— at least it would be a change from the usual fare—he would have no part of it. No one in San Francisco had heard of Frances, he maintained, and not many people knew *Turandot*. I told him it was time they did.

On getting back from South Africa, I found that the season was not yet completely decided upon, so I put in another plug for Frances, but there was still no interest. I had gotten very keen on the idea by this time and was going to try to muscle it through. There is so much wheeling and dealing that goes on in the concert business that I thought I'd try a bit of it on my own, just for the hell of it.

My friend Florence Atherton Irish had asked me to address the annual Los Angeles Opera Guild lunch, at which a professor from the university always gave an analysis of some opera. I agreed to speak on condition that there would be an analysis of *Turandot*. When she asked why, I told her the whole story, and she promptly entered into the spirit of it and called her counterparts in San Francisco, telling them to bombard Dario with talk of *Turandot* and Frances.

When I got to San Francisco a little later, Dario said he was surprised to find there was quite some interest in *Turandot*. "They did an analysis of it at the Los Angeles Opera Guild lunch," he told me, and admitted he was thinking now of putting it on.

"Fancy that," I said. But my project almost came to naught some time later when Dario told me he couldn't do *Turandot* after all, because the sets had to come all the way from Dallas and were prohibitively expensive. So I called John Rosenfield and gave him the story. He knew the set designer and said he would try to persuade him to let the sets go for just the trans-portation costs. He'd tell him it was either that or they would stay in the warehouse. As soon as I got back to New York Frances called to say she was to play *Turandot* in San Francisco. I must say I felt very pleased with myself.

While I was still in California, I did a concert in Apple Valley sponsored by John Charles Thomas, the famous baritone, who had retired and was running his own series. Afterward he showed us the memorabilia of his ca-reer, and I was astonished to discover that he was none other than Jean Charles, the handsome baritone at le Theatre de la Monnaie in Brussels when I was at finishing school, the singer with whom all us girls were madly in love.

I went to San Francisco for the *Hänsel and Gretel* rehearsal. This produc-tion was going to be very different from the one at the City Center. For one thing, instead of Mr. Arshansky's rather terrifying makeup, I was going to be a clown, with a bright orange witch's costume, a pointy hat, long green hair, and two-inch silver fingernails. To construct the nails, they put a sort of collar under my own nails and painted layer after layer of an acrylic powder that became hard as steel and gave me great claws like the Wolf Man. I had to have this done some time in advance so I could get used to them and, believe me, they took some getting used to. It was practically im-possible to pick anything up, and dressing and undressing took hours, not to mention going to the bathroom. I was covered in scratches, and making up the face—forget it! Every time I went out, people in the street would turn and gape at my two-inch silver nails.

For another thing, I was going to fly. They had rented the *Peter Pan*

equipment from England. Wherever this equipment goes, an English operator goes with it, as it belongs to an English cartel. The one that came this
time had such a thick Cockney accent that no one could understand a word
he said, so I had to stay around to translate for the stagehands who were
helping him set up.

Learning to fly was rather nerve-wracking. I was strapped into a harness
through which I put my arms and legs, and which was tightly belted around
the middle, then I was suspended on a wire that hooked on between my
shoulder blades. I had to clamber up a scaffolding to a platform near the
proscenium arch on one side of the stage. It seemed about a hundred feet
high by the time I got there. The wire attached between my shoulders went
around a great system of pulleys, and in the opposite wing was our Cockney friend holding the far end.

He told me that when he dropped his hand, if I went all loose and relaxed, I would just lift off; otherwise, if I tensed up it would hurt. It was
all very well going slack at that height and trusting your life to a bit of
piano wire. Of course, when his arm dropped I tensed up, which made
me shoot off the platform like a rocket and nearly pulled me limb from
limb. After the first day's practice I was stiff as a board, but it had to be
mastered, and it gradually got easier. Eventually it was lovely, like a
bird taking off, and I was able to do all sorts of fancy maneuvers in
mid air.

The witch appears only in the last act of the opera, but since this equipment had cost so much to install, our sponsor thought it should be used
more, so the witch was duly written into the middle of the father's aria,
which starts in the usual way:

> *A witch within this wood doth dwell*
> *And she's in league with the powers of hell.*

When he came to the line "Away to the Witches' Ball we go," I shot
out over the audience from the top of the proscenium and screeched out,
"It's terribly expensive, but frightfully chic." This was so unexpected it lit-
erally stopped the show, the orchestra, and the father, so we had to do it
over again.

It was difficult to sing while I was done up in that harness and flying
about, and my voice wasn't at its smoothest and best, but it didn't seem
to matter. I made a lot of witchlike remarks, laughed maniacally, and
made a great deal of noise. It turned out a tremendous romp. The chil-

dren loved it, more I think than at City Center, where some of the little ones were frightened by my horrendous makeup. This time they all seemed to go for the clown. Our sponsor was delighted with it, although his Madame had not come—it was all too lowbrow for her. He immediately engaged me again for the following season. It was either that, he said, or he was not going to put up another cent for any more *La Bohèmes* and *Rigolettos*. Good for Daddyo; he'd started to put his foot down.

Sure enough, we did it all again the following season. I really made that role my own, I think, although there were those who said I'd ruined *Hänsel and Gretel* forever.

I spent that summer working on a new piece of special material, a talk on Alban Berg's opera *Wozzeck*, in the same style as the discussion of Wagner's *Ring*. I had heard the first performance of *Wozzeck* in London about twenty-five years before, at which time there was a terrible uproar. Letters to the *Times* of the "How dare you, sir!" variety came from our old friends Pater Familias and Pro Bono Publico. That was one of my reasons for doing it. I remembered that when Wagner first came out with his operas the same thing had happened. They even had fistfights in the opera houses and threw rotten eggs at the performers.

That summer, too, Mother developed a lump in her breast. Since she was very old by this time, the doctor thought it safer to remove the whole thing. So Aunt Jessie arranged for the operation to be done at the Yateley Cottage Hospital, where it would come under socialized medicine.

One thing about old Mum, she was as strong as an ox, she had never spent a day in bed since I could remember, and she never seemed to worry about the ills of the flesh. The uncles told me she went off all by herself, not in the least upset about it.

I went over to England early to be with her and arrived the day after the operation. When I called the hospital, the matron asked if I would please come and do something—Mother was driving them all mad. Apparently, the night before the operation Mother had been given a sedative. The next morning she was still asleep, so instead of waking her up properly, they did the necessary, then gave her the next lot of sedatives, wheeled her in, and the deed was done. In due course Mum came to, looked at the clock, saw that it was the afternoon, and started to raise hell. The operation should have taken place that morning. All they did was leave her lying there, giving her sleeping pills, which made her feel rotten. When were they going to do something?. . . Why didn't they get on with it?

When they got her quieted down, they told her the operation had already been done. "Why didn't you tell me?" she said. "I can't feel anything." They said it was because she was sedated. That held her fairly well till the next afternoon. The odd thing was that she never made a mention of any pain from the operation—it was that her bottom hurt, the back of her heels were sore, there was no air in the room, she didn't like staying in bed, and she was going to get up. No one could stop her, so they got her dressing gown and slippers on, and off she went into the garden.

At this point I turned up and they told me wearily where she had gone. "But," I said, "she was only operated on yesterday."

"I know," said the matron.

"Oh, so do I," I told her, and went to look for Mum. There she was, seemingly as right as rain, telling the gardener what he was doing wrong. She stayed in hospital for two days and then went to Aunt Jessie's, which was just over the road.

Aunt Jessie, who has never been known to get angry with anyone, said, "God forgive me, but sometimes she drives me mad. If the door is shut it is stuffy, if it's open there's a draft. I have opened and shut it about eighty times today."

With Mother everything was wrong with everything, except the things that really were wrong, and these were never mentioned. The only time she ever alluded to her operation was later when she couldn't get a bra to fit that didn't make her look lopsided, but that wasn't the fault of the operation, that turned out to be the fault of the bra manufacturer.

Mother recovered rapidly and went back to Canada, and I went on to St. Andrew's Hall, Glasgow, as a sort of tryout before the Edinburgh Festival. I was a little apprehensive that the number on the bagpipes might cause offense, bagpipes being sacred to the Scots, but in Glasgow it was the hit of the evening. In Edinburgh I got cold feet and substituted "How to Play the French Horn," just to be on the safe side.

The Caledonia Hotel in Edinburgh was full of artists appearing at the Festival—Eugene Ormandy, Firkusny, Set Svanholm and the Swedish Opera Company, Walter Susskind, Victoria de los Angeles, Alfred Deller, Maria Callas, Dudley Moore in his "Beyond the Fringe" days, and hosts of others. On the first day there was a great uproar. Maria Callas had gotten into a row with the woman in the beauty parlor, who had not done Madame's hair to her satisfaction. There were so many repercussions that Callas canceled the last opera she was to be in and went off in a huff. Then there was a piece in the newspaper about Victoria de los Angeles's husband and manager, Mr. Magrina. The paper misspelled his name McRina and remarked how pleased they were she had a Scottish husband.

Gene Rankin was not with me this time, so Wilfred van Wyck had engaged Joseph Cooper to play for me. I was a little nervous for fear he might be a "pupil of Leschetizky," but he turned out to be a remarkably fine pianist and a great wit into the bargain. His wife, Jean, who was as light-hearted as he, took care of the props and served as dresser and stage manager.

Before long, Jean's cousin, Irene Ravensdale, turned up to join our group. The eldest daughter of the late Lord Curzon, she was a baroness and the first woman ever to sit in the House of Lords. An elderly but very handsome woman, Irene Ravensdale reminded me of my aunt Jessie. She announced that since she was the only one with a car she was going to join our gang and be the chauffeur.

My concerts, which were in Freemason's Hall, were crowded to capacity, with people sitting within three feet of me on the stage. After wonderful concerts all day, the audiences were happy to come and have a laugh with me at night.

The reviews for my first concert were good, which was a relief, because I still wasn't sure I would be accepted in such august surroundings. When I mentioned my misgivings to the Lord Provost, he said I was bringing in a great deal of money, and that was as acceptable as I need to be in his book.

One afternoon a Mrs. McPherson turned up to say that she and a busful of women had come down from Glasgow to see the show and they would like me to please do the bagpipes. So after explaining the circumstances to the audience and asking their indulgence, I did. This started a lot of fun with the Public Relations Department. I was dressed up in full Scottish regalia, and they photographed me marching in front of Edinburgh Castle, playing "The Road to the Isles," which was the only tune I could play at the time, and the pictures appeared in papers all over the country. I was even taken in hand and given a lot of help by a grand old gold medalist piper who said, quite rightly, that if I was going to pipe I should learn to do it properly.

What I enjoyed most at the Edinburgh Festival was the Tattoo. I've seen the Aldershot one and several others, but here the setting was breathtaking. It was held on the parade ground in front of the castle, a great battlement silhouetted black against the night sky, with the moon-lit hills rolling away behind it. The Tattoo glowed like a jewel in this setting. There were pipe bands, brass bands, the Canadian Mounted Police doing complicated maneuvers on their beautiful horses, and foreign regiments in strange and exotic uniforms, some mounted on camels. There was dancing of all sorts and fancy marching, and at the end everyone came on for the grand finale. Then the groups marched off one by one, bands playing, pipes skirling, and drums beating, and as they went, the lights and the sound faded into the distance until all was dark and silent. Then a pin spot picked out one lone piper high up on the ramparts playing a pibroch, a beautiful eerie lament, until it, too, faded out and the sound gradually died away.

While in Edinburgh, I received a call from the hotel desk to say that a Miss Deirdre Hibbert was there to see me. She was a girl who used to turn up at all my concerts in Sydney, Australia. She looked about sixteen but was actually nineteen or twenty, and she hardly ever said anything. Goodness knows how she got to Edinburgh, but she was going to all my concerts this time, too. As she had no job, I asked Wilfred van Wyck if he could find her a place in his office, which he did. That was just the beginning, of her career and our friendship.

After the festival I went back to London. In the excitement I had forgotten that the Albert Hall concert was coming up in two weeks, so it was high time to get busy. When I went to the hall, it was terribly exciting to see my poster on one of those great hoardings on which I remembered seeing the names of artists like Paderewski, Caruso, Chaliapin, Tetrazzini, and all the heroes and heroines of my youth.

When I asked Mr. Hopper for fifty complimentary tickets and suggested some newspaper advertising, he said this was out of the question. I thought this was a bit thick, since I'd booked the hall. I was starting to expostulate when he said it had been sold out for days. I couldn't believe my ears. Mr. Hopper said he could have sold a lot more tickets and that there was even scalping going on. It was the most exciting thing that had ever happened. I rushed off to tell Wilfred van Wyck, and I think he was a bit sorry he hadn't managed the concert on a percentage basis.

I was in a daze for the next two weeks, interspersed with terrible bouts of cold feet, although everything was well rehearsed and ready to go.

It was in the fall of 1957 when the great day arrived. People had started to queue the night before for standing room, there were two thousand people in the gallery, and every seat was taken. I walked on, and I never saw anything like it. There were people right up to the organ in back of me, the stage all around me was full, there were even people sitting in the aisles; you couldn't have gotten anyone else in with a shoe horn. Because it was all so marvelous, that was the best concert I ever did.

Afterward, everyone I'd ever known came backstage—old school friends not seen in decades, people who had been students at the Royal College of Music with me, relations, fellow artists, old friends from the orchestra days—and there were masses of flowers and champagne. It's the one and only time in my life that I really felt like a queen!

In the middle of all this Mr. Hopper phoned to say that the hall's trustees had decided they would present me themselves in future, at any time I wanted. The trustees had presented only sixteen artists since the hall was built, all of the highest caliber. I would be the first one not in the grand tradition to be thus honored. (I went back to the Albert Hall five years later in 1962.)

Afterward, Irene Ravensdale gave me a beautiful reception at her house, where I met a lot of new people and some old friends. Aunt Jessie was there with all the Brown uncles; even my first husband was there with his second wife, whom I found perfectly delightful, though he was not so delightful. Irene had insisted he come, as she said she had paid enough money to the Arts Council to entitle her to do so, and you could plainly see that it had punctured his self-esteem. Stephen Potter, the author of *Gamesmanship* and the most delightful, witty man, was there with his wife, who ran a matrimonial agency that was said to be much patronized by the aristocracy. He suggested that she try and find a suitable husband for me, which I thought was a great joke at the time.

Looking back, it probably wouldn't have been a bad idea. I've always had the most ghastly taste in men. The ones I've liked always have something radically wrong with them, and I've passed up some very good bets because I didn't love them. On looking around, *l'amour* doesn't seem to be any basis at all for matrimony. A clear head and sound judgment probably get you further. At this particular time I was cracking on all cylinders, so Mrs. Potter might have come up with someone really worth having. In my next incarnation, when it comes to matters of relating properly to the right people, I'll have myself computerized.

I had about three weeks before I was due in South Africa, and all the shows were rehearsed and ready, so there was nothing to do in the meanwhile but have a good time.

Irene arranged for me to go to the House of Lords to hear her speak. It's the sort of place I had read about so much in history books, that somehow it never seemed quite real. It wasn't a bit like what one would imagine. On the Conservative benches were a lot of old men sound asleep, and on the Labour benches was a knot of men talking and laughing uproariously. If we weren't where we were, I would have said they were telling dirty stories. Irene gave a most interesting speech on the Boys and Girls Clubs of the East End, which in no way disturbed the sleeping men on the Conservative benches, and the Labour jokes continued sotto voce behind the hands. The atmosphere was very relaxed.

Irene later arranged for me to see the investiture of a new peer. First, a man in a full wig came on, preceded by someone carrying the mace. Garter King of Arms was there in full regalia, wearing a tabard with the royal coat of arms, knee britches, and buckled shoes. He carried a wand and was attended by heralds and pursuivants. Then three men entered dressed in long crimson robes and fore-and-aft Duke of Wellington type hats. The one in the middle was the peer-to-be and the other two presumably his sponsors. They kept taking their hats off and putting them on and walking back and forth to the man with the mace. It was like a cross between High Mass and Gilbert and Sullivan. It was impressive, but did not disturb the slumber of the old men on the Conservative benches.

I was reminded of High Mass because I had just been to Yateley to see the family, and my uncle Llewyn's brother-in-law, Arthur Coleridge, who at the time was interested in Roman Catholicism, took me to High Mass at the Farnborough Abbey, on the occasion of the visitation by some cardinal. I'd never been to a High Mass before, being Church of England, and I thought it was an incredible performance. After endless repetitions of taking off and putting back on the cardinal's mitre, I started to get the giggles. If that mitre came off one more time I was afraid I'd disgrace myself. Arthur was very annoyed with me, and I don't blame him. It was certainly spectacular and beautiful, and the vestments were magnificent, but I couldn't get out of my mind that the whole routine would have been very effective as a change of pace in the Edinburgh Tattoo.

It is one of the drawbacks of my kind of existence that you always have to move on, making new friends and losing touch with the old ones, and becoming after a time, very rootless. I suppose that is one of the reasons performers never seem to want to give up, and will struggle along till their last breath. Having not had the opportunity to develop roots, they wind up with nothing else in their life but performing.

CHAPTER 24

I build Valhalla, break with Boomer, take a sabbatical, and go into a slump

After a short Canadian tour I returned to England to do a twenty-five-city tour. I was amazed to discover that our tour manager was none other than Deirdre Hibbert. I had never seen such a change in anybody. When she had first turned up at the Edinburgh Festival practically all she'd say was hello, yes, no, and good-bye, but now she was a very self-possessed young woman who had turned into one of Wilfred van Wyck's most capable employees.

After finishing my tour I had a little time to spare before going back to New York, so I went to Nice to visit Cousin Maud, the last remaining daughter of one of the Beaky-Bullys, Aunt Nell. The plane from London to Nice was full of lovely southern women who turned out to be "The Catholic Ladies of Memphis, Tennessee," visiting the shrines of Europe with their parish priest. I had never been to Memphis, so we started chatting about the city and about what I was doing, and so forth. They promised that if I ever played in Memphis, they would be there.

The funny thing was that, when I got back to New York, I discovered that my first booking for the fall tour was—of course—Memphis. When I got there the manager said, "I was in two minds about booking you here, because I wasn't sure you would go, but we're nearly sold out. You must be a Catholic." I think the whole planeful must have turned up, and they gave me a wonderful time.

That spring I went to New Hope to rehearse the part of Lady Bracknell in Vivian Ellis's *Half in Ernest*, a musical version of *The Importance of Being Earnest*. The plan was to start at the Bucks County Playhouse, tour all summer, and hope to go to Broadway in the fall. It was an enchanting show, but we were beaten to the punch by another version of the same play, called *Ernest in Love*.

At any rate, when I got to New Hope I met Al Boell, an architect, contractor, builder, and genius. He was interested in building a really modern house. The idea took my fancy, so I bought two acres of land near New Hope and the project was on.

I do this kind of thing continually. I get a gut feeling that whatever it is must be done now, and although it may make no sense at the time, in the end it usually turns out to be the right thing.

When Boomer came down for the opening of *Half in Ernest* and found out about the house, he was perfectly furious with me. This was a side of him I had never seen before, and I never quite knew what brought it on. Perhaps because I had always consulted him about everything and taken his advice over everyone else's, he was angry that I had taken such a radical step without telling him. But it had all happened so suddenly that I hadn't had the time to tell him. Anyway, after this our relationship suffered, for which I was very sorry.

Al Boell and I burned the midnight oil over the plans for the house, as I was about to go to Australia again. When they were finished, the living room looked rather small compared to the bedrooms, so I suggested Al put one-tenth of an inch on two sides of the living room, and off I went, thinking I would come home to a nice, reasonably sized country house. When I walked into the finished house I nearly fainted. It was perfectly beautiful, but the living room was enormous, with a cathedral ceiling, yet. I had not realized that one-tenth of an inch on the plans represented ten feet!

So I had a mansion. Nonetheless, it was beautiful. My old friend Audie Kellogg came to be my secretary and we had some very pleasant years in "Valhalla."

Deirdre by this time had left van Wyck and gone to Toronto, and she was the secretary to the manager of the Prince George Hotel when I was summoned to Toronto to do the show for the International Convention of Zonta Clubs. It was to start on a Monday, and my performance would be on the Friday, so I thought I'd take the week off and take in the whole thing. On Monday at about 2:00 P.M. I went and registered, all done up in my business suit. I pinned on my ribbon and badge and had moved about a yard when a phalanx of women appeared and said, "There's Anna."

Our lot wanted to know, "Who are they?"

"Akron, Ohio."

"So introduce us." I did, and went a yard further when another lot appeared. Same thing.

"There's Anna."

"Who are they?"

"Dallas, Texas." I introduced them. This went on all afternoon, until it finally occurred to me that if I went to meetings all day with the home team and sat up all night celebrating with the visitors, by Friday I would be hoarse as a crow.

So I phoned Deirdre at the Prince George Hotel, one block up the street, and booked a room there instead. After a pleasant evening visiting, I sneaked out at midnight to the Prince George, where, as soon as I got into the lobby, a beribboned and pinned woman came charging up and said, "Are you saved?"

"I don't think so," I said. "I'm at the Zonta Convention down at the Royal York. Who are you?"

"Jehovah's Witnesses," she said. So I Zontaed all day and was saved all night. It was quite a week.

I asked my friend Winifred Stewart to play for me on Friday. She was the one who had played all the club dates with me at the Royal York so many years ago, and I thought it would be fun to work there again after all this time. So there we were on Friday, all elegantly coiffed and gowned, with our mink stoles on, feeling pretty pleased with ourselves. We rang for the elevator and up came a little old operator. He took one look at us and said, "My God! Are you two still working here?" It was the same old chap who used to ride us up thirty-five years before. That certainly punctured our balloons!

Not long after I got home, Deirdre came to Valhalla to say good-bye. Her mother had died, and she was going back to Australia to take up nursing. It seemed she would finally be home after all her wanderings. Famous last words!

Everything went on as usual for the next few years. I went to the Orient, New Zealand, and England, and once again to South Africa. While I was in England I met Neville Cardus, the famous music critic for the *Manchester Guardian* and also the world's expert on cricket, and he gave me his book, *Composers Eleven*. I was sitting on the plane to South Africa reading when I spied across the aisle an incredibly handsome man with a beard who I thought was giving me the eye. But he suddenly got up and said, "I see you're reading a book by Neville Cardus." I told him yes, he'd given it to me. "Oh, do you know Neville Cardus?" he asked. I said yes, he's a very good friend. "Do you know he's the greatest expert on cricket in the whole world?" he said, and proceeded to talk and talk about cricket—where he'd played cricket, how he'd played cricket—we had cricket for hours and hours and hours.

Finally the plane came to a halt in Johannesburg, and I walked up the aisle and down the gangplank with this man beside me still talking cricket, right into the arms of the concert manager, who looked at me in amazement. I said good-bye to my friend and hoped we'd meet again. This was shot by the photographers there to meet me, and Percy Tucker, the manager, said, "How in the world did you manage that?"

"Manage what?" I asked.

"To meet him," he said.

"Why shouldn't I meet him? He must be an ex-international cricketer. We've talked about cricket for three solid hours."

"International cricketer, hell," said Percy. "He's only our most important music critic, Oliver Walker, and a very tough one at that. According to what he says, so the tour goes." Oliver Walker was very kind to me in his reviews, but I'm sure it was knowing Neville Cardus that tipped the scales.

While I was in Johannesburg, problems that had been brewing for some time between Boomer and his partner, Edna Giesen, came to a head over complaints I had made about my fees and other matters. I tried to get to the truth, but the ensuing fracas merely resulted in Boomer being fired. He started his own agency, and I was hoping to sign with him again, but I discovered when I returned to New York that, although the management had broken up, I still had to fulfill all the dates they had booked for me for the next several years.

Boomer did very well on his own, but he didn't speak to me again for twelve years. I was so fed up with everything I left my house in the capable hands of Audie Kellogg, who rented it to MGM to make commercials in, and I took a one-year sabbatical in England.

When I first got to London I was staying in a very expensive hotel on Bond Street when I ran into an old friend from my Royal College days, Florence Mudie. She was horrified when she discovered how much I was paying and suggested I come and live in her boardinghouse in Tregunter Road, which she rented to musicians. I could have her front living room and bedroom for the same amount per week that I was paying per night at the hotel. So I moved in.

The Tregunter Road house was one of those great big Edwardian houses in South Kensington that must have been very grand in its heyday, but was now damp and cold and showing signs of neglect or hurried and cheap patchings. There appeared to have been only one bathroom originally. The upper-class Edwardians, for all their elegance, never seemed to be that keen on washing, or maybe they had so many servants rushing up and down with jugs of water that it wasn't necessary to have several bathrooms.

My flat had a living room with a fireplace, and a kitchen made from what was once a dressing room adjoining the bedroom, which had a balcony. Florence had a great talent for adapting things, and she had certainly adapted this in a slightly Rube Goldberg manner to be a very livable flat, if one didn't mind the main staircase going through it.

My private bathroom was really the masterpiece. It was on the balcony off the kitchen. The balcony was the usual wrought-iron type stuck onto the front of the house, but this one had been enclosed by what amounted to a wooden box, and plumbing had been installed, including a beauteous Victorian bath standing on ball and claw legs. The only trouble was there was no insulation, so by the time I had run my hot bath it was usually stone cold, either because of the wind whistling through the walls and cooling the water, or because of rain running off the leaky roof into the bath. A hot bath was a seeming impossibility, until I had an idea.

I went to the hardware store and bought a bale of insulation, one of those huge garden umbrellas, and a Christmas tree stand. I wrapped the bath up in the insulation, put the umbrella in the Christmas tree stand and stood it in the middle of the bath, and washed around it. It wasn't perfect but it worked, better than before, when I would sit in the bath holding an umbrella up with one hand and trying to wash with the other. Except for the fact that I would frequently be caught by the other boarders as I rushed across the main landing to get my clothes in the living room, where I kept them so they wouldn't smell from cooking odors, the flat turned out to be quite comfortable.

The house, however, was total pandemonium. There were flute players, horn players, guitarists, timpanists, pianists, and Florence's sister Anne, a violist, all going day and night, but it really didn't bother me. When I was with my first husband and we had all those musicians around, not to mention the practicing of the French horn, I learned to turn my ears off to anything I didn't want to listen to. I can do it to this day, and it's very useful when I get stuck with people who talk my ear off. If I say, "Really? Too bad! You don't say!" and similar things, I'm fine, because they don't want to hear what I think, anyway.

About this time I met an extraordinary man whom I shall call Tim. He had something to do with movies—a technical director, cameraman, goodness knows what. He was attractive and exceedingly good company, but I felt in my bones that he was a bad lot.

All the men in my life, not that there have been very many, have always been of the all-wool-and-a-yard-wide type right from the beginning. While my girlfriends would be into romance, high drama, ecstasy, despair, and heartbreak, I would be jogging along quite happily with my current boyfriend. Although I never went through terrible disasters, I couldn't help feeling I wasn't having as much fun as they were. So here comes this fancy fellow, and I thought what the heck. Why not for once?

He had to go to Majorca to look for movie locations (so he said) and wanted to take me with him. So I went. I met all sorts of weird people and I had a marvelous time, but when we got back he wanted me to move in with him. No fear! So he moved into a vacant room in our place. As he said, you can't stop people moving into a boardinghouse, can you?

It wasn't bad. He did whatever it was he did most days, so I didn't see too much of him, but on Sunday mornings we'd have brunch starting with Bloody Marys in my living room. One Sunday we were sitting there in our dressing gowns, when there was a knock on the door. Who should it be but Deirdre! I nearly went through the roof! What had happened to the nursing? I had her first-year graduation picture and thought she was set for a career.

She had gotten fed up with nursing and come back to England to try something else. She was staying with her dotty aunt and had heard that I was back, so she had come to see me.

Well, I could hardly take the high parental tone that I had erstwhile taken with her under the circumstances. I mean, it was a fair cop, wasn't it? So I sent her round to the pub to get more gin, and she joined the party. Thus began the next phase of our friendship.

At this point I was just about to star in what turned out to be probably the worst play ever written. It was supposed to be a farce and was called *Papa's All-Purpose Speech* and later, *Spoof.* It was about a middle-aged British woman who goes to Africa and becomes the head of a small state called Bunga. She goes to America seeking aid for Bunga and gets mixed up with the presidential election. It was just awful. I can't think what induced me to do it, or for that matter how it ever came to be put on.

The only thing about it that was any fun at all was writing the one number in it, which was supposed to be the national anthem of Bunga, the "Bunga Boo." I wrote it, the musicians in the boardinghouse played it, some old friends from college days who were at Covent Garden sang it, and the thirteen-year-old son of the keeper of the boardinghouse next door, who was a terrific jazz drummer, did the rhythm. I ran the recording session, and it turned out great. But the rest was a disaster.

We went on a two-month provincial tour that finally conked out in Golders Green, a most suitable place, because that's where the crematorium is. We were booked for St. Martin's Theatre in London, but I went in instead with my usual old show. So after all this effort to get into the theater, to diversify, to broaden my horizons, here I was right back where I'd started, only this time it was eight shows a week!

Between Golders Green and St. Martin's Theatre, I was back in Tregunter Road. Tim went on and on about going to Spain to see the bullfights and why didn't I forget about everything and go too. I could see then why I don't get on for long with charming and macho men—I have to give them my undivided attention. This was fine when I had nothing to do but think of him, but now when I had only two weeks to get ready for my show at the St. Martin's Theatre, he was driving me crazy. I promised that if he would go to Spain first, I would join him later. Thankfully, he did. Deirdre then moved into Tregunter and was a great help getting the show on the road.

The St. Martin's run went very well, but luckily I was only booked in for a limited run, as I was pooped after all that "spoof."

Lady Ravensdale arranged that I should do a benefit at St. James Palace for Princess Alice of Athlone and the Girls' and Boys' Clubs of the East End. This turned out to be quite a seller, so instead of an *intime* held in the throne room, it was to be held in another great room in the palace. The organizers were a bit doubtful whether the floor of this room would stand up to the weight of the audience, so the day before, all the servants of the palace were sent in to jump up and down. Luckily the floor held; otherwise it would have been a bit hard on the servants.

On the night of the concert, all the women were ablaze with diamonds and gorgeous gowns, although a lot of the older ones looked as if their gowns had been made out of the drawingroom curtains. Princess Alice looked charming and was partnered by Sir Malcolm Sargent, chic as always, in his immaculate tails, with ribbons and stars blazing across his bosom. It was an elegant turnout.

During this period I also went to Ireland for the first time, to play the Theatre Royal Dublin on a Sunday afternoon. It was pouring rain and was so dark it could have been 7:00 P.M., so I doubted if anyone would come. I needn't have worried. It was packed with the jolliest audience in the world.

Later I played in the Brighton Pavilion, the former palace of King

George IV, which was designed in the Indian style and is covered with gingerbread minarets and Taj Mahal type domes. It looks very baroque, even more so because it is flooded in rainbow-colored lights that change constantly. I was glad I wore a plain black dress for my concert, because when I went on, the spotlight was red, the foots blue, and floods of every color shone all over the place. The next time I looked the spot was green and the foots were blue. We were changing color constantly, inside as well as out.

My last concert of that 1962 season was in the Albert Hall, and once again I had a tremendous house. So I was back to square one and considered myself lucky not to have permanently gone down the tubes with *Spoof.*

Meanwhile, Deirdre and I were leading quite a pleasant life in Tregunter Road, which happened to be just two streets away from where I had lived with my first husband. One night I went down to the local pub, which was the same one he and I used to frequent. It hadn't changed one iota. In fact, there behind the bar was the same barmaid. We had a lovely gossip. She told me she had married the boss and was now the "madam." Then she said, "They'll all be in soon."

"Who?" I asked.

"Oh, the same lot. They 'aven't changed the clients here in thirty-five years or so, except some 'as passed on." And sure enough, in they came, a lot of the same people I used to know. It really was quite fun. Deirdre and I would go down several nights a week and play darts and the piano or whatever.

I might have been there yet, except one night they kept the BBC open after midnight, as the president of the United States was going to make an announcement. It was the Cuba crisis. All the people in the pub started saying, "Oh, fancy them doing that without consulting us." And I suddenly thought, "I'm not us, I'm *them.* It's time I went home."

CHAPTER 25

Deirdre's Wedding. The second Broadway show

So I packed up everything and went back to Valhalla. Deirdre stayed in London and went back to work for Wilfred van Wyck. Soon after, Audie Kellogg's parents became sick and she had to return to California, so I sent for Deirdre to be my secretary, and she moved into Valhalla.

Being very pretty, Deirdre received plenty offers of marriage, but she elected to marry one Fred Prussak, who used to be one of Edna Giesen's salespeople. She was about a foot taller than he, and they looked most extraordinary together.

The wedding party was held at Valhalla, which was all spiffed up for the great event. There was a three-tiered wedding cake and pink champagne, in addition to all the usual drinks and noshes that go with a wedding. Frank Bartholomew, my new accompanist, was going to give the bride away in his morning suit and striped pants, and I was going to be the mother, in beige flowered silk—very matronly. The justice of the peace was a very large woman who kept one of the local groceries, and the ceremony was to take place in her parlor behind the shop. Deirdre was wearing a suit, with a white box hat topped with a pouf of white veiling. Why this, I don't know, because at five feet eleven inches she was already towering over Fred, and the hat and her high heels added a good five inches, but I must say she looked absolutely stunning. Fred gave me a huge corsage of white orchids, which, pinned on my large bosom, made me look more matronly than ever.

Off we went to the grocery store, and there in the back room was the justice of the peace in carpet slippers and an apron, with her husband as an acolyte. Frank walked smartly up with Deirdre, gave the bride away, and came back and stood beside me. He took out his handkerchief and started blowing his nose and wiping his eyes. My goodness, I thought, I hope he hasn't got the flu. The justice of the peace looked at him and said, "You mustn't be upset; you're not losing a daughter, you're gaining a son," which sent Frank into another paroxysm of nose blowing. I realized then he was laughing.

When I got him outside, I said, "What's the matter with you?"

He said, "Here we are, all dressed up to the nines, looking as if we should be in the cathedral with organ and full choir, and I see the back view of Deirdre and Fred, being married by the carpet slippers against a background of crates of Campbell's soup. It was too much for me."

Luckily the justice of the peace didn't hear this. She said to Frank, "It's so nice to see such a devoted family. May we come to the reception?"

When we got back to the house it was bedlam, so I put the justice of the peace into a comfortable chair and told one of the waiters to keep her glass filled while I attended to the other guests. Well, I needn't have bothered. While we were away they had been very adequately attending to themselves. After someone mentioned that one of the guests had ripped off the top layer of the wedding cake and fallen into the lake with it, I insisted Deirdre and Fred cut the rest of the cake before anything else happened. After seeing that the justice of the peace was being suitably primed with pink champagne so as not to be disillusioned with our "devoted family," I just joined the others and let her rip.

Finally the bride and groom went off, and the justice of the peace was put into the back of a car by several of the guests and drove off bowing and waving to left and right like the Queen, to great applause. Bit by bit they all left, including the caterers, who promised to come the next morning to clean up. I was finally alone amidst an absolute shambles.

Just then the telephone rang. It was an old friend I hadn't seen for years who was in the vicinity. "I'd love to see you," I said, "but you're going to be surprised." He certainly was surprised.

"What's been happening, a riot?"

"No, just a wedding." I gave him some pink champagne and told him about it.

"Well, you can't stay in this mess," he said. "I'll take you to dinner."

So we went out, but when we got back the house was ablaze with lights, and some neighbors and the police were there. "Where have you been?" they said.

"Out to dinner, where else?" I said. "And what on earth are you doing? Have I been burgled?"

Apparently Deirdre had started wondering if I was all right alone in the house, so she called. Of course, I wasn't there. She thought perhaps I'd had too much champagne and passed out or fallen downstairs, so she called my neighbors and asked them to go over and look. They called back to say they couldn't get in. Deirdre said, "She might have gone out. Go and see if both cars are in the garage." They called back to say both cars were in the garage. She said, "Go and get the police."

So they got the police, who broke in and said, "The house is in a frightful state, but there is no one there." Maybe I had been kidnapped, so they called for more police.

It was about this time that we came back from dinner, to find almost as much of an uproar as there had been in the afternoon. Everyone concerned was absolutely furious with me, and I was equally furious with them for being so ridiculous.

But that's my Deirdre. She worries about her friends and her pussycats and her relations and Fred and me, which is a very nice trait in a person, although I must say at times I have known her to overdo it.

Valhalla was a wonderful place to have a wedding, or a party, or any other sort of entertainment, but the upkeep was enormous, it was much too big for me, and it was too far away from New York City. So I sold it to a wealthy Hungarian. Everybody asked how I could bear to sell it, but then I'd had lots of fun building it with Al Boell, I'd lived there off and on for seven and a half years in the greatest of comfort, and I felt it was time to move on.

This was just about the time I was finally getting disentangled from Edna Giesen, and who should I run into but Jack Petrill, the man who had put on my first Town Hall concert so many years before. Not only did he get me an apartment in Carnegie Hall Mansions, where he was living, but he decided to put me in a one-woman Broadway show at the Forty-first Street Theater.

He still had all his old enthusiasm. I didn't know how he intended to get the backing, and I was really afraid to ask, but it didn't take much in those days anyway, because I wrote the show and performed it myself, and I don't think Jack took much of a salary.

The show was my usual sort of thing, except we had dramatized *Hamletto or Prosciuttino*, which was a mythical opera of *Hamlet* by Verdi that I had cooked up. I used to do it sitting at the piano the way I do the *Ring*, but Jack thought it would be more in keeping if I dramatized it, more suitable to the theater. So there I was in scarlet tights and a very, very short jerkin with Russian sleeves. "Elsinore" was a flight of steps up to a very small platform, and my father's ghost *("Il mio padre's spook")* was a Chinese Mandarin mask on which we put a green spotlight. I played all the parts, rushing up and down the stairs, hiding behind the arras, swishing a sword. It was a very exhausting athletic effort. Of course, we opened at the wrong time of the year (June), but we opened.

Afterward we had a party at Sardi's to wait for the reviews. I was very self-conscious, because everyone there knew it was a first night, and since it was so late in the season there was nothing much else to do, so everybody was looking at us. What surprised me most, though, were comments from people in our party about what beautiful legs I had. This was the first time they'd had a good look at them on the stage. I remember thinking to myself, "What a stupid idiot I am! I wait until I'm fifty to find out I've got beautiful legs. Maybe I would have done better to have run around all this time in a yashmak and miniskirt."

When the reviews came in I wanted to slide under the table with embarrassment, but they turned out to be raves! Each one that came in was better than the last. We did super business until August, when the weather got hot and everybody went out of town.

Now that I was no longer with Columbia Artists, who were devoted mainly to concerts and opera, I signed with Ashley Famous, an enormous corporation that managed stars of the utmost magnitude in movies, TV, and theater, but only marginally in concerts.

My first tour was with a road company of *Gigi*, where I played the part of the aunt, who is a retired courtesan. It was a musical with lyrics set to familiar music by Bizet, Offenbach, and similar composers, and was actually a very nice show. I began to have visions of getting somewhere as a character actress in the theater, perhaps following in the footsteps of Margaret Rutherford. The pipe dreams one has.

After quite a long time on the road, we got to Detroit and they hated us. They particularly hated George Hamilton, and since I suspect the whole package was put on in order to present him as a stage actor, after Detroit we closed.

I discovered while on tour that success as a concert artist does nothing for you in the theater. It seemed I was starting again from scratch, with different theaters, different bookers, different advertising, different critics, and a different audience. People knew about my recent Broadway show, but that was it.

After Detroit I went back to New York and sat about doing nothing. Ashley had all the stars in the firmament, so naturally nobody was interested in me. But then in December, at the annual concert managers' convention, someone asked, "Whatever happened to Anna Russell? Is she dead?" The Ashley Famous concert manager said, "No, we've got her," so off I went on another concert tour.

Since all the best local managers booked from Columbia Artists, I now did all sorts of ghastly club dates, much like my first tour many years before, although a few of my old bookers took pity on me, so I still had some good dates. But then I met Newell Jenkins, who invited me to join his production of *Archifanfanno King of Fools,* by Karl Ditters von Dittersdorf.

Newell was the founder and conductor of the Clarion Orchestral Society, which I suspect was more for art's sake than for profit. I believe he was heir to one of the great toothpaste fortunes and spent most of his time unearthing neglected or long-forgotten works and presenting them. I liked this, for I am afraid I have a strong streak of dilettantism myself, but I've never had enough money to indulge it. He was planning to do a concert version of this opera, which was written by a contemporary of Haydn and Mozart.

The story was about a king who had become bored with his kingdom, so he invited all the classic vices to visit him—Rage, Vanity, Avarice, Prodigality, Prudishness, and Frivolity—with, of course, due results. Newell thought I would be perfect to play Frivolity. Eleanor Steber and various other members of the Met would be in it, and Archifanfanno would be played by David Rae Smith of City Center Opera. But when he sent me the score, I saw at a glance that it would be impossible for me.

Garbata, as the character was called, was a high soprano role, way out of my range. Not only that, but the English translation was by W. H. Auden, and I didn't think I could do credit to his poesie.

When I phoned Newell to say I was very sorry but I couldn't do it, he said, "Don't be in such a hurry. Come over and we'll discuss it." He suggested, for one thing, that I sing the part an octave lower. "The last time this work was performed was when Haydn conducted it in 1798, and Archifanfanno was sung by a castrato, so there's no reason we can't have a baritone Garbata." As for my concerns about Auden's translation, Newell said, "Oh, well, write some funny lyrics to your numbers. He won't mind; he's a friend of mine." And, in fact, he didn't mind, so there I was, playing Garbata after all.

Although it was a concert version, we were costumed to the nines. I wore a cap and bells outfit, with bells on the huge padded horns on my cap, and bells on every point on my costume. It was quite a help in my comic numbers, but I had a terrible time sitting still enough not to jangle during other people's arias. The show was a tremendous hit and we got wonderful reviews. One review said, ". . . and there was Anna Russell, whooping and hollering and covered with bells, which strangely made a very good change of pace."

At the party after the show I met David Smith's patroness, Hannah Bierhoff. I had no idea people had patronesses in our day and age—I thought they had gone out with Queen Victoria. Hannah was a small, slim, beautifully turned out and extremely amusing woman of ninety-two. After her husband died when she was between sixty and seventy, she went on a world tour with Fritz Kreisler and his wife and then lived in Hollywood for a number of years. She had always been waited on, but she was struck by the fact that everyone in California could cook, so she went to school and in no time at all became a remarkable chef.

At the end of the party she said, "I like you and I am going to adopt you as one of my grandchildren."

"Grandchild!" I said. "I'm in the grandmother age group myself."

"At my age," she said, "I make everyone a grandchild, which means I shall expect you to dinner at least once a week, and if you don't come, I shall call up and see what's the matter. What do you like to eat?" I settled for filet and strawberries. "That will be fine," she said. "When you want a change just ask for it."

Those dinner parties were the greatest fun. David was usually playing host, and she would have all sorts of fascinating people, all very young. I was by far the oldest of the "grandchildren." She did all the cooking. "Anna is steak and strawberries," she would announce, "and Dick is grilled sole," and on would go the one-woman restaurant. If she wasn't entertaining, she would be at the opera or a concert, and during the day she would think nothing of hopping on a bus or the subway. I once met her daughter, who was a real old woman and who could easily have passed for Hannah's mother.

Newell Jenkins's next project was *L'astutzie Femminili* by Cimarosa, which in the new version was called *The Ladies' Game, or How to Get Your Way With Men Without Them Finding Out.* Newell asked me to write the libretto based on a verbatim translation from the Italian. It was the same old Mozartian plot with the beautiful girl, the lover, the lawyer, the maid, the duenna, and the silly old man, only this plot had rather a twist. After they all pretend to be someone else to bamboozle the old man (Gianpaolo Lasagna), he finally turns the tables on them and wins the day.

When it got into English, there seemed to be a lot of patter songs in it. For example, Bellina, the heroine, who intends to marry three husbands, sings,

> *When I'm young and I'll have him wealthy,*
> *Later on he must be healthy,*
> *When I'm old I will content me*
> *With a husband who is twenty.*
> *Though he may not have a cent, he*
> *Well may be a popinjay,*
> *May be vain or spoilt or gay,*
> *I will love him anyway.*

It really turned out quite funny, even as a concert version. I wish someone would put it on again. It has only six characters and the music is charming.

Apart from this kind of project, I was doing the usual concerts and a lot of summer stock. I had moved out of the dismal Carnegie Hall Mansions into a lovely big apartment which was only a few blocks from Deirdre and Fred, and my dear Myrtis Clare, who had looked after me on and off since I lived on Fifty-second Street, came back to take care of the place.

In the summer of 1963 I got together with Joan White, whom I had known since my childhood holidays with the Farquharsons, and cooked up a show for the Berkshire Playhouse in Stockbridge, Massachusetts, which she ran. For a long time I had had the idea of making one of the old Victorian melodramas into a musical, not the way they are put on now, with a lot of slapstick interspersed with parodies of current popular songs, but played for real, with an elegant production.

Melodrama is a theatrical phase that came after sentimental drama, and is so dripping with feeling it is ridiculous. The one we chose, however, *Lady Audley's Secret,* had a very good plot. In fact, it could have been one of the first whodunits. It is about a beautiful girl whose husband leaves her temporarily in order to go to India and seek his fortune. She gets bored, so after putting a notice in the paper announcing her death, she goes to the United States and marries a rich old man, Sir Michael Audley. The husband returns, finds that his wife is dead (or so he thinks), and with a broken heart goes to the United States to visit an old chum, who happens to be Sir Michael's nephew, and who is engaged to his daughter Alicia. You can see what that might lead to, and with the help of a scoundrelly drunken groom and a smart little maidservant, it certainly does. The skulduggery is tremendous. When the action becomes so heartrending as to be unbearable, the four men put up masks, form a barbershop quartet, and sing about the dire happenings until the audience has gotten itself under control.

The sets, which Robert Paine Gross did, were all painted black on white ground. Such little furniture as was needed was antique red velvet and gold, and the gowns, which looked very rich and ornate from the front, were actually painted on some special sort of canvas. It all looked simply gorgeous, including the olio curtain, which was covered with ads that had been sold to the local tradesmen, done in true florid Victorian fashion.

The show was a great hit. The Boston papers came and covered it and gave us splendid reviews, and the show was held over, a very rare occurrence in summer stock.

When the people at City Center Opera saw it (thanks to our great p.r. person, Mary Jean Parson), they took us over and rehearsed us to go into the World's Fair in Flushing Meadows, New York. When we opened, the pavilion the theater was in wasn't nearly finished. There was no marquee, no mention of the show at the main gate, and there was a press embargo on the whole fair. If we had ten people who had wandered in by accident, we had a good house. I don't know what City Center lost, but all the shows lost money, in some cases millions. In a very short time the whole fair went down the tubes, *Lady Audley* with it.

That fall Ed Rubin of Ashley Famous came up with an Australian tour. This was going to be an eight-shows-a-week proposition—four weeks at Her Majesty's in Melbourne, six weeks at the Phillip Street Theatre in Sydney, and a couple of shows in Canberra. Since Deirdre was bored with Bloomingdale's and felt like a trip home, I took her along as my secretary. One could afford secretaries in those days of reasonable air fares.

So off we went to Australia again. While we were in Sydney, one of Deirdre's friends took us on a Sunday drive to a new housing development called Sylvania Waters. It was a combination housing development and marina built on a series of man-made islands surrounded by concrete and linked together with a ring road. I suppose the islands were originally made of garbage, as most reclaimed land is. The islands were divided into fifty-foot lots on which one could erect the mansion of one's desire. The lots were deep enough to have a garden, at the end of which was the sea wall, where one could tether a motor boat or dinghy. The houses already inhabited were an extraordinary selection—miniature Taj Mahals, Venetian palazzos, Tudor manors, glass-and-chrome marvels.

Just for fun we looked over some of the houses that were for sale, and I was captivated by a house at the end of one of the islands. Since it was at the end of the island, the lot was pie-shaped, and so was the house. I found it had been built on spec, but nobody liked it, so it was going for at least $15,000 less than all the palazzos round about. I couldn't think why this was; I thought it was the nicest house there. I smelled a bargain, so we searched out the real estate man, who turned out to be a "fairdinkum Aussie" with that incredible accent locally known as "strine." (*Strine* is a very popular book in Australia, purported to have been written by one Afferbeck Lauder—alphabetical order—and dedicated to getting the Australian accent down on paper phonetically. I think he was actually a newspaperman by the name of Alistair Morrison.)

When I told the real estate man that I could be interested in buying the house, he looked at me as if I'd lost my marbles. "Nah, yer don't want that; the wallsign strite," he said, and started a spiel on all the other goodies he had for sale. I insisted that was the only house I was interested in, and I could see immediately that he thought I was a silly pommie barstid (common Australian term for an English person), and that he was determined for my own good that I was not going to buy it.

"The wallsign strite," he said again. "I telltha bilda sorphous rokka, or davvy zed red. Godger woomba levy, twoodja? So ya naw wodder sair twim? 'Hagger nigh sellut? The wallsign strite.' E sedomia got assella tenny cos. So fyoo likit, you gotta bargain." (Translation: "The walls ain't straight. I told the builder he's off his rocker, he ought to have his head read. God, you wouldn't believe it, would you? So do you know what I said to him? 'How can I sell it? The walls ain't straight.' He said to me I've got to sell at any cost. So if you like it, you've got a bargain.")

"Too rite! My word! I'll tike it!" I told him.

"Stone the crows!" he said.

CHAPTER 26

Off to live in Australia

After the Australian tour finished, we went back home, Deirdre to the Arden counter at Bloomingdale's, and me to the odd concert, summer stock, and bits and pieces of TV, game shows, and talk shows. I was doing all right, but I wasn't going anywhere except in circles, and Deirdre couldn't seem to penetrate the higher echelons of Elizabeth Arden and was getting homesick.

So we decided to burn our boats, give it all up, brush the dust of New York from our feet, and all the other rubbish people talk about when they are feeling frustrated, and we were going to live in our house in Sylvania Waters.

Myrtis, my cleaning lady, took a very dim view of the whole thing. "Going to live in a heathen place like that at the end of nowhere at your time of life—you must be crazy," she said. In spite of that, I had all my things crated, and sold some very beautiful but large chests at Parke Bernet. The only things remaining were the beds and that weird collection that is always left when one makes a major move—two plates and a milk jug, cracked, from Grandmother's beautiful Wedgwood tea service; a collection of hideous vases from relatives of one sort or another; an old, very tarnished samovar that belonged to a great-uncle who once visited Russia; jelly molds; ten dessert plates of different sizes and shapes; a teapot with no top; a teapot with a top and a chipped spout; cups with no saucers, saucers with no cups, cups with no handles; some enormous Victorian platters; dozens of cake plates, wine holders, candlesticks, little boxes, unmatched cutlery, pots and pans and things to make little cakes in; mixers and toasters and gadgets and things bought at rummage sales; and whatnots from friends and things that aren't even identifiable. No matter how many cupboards there are, they are always full of this kind of junk. This, of course, is before I learned from Aunt Jessie the gentle art of getting rid of things.

We piled all this stuff in the dining room, which was painted brilliant Chinese green, including the ceiling, and then we sent our invitations to everybody we had ever heard of in New York.

Grand Farewell Party and Rummage Sale.
11:00 A.M. till lunch, Bloody Marys.
Bring your own sandwiches.
After lunch onwards, French Seventy-fives.

Deirdre was going to look after sales, and Gene Rankin and another friend were coming into town and would do the bartending.

When Myrtis came on Saturday to give the place a last dust-over, she looked at the collection in the dining room and said, "Why don't you give the garbageman ten dollars extra to cart it all away?" I could see her point. It looked awful, particularly against the Chinese green dining room.

Sunday morning at eleven I opened the door to admit a mob of people, many of whom I'd never seen before. They were all immediately provided with Bloody Marys, which were handed from the kitchen bucket-brigade fashion. I don't know whether it was on account of the drinks, but all the junk in the dining room quickly vanished, as if a hoard of locusts had been in. Then people bought the light fixtures, the locks on the doors, and everything that wasn't nailed down. We had actually expected to make only enough money from the sale to pay for the liquor, but in the middle of the afternoon Deirdre whispered in my ear, "Do you know we've made over $900?" I nearly fainted.

When Myrtis came to do the final dusting the following morning she said, "I see you took my advice and got the garbagemen to take it after all. What did they charge?" I don't think she believed me when I told her what happened.

There was only a day left, so Deirdre and I went off in different directions saying good-bye. When I got home that night and looked through the hole in the door (there was a hole because someone had bought our safety lock at the sale), there was Deirdre lying unconscious in the hallway. Or was she dead? After I called Fred to get the doctor, I applied a wet cloth and she started to come to.

All this dragging out of junk from our sale had left the floor very slippery. She had come in, skidded, hit her head, and knocked herself out. When we got her to the hospital we found that she had cracked the bone in her shoulder. She was able to leave, luckily, but all bound up, with her arm in a sling.

We went to Australia by cargo boat, which didn't have the facilities and amenities of passenger boats, so it took the combined efforts of Fred and myself to push and tug the poor invalid up a very shaky, laddery type of stairway to get her onboard.

Deirdre's brother George and his wife, Frieda, met us at the ship and drove us out to Sylvania Waters. There was nothing in the house except a beautiful vase of flowers from the neighbors and some cleaning equipment that the Nelsons, next door, had kindly put under the sink for us.

Our first few months in Australia were awful, just like swimming through mud. For example, we were told it would be months before we could get a telephone. Fortunately one of our neighbors introduced us to a great big jolly police detective who lived nearby. He went to the phone company and told them a story about these two poor women all alone, with no man to protect them, windows bare all around the house because they couldn't get curtains for many weeks. It wasn't safe—there might be prowlers. This is where male chauvinism, which is rampant in Australia, really worked for us. He spun them such a gorgeous yarn that they relented and installed the telephone the next day. This is typical of Australia—you have to resort to guile and stealth to skin a cat.

Deirdre got a very good job right away in a big department store at the Elizabeth Arden counter. The fact that she had worked for them in New York made her quite the star and it was obvious she was destined for advancement. Being back in her old hometown with her family around also boosted her confidence no end.

On the other hand, I was discovering the truth in the saying that you never really know what a place is like until you live there. I had been very successful on my three previous visits to Australia, but then I was imported at great expense from the United States. Now that I was there to live, I was considered a local, and local performers get no recognition at all.

To do well in Australia it is a good idea to be a jockey or a builder or a plumber. Even a carpenter or housepainter would be all right, but actors come very low on the totem pole. Tyrone Guthrie summed it up when he said, "Australia is loaded with every kind of talent imaginable, except talent for booking, displaying, or in any way promoting talent." All I was able to get at the time was a fifteen-minute radio spot on the ABC "Morning Call" every Wednesday for the princely sum of thirty dollars.

I was beginning to regret having come to Australia. It looked as if I was never going to work again, and my money wasn't going to last forever. The house was too far out of town, and I'd left all my friends in the Northern Hemisphere. I was nearly fifty, and in Australia females are over the hill at forty-five. And on and on and on. I must have been a pain in the neck.

Deirdre, on the other hand, had burst out of her cocoon and certainly didn't need me anymore, and she complained that my friends, who had known her as my secretary on the last trip, patronized her. When they came over she would clam up and sit around looking sulky. Anyway, we had a big fight and Deirdre moved out.

For a couple of days I felt more depressed than I ever had before, but the fact is that deep down I rather enjoy my own company. The fact that I wasn't working had its social advantages, though. Instead of working during the hours that everyone else was playing, I could now have fun when everyone else did, and I became great friends with the Nelsons next door. They were both great gardeners, and George grew wonderful orchids. My place was nicely landscaped by that time, too, and I liked pottering around in the fresh air, so George and I used to do a lot of chatting over the back fence. He had a stentorian voice, and in that respect I can give as good as I get, so I guess we got pretty noisy. Nancy suggested that we hire a tent and set up shop. "The way you two go on together, you'd make marvelous evangelists." That's what we became known as—the Evangelists.

Their neighbors were the Roughsedges. He was an American and she was French and very vivacious. They and the Nelsons both had swimming pools, and we used to have the most wonderful Sunday parties. We were really too far out for people just to drop in, so on Sunday we would all invite our friends, who would start at my place with breakfast and Bloody Marys. Then the whole lot would move next door for a swim in the pool and lunch with the Nelsons, then we'd sunbathe, drive around, go out in boats, or rest, and finally converge at the Roughsedges for supper and, if warm enough, more swimming.

In spite of its charming aspect, Sylvania Waters was suburbia, and there is nothing more suburban than the suburbs in Sydney. It was dullsville incarnate. No one seemed to communicate very much; they mowed the lawn, washed the car and, I should think, bored themselves to death. There was very little community spirit, and if it had not been for my two neighbors, with their swimming pools and their *joie de vivre*, I would have gone into a decline. On hot weekends by nine-thirty every light on our island, and indeed in Sylvania Waters, would be out except mine and my neighbors'.

When the Nelsons started making plans to leave Sylvania Waters, and the Roughsedges decided to go back to the States, the prospect of being left alone in suburbia was so unnerving that one night I called Aunt Jessie long distance in England and asked her to come and visit me. She was at this point eighty years old and into building old folks' homes. She had already built one in Yateley, Surrey, the old Brown hometown, and had recently sold her cottage and used the money to buy a tract of the cheapest land she could find in England, which happened to be in Reepham, Norfolk, and was putting up another old folks' home. She agreed to stay with me for a year while it was being built.

A week later I got a cable saying she was arriving at seven the following morning, on a direct flight from London. I gathered together a few people, and off we went to meet her. Since there were seven flights arriving at the same time, the airport was jammed, so I asked the woman at the Customs desk if she could make an exception and let me go and collect my eighty-year-old aunt, who had just had a twenty-eight-hour flight. She said yes, and I was just about to go in when I spotted Aunt out on the sidewalk, having an animated conversation with a bus driver and clutching a moderate-size suitcase.

"How clever of you to get out so quickly," I said. "Now shall we go and claim the rest of your baggage?"

"What baggage?" she said, brandishing her suitcase. "It's all in here."

"But you're staying for a year," I said.

"I know," she replied. "Everything I own in the world is in here."

She had one suit on and one in the suitcase, three changes of underwear, one pair of shoes on and one pair packed, her brush and comb, and her washing things. She was never known to wear makeup, so she had no beauty products, but she had found room to bring a beautiful Nepalese tunka as a present for me.

We all cavorted home and had a big breakfast in the garden. Aunt was sparkling with enthusiasm as usual. Being a great gardener, she was fascinated by all the plants in my garden, which were quite different from those in the Northern Hemisphere. It was now about 10:30 A.M., and the guests left. I said, "I've turned your bed down, Aunt. I expect you'll be looking forward to a nice sleep."

She looked horrified. "I never went to bed at ten-thirty in the morning in my life," she said.

"But you've been sitting up on a plane for twenty-eight hours."

"I dozed," she said. "I'm not a bit tired. I would love to see an Australian nursery garden. Are there any round about here?"

There was one down the road and nothing else would do, so off we went
and were there for three hours. I think she examined every plant in the
place. The nurserymen were trailing around after her, fascinated. My aunt
has always had instant charisma, and I could see that, eighty or not, it was
still there.

I finally got her to bed at 10:30 p.m. She slept the whole of the next day
and woke up the day after at 7:00 a.m. raring to go.

A few days later we were invited to dinner at the Murphys. They were
thrilled with Aunt, and Aunt was thrilled with Australia. "The only thing I
shall miss," she said, "is my bicycle."

"Your bicycle!" said our host, looking at this elderly person.

"Oh, yes," she said. "I've never been able to afford a car, so I bicycle
everywhere. Always have. Still do."

"Well, actually," said our host, "my two daughters have recently taken
to motorbikes, and we have a bicycle you could have."

If you had given her a million dollars, she couldn't have been more
thrilled. They were going to clean it up, and the next day they brought it
over.

The wheels had blue spokes and red rims, the framework was bright purple, the handlebars were bright green, the saddle was upholstered in fuzzy
velvet, and there was a foxtail waving from the top of an antenna.

Mr. Murphy was a little bit embarrassed. "There was so much dirt on
it," he said, "that till I cleaned it up I had no idea it was going to be so
gaudy. I'll take it to the garage and have it painted black."

Aunt was stunned. "Certainly not. It's very creative, shows a lot of
imagination. Your daughter must be a very talented girl," she said, thereby
making the Murphy daughter her slave for life.

So she bought a bicycle basket to hitch on the handlebars and said, "I
shall now do the marketing. You make the list and I will go and get everything. That will be my contribution." Every morning off she would go,
thereby electrifying placid, boring Sylvania Waters.

The whole thing caused such a stir that it reached the ears of Di Arthur
of the *Sydney Morning Herald*, who came to interview Aunt. Before long an
article came out revealing that Aunt Jessie wasn't some silly old nut who
rode a bicycle, but had been, in fact, the first orthopedic nurse, in the days
before the First World War when Dr. Jones and Hurse Hunt invented or-
thopedics. They began by shoving the feet of clubfooted kids into plaster of

Paris and bending them straight. When they came out of the plaster weeks or months later they were okay, but of course this was not okay with the medical profession, just as chiropractic isn't now, but they progressed farther and are now in the bosom of the medics. Aunt, newly trained as a nurse at Guy's Hospital, had ridden around the country on a motorcycle getting doctors to set up weekly clinics for clubfeet.

This article caused all sorts of excitement, and our house became like Grand Central Station, with the quadriplegic people and every society for the handicapped coming to see Aunt. She was in her element.

All Aunt Jessie's life she has been able to get the most enormous amount of publicity without trying or having the least interest in it. The Yateley Textile Printers are a good example of this. She was a very good artist, so she went to the Royal College of Art and learned hand block-printing on textiles, after which she took three of her polio after-care girls, who were crippled, and set them up in her garage with the appropriate tools. They started hand-blocking, using designs that Aunt had collected in Nepal, Tibet, and such places. Everyone wondered what she was up to, so of course it attracted the press, then somehow the Duke of Wellington became the patron and money was raised for a proper building. Then the company made some fabrics for a small room in Buckingham Palace, which made them "By Appointment," then they got a Nuffield Grant, then a Gulbenkian Grant, then someone built hostels around the factory for the girls, since by now there were some eighty of them employed and it had become a flourishing business. Aunt by this time was bored with it, so she handed it over to the British government, which has been running it for some twenty years now. The original three girls stayed with it until they retired.

Although Aunt Jessie is the greatest attention getter I have ever known, she has always been completely oblivious of the fact, just as she would see nothing peculiar about an eighty-year-old woman riding around on a psychedelic bicycle. I was very glad to see she hadn't lost her touch.

I began to get a few dates on TV game shows and talk shows, and parts in dramas—nothing showy, but they kept the wolf away from the door. Then I started in *Breath of Spring* at the Independent Theatre (the film version is *Make Mine Mink*), after which Eric Cartwright from the Australian Arts Council approached me to do a tour of New South Wales. I had run into an old friend, Colin Croft, who had been very kind to me on my first Australian tour, so I asked him if he would like to do a two-handed show with me. He agreed and found a very pleasant pianist with one leg, Charles (Chicker) Field, and we all set to work pulling a show together.

Col had been in the theater all his life. He started at five or thereabouts with the Young Australians, a nationally famous show done by a lot of young boys. Col could do anything from Shakespeare to tap dancing on roller skates. He had a nice singing voice, was a good comedian, and knew everything there is to know about the theater. I learned a great deal from him. He constituted himself as our director, and would get absolutely beside himself with rage at me from time to time.

Up until then, having always played by myself, I was used to sauntering onstage from anywhere at all and addressing myself straight to the audience. This would drive him mad. "Will you please come on the way we rehearsed it," he'd say. "You aren't an actress; you're just like a bloody evangelist."

When we finally got our material together, it reminded me of the style of my first club date act at the Royal York in Toronto. In fact, it was Mum and Dad's Old Vaudeville Show. Col and I sprang on in full evening attire with an opening number and a little dance, we had a few funny skits and a few solos, and then in the second half we did our big number, "The Prince of Philadelphia, or How to Write Your Own Light Operetta." I had longed to do this sort of skit before, but it needed a baritone prince, so this was my chance. I played all the female parts (the ladies dancing, the heroine, the prince's stepmother, the Zingarella), and Col played all the males (the prince, the soldiers, and the innkeeper). I made all our hats and shakos out of blond linoleum trimmed with those pink bobbles that are usually found on lampshades.

The show finished with my talk on the *Ring,* followed by a striptease by Col from utterly square evening clothes to purple shorts covered with beautiful wool embroidery, followed by, I'm afraid, slightly vulgar audience participation. I must say it served the purpose, though.

We played in some strange places. In one I had to use the ladies' toilet as a dressing room but had to get out at half time for the audience, and Col had the woodshed at the bottom of the garden.

We called our first tour "The Rainmakers." There had been a bad drought, but it just so happened that five or six towns running, as soon as we got there it rained. It was quite a joke. Then we went to Bourke.

"Back of Bourke" is an expression like "To Hell and Gone"—miles away from anywhere. When we got there and told them of our rainmaking proclivities, they roared with laughter. "But that is so ridiculous," they said. "It hasn't rained in Bourke for a year."

People had come in from the outback for hundreds of miles to see our show. Afterward they had a terrific party for us, which went on till all hours. By the time we got to bed about 4:00 A.M. it hadn't rained a drop, but at 4:30 I was wakened by a crash of thunder. Such a storm you never did hear. The rain came down like Niagara Falls.

In the morning the place was a swamp. The two or three little paved streets of Bourke were okay, but they all ended in a sea of mud. We heard later that everyone who had come in to see the show got stuck in Bourke for weeks, and our poor little Cessna plane got stuck in the mud, too, so we had to go on commercial flights until it got unstuck.

After New South Wales we toured Victoria, then Queensland. In some places in Queensland we would drive all day without seeing a tree or blade of grass—nothing. One could have been on the moon. "Who," I asked, "is going to come to a show out here—Martians?" It was mining country, and we would come to a little collection of houses and play in a hall with a tin roof. Everybody would come, including babies in perambulators, who would be laid on rugs in front of the stage. All these people had in the way of communication was the nine-till-midnight classical radio station, so they were a surprisingly good audience. But what a place to live!

CHAPTER 27

Boomer reappears and I repair to the Funny Farm

After sixteen months on the road and a run in Sydney that got fine reviews, I decided to quit performing for a while and settle down to finish some writing chores that needed doing. I found, however, that once my time was governed neither by the regular nine-to-five schedule nor the eight-thirty curtain, my timing became more and more erratic, until I lost touch with it altogether. It's hard to concentrate when the telephone rings every five minutes and the neighbors drop in, so I'd start writing at ten at night, intending to do two or three hours' worth, and the first thing I'd know, the birds would start twittering and it would be getting light, and I would go to bed at seven-thirty or not at all. If I went to bed, the telephone would start ringing at nine. I would answer in a sleepy, cranky voice with one eye open, then clamber back into bed, usually forgetting what the call was about. Then at 4:00 P.M. I would wake up, ravenous for breakfast and ready for a hard day's work. I got a lot of writing done, but people began to ask did I feel all right, was anything the matter, where had I disappeared to, why did I sound so peculiar on the telephone?

Then one day I made a date for dinner and a concert with Deirdre. I forgot about it, of course, and was having breakfast in my dressing gown when she arrived. Naturally she was annoyed. "Insomnia's all very fine," she said, "but this is ridiculous. I think you had better have a medical check-up." And all of the sudden there I was, in a psychiatric clinic.

I don't know what I expected, probably stone walls, barred windows, prison matrons, and a lot of weird inmates. I was quite amazed when it turned out to be more like a hotel. There was a regular reception desk and a large lobby with sofas and armchairs. People were sitting there, looking exactly like people who sit in hotel lobbies the world over—old women knitting, businessmen gabbing, teenagers, even a couple of women with babies. A charming nurse, looking more like an airline hostess, showed me around.

There was a cafeteria, a TV room, a music room, the occupational therapy room, the laundry, and the garden, with two barbecue pits and a Ping-Pong table. Then I was taken to my room, which had the usual hotel furniture and a nice view of the harbor. There was wall-to-wall carpet throughout, and planters full of greenery here and there, all very pleasant so far.

I unpacked, spruced myself up a bit, and sat down to await developments. After a while a nurse came in and, fixing me with a penetrating stare, started to ask me the most extraordinary questions, writing my feeble answers down on a pad. I asked what all this had to do with insomnia. "You are here," she said, "to find out what is causing it. The psychiatrist will come and see you as soon as he has read this." After taking my blood pressure and temperature, she bustled out.

I had been to a psychiatrist once many years before, when my husband sent me because I was being more than usually tiresome, and I have known quite a few in New York. They were all rather froglike men with guttural, middle European accents and thick, horn-rimmed spectacles. The one I went to sat like a fat Buddha in complete silence while I thrashed about on the couch talking absolute nonsense and feeling a perfect idiot. I wasn't looking forward to this part much, when in came a tall, perfectly normal-looking Australian, who introduced himself and said I was to have a session with him every day. I told him I was perfectly hopeless on the couch. He said it didn't matter, as he didn't use one anyway, and he would see me in the afternoon.

At lunch I was put at a table with four other people who promptly introduced themselves as Fred, Herbert, Dora, and Phoebe, first names being used exclusively in this emporium. In two minutes I found out that Fred was a practicing psychologist suffering from hypertension due to overwork, Herbert had had a nervous breakdown after getting an honors degree at the university, Dora was a nurse who had got fed up with the long hours and become depressed, and Phoebe was an actress (whom I'd previously met) who was suffering from acute anxiety over the rotten state of Australian show business. I told them I was Anna with insomnia, I didn't know why, but now Phoebe had mentioned it, probably also on account of lousy Australian show business, and then we carried on as if we had known each other for years.

I had my chat with the shrink in the afternoon. We talked about me. Let's face it, everyone likes to talk about themselves, only one can't do it as a rule because it bores everyone so, but there it was encouraged, and it was rather fun. When I came out of the session everyone was engaged in occupational therapy, but I was excused because I had brought a typewriter and a typing instruction book, so I could do that instead. Later we had dinner, watched TV, and went for medication. I was given what looked like three big jellybeans, two big white pills, two little yellow ones, and a green one. It was lucky I was in my dressing gown, because I just managed to get to my room before I went out like a light. At seven the next morning I'd just got as far as my pants and bra when the nurse brought a repeat of last night's dose. I took them and keeled over on the bed just as I was and didn't wake up till lunchtime. That night it was the same. Sleep I was now getting.

The next morning I asked if it was possible to have the pills after break-fast. No, I must take them at once, so I obediently did. Luckily I was al-ready dressed. I just managed to negotiate the stairs down to the cafeteria, I missed the chair and sat with a bump on the ground, I couldn't aim the jug at my coffee and poured milk all over the floor, and I would have gone to sleep with my face in the bacon and eggs if Fred hadn't pulled my head up just in time. I felt rather embarrassed, but Fred said not to worry—they do it to all the new admissions.

Apart from the shrink every day there was group therapy on Tuesdays and Thursdays and psychodrama on Wednesdays. The first group therapy was a disaster as group therapy, I suppose, but otherwise it was hysterical. There were Fred and Phoebe who had done it before, five of us who hadn't, and a rather terrifying nurse taking the session. Fred made a few vague opening remarks, which Phoebe said she didn't agree with, and everybody clammed up for about ten minutes. Then the nurse started prodding energetically at each of us in turn, only to elicit a few grunts and noncommittal remarks. When she came to me she said, "Say what is in your mind at this actual moment," so I said, "I haven't an idea in my head," which was true. Nor had anyone else, apparently.

Just then she was called to the phone. As soon as she went out everyone started gabbing a mile a minute. I was in the middle of telling them about a week I spent once at the New York Infirmary, and we were all shrieking with laughter, when she came back and we all clammed up again and sat shaking and sniggering. She asked what the joke was, but we couldn't tell her, as it wasn't relevant to the therapy, to say the least, so she got rather peeved with us and ended the session.

I discovered the next day it had all been reported to the shrink, which made me realize that there is no place for levity in group therapy. One is there just to communicate. We communicated better after that, but I'm afraid merriment still erupted from time to time.

Then there was psychodrama, where one is supposed to act out one's conflicts. Since Phoebe and I were professional actresses, no one else was game to try, so they told us the problems and we acted them out. We were husbands, lovers, queens, girlfriends, boyfriends, children, nasty neighbors—you name it. I don't know that we did much for anyone's problem, but it was very good practice for us, and everyone seemed to enjoy it.

After two weeks I was weaned off the pills and sedation and got injected with what looked like about half a cup of vitamins every day, which made me feel marvelous, except for my rear end. I was asleep by eleven, up at seven, busy as a beaver, and having a very good time. There was no cooking or housekeeping. We could go out if we wanted to but it wasn't mandatory, so I had a gorgeous excuse to refuse invitations that were boring, like addressing women's clubs, while still being able to accept interesting ones. I trotted out all my best neuroses in the hope that they would keep me there long enough to finish my writing chores and work up some speed on the typewriter. I figured even if they couldn't shrink my head to their entire satisfaction, which was a pretty tall order at my time of life, at least I would have something to show for my stay there.

The beauty of it was that it all came under medical benefits, so the whole deal cost only about thirty dollars a week, which was a darned sight less than living at home. That was the only thing I found that Sydney had over New York. There it paid to be crazy.

As I became busier with my work, the house in Sylvania Waters was simply too far out of Sydney, so I sold it. The fact that "the wallsign strite" wasn't a problem this time, because I had coped quite well with the odd-shaped bedrooms. I had no trouble selling the house for half again what I had paid for it.

I moved into North Sydney and in due course bought an apartment overlooking the harbor and the Opera House.

The Sydney Opera House! I think I have collected over the years all the information both public and private on it, by stealth and guile and a lot of snooping. I grant you that the *Nibelungen Ring* is funny, although mythical, but it is not a patch on the story of the coming into being of the $113 million Sydney Opera House.

The *Sydney Morning Herald* summed it up: "The Opera House is regarded by many as Australia's greatest architectural masterpiece but by many more as the nation's greatest farce." It started when the trams were replaced by buses on Sydney's streets, and the trams were left to molder away in the Tram Shed on Bellelong Point, a peninsula sticking out into the harbor. The Tram Shed was a great U-shaped crenellated Edwardian building.

Eugene Goosens, at the time the conductor of the Symphony, remarked one day (and I don't mind betting he lived bitterly to regret it) that someone should "get rid of the streetcars and put a stage and orchestra pit at the flat end of the U; it would probably make a quite good opera house, as the shape would be good acoustically." This caused a great deal of merriment, comic songs at the Tivoli, funny bits in the papers. The only person who took it seriously was Mr. Cahill, the first Labour prime minister of New South Wales, who probably thought the project would get him a few more votes.

Like many politicians, he got it arse backward and thought it was Bennelong Point that Goosens was talking about and not the building itself, so the first thing he did was to pull down the Tram Shed and instigate a world competition for a plan for a new Opera House.

On the selection jury were Australian architects, two English ones, and a very "in" American—Saarinen, the roof man. Saarinen was three weeks late for the judging, by which time the others had made their selection, but he didn't agree and asked to see the rejects. Among them he found a picture of a crazy roof by a Danish architect, Bjorn Utzon, which he declared the winner. Because he was such a big cheese, he overrode the rest of the jury.

So they had a picture of a roof, but no working plans. They then hired the great architectural engineer Sir Ove Aarup to design the podium to support this roof, but the podium began to sink as soon as it was built, because Bennelong Point wasn't solid, it was mostly fill. The builders took the podium down to put in a storm drain, then built it up again quickly so Mr. Cahill could dedicate the plaque before he got voted out of office.

The podium was up, but the problem was how to build the roof. This sort of thing went on for eight years. At one point Utzon was fired, causing a terrible row. By the time it was finished it covered seven acres and was a great empty concrete whatnot described by the press variously as "the Beast of Bennelong," "the Ship of Fools," "the Bunch of Huns," and "the Danish Pastry." The cost was now up to about $60 million.

Next was a big uproar involving the Australian Broadcasting Commission, the outcome of which was that the big hall originally intended for opera would now become the concert hall, and vice versa. So the stage machinery was taken out and junked, thus leaving an empty space in the large sail, though not for long.

The possums found it cozy to live and breed in, so they appointed an official possum catcher to go up and collect them in a sack and decant them into the zoo nearby. Before he could get back they'd usually have beaten him to it. Even after the hall was finished people watching a concert would occasionally catch sight of a little possum running along the molding up by the ceiling.

The smaller hall, which became the Opera House, didn't fare much better. The pit, which was right under the stage, held only thirty-five musicians—any more and they would be in danger of being decapitated by the stage revolve. The revolve was taken out so sixty-two musicians could be accommodated. The hall was somewhat small, so they put in a rear gallery, which turned out to be above the masked top of the proscenium. As one critic put it, "The audience has increased, but the spectators have not."

From the beginning the whole project had been sheer Gilbert and Sullivan, but now it turned Alice in Wonderland. The Opera House had been abuilding for fifteen years when someone suddenly realized that there was no parking and there wasn't an inch to spare on Bennelong Point, so the uproar started all over again. Everything was suggested—a monorail over Sydney from the city parking, a fleet of gondolas starting from the amusement park at the other side of the harbor, mooring the old aircraft carrier HMS *Terrible* alongside and having floating parking, putting ramps up the front steps (seventy-five) and having drive-in opera. They almost settled on gouging out 60,000 square feet from the adjoining cliff and growing vines down the side so it wouldn't be an eyesore, à la Hanging Gardens of Babylon, but the Botanical Gardens on top of the cliff scotched that, as it would have interfered with the roots of their Morton Bay fig trees.

Finally they didn't do anything. The government said, "She'll be all right, mate," and pretended the problem didn't exist, so people got there as best they could. The Queen was to come to the opening of the Opera House with the *Magic Flute* as its first production.

A few months before the opening the manager called me in and said, "Could you do one on the *Magic Flute* like you do on the *Nibelungen Ring?*"

"Whatever for?" I asked.

"We could record it and put it in the souvenir program. It would be different." Did you ever hear of a more peculiar way to celebrate the opening of an opera house? But that's what he wanted, so I did it, along with *Nabucco* and *Tannhäuser*, which they were also doing that season.

So that is how I came to make the first LP ever recorded in the Opera

House studio. No one at that point was quite sure how the equipment worked, so someone sat on a chair in front of me sticking one of those long, thin directional microphones into my face. It was the weirdest recording session I have ever been mixed up with.

The Opera House has turned out to be a super fun house for Sydney. They hold a lot of conventions there, and it's pretty good for a lot of things, except, of course, opera and ballet. I mean, what opera can you do with sixty-two musicians in the pit? As for ballet, there are no wings on the stage, so you do a *grande jetée,* crash up against the concrete, and kill yourself.

If they had been practical they would have put in slot machines and gambling. Australians by and large vastly prefer that to opera. They could have had a $100 minimum room where tiaras and tails were obligatory, which would soon attract the international set. This would be so profitable that there would be enough money to build a proper place for opera and ballet, which, I suppose, would be called the Casino.

One day I picked up *Time* magazine to find that two of my records, now called the *Anna Russell Album?* had just been re-released, and there in *Time* was a wonderful review and a picture of the album cover, which was hilarious. No one had consulted me, and I never found out who was responsible. Shortly after, Boomer wrote me a letter saying I had been away too long and should do another tour of the States. After all the vicissitudes I had been through in Australia, how marvelous it would be to be back with him again, earning the fat American fees I hadn't seen for a very long time. I agreed, and he booked a tour for the following year, which was 1974.

Before that, though, I was called on to play Madam Armfeldt in *A Little Night Music* for Williamsons' Theatres in Sydney. At first I turned it down because it would be running the same time as my tour for Boomer, but they really wanted me for this play, so they decided to put in Doris Fitton as an understudy for me while I was away.

All the costumes and sets came from New York, where the original was still running, and George Martin came from the Hal Prince office to direct the Sydney production. George had a most unusual method. Instead of blocking the whole thing out as most directors do, he started at the beginning and each day added on a little more. I liked this much better, because I always forget what's been blocked.

But he was very tough on me, which made me nervous at first. He said, "I don't want any of your tried-and-true comic gags in this show. It will ruin the whole thing." I finally understood that he meant it had to be played as an ensemble rather than a star-dominated show, so I plugged along and kept a proper low profile. After we opened I was allowed a few little extravagances, but I saw what he meant.

After we had been running a few months it was time for me to go to New York. After six years away, it was just like coming home. I asked myself why I had made the move in the first place. There was Boomer again, still his jolly, laughing self, although his health was no longer good. And there was Bob Sherman's Saturday morning program on WQXR, which I've appeared on countless times since I first started out.

I am now a fat old granny type with white hair, while Bob still has all his hair without a gray streak in it, he has a trim, athletic figure with not a line in his face, and he could easily pass for a man in his middle thirties. I know he isn't, because his son was there last time taking pictures, and the two of them looked about the same age.

After an appearance with Bob I got some very funny mail. One woman, who I'm sure meant it in the nicest possible way, wrote, "I was amazed to hear that you are still at it. I used to go to all your shows, I don't know how many decades back. I thought you'd passed away years ago." Boomer told me that every manager he'd booked me with said, "Good heavens! Is she still alive? Where on earth has she been?" I'm afraid it's a sad fact that you can be the Queen of the May in any other country in the world, but unless you show in New York or Hollywood, no one in the States knows you exist.

By the time I had finished my tour and come back to do Avery Fisher Hall, Boomer had had a massive heart attack and had retired to his house in Florida. He sold his business and handed me over to All Arts Presentations. Dear Boomer, what a character he was! He could be ruder than anybody I ever met, and he had an earsplitting laugh that usually came in at the wrong moment, as he had absolutely no tact, but he was unfailingly cheerful and very good company.

When I went around to All Arts Management, I discovered it consisted of three men. One was tall, one was middling, and one little. They all had long, dark hair and beards, and they wore jeans, funny sweaters, and stocking caps with big pompoms on top. Unless they were all together and I could recognize them by height, I couldn't tell one from the other. They did an excellent job, however, and Avery Fisher Hall was sold out.

On the way back to Australia, while stopping over in Los Angeles, I was addressing a gathering in the Ambassador Hotel when suddenly Wagner, our stage manager in Sydney, came striding in.

"I thought I recognized that voice," he said.

"What on earth are you doing here?" I asked. Apparently he was squiring a group of Aussies to California, and he was waiting in the lobby with his group to catch the limo to the airport when he heard my stentorian tones.

"I knew that voice could belong to only one person," he said, "and I'm glad I caught you. You'd better get back to *Night Music* in Sydney double quick, as they are having a lot of trouble."

Luckily I'd been over my script from time to time and had hummed through "Liaisons," because when I arrived in Sydney I was driven straight to the theater with all my baggage and jet lag. I didn't even have time for a shower.

There had been a few little changes during the two months I had been away, and the orchestra hadn't played "Liaisons" at all during that time, but the final touch came when the dining room table sailed out with us all sitting around. In the middle of the scene I looked down, and there were cards with my part written on them, stuck all over the tablecloth for my understudy. That nearly threw me, but in a day or two I'd completely settled down again, as if I'd never been away.

CHAPTER 28

I join the circus

Back in the States All Arts gentlemen had said they would like to manage me if I moved back, so I decided I would. I couldn't go for a couple of years, as I had to finish my commitments in Australia, and the new management needed time to promote me and book a tour, but I started to get prepared. As to how to move, I remembered something Aunt Jessie had said before she returned to England: "It is fine to collect a lot of possessions when you are young, but by the time you are about sixty, get rid of them. If you don't, by the time you reach my age they will have buried you."

She had left Australia some time back, after staying exactly a year. As she explained, "I am now eighty-one, and I might become senile at any moment, and I do not wish to become senile in a foreign country." Besides, her old folks' home in Reepham needed her attention. So she packed her little suitcase with exactly what she had brought with her, gave away everything she had acquired in Australia, and went on her way rejoicing. Some years later, when she was settled in her new quarters with her raised garden, she wrote to me and said, "I've only got one thing to look forward to now, and that is dying. Isn't it exciting? I can't wait to see what happens."

When I was wondering how I was going to get all my stuff across the ocean again, I remembered what Aunt Jessie had said and knew that she was right, so I took a deep breath, made a deal with my old pal Elizabeth Orme, and flogged the lot. Some very valuable things, like my precious Chinese porcelain, were sold at a fine art auction, where they put out an elegant color brochure of what was to be sold. The first weekend, when some of the things I'd lived with all my life went off, I must confess to a slight twinge or two, but I discovered by the next weekend I had forgotten what they were, and the checks kept mounting up.

I sold my apartment and everything else except my music, a few books and records, and a very few clothes, which I sent on to Unionville in a crate. By the time I had cleared the decks I found to my surprise it was absolutely wonderful. I didn't have to practice, since I had no piano, or vocalize, because as far as I knew I might never work again. There was no housework, as my apartment was virtually empty, and my wardrobe was so limited that I never had to worry what to wear. I finally realized what Aunt Jessie meant about being strangled by possessions. She had never owned anything in her life, which is why she had always been completely free. Until I got rid of everything, I didn't realize how very little I needed.

The last job I did before I left Australia was with the Ashton Circus, which is to Australia what Ringling is to America. It had been going for about 150 years and was still full of Ashtons, who were famous aerialists.

That season they were putting on a very successful show called "The Clown Who Lost His Circus," which combined the circus proper with the traditional British pantomime. They were based on fairy tales such as Ali Baba, Dick Wittington, and Cinderella, with vaudeville acts and slapstick comedy thrown in. These aren't performed much nowadays, but when I was little, part of Christmas was always the pantomime. Every town in England had one, right up to the grand, spectacular one at the Drury Lane Theatre in London.

The Ashton show was about a poor clown who had lost his circus and traveled the world looking for it, and all the circus acts were tied in with the story. The Dame was played by Slim de Gray, a popular Australian comic who had been around for a long time, and my pal Colin Croft was the villain, the Knave of Knives. At the end of the Sydney run Slim got sick, so Col became the Dame and persuaded the Ashtons to let me be the villainess for the Canberra run.

Most of the pantomime actors stayed in hotels away from the circus, but Col thought we should do it properly and actually live with the circus. So we each rented a trailer, the Ashton truck came and hitched us up, and off we bumped to Canberra, where we were lined up on a great big common alongside a lot of huge caravans belonging to the circus hierarchy. The Ashton grandparents' caravans were the height of luxury, with kitchens, showers, and toilets, much like today's mobile homes. Our poor, cheap little trailers looked very pathetic by comparison.

Once we'd all arrived, a huge vehicle appeared, like an enormous furniture van with little doors all over it, out of which leapt a lot of little men. These were the roustabouts, who were going to put up the tent. First they unfolded a huge piece of canvas and put it flat on the ground, then they put down some very, very long poles. A lot of banging with mallets went on, then they draped piles and piles of huge chains all over the place. It really looked a mess. I couldn't imagine how it was to become a tent. But then suddenly, what looked like four army tanks appeared, bright orange in color. They stationed themselves at the four corners of this confusion, facing outward, and on a signal they started. All at once the poles reared, the canvas smoothed out, the chains tautened, and lo and behold, there was the tent. I never saw anything like it. From the time the roustabouts came out of their beehive till it was up, couldn't have been more than two hours. Then the carnival people started setting up the carousel, the rides, and the sideshows, and what in the afternoon had been a vast expanse of grass with hardly anything in sight, had become like a wild west town.

Since my part was a clown and I had no idea of the makeup required, all the other clowns got together to help me, which is apparently a traditional ritual for newcomers. They were sweet, and some of them were very, very old. There was one family of musical clowns from Germany who played all sorts of strange brass instruments I'd never seen before. The old father, who was eighty-two, had been in the circus since he was a boy. Although he had lived in Australia for over forty years, he still had a thick German accent. His sons had been born in the circus and had never known anything else.

Since I had a Dracula son, we settled on a witch makeup, which turned out to be huge rubber eyelashes going right up to my temples, with green spangly eyeshadow and a huge Cupid's bow mouth starting at my cheekbones. The paint was very thick and made me totally unrecognizable.

After a few days I found myself in another world completely. The public became "them" and I became "us." There were two shows daily and three on Saturdays and Sundays, but it was after the show, when "they" were gone, that life really started. There were barbecues and parties and a lot of little kids practicing different routines, because that is where the new talent comes from. Anyone could try anything. I had a swing on a trapeze and a try at standing up on a horse. Of course, I was much too old for that, but everyone was encouraged to try, and if in the process they had an accident, they got up and tried again. If they killed themselves—well, that's Fate!

There wasn't a great emphasis on cleanliness. There were only two lots of lavatories on the place, one for each. The women's had two toilets and two washbasins, and not everyone's trailer was luxurious. Our tanks held very little water, and if we wanted more we had to get it ourselves, which was rather a long walk, so it wasn't long before we were also quite happy to make do with a lick and a promise.

Col and I were frequently invited out, as we had a lot of friends in Canberra, so we arranged, more for our hosts' protection than anything else, that we should go and have a nice hot bath before the other guests arrived. One or two friends would even offer us the courtesy of their laundry, and we would arrive with bundles of dirty clothes. Given the right circumstances, I think it wouldn't take me long to turn into a gypsy.

One night one of the Ashton sons turned up out of the blue. Some years earlier he had left the circus and gone into the trucking business, much to the family's disapproval, as he had been the trapeze lot's main catcher. There were great rejoicings at his return, and that very evening, though he hadn't done it for years, up he went on the trapeze, flinging people around as if he'd never stopped. Afterward his legs were all bleeding and his wrists were all chafed, and he looked a mess. It didn't faze him a bit. "I'll be all toughened up again in a week," he said. The outside world, though, that he couldn't take. "It's far too dangerous," he said. They all agreed, and rushed off to turn cartwheels on a galloping horse or hang by their teeth from the roof of the tent.

I had a lovely time and hated to leave. When we did leave, Col and I were both presented with gold medals with the Ashton crest on one side and our names engraved on the other. No one else in the pantomime got one, because they stayed outside, so they were not "with it and for it," but our caravans had rested in the right place, alongside everyone else's, which made us true circus folk. If we showed our medals to any circus in the world, they would be honor bound to give us a job, even if it was hosing down the elephants or cleaning the garbage cans. It's nice to know if I am down and out there is somewhere to go.

CHAPTER 29

I settle in the old home town
and embark upon the World Farewell Tour

I got back to Unionville a few days before Christmas and called my three managers who told me that I was to emcee the P.D.Q. Bach Festival at Lincoln Center on July 28 and 29 and introduce the new musical nuts.

This was the first I had heard of it. "But we wrote you twice to Australia about it," they said. "That of course," I told them "doesn't mean a thing." Today it would be hard to say who has the worst postal service in the world.

I had brought nothing home in the way of a concert dress, and I couldn't get anything in Unionville before Christmas. So what to do? Suddenly I bethought myself of a gift I had been given ten years before when I lived in New Hope, Pennsylvania. New Hope was somewhat of a summer resort, and a lot of shows would come in. This time it was female impersonators, one of whom did a dance where the stage was filled with swirling pink chiffon but you couldn't see anybody in it if you see what I mean. Rather like Sally Rand and her fans. It was a very clever routine but when they came again, this routine wasn't there. I asked about it and they told me that the chap had got too fat to be in the show but he had opened an antique shop up the street. So I went and bought a chandelier for my house from him and when I went to pick it up there was this pink chiffon outfit which he gave me. It was permanently pleated and must have had at least forty yards around the hem.

This was just before I went to Australia to live. So I shoved it into a pillow case, where it remained all the eight and a half years I was away. I seemed to remember it got stuck in with my orchestrations. So there it still was in with the music. I hauled it out of the pillow case to find it was still permanently pleated and uncrushed. I put it in the washing machine and it came out clean as a whistle. It is practically indestructible and I have worn it ever since. Some years later I was wearing it in London and was telling this story when there was a sudden uproar in the audience. The fellow who gave it to me was there. They almost had to get the ambulance for him. I don't know how it got in with the orchestrations, but wasn't it lucky I kept it? I'd gotten rid of nearly everything else.

Then I went off to California to share an apartment with my former secretary, Audie Kellogg. She is one of those friends I might not see for years and years, but when I do, I am at exactly the same point with her as when I last saw her. We rented a lovely apartment with a great big beautiful patio on which we had millions of plants. She had some lovely things, including a collection of blue and white Chinese porcelain. It's lucky I'd sold mine, or we would have been awash in it. I got a few bits of furniture and a grand piano, which I still have, and we were in business.

I had enough work to keep me going and lots of time to potter about and see my friends. That fall I did some shows in England and visited Aunt Jessie in Sun Barn Walk, which by then was full of contented seniors. The following season I appeared at a number of summer festivals and played Madame Arcati in Coward's *Blithe Spirit* and Helga Ten Dorp in *Death Trap.*

Living in Australia for eight and a half years had made me a sort of Rip van Winkle. Not only had I never heard of most of the current artists, but all the great old concert managers had given up or died, except for Hugh Pickett in Vancouver, Harry Zelzer in Chicago, and Pat Hayes in Washington, D.C. Conversely, it took about two years for the penny to drop that I was still around. So I played Vancouver for Hugh and Chicago for Harry and thought I was going to Washington for Pat Hayes. What actually happened was quite different.

In Washington I was met by a completely strange young man named Keith in a large, chauffeur-driven limousine, and was conducted to the New Watergate Hotel and ensconced in an enormous apartment. Keith told me to sample the elegant restaurants in the hotel and to charge it all, and if I wanted to go anywhere, the limousine and chauffeur were at my disposal downstairs, and they had put only domestic champagne in my fridge, and he hoped that would be satisfactory. I wondered to what I owed this elegant treatment. The concert business was never like this.

The next day I saw Pat Hayes at an interview, so I asked him what on earth was going on, and who were these people. He told me, "It's a very big rock booker, Cellar Door." I asked why a rock booker would be interested in me, and he said they were now booking concerts at Kennedy Center to upgrade their image. "You, my dear," said Pat, "are what a rock booker considers a concert artist."

When I got home and told my manager how nicely I had been treated, he said, "You went down pretty well, too. They called and said you were quite satisfied with domestic champagne and didn't break the place up or steal anything. 'And I don't even think she was on anything,' they said."

After several more months of touring, I decided to move back to Toronto, because I was living too far from most of my work. Besides which, my three managers had decided to part company. One went to the coast, the other into jazz booking, and I stayed with the short one who was all right for a time. Then one day he decamped with the money and has not been heard of since. I then met Arthur Shafman, who was managing and producing at the Bijou Theater on Broadway. He was currently producing *The Elocution of Benjamin,* a one-man show with my old acquaintance Gordon Chater. It was a most remarkable show, and it did my heart good to see Gordon having such success on Broadway after the shabby treatment he got in Australia. That's the worst of Australia: it never appreciates what it has until it's gone. Arthur is now my manager and a better or more charming one I could not wish for. I have been very lucky in this respect— Alpha and Omega, that is Boomer and Arthur, the beginning and the end— although I have had some terrors in between.

At first I was going to move into an apartment in downtown Toronto, but then my friend Mildred Temple suggested I move into Heritage Village in Unionville.

Heritage Village is built very much on the idea of Aunt Jessie's senior citizens' place, Sun Barn Walk. Aunt had a theory that everyone should have a front and a back door and facilities for gossiping with one's neighbors instead of being shut up in a high-rise. I think she is perfectly right. I see much more of my neighbors than I ever did in my huge apartment in the Park Labrea in Los Angeles.

After I moved into Heritage Village I stopped working in the summer. As a matter of fact, at seventy-one it was time I stopped working altogether, so I planned to start my farewell tour the following November.

That summer I got bit by the gardening bug. The neighbors warned me to take it easy, but of course I didn't listen. The first day I started at 6:00 A.M. and went on till it got dark. When I woke up the next day I couldn't move. I had not taken into account that the muscles I use skipping around on stage are not the muscles I use hunkering down weeding or digging a hole with a spade or lugging bags of manure. After two days of hobbling around I went about it more gingerly, and I discovered I had quite a green thumb.

After spending my entire days in the garden and ruining my fingernails, I won the trophy from the Unionville Horticultural Society. That summer I continued to garden furiously every day whatever the weather, in spite of warnings from my neighbors about possible strokes or heart attacks. "Oh, no," I thought, "that won't happen to me." Well, *that* didn't, but something else did, probably to pay me for being a smart-ass.

It was a lovely Sunday afternoon and everyone was sitting in the garden having tea under their bright umbrellas, except of course me. I was running around attending to my hanging flower baskets. When I came to put up one in the corner, the hook came loose, the basket came crashing down, and I came crashing after it, still clutching the basket. My head hit the concrete patio, and although I didn't knock myself out, blood started pouring all over the place.

Everyone rushed to my rescue. Someone called the hospital and the ambulance came whizzing up. I was laid on a stretcher and whipped off, blood still dripping. I was in the hospital emergency room settling in for a long wait when suddenly a nurse rushed in and whispered to the doctor and nurse, and they all turned to look at me in horror. Apparently, after I had left home, my neighbor Eva in the next apartment had heard my phone ringing every five minutes. Since I had left my door open, she went in and answered the phone. It was Deirdre calling from Australia. I was going on my holiday the next week, and she wanted to find out my flight number. Eva, of course, told her I'd had an accident and been taken to hospital. That was all it needed.

She asked Eva to find the number, then Deirdre called the hospital and went into her hospital act, which can put the fear of God into anyone. She told them she was Sister Prussak calling from the Royal Prince Alfred Hospital in Sydney, Australia, and did they know that I am a world-famous artist so must in no way be allowed to become disfigured. If there is any chance of this I must go at once for plastic surgery.

She scared the poor darlings within an inch of their lives. They didn't know who I was from Adam, but to be called in that imperious manner from the other side of the globe just about put them into shock. On account of the uproar Deirdre had started, the doctor called a plastic surgeon in Newmarket, some thirty or forty miles away, and got him out of bed at 11:00 P.M. on Sunday to sew me up. As a result, I was left with no visible scars at all. The main gash follows my right eyebrow, and a smaller one at the side of my eye melds with my general wrinkles.

The next week I went to Sydney as scheduled and, as usual, had a lovely holiday with Deirdre. Now that she is a middle-aged woman it seems amazing that Deirdre was once that funny little girl who was so shy and never said anything. When I found myself *in loco parentis*, I would worry and fuss and nag because she would never finish anything. She would chop and change and never carry a project to its conclusion. I can appreciate now what poor Aunt Al Schuyler went through when I was suddenly dumped on her, a lumpy teenager who wanted only to sing comic songs and play the ukelele, when she wanted to prepare me for life.

As soon as Deirdre got out from under my bossy presence in Sylvania Waters and went on her own, she never looked back. She went all over the country training beauticians for Elizabeth Arden, then she finished her nurse's training, winning a gold medal upon completion. After that she became some big deal in the nurses' union, which required her to get up and harangue the mob in the Sydney Town Hall. She started something called the Scar Clinic at the Royal Prince Alfred Hospital, then she opened a salon in the Strand Arcade. She writes a column for a national magazine, she's on TV and radio, and she has become a very good speaker and a most self-reliant person.

That spring, all within two months, my two remaining uncles and Aunt Jessie died. Uncle Eric, who was one week off being a hundred, and Aunt, who was ninety-six, both died in their sleep. Uncle Llewyn, the young and spiffy one, died at ninety-something after a short illness. A couple of years before, my mother's younger brother, Uncle Bryer, died in Unionville at ninety-three. Thus it was forcibly brought home to me that I am now the family antique. For years I have been playing antique roles, but I always thought I was acting. Now I'm really there.

So in the fall of that year my manager and I decided to start my farewell tour. It's amazing how announcing a farewell tour gooses up the bookings. I've never been so busy in all my life. In 1984 I started January 5 and finished a week before Christmas. Even my August holiday in Australia turned into a round of interviews and performances, thus confounding everybody there who thought I was just Deirdre's nice old mom.

Although I have any number of places left to do farewell performances in, the crowning glory of this last tour has to be my sold-out concert in Carnegie Hall. I am of the generation that looks on Carnegie Hall as the goal, the Mecca, the *ne plus ultra* of musical endeavor. I was brought up on movies in which some poor immigrants have a talented son who plays the violin or piano or composes, or whatever, and the family slaves to pay for his tuition. He has a devoted love who sticks through thick and thin. Then he is accidentally heard by a great impresario, who sends him to Europe, where he falls into bad company and drinks too much, This, of course, ruins his love affair, and almost his life.

All is nearly lost, but not quite. There follows a sequence of ships and planes and trains hurtling through the night, with names of world capitals zooming across the screen, then there he is, at Carnegie Hall, playing to a standing-room-only house, in full evening regalia, and all ends happily with his new life of success and world acclaim.

There were only two things a bit off about these movies. One is that I never in my life saw a Carnegie Hall audience all in full evening dress, and the other is that the conductor is never moving his baton according to what the orchestra is playing. Whatever Hollywood teaches its stars, it never teaches them to conduct. But never mind, Carnegie Hall is still the most wonderful place to perform.

To make things even more exciting, not only was my farewell concert at Carnegie Hall sold out, but a whole congregation of my friends came from all over the world to see my show. Friends we'd met on our Mediterranean cruise who were also celebrating their thirty-fifth wedding anniversary; Deirdre and Fred, who were celebrating their twentieth; Deirdre's niece, Linda, from Australia and Boomer's niece, Mary Boomer, from Florida; Gene Rankin, Dorothy Lee from Rehearsal Club days, friends from To-ronto, and on and on. I had suggested they all stay at the Mayflower Hotel, since that was where I always stayed, and the manager decided to put us all on one floor, which turned out to be great fun.

My friend Cynthia Lake took over the Carnegie Hall Bar to put on the most lavish party after the concert. When I came offstage, however, I was stuck in the artist's room for nearly an hour greeting people while the rest of my friends were entertaining themselves in the bar. This room is at the end of a cul-de-sac, but Mary Boomer managed to find a backstairs way that the cleaners use, and sneaked me the odd drink, so that when I finally got to the party I was doing as well as everyone else.

So here I am, finishing, as is suitable to my age group, sold out at Carnegie Hall. That's it. Thanks for reading, if you ever got this far.

LOVE,

ANNA